Chameleon

Chameleon

A NOVEL

RICHARD HAINS

B
BEAUFORT BOOKS
NEW YORK

Library of Congress Cataloging-in-PublicationData

Hains, Richard.
Chameleon : a novel / Richard Hains.
p. cm
Novel.
ISBN13: 978-0-8253-0510-8 (alk. paper)
ISBN–10: 0-8253-0510-1 (alk. paper)
I. Title.

PR6108.H43C47 2006
823'.92—dc22

2006001678

Published in the United States by Beaufort Books, New York
Distributed by Midpoint Trade Books
www.midpointtrade.com

2 4 6 8 10 9 7 5 3 1

PRINTED IN THE UNITED STATES OF AMERICA

To Jocks

Chameleon

CHAPTER ONE

"Since 9/11, no one seems to want my money," Boris Posarnov said, in an unmistakable Russian accent.

"Which is why our bank is different," nodded his breakfast partner, Ernest Johnston, reassuringly. "We are able to provide you with services others cannot. After all, since you are one of my most important and innovative clients, it is my job to find solutions to your problems, is it not?"

Johnston's blue-and-white-striped shirt was set off by a white collar and cuffs, just visible under a single-breasted Brooks Brothers suit. A pale yellow tie and improbably red braces completed the ensemble, which identified its wearer as the successful American investment banker he was. Part entertainer, part financial advisor, and part confidant, Johnston played an important role within the Bank of Manhattan, one of the fastest-growing and most prominent investment banks in the United States. His job was to sniff out and extract money from rich people, or as the industry more euphemistically phrased it, to develop and nurture high net worth banking relationships wherever he found them. This morning his search had taken him to London.

Posarnov chose to ignore Johnston's rhetorical question, remaining silent until the young Claridge's waiter, resplendent in his spotless livery, finished placing a pot of tea onto the crisp white tablecloth and moved away from them.

"So how do you propose to legitimize my money, given this regulated world we're now living in?"

Johnston leaned forward conspiratorially. "It just so happens that a unique opportunity has arisen in the government bond market. It is ideal for your needs and I anticipate that we can move your company's entire thirty-five million dollars through the market in two or three days, start to finish."

"And the risk?" Posarnov remained skeptical.

"That's the joy of this transaction. There is no risk. Your capital is completely protected. The bank needs the U.K. Trading Company to play a minor role in a large government bond purchase we want to initiate for our own account, and, in return, we are willing to guarantee one hundred percent of your company's capital."

At last, Boris smiled, his normally dour expression softening. "Well, I cannot ask for anything more than a capital guarantee from your Bank. This is most certainly very encouraging news. But the fees? What will they amount to?"

Johnston leaned back expansively as he delivered his final selling point. "Other than a fee for me personally for facilitating this unusual transaction, there will be none, since the Bank needs your company's compliance in order to circumnavigate one or two of the SEC's rules and regulations." He waved a dismissive hand. "Nothing important, just technicalities."

Boris fingered an unlit Cuban cigar as he surveyed their opulent surroundings. One of London's finest dining rooms was an appropriate setting for one of Russia's most successful and creative businessmen, he thought to himself. He loved England now that he had taken up residency, and he wanted to be treated with the respect a man of his position rightfully deserved. Money could buy such respectability. All he needed now was a mechanism to enable him to freely spend his ill-gotten gains in the leading commercial and social centers of the world. He was on his way.

"I like your terms. Let's do it!"

Their business concluded, the two men addressed their eggs Benedict with gusto, both more than pleased with the proposed plan.

Queens, New York

Robert Baldwin preferred to have breakfast with his wife and two young daughters rather than rush into the office at the crack of dawn. A conscientious man of strong principles and clearly defined ethical standards, he was one of the most effective senior employees at the Bank of Manhattan. If work needed to be done, he would simply stay at the office until it was completed, no matter what the hour, so he allowed himself the luxury of going in later than the traders.

When the telephone rang, he was not altogether surprised. The office often called him at home. What did surprise him, however, was who turned out to be on the other end of the line.

"Robert," Ernest Johnston began, "sorry to trouble you at home, but I wanted to discuss the bond auction idea you ran past me last week."

Baldwin was quick to respond. "Mr. Johnston, sir, I appreciate your position on that, and as I said, I completely agree with you. I have advised Jon Phillips that we cannot proceed with the transaction he was proposing, given the regulatory issues involved."

"That's why I'm calling. I have subsequently had legal advice from the bank's lawyers and it is our intention to proceed as per Phillips's proposal."

Baldwin was rattled by this. As head of the Bank of Manhattan's Compliance Department, he was responsible for protecting the bank from any regulatory or client risks. "But I thought we agreed that the proposed transaction would violate SEC regulations."

"We did, but it seems I misunderstood how the regulations would apply. The board has approval from our lawyers, and it is our intention to move forward. I am in London, and I have secured a major U.K. client to provide the necessary thirty-five percent assistance in the auction."

"But, sir," Baldwin began.

Johnston interrupted. "Robert, I did not call you to debate this issue. I called you to inform you as to what the board's position is. Am I understood?"

"Yes, sir," Baldwin replied reluctantly. Despite his senior position within the bank, it was not his place to question policy decisions set by the board. He now had no choice but to take the steps necessary to ensure all the appropriate structures and documentation were in place for Phillips to make his unprecedented move in the upcoming government bond auction.

Alphabet City, Manhattan

Although it was nearly dawn, it was as good a time as any to complete the day's business. Georgie McWilliam was working his way through the receipts for the evening's take as he waited for his visitor to arrive. His nightclub in lower Manhattan, the popular Easy Bar, was the perfect front for his drug and prostitution rackets. He was a small player in a vast market, but he had ambition. Trading conditions had gotten better following the slump after 9/11, as the financial markets recovered and property prices soared. New York was once again booming, and people had begun to feel rich again. Young urban players were back in the game, discretionary spending was up, and McWilliam was perfectly positioned to take full advantage of it. He made his money giving people what they wanted, and what they wanted was drugs and girls. Someone had to do it, he mused, as he finished the last of many Jack Daniels and contemplated the various ways in which he would expand his empire by maximizing the tools of his trade — his vast client list; his expanding book of pretty, but impoverished or drug-addicted young girls; and, most importantly, his high-quality and reliable cocaine connection.

There was a knock on the door, and James Remini entered the

room, dressed entirely in black, his long graying hair neatly pulled back into a no-longer-in-fashion ponytail. McWilliam was surprised to see him in person, a rare occurrence these days. Remini barely acknowledged McWilliam's effusive greeting. "Give me the money, George, so we can get this thing done."

McWilliam tried to lighten the mood. "So how have you been, my friend? It's nice to see you in person. A rare honor, indeed."

Remini glanced at him dismissively. "I do not want to appear rude, but I am not your friend," he replied, accurately. "I am here tonight only because my courier let me down, so I have been forced to do this myself. I do not expect to be making a habit of it. Where is the money?"

Since leaving the CIA, Remini considered himself an international financier, and he did not like to be reminded of the drug-dealing business he maintained simply because it was too lucrative to give up. He was distinctly unhappy at finding himself delivering cocaine in the wee hours of the morning to low-life, second-rate players like Georgie McWilliam.

McWilliam removed several large bundles of cash from his desk drawer. He handed them to Remini, who casually tossed them into the gym bag he had brought with him.

"It's all there, baby. Aren't you gonna count it?" McWilliam asked.

"One thing I know for sure is that you wouldn't be stupid enough to shortchange me. The money will be checked, and if we find anything missing, you will live to regret it." This was said more as a statement of fact than a threat.

"Hey, slow down, Jimbo. I've been doing business with your syndicate for a long time. We should trust each other by now. Take it easy and pass me the coke." At this point, McWilliam wanted to get the transaction over and done with almost as much as Remini.

Remini removed eight small plastic bags from his gym bag and placed them in front of McWilliam. Picking up a small penknife, McWilliam selected one of the bags at random and punctured it. He dipped his finger into the cocaine and massaged it into his gums, rubbing the last of it on his front teeth. Like a connoisseur of fine wine, he hesitated for a moment to savor the drug before making any comment. Remini stood impatiently, waiting for McWilliam to accept it so he could leave.

"Tastes good, my friend," McWilliam finally nodded. "As always, it's a pleasure doing business with the Remini network."

Remini didn't bother to be polite this time. "Please do not refer to me like that and, once again, I am not your friend." But McWilliam had returned his attention to the cocaine, poking his finger into the bag to get another bump. By the time he looked up, Remini had gone.

Upper East Side, Manhattan

Jon Phillips approvingly observed his taut, muscular reflection in the floor-to-ceiling windows of his starkly contemporary bedroom, oblivious to the magnificent late-night view across Manhattan. He was standing beside his king-sized bed as a young, naked model enthusiastically performed oral sex on him. She was doing a good job of it, considering how she was positioned at an awkward angle in order to accommodate Jon's girlfriend, whose head was buried in her crotch. As Danielle lifted her head from between her friend's legs to reach for the bedside table, the girl broke her rhythm momentarily, whimpering in disappointment. Grabbing a small vial of cocaine, Danielle sprinkled some of the white powder onto her friend's abdomen. She then dipped her tongue lasciviously into the cocaine and, parting her friend's lips, gently but expertly licked it onto her swollen clitoris. Her friend gave a muffled moan of pleasure, her mouth still jammed full of Jon's hard cock, as she forcefully pushed herself toward Danielle's eager tongue.

Realizing her attention had shifted, Jon removed himself from the girl's mouth and wandered over to position himself behind Danielle. Her bottom lifted reflexively as he approached. She knew what to expect. She barely broke stride as Jon began pumping her vigorously, all three now moving in a quickening rhythm of heightened sexual arousal. When the phone rang, Jon was only momentarily distracted. If it wasn't important, whoever was calling would leave a message. When the ringing began again a moment later, he reluctantly removed himself from Danielle, who quickly replaced him with her own probing fingers, and walked toward the bedroom door.

As he left the room, he addressed the girl writhing wildly with pleasure under Danielle's ministrations: "Baby, do me a favor and finish off Danielle for me, will you?" Neither of the girls acknowledged Jon's gratuitous request. There was no indication they had even noticed that he'd left.

Jon stood naked and still erect at his desk in his spacious living room. He picked up the phone on the sixth ring, knowing who it would be and what it would be regarding. "Yes, Anthony," he said somewhat brusquely, in a broad Australian accent that bore traces of his decade in New York. "What's going on?"

"Sorry to bother you at such an ungodly hour, old chap, but the bonds have reached your level," replied the caller in a clipped, upper-middle-class English accent.

The loud panting and groaning sounds emanating from his bedroom were escalating into screams and Jon, although a little piqued that their activities weren't grinding to a halt in his absence, was keen to get back into action. These young girls were almost insatiable, especially when they were entertaining each other sexually. The new Les-Curious phenomenon that had caught on with his girlfriend's trendy circle of friends in Manhattan was indeed a wonderful thing, thought Jon, as he wrapped up the call.

"Sell $500 million of the August 2015s, if you can get them away at this level in London. If not, I'll deal with it here in the morning. Book the trade to Bank of Manhattan, New York account." The phone was down almost before he had finished speaking. He certainly wasn't going to hang around waiting for a reply. He'd given his London desk an instruction and that was enough.

He headed back into the bedroom. Danielle now lay splayed out on the bed, her girlfriend between her long, slender legs,

vibrator in hand. Jon did not hesitate. It was time to fuck Danielle's
friend while she devoured his lissome and voracious girlfriend.

Fleet Street, London

Penny felt exhausted, although it was barely nine o'clock in the
morning. She sat surrounded by the clatter of a London tabloid
newsroom, massaging her temples. Another late night featuring too
much alcohol, too much sex, and not enough enjoyment. She had
gotten to the point where dinner was nothing more than a two-
hour audition during which she decided if the guy merited screwing
after dessert. If he measured up, it would be straight back to her
place in West London. Penny preferred sex in her own bedroom.
Of course, there was always the risk that her partner might want to
stay over, but she had become adroit at inventing an early morning
meeting or whatever excuse was needed to make him leave. Sex was
a pleasurable enough distraction, but she couldn't tolerate awkward, post-coital pleasantries.

She got up from her desk and paced around the newsroom,
breaking her self-imposed rule to never eat a pastry from the com-
munal tray of Danish. Maybe a few carbs would get her going. On
the other hand, why bother? The story she was working on was
hardly worth the calories. Yet another breathless account of some
grade-B celebrity's recently exposed lifestyle issues. As in, who
cared?

She settled down to put the finishing touches on today's write-
up of the latest celebrity du jour, wondering at what point the public would lose interest in these ersatz, interchangeable media
creations. Apparently never, a rather depressing prospect, although
one that would at least keep the British public buying her trashy
tabloid newspaper to read her equally trashy stories.

Penny had long since tired of writing simply to fill the daily
pages of her newspaper, but every time she attempted to raise the
bar, her efforts were frustrated by an editor whose interests did not
extend beyond tits, money, sex, and scandal, preferably involving

names in the news. She'd made the mistake early on in her journalistic career of going for the higher pay and plentiful bylines offered by the tabloids and, over a decade later, had become pigeonholed in that field. She was now seriously looking for an opportunity to shift gears in her career, a shift to something that would allow her to take advantage of her Cambridge degree instead of her ability to chat up the latest lame overnight sensation. Right now it seemed about as likely to happen as finding a man who would engage her interest for more than just a few hours.

CHAPTER TWO

Wall Street, Manhattan

"Jon, you don't have to go through with this crazy bond auction scheme. Stop while you still can," urged Robert Baldwin, leaning across the bank of flashing monitors on Jon's desk. The desk was slightly elevated, allowing Jon to look down on all the other traders, barely distinguishable behind the monitors at their workstations.

"Robert, for God's sake, this is Wall Street, not Main Street. It's a great opportunity. You and the bank will be thanking me. You'll see." Although they spoke quietly, there was little chance of anyone overhearing their conversation through the volume of noise created by the hundreds of traders, analysts, and brokers surrounding them. Nonetheless, Robert moved closer, his voice lowered to an urgent whisper.

"I know you're good. But no one's that good. I can't force you not to go ahead with this, but as a friend and colleague, I'm telling you, the risk is just too great. There are very good reasons why no one's ever managed to corner the U.S. government bond market."

"So . . .?"

"So!" Baldwin virtually spat the word. He caught himself, regaining his composure, but his whisper retained its level of urgency. "If you succeed, you'll be making the bank responsible for over ten *billion* dollars of government bonds, in the space of five minutes! Why on earth would you want to take all that risk?"

"Because that's what we do in this department. We take risks." Jon smiled at his friend's worried expression. "And I'll be raking in ten or fifteen times more for the bank — not to mention myself — than if I just played by the rules, as usual. How does a profit of seventy or eighty million dollars, instead of five or six, sound to you?"

Robert looked toward the floor, shaking his head. "That's the problem. All you can think about is what happens if it works. But it's my job to think about what happens if it doesn't, and what I'm thinking is it could ruin you and compromise the bank. I just don't get why the board doesn't see that."

Shrugging, Jon turned back toward his screens. "It will work, Robert. And it's precisely because we *can* do it this time that we *should* do it. It's called seizing the moment, my friend."

Baldwin could see he was making no headway. "Fine. It won't be my responsibility anyway. If Johnston's gotten the board to approve it and they've even found you a partner — God knows how — to do it with, then it's not for me to stand in the way of this scam."

"Scam? Let's not get melodramatic here. Everyone but you realizes that rules exist to be bent. Notice that I didn't say broken — just bent."

Baldwin could not let it go. "You do realize how much things have changed since 9/11, don't you? Sometimes I think you just don't seem to get that we're no longer living in the Nineties."

"That's where you're wrong. Nothing has changed. We're still all part of the same food chain. The predators are still out there, and the lower down you are, the less likely you are to survive." Jon had raised his voice, and was gesticulating to make his point. "Like the sharks that we are, we have to keep moving forward just to stay alive. Stand still and you're a goner."

"Maybe your attitude hasn't changed, Jon, but the bank's has. Be careful, no one is irreplaceable. Not even you. Don't say I didn't warn you, old buddy of mine." With that, Baldwin turned and walked away, ending the discussion.

Jon watched him, thoughtfully, as he threaded his way through the maze of desks. One of a handful of African-American senior executives within the corporate ranks of the Bank of Manhattan, Robert Baldwin was Wharton-educated, very bright, highly respected, and not to be ignored. The rare employee who consistently put the bank's interests ahead of his own, he was a twenty-two-year company veteran, and as head of the Bank of Manhattan Compliance Department, he was effectively the bank's watchdog.

Years ago, when Jon had been a junior bond dealer operating within a small trading department, compliance had played virtually no role in what he did. But as Jon's proprietary trading activity grew and the risk involved spiraled, Baldwin's department was given the added responsibility of monitoring all the bank's proprietary positions — the trading done on its own behalf versus that of a client's. They had to make sure that the game everyone was playing was based on a clear and rigid set of understood rules, and that no undue risks were being taken; freewheeling traders like Jon chafed under their constraints.

Still, Jon was momentarily unnerved by the vehemence of his friend's warning. Despite his bravado, Jon knew very well there was no going back from the move he had planned. He sat motionless at his desk overlooking the trading floor of the bank. One of the largest in the world, it was designed to accommodate the maximum number of profit centers in the smallest possible area. The floor had very specific, very complex territorial divisions. The men and women who spent their days there rarely strayed out of their designated area; to do so was regarded as foolhardy. Only the most ambitious or stupid would dare infringe upon another occupant's personal space, relationships, or precious client lists.

Few individuals had complete access to all these fiercely protected departments and their staffs, and even fewer understood all their various functions. One such individual was the head trader, a position commanding a great deal of influence and respect. It had required eight of the ten years Jon Phillips had worked at the bank for him to single-mindedly maneuver his way into that position. Doing so had taken a toll, turning him into someone his parents hardly recognized on his rare visits to the cattle farm outside of Melbourne where he'd grown up. Of his three siblings — two younger sisters of whom he was fond but had little contact, and his younger brother David — only David had remained his steadfast, if long-distance, confidant and supporter throughout those years, at least whenever Jon could track him down.

At the bank, with the possible exception of Baldwin and one old drinking buddy from his London days, there was no one with whom Jon could let down his guard. As ringmaster, his task was to see that all the various acts were being performed simultaneously and to the same tune. He accomplished this with a mixture of arrogance, sarcasm, brilliance, and flair. Consequently, he was universally envied, not necessarily liked, and usually respected. After all, his was the position most still aspired to, notwithstanding the fact that proprietary trading wasn't quite what it used to be.

The Bank of Manhattan was typical of all modern-day New York-based financial institutions. Steeped in a tradition dating back to the city's humble beginnings, the bank had grown to staggering proportions over the previous decade, its tentacles spreading well beyond Wall Street. From its vast European headquarters in London to deep into Asia and the Pacific Rim, its influence was now felt almost everywhere in the world.

As head of proprietary bond trading, Jon routinely used huge levels of debt to buy and sell U.S. government and corporate bonds and their derivative products, financial futures. The bond trading department had historically brought in much of the money funding the bank's global expansion, and was the source of huge profits during the bank's steady rise to market dominance in the 1980s and the 1990s.

Lately however, the winds had begun to blow from a different direction. It was believed money could be made in ways without incurring the risk involved in proprietary trading. Largely driven by a stock market that had enjoyed a run of uninterrupted gains in the 1990s, the international financial markets had been shifting to equity-related services to fund their continuing expansion. As a result, the proprietary departments of the major banks were rapidly being wound down. Jon was all too aware of the shift. As long as he stayed at the bank, he was determined to hang on to his position as a big gun, and so far he had been successful. The only way to do this was to keep making large trading profits for the bank, which were becoming ever more difficult to find because growing competition caused the markets to become more efficient and stricter regulatory laws clipped his wings.

The truth was that at the age of thirty-eight, Jon was ready to move on. To what he wasn't sure, but he *was* sure that he was fed up with being consumed by his work — the long hours, the self-protective isolation, the ongoing internecine warfare that could, and often did, turn ugly. He'd been living on the edge for so long that he was not even aware he was teetering on a precipice. He was no longer manipulating the financial markets; they were manipulating him. For too many years, he'd cancelled more holidays than he'd taken. Nights out were constantly interrupted by his obsessive attention to where the foreign markets might be trading at any given moment. Rarely was his hand-held futures pager out of reach.

There would be other holidays and many more nights out; what he found himself regretting were the relationships he'd let slip from his grasp. He had left his Cambridge girlfriend, Victoria, in London; intense as it was, their affair hadn't survived his move to New York. In those early days, ambition had been his clear priority. Other girlfriends had come — but always gone. Lately, there were times when he would sit at his desk and wonder what might lie beyond the world of bonds, bonuses, fashionable clubs and restaurants, and pretty young girlfriends whose names he barely learned before they disappeared. He saw himself getting older, and felt he was doing it without any real dignity. Something had to change.

Jon shook himself out of his reverie. It was not a good idea to be off-guard while at work, even for a few moments. So far, the week had been an unusually quiet one, but this Friday morning things could be getting interesting very soon. He sipped from his Starbucks coffee mug as he scanned his screens, looking for material movements in the European markets, and any major news items that might affect the U.S. financial markets, which were about to open.

Eight o'clock in the morning on Wall Street is recognized worldwide as the starting point of a new financial day. At the Bank of Manhattan, it was now time for the morning briefing to begin. As dozens of traders looked up from their workstations, Jon stood to begin the address he gave daily, as head trader. Underneath their frenetic activity, the traders had been waiting for him to make the start of their day official. Hurriedly, they wrapped up their phone calls and conversations in order to give him their undivided attention.

Jon waited for complete silence, his large, blue eyes missing nothing. He was dressed immaculately in a dark blue, hand-tailored Italian single-breasted suit, his white shirt lightly starched, its cuffs held together by two gleaming kangaroo-shaped sterling cufflinks. Compared with his colleagues, he was rather formally attired. The technology boom had brought with it more casual attire. A business suit was no longer required in most trading floor environments, although this was beginning to change back again, following the tech boom's spectacular bust.

The topic of today's briefing was the U.S. government economic statistics relating to the state of the labor market, due to be released by the Labor Department at exactly eight-thirty that morning. Trading floors across the globe would receive the information simultaneously. It would then be analyzed and interpreted a thousand different ways by tens of thousands of different dealers in a hundred different languages.

The non-farm payroll employment figures were always of particular interest to Jon, as a bond trader, since they often had a substantial influence on the direction of the U.S. government bond market, the largest and most influential financial market in the world.

"The September long bond appears to be damaged," he began. His distinctive accent — Australian with a New York cast — was exaggerated by the squawk box amplifying his delivery. "Sentiment is weak, based on the belief that the Fed is going to substantially raise rates in excess of one hundred basis points over the next six months. This is reflected by where the short end is already trading. It looks a little pessimistic." Typical of the industry, Jon's speech was larded with technical jargon. The financial markets were designed to keep the insiders in and the outsiders out; a protective mechanism intended to maintain the status quo of the marketplace. "Our analysis suggests sentiment is very weak and bottoming," he continued. "This is constructive for the treasury market. Open interest suggests the shorts have got hold of the market. I don't wear it, the momentum players haven't made a dime all year, no need to think they're going to make money now. The bottom line is the market is too damn nervous and underweight. The trade looks long, and timing will be critical, so we're looking to use . . ."

Suddenly, Jon stopped short. His pause hung in the air. An initial paranoia among his audience was replaced by a wave of relief as each of them gratefully realized they weren't the source of the interruption. One by one, all eyes shifted to follow Jon's steely gaze. The target of his wrath, two young traders who had just quietly entered the room, were now visibly uncomfortable in the unwanted limelight and shuffled sheepishly toward their desks. Not only were they late, but one sported a black eye and some visible bruises, and the other had a bandaged nose. By now, the entire floor was focused on them. The silence was pronounced.

Jon made no attempt to hide his irritation. "I don't give a damn what you two wise guys do in your spare time, so long as you don't bring your bad habits onto this trading floor. You're late and you're disrupting my meeting." The traders looked helplessly around for some sign of support or sympathy from their colleagues. None was forthcoming, as Jon continued. "Apparently you went out looking for trouble and it found you. Let's see." His eyes scanned them. "Did we get any blood on our Gucci loafers? What a terrifying pair you two make, the other guys must still be quaking in their boots." This sally produced a few audible sniggers. Jon showed no sign of letting up. "Hmmm . . . Or perhaps the two of you simply let a quiet night of rough sex on the home front get out of hand?" Jon knew he was pushing it but was, in fact, beginning to enjoy himself. "If so, do us all a favor and take it a bit easier on each other next time 'round. You might not get as much out of it, but at least you'll be able to come in on time."

The floor erupted with laughter, as both men sank into their desk chairs amid heckling from their colleagues. Jon reverted to the job at hand, all business again. "As I was saying, the trade is long and we'll use any weakness after the figure to buy it. Are there any questions?"

This was asked rhetorically, only as a way of finishing the briefing. Now was not an appropriate forum for a question-and-answer session and Jon did not wait for a response. "Thank you."

The trading floor settled back into its usual rhythm, the dealers busily squaring up their positions. Given the importance of the non-farm payroll figures, traders were generally reluctant to second-guess what they were going to be. Instead, they marked time by calling their many clients, both international and domestic, to advise them on the scenarios that might be triggered by whatever numbers were released. Anticipation grew as 8:30 A.M. approached.

Ellen, one of Jon's team of three traders, waited until the noise level in the room had again risen before turning to Jon. "Well, you certainly handled that situation with a high degree of professionalism and decorum," she drawled.

He merely shrugged.

"Seriously, Jon, you can't say things like that anymore. You'll get in trouble."

"You know what; I don't give a flying fuck. This whole p.c. shit has gone too far. If they can't take it, too bad."

Ellen gave him a long look, but did not reply. In her thirties, she made a point of wearing scruffy clothes and provocative buttons that only she could get away with, due to reverse political correctness. Today's button was "All Men Are Rapists." She was overweight and had an attitude to match her size. Responsible for coordinating the settlement procedure and the minute-by-minute management of the profit-and-loss account, she was more competent than most of the men on the trading floor, and also more masculine. Gay and openly proud of it, she was secure in the knowledge that her job was protected by the extraordinary lengths to which the bank went these days to outline and enforce their intolerance toward behavior that might even vaguely resemble discrimination or intimidation. Gone were the days of the leering, bottom-pinching senior officers of U.S. financial institutions, although there was no way of muzzling the private discussion and speculation about Ellen's sex life.

Jon decided to ignore her sarcasm. "Well, they should learn to come in on time."

Ellen wouldn't let it go. "Come on, Jon, why do you have to be such an asshole?"

"Why? I'll tell you why! Like everyone else here, I'm in this for one reason and one reason only — the money. And that means the bonus. So I'm going to do whatever it bloody well takes to see to it that everyone pulls his weight. I'm not here to make friends. If I were looking for friends, I wouldn't surround myself with this bunch of pricks."

"And fuck you, too. Pricks? Jesus! I thought you Australians were nice guys!"

Jon smiled. "Let's face it; we're all a bunch of overpaid thieves. The only thing missing from our costume is the little black Zorro mask."

"Speak for yourself. Not everyone who works in the financial markets is a thief. You're too damn cynical."

Jon's attention had already shifted back toward the screens. The employment data would be arriving at any second. He turned to the other two members of his team, Tony and Gary. In their twenties and casually, but neatly, dressed, they were responsible for executing all proprietary positions for the team, generally on specific instructions from Jon. After which, Ellen entered the information into the bank's computers. Although at this stage Tony and Gary's primary job was to support Jon, they aspired to one day fill his shoes, knowing achieving that heady ambition would guarantee them recognition, respect, and riches. Wall Street's very own three "R"s.

"What's the figure? Has anybody got the bloody figure yet?" Jon was all business now.

Nobody spoke. Instead, every eye was focused on the array of computer monitors crowded in a jumble at each station, constantly providing the individuals seated in front of them with every kind of information imaginable. At precisely 8:30 AM, every screen simultaneously printed out "Govt. Non-Farm Payrolls 250,000 October. Previous fig. UNCH."

The room erupted into a frenzy of activity. Only Jon's group remained calm as he and his team continued to watch their screens. Unlike the traders, who dealt with clients, they bought and sold solely for the bank's own account, using the market's volatility to their advantage in doing so. As the seconds passed after eight-thirty, the market quickly assessed the figure and the breakdowns. The price of the thirty-year benchmark U.S. government bond future promptly began to fall, a result of investors selling futures in anticipation of higher long-term U.S. interest rates.

The weakness in the futures market gathered momentum. The market perceived the strong economic figure it had just received as a negative, since the independent Fed, the Federal Reserve Bank of America, would be likely to raise interest rates in order to slow a rapidly growing economy. The Fed had a basic policy of maintaining a "Goldilocks" economy at all costs: not too hot nor too cold, it had to be just right. It was regarded as the engine room of the global economy, and Owen Taber, the Chairman of the Fed, had the responsibility of keeping this engine finely tuned. The nation and its financial markets held their collective breath each time Taber spoke publicly about the state of the U.S. economy.

Tony watched his screen intently. "The figure is strong," he said, stating the obvious and thereby irritating Jon. "We are pretty weak, Jon, the futures are down two big points and they're dumping them. They hate that figure."

Jon raised his eyebrows dismissively at Tony. "Perhaps you

could tell me something that everyone in this room doesn't already know." He shook his head impatiently and turned back to his monitor.

Tony glanced at Jon apologetically. His boss had again become the focus of everyone's attention. When market prices were highly volatile, as they were now, clients, sales people, and traders all looked desperately for direction. The head trader was expected to provide that direction. His job was to sort out what would happen next and to position the bank accordingly. Jon's team awaited his instruction in respectful silence.

Most trading floor occupants were experts only on what had already happened. For a proprietary trader, it was this very nervousness and volatility in the market that created opportunity. Jon thrived in this environment. Now his eyes were fixed on a series of screens; he was oblivious to the noise all around him. He was calm and his manner was deliberate. His focus was complete.

Various scenarios flowed through Jon's brain as he ran through every possible situation, calculating the odds of each outcome. Risk, reward, profit, loss, stop loss, break-even. A few moments later, he knew exactly what had to be done. Jon shouted across the trading floor toward the option desk. "Hey, Delboy! What are you seeing on your screen, pal?"

The traded option desk was run by a man in his early forties, who was as formally, if not as nattily, attired as Jon. Known as Delboy or Del for short, after a crooked but lovable Cockney character in a British sitcom, he was an old friend from Jon's early days on the London Stock Exchange. A sharp, quick-witted east Londoner, Del was one of the trading floor's great characters. Like Jon, he too was not inclined to operate under the new behavioral guidelines; ingrained habits were hard to break. Considered a little past his prime by traders more than a decade younger than he, Del was a predator from the eighties who nonetheless remained highly effective.

Hearing Jon's shout, Delboy looked up, a wicked smile on his face. "What am I seeing?" He repeated. "Nothing much other than the reflected image of the world's greatest living lover." His words were delivered in a distinct east London accent.

Jon laughed. "Uh huh. Perhaps you could elaborate on your amorous exploits later on over a beer. But for the time being, I was wondering if you had a view."

"You know me, Wallaby; I always have a view on everything."

Jon's nickname while working on the floor of the London Options Exchange in the 1980s had been Wallaby, derived not from the Australian marsupial but from the astonishingly successful Australian rugby team of the same name. "Then tell me, what do the September one hundred and ten calls look like?"

Delboy glanced toward his screen before answering in a fake, exaggerated Cockney accent. A few traders were starting to take notice of their exchange, and Jon and Delboy were not above putting on a show for them. "Oh, those. For you, Wal, they look fifty-four to fifty-six and I'm told they're better bid. What do you wanna do, my son?"

"What sort of size are they in?" Jon asked.

Delboy hesitated momentarily. "Given they're better bid, you'd be able to knock 'em out at fifty-four in about a gorilla, and buy 'em at fifty-six-ish in a monkey."

Jon nodded. Delboy was referring to the number of option contracts the market would be willing to buy or sell at each price. Jon's team was by now closely following the conversation. They, along with the other members of the trading floor within earshot, were hoping to glean some valuable tidbit of information, but were looking increasingly baffled by the unfamiliar, 1980s references. This was exactly what Jon and Del intended; it was a way in which they could assert — even flaunt — their experience and apartness.

Jon was now openly playing to their audience. "How do they look to you at fifty-six, Del?"

"To be honest, Wal, if you fancy going long, they're very buyable, but I'm not sure it's in your size, me old pal. In my view, these things look budgerigar, vol is currently very low."

Jon acknowledged Del's comment without question. He turned to Tony. "Tony, can you please check out in what sort of size the benchmark treasuries are being offered at?"

Tony picked up the phone. Jon turned back to Delboy.

"Delboy, why don't you tell these young, naïve, and unseasoned boys and girls what we're talking about whilst I have a look at the physical bond? You and I have an obligation to educate the inexperienced. Tell them what a monkey is."

"Okay, Wallaby, I suppose someone's gotta do it." Both men smiled. "As everybody knows, a monkey is a small gorilla; in fact, it's half its size. A gorilla, of course, is twenty Hawaii's, and everybody knows what a Hawaii is." Jon nodded. "So, two monkeys equal one gorilla, and a monkey is ten Hawaii's." A gorilla meant a thousand, a monkey five hundred, and a Hawaii, as the fiftieth state admitted to the union, was fifty.

Jon nodded again. "Thanks, Delboy, that's quite clear. Now could you also explain to my team here why you think these options are budgerigar?"

"Sure. It's simply because they are . . ." Delboy mimicked a bird — an Australian parakeet — chirping, ". . . cheap, cheap."

This raised a laugh at the surrounding desks, but with a typical shift in mood, Jon suddenly tired of the banter, his lighthearted tone shifting back into business mode. "Thanks, Del, but I think I'll stick to the physical bonds." He swung around to Tony. "Could you please check what price the benchmark 5 3/8% Feb 2031s are trading at? I'm looking for the offer," he said brusquely.

Tony immediately called the market-making team on the other side of the floor, then after listening, held his hand over the receiver. "They're offered at 109 and 8/32nds in 100 and 11/32nds in 250."

As Jon began to respond, his right hand instinctively moved up and tapped his left shoulder, an old habit. It was a gesture from his days trading stock options on the floor of the old London Stock Exchange next to the Bank of England, used to signify his status as a buyer. "Buy 250 at best."

Tony quietly followed Jon's instruction and on completion yelled out to him, "250 you buy at 109 and 11/32nds."

"Thanks, Tony. Book 'em, proprietary account No. 1." Jon had just purchased $250 million worth of thirty-year U.S. government bonds for the bank's proprietary account and his day was gathering momentum. "Tony, where does that leave them?"

Tony had his ear to the phone. "The futures are a little firmer. He'll offer another 250 at 109 and 13/32nds."

"Take them again at thirteen." Once more, Jon's right hand moved instinctively up to touch his left shoulder.

Tony did not remove the telephone receiver held to his ear. "You've got 'em at thirteen. You are now long 500 at an average price of 109 and 12/32nds. That's a yield of just over 4.74%."

Jon nodded. Now his purchase amounted to five hundred million dollars worth of thirty-year U.S. government bonds, a position consistent with what he'd outlined in the morning briefing. By Jon's standards, buying half a billion dollars worth of highly liquid, but not-so-recently issued benchmark thirty-year U.S. government bonds was not a large trade.

The early excitement generated by the monthly non-farm payroll figures was now dissipating. The floor settled back into its normal stride, dynamic but not frantic. Jon concentrated on the second-by-second technical analysis of the price action in the bond futures market. He was searching for the appropriate price levels to either add to his position if the market continued to fall, or to reduce his position by taking profits if the market moved higher, a process known as technical analysis, or charting.

Jon earned his substantial salary and bonuses by combining this price action analysis with other economic and fundamental data in order to take advantage of opportunities within the market. It was also up to him to balance the economic and psychological factors in the market, and then make a judgment as to how each would affect the price of government bonds. It all added up to a constant battle with the marketplace.

Later in the day, his mouth half-full of the sandwich passing for a late lunch, Jon grabbed one of the constantly ringing phones. Upon hearing the caller's voice, his face lit up. "Da . . . David?" He blurted. "Where the hell are you? I haven't heard from you in weeks."

"Sorry, Jon, I'm in Mongolia. I kept meaning to give you a call, but the camp's satellite telephone broke down so I had to wait for a lift into UB."

"Ulaanbaatar? You're still in that Godforsaken place?"

Jon and his younger brother were alike in many aspects, their wanderlust taking them to opposite ends of the globe, far away from the family's cattle farm. The bond between them was partly forged by the fact that neither had chosen to fulfill their father's wish that they succeed him in running the farm. They shared the same handsome features and were both tall, with dark wavy hair, and a presence that got them noticed in a crowd. While Jon had chosen a course of economics and law at Melbourne University, David had majored in geology, set on becoming a wildcat exploration geologist. In his attempt to stake a claim in the gold mining industry, David had worked his way across some pretty inhospitable regions, from the Australian northwest to southern Africa, the tropics of Indonesia, war-torn Angola, and now, the frozen steppes of Mongolia.

"Yes, still! I've been in the field for over two months."

Jon didn't hesitate. "And now you're taking a break? Fabulous, mate, you're coming here. I need to see you."

"Jonny, I called you for a reason. I can't. I'm going home. I'm getting married."

Jon sat in silence, stunned by the news. It had caught him completely off-guard. He felt that David had somehow trumped him, in beating him to the altar. "What can I say? I'm surprised, but thrilled. Good move. I assume its Lucy, right?"

David laughed loudly. "Of course it is. Couldn't imagine myself with anything but a nice, wholesome, Aussie chick. Those fast, high-living New York birds are out of my league, mate. Couldn't afford 'em, even if I wanted to. I'm pretty excited, actually."

"You are a lucky man. Are you going home for good?" The big question, one the brothers had asked themselves and each other on many occasions.

"Yep. Settling down, finally. Mum and Dad are happy, needless to say."

A flash of envy washed over Jon. "I bet they are, mate. Mum will be beside herself and Dad will finally have one of us running the farm."

"Not too fast, Jonny boy. I'm still not one hundred percent sure where I'll be living. But the farm's certainly an option and Dad's already on my case."

"We really need to get together. Changes happening all around. Come over here, David. On your way home."

"Jonny, I'm in fucking UB, not L.A. It's hardly on my way."

As usual, Jon's accent broadened while talking with his brother. "Who gives a fuck? You're getting married, I'm thinking about making some career moves, and we need to get together. Come here for a wild one. A million drinks, a few birds, that sort of thing. Let's tear up the town before you settle down. Fuck you, you're coming to New York, and I won't take no for an answer."

In fact, David liked the idea. He might have traveled to some of the most exotic corners of the world in the course of his work, but a bachelor blast in New York City with the brother he never saw enough of appealed to him. "Mate, it's not the silliest idea I've heard all day. I'll think about it."

"It's a yes, then. Fabulous! The spare room's already waiting for you."

And that was that. Jon grinned as he hung up. This Friday was turning out to be a very good day.

Chapter Three

The serenity of the early Saturday morning was abruptly pierced by the ringing of a telephone. The sun had just risen on a cloudless day outside the luxurious confines of the condominium building. Taking up one-third of a floor, the airy apartment was decorated in an uncompromisingly minimalist style, conveying the essence of chic, contemporary design. Its views reached well beyond the Hudson and the East Rivers, encompassing the full Triborough experience.

As dawn washed over the ample, open-plan living room, the telephone refused to give up, repeatedly shattering the early morning calm. Frank Sinatra was crooning, "I Get a Kick Out of You" from a stereo located somewhere beyond the large, unconscious figure sprawled half-on and half-off the sofa. Long hairy legs protruded from a crumpled cream-colored, lace-and-taffeta evening gown. Mascara-laden eyelashes fluttered in an attempt to reach consciousness.

It was Jon, awakening to a new day. He propped himself up with a start, then tried several times to blink, unsuccessfully, before reaching up to peel off the mascaraed fake eyelashes welding his eyes together. In the process he smeared red lipstick across a pale cheek sorely in need of a shave. A dark wig, cut in an even fringe, lay crookedly across his forehead.

Slowly looking around, he struggled to get his bearings, adjusting an arm that had been twisted uncomfortably beneath his torso. Danielle slept next to him on the sofa, her head resting heavily on his artificially padded chest. Like Jon, she was thoroughly disheveled. He regarded her for a few moments, then looked across the room to take in a man passed out on the floor, still clutching a trumpet. The man wore an ill-fitting blonde wig, cut straight and styled in a short pageboy. He was dressed unfashionably in a brightly colored, seventies-style knitted sweater and beige slacks. After registering the man's presence, Jon scanned the apartment. Half-empty bottles and overturned glasses littered the floor in post-party disarray.

The phone persisted, unrelenting.

"Make it stop," the man on the floor pleaded.

Jon still seemed unaware of the ringing. Finally, he slid Danielle's head carefully off his chest and settled her against the cushions. She exhaled the smallest of sighs and snuggled into the warm indentation of his form on the sofa as he shakily stood up.

Yet another ring prompted him to search for the cordless handset. It was nowhere to be found, so after unsuccessfully struggling to place a headset on top of his tousled wig, he stumbled over to the console unit on the granite kitchen counter and hit Speaker.

"Did I wake you?" The voice on the phone asked cheerily.

"No, no," Jon replied. "I was just . . . I've been out running I just got back in."

"Running? Who are you kidding?"

"David?" Jon was now on firmer ground. "What's up? Do you know when you're arriving yet?"

"Yes, that's why I'm calling. I've organized a flight to Beijing, and from there I'll get on a plane to New York. I should be there late afternoon, a week from the day after tomorrow. I'll just catch a cab to your place."

"See you then. Can't wait." And with that, Jon hung up. He

and David shared the habit of abruptly terminating telephone conversations, rarely offering a "goodbye."

By now the other two occupants of the apartment were beginning to stir. Danielle got up, stretched and yawned noisily, then stumbled across the room to turn off the stereo just as Frank was starting in again on "I Get a Kick Out of You." Sweeping aside an ashtray and some glasses, she sat down and dumped the contents of her handbag out on the dining room table. Sorting through the pile, she fished out a large packet of cocaine, cut herself a line, rolled a ten-dollar bill, and snorted it. With a sigh, she tilted her head back and closed her eyes, waiting for the drug to take effect.

Jon gave her a look. "And just what do you think you're doing?"

Danielle's eyes opened, then narrowed, looking him up and down. "Having breakfast."

"Oh, for God's sake, can't you pass on the drugs even for a moment? It gets to be a bore."

"No, as a matter of fact, I can't." She got up and walked slowly over to Jon, and in one fluid movement, slapped him across the face. "Nor do I choose to."

"And what did I do to deserve that?"

Danielle raised one finger to her right nostril and sniffed loudly. "For one thing, you look like my goddamned mother in that ridiculous dress. And if you're my mom, I don't even want to think about what that would make me."

"A drugged-up lush with a very well-dressed mother, I'd say."

She slapped him again, harder this time. He was unmoved, it didn't really register. Annoyed, she grabbed him, thrusting her pelvis into his, and kissed him passionately on the mouth. Nothing.

After a few moments, she broke away. "You know, if it wasn't for the sex, I'd throw you the hell out of my life."

"If it wasn't for the sex, you wouldn't be in it."

She drew back her hand to hit him again, but this time he caught her arm. She hissed at him. "Fuck you!"

But Jon was too hung over and tired to play her games. "The

door's over there. Now get the hell out. I've had quite enough of you for a while."

For a fleeting moment, Danielle looked shaken. She was a woman used to having complete control over her lovers, and, for that matter, almost everyone else. Jon could make her feel vulnerable, however, an emotion with which she was relatively unfamiliar and distinctly uncomfortable. He had correctly intuited it was the only way to play her when they'd first gotten together several months earlier.

"I'll go when I want to go. No one tells me what to do. Anyway, I'm sick of you and your crazy friend. I'll be back for a piece of you later, when I don't have to share you with your nerdy pal." She glanced dismissively at the man still lying, semi-conscious, on the floor. "Call me when you realize you can't live without me, and do try to wait at least until I get home."

Jon nodded toward the door. "Don't flatter yourself."

"I don't need to; I've got everyone else to do that for me. Anyway, I'm off. As always, Jonny, it's been a whole lot of fun. Ciao, baby."

Jon turned away from her. "Bugger off, for God's sake."

She grabbed him again but this time, kissed him gently and affectionately on the cheek. "You know you love me, Jonny, and I know you couldn't live without me." She picked up her handbag, swept its jumbled contents back into it, and left, blowing a kiss in Jon's direction. Jon smiled, in spite of himself.

The man on the floor — an old friend of Jon's — was now awake, although so shaky he had to steady himself on the wall in order to get on his feet. "I tell you, Karen, that chick is pretty as a picture, but she's a dangerous one. Surely not the type you'd take home to meet mummy."

Jon nodded in agreement. "Damn right. Mum keeps telling me to settle down, but just imagine what she'd do if I turned up with that little designer number. No, she's strictly late-night New York."

"Well, boys will be girls." Timmy was now wide awake, and grinning.

Contemplating each other's appearance, they burst into simultaneous laughter. "I certainly hope we raised one hell of a lot of money last night. Who would have suspected Karen and Richard Carpenter still had so many fans!" Jon managed to get out, through his laughter.

"Yeah, our number was definitely the biggest hit of the whole shindig," Timmy replied, when he'd recovered himself. "But I don't think my outfit won me any points with those society dames."

Jon was still laughing as he ran his hand over the dress he was wearing. "You know, there's nothing quite like the feel of taffeta in the morning," he vamped.

Timmy moved toward the kitchen. "You sure as hell know how to live well in this city. Any chance of a job at the bank for someone like me?"

Jon smiled. "Mate, I'm sorry to say your timing is off, given that I'm currently working on my exit strategy."

Seeing that Jon was serious, Timmy gestured toward the expanse of Manhattan sky visible across the living room. "How can you possibly want to give all this up?" he asked, with genuine disbelief.

Jon sat slumped in his chair, his long, hairy legs protruding awkwardly from his taffeta evening gown. "What I do is not quite as easy as it might look. Plus, I've come up with a plan for making a whole lot of money in a very short time."

"How do you do that? I thought all the easy money scams went out with the . . . umm . . . well, with the Carpenters." Timmy laughed. "So what's this plan?"

"Look, I've just woken up on my couch in a dress that I'm not sure even Karen Carpenter would ever have worn, I've thrown my bird out of my apartment 'cause I couldn't face her one minute longer and, without wanting to be rude, I really can't be fucked talking about my work right now."

"Jonny, we never talk about what you do. Just give it to me in shorthand. Who knows, maybe there'd be a buck in it for me."

"Mate, I'd love to cut you in, but this deal can only involve the bank and one other large London-based client. That's the beauty of it. It doesn't involve anyone or anything else," Jon replied.

"But what's the angle? How are you going to make your killing?" Now that Jon had piqued Timmy's curiosity, he wasn't about to give up. "It can't be as simple as all that, nothing is anymore."

"It is and it isn't." Jon sighed, pausing before launching into the explanation that his friend seemed so keen to hear. "I'll start with the basics. Every three months the U.S. government has to borrow money from the public — well, that is, financial institutions — both in America and overseas in order to fund its spending programs. When it borrows this money, it does so by issuing government bonds. These government bonds pay a fixed annual interest rate and they each have a specific date when the government has to pay back all the money it has borrowed. Normally, the government borrows over two-, three-, five- and ten-year periods."

"And that's what you do, right?" Timmy interrupted. "You buy and sell these government bonds for the bank as their price goes up and down?"

"That's it, baby," Jon nodded, pleased that Timmy was following his explanation. "The bond prices go up or down depending on the U.S. economic conditions and investors' expectations at a given moment in time. What I'm trying to do this time is to buy a huge number of these newly issued ten-year government bonds all at once during the bond auction the government is having next week. There's no other way of buying such a large number of bonds so quickly."

"What does 'huge' mean in your Wall Street language?" Timmy queried.

"That's a fair question, but I'd ask you not to mention the answer or what I'm planning to do to anyone," Jon said, suddenly cautious. "I need to be very discreet about it."

"And, like, who am I going to tell? The only kind of bond my crowd knows about is bonded whiskey and they don't even get to see all that much of that."

Jon laughed, reassured. "Right you are. Okay then, what I want to do is to buy between ten and fifteen billion dollars worth of the ten-year government bonds all in one hit and, as I said, the only way I can do that is via one of these quarterly auctions."

Timmy was stunned. "Fifteen *billion* dollars of government bonds? That seems an awful lot of money you're spending here. Exactly whose money is it?"

"It's all the bank's money, although I need this other client of the bank's — the London-based company — to take, in addition, a large chunk of bonds I'm technically not allowed to take. The bank will bear all the financial risk, and the London client is just in it to front for the extra bonds that I'm not allowed to buy in the auction. As you can gather, it's not strictly legal."

"I love it!" Timmy said, responding to Jon's excitement. "The bank puts up all the money, takes all the risk and you get all the glory."

"That's it." Jon's heart quickened at the mere thought of it. "With a position that big, I take control of the bond auction, which gives me temporary control of the whole government bond market. Then, once I artificially push up the price of the bonds after the auction, I plan to sell them for a tidy profit. And since I get paid on a bonus system, my fortunes and the bank's are connected, so I'll be getting a big piece of the action."

Timmy was looking puzzled. "But how can you manage to push up the bond prices, all on your own?"

"The effect of a few floated rumors about what's happening in the market is amazing," Jon replied, smiling enigmatically. But he was beginning to tire, the revelry of the previous evening catching up with him.

"I get it. But Jonny, just one more question. May I ask just how much you expect to bag in this scam?" Timmy wanted to at least fantasize about the rewards his friend's ambitious scheme could net him.

"It's almost impossible to know, but I'm hoping my cut may be as much as eight or nine million." Jon knew that to someone like

Timmy, such numbers had very little reality. This was confirmed by Timmy's reaction.

"Wow! That's crazy, man! I'm the penniless musician-type, but I think I get the plan. You're using this auction process to get a shit load of these new bonds so you can manipulate the market by pushing their prices up and then selling them all at a price higher than what you paid for them." Timmy was justifiably proud of his summary.

Jon nodded. "You are very good, Timmy. That's it, exactly, and I'll have a big bonus check to facilitate my early retirement from the bank." He yawned as he stood up, now feeling his largely sleepless night in every muscle. "Hey, mate, you're out of here. I've got to get myself in order. I've got an important date at the racetrack in about . . ." He checked the clock on the stove, "three hours."

Reluctantly, Timmy packed up his wig, gathered his belongings and left, wishing Jon luck on his way out. Jon stood in momentary silence. He caught his reflection in the panoramic living room windows and saw how ridiculous he looked. Quickly, he unzipped his dress and stepped out of it. Naked, he wandered into his bedroom and studied himself critically in a full-length mirror. Better, he thought, but he still needed to wash away the indulgences of the previous night, not to mention what was left of his makeup. He headed for the bathroom and turned on the seven-headed spray in his granite-lined shower, the morning's phone call on his mind.

He longed to spend some time with his brother. Although he'd grown used to being an outsider, first in London and then in New York, he immediately felt at home wherever he happened to be when his little brother was around. The timing of this visit was perfect, just when he really needed a steadying presence, someone simpatico with whom to talk over his next move. The bond auction would free him from what he was coming to regard as a straight-jacket — his job — but what then? If anyone could help him figure that out, David could.

Funny how although so different, they were, in all the important ways, so very much alike. It was in the genes. They'd grown up as country lads, in a town called Mansfield in northeastern Victoria. Snow in winter and bushfires in summer — it was regarded as difficult country, with its harsh and mountainous terrain. Made world-famous by the movie based on AB "Banjo" Patterson's epic poem "The Man from Snowy River", the region bred a particular type, hardy and self-sufficient. Jon and David had been raised to believe in the virtues of hard work and responsibility.

Their father was a tough, fourth-generation Australian, quick to point out that his father had participated in the first landing at the infamous Gallipoli Cove in 1915, during the early days of World War I. Every year, Australians celebrate the fortitude of these men — most of whom were ordered to their slaughter by incompetent British commanders — by marching through the streets of each major town and city. Forever etched into the calendar on April 25 as ANZAC day, it is an important public holiday in Australia, a day both Jon and David noted, if only in passing, wherever they found themselves. Jon firmly believed in the saying about taking the boy out of Australia but not Australia out of the boy. In some profound way, the longer both Jon and David spent outside Australia, the more Australian they became.

Toweling himself dry, Jon had to smile when he thought of how he often described going into work as going into battle. In fact, when compared to David's hardscrabble nomadic existence, he'd been leading a pretty cushy life. All his battles were interior ones, whereas David's life had actually been in danger on more than one occasion. A couple of phone calls ago, he'd told Jon about the long, bleak winter he'd just endured in Ulaanbaatar, the coldest capital city in the world. The winter months in the field had apparently been brutal. Still, in an obvious attempt to appear upbeat, he'd made a point of noting that the Mongolian people were friendly, and that the new, democratically elected government was doing what it could to accommodate ambitious western entrepreneurs. To him, this meant there was a growing group of ex-pats, predominantly Australians, Canadians, and Brits, with whom to have a good time during breaks from the isolation of the mining fields.

Back when they both were coming of age in the early eighties, the gold market had been one of the world's most important. Fortunes were being made and lost on an almost daily basis, as promoters looking for a fast buck used the huge interest in gold to publicly list gold companies, stake claims in exotic regions of the globe, and sell to private investors. They would then speculatively trade the daily fluctuations of the metal's spot price. It was during those heady days that David had left Melbourne, right after graduating from the university, to try to tap into the opportunities gold prospecting offered.

The rise and fall of interest in gold was a paradigm of the ill-fated boom-and-bust cycle in the technology sector that would take place some fifteen years later. Jon thought the two sectors had a great deal in common, starting with the fact that both relied on what might be more than what was. And in both, investors were seduced by the allure of the almost-unlimited wealth associated with finding the "big one." David was fond of quoting an old saying in the mining industry; something to the effect of the best way to ruin an untapped gold mine is by extracting the gold, since the promise is greater than the economic reality. Similarly, in the technology sector, the reality almost never matched the promise, and investors were all too often left holding worthless share certificates they had paid a fortune for.

Although the careers they'd chosen seemed very different, there were, in fact, some striking similarities. Each brother possessed the ambition and optimism necessary to succeed in his world. Without optimism, a geologist had little to drive him. It was always the next drill hole that would prove him right and make him rich. For a while, David experienced mixed success, but the 1990s proved to be a difficult market for gold. As its price fell from over $700 an ounce in the early 1980s to less than $300 an ounce in the late 1990s, David's prospects dimmed and he began losing his all-important positive outlook. While Jon had thrived during those years in the unprecedented prosperity of the financial world, David had begun to tire of the conditions under which he was forced to work; the loneliness, the diminishing commercial prospects, and the long absences from home. Jon missed little about living in Australia, but he was glad for their father's sake that at least David would be going home. And if he could also be persuaded to take on the farm, better yet.

Chapter Four

The week was going much too slowly for Jon. He was having a hard time concentrating on anything but next Tuesday's auction. Today had been quiet, with the stock market holding steady and no major U.S. economic releases to move the bond market one way or another. Bored, he killed time by flipping through the bank's vast array of reports and recommendations put forth by their various highly touted and highly paid senior advisors and analysts. This activity always set him off, and today was no exception. Impatiently flinging the glossy folder he'd been skimming into a wastebasket, he called over to Tony.

"So, Tony, how many senior economists would you say we have on salary here?"

"Well, including only the celebs, I'd say about four: Barlon, Brian, Kirsty and Chester," replied Tony, eyeing Jon quizzically.

"You're absolutely right. Would it surprise you to know that not one of them agrees with any other? They spend half their fucking lives elbowing their way onto any television screen that'll have them, or fighting to the death for column inches in the Journal, all without ever having to account for their views in any significant way." Jon shook his head dismissively and sighed. "They aren't fund managers or investors; they don't actually trade their opinions. All they do is pontificate about what our clients should do with their money. And if they're wrong, not only will it not matter, but they'll also deny it. They're never held accountable. What is the point of these ridiculous people?"

"Those are Wall Street's biggest gurus you're trashing," Tony reminded Jon.

"But it's incredible, isn't it? Kirsty says the Dow's going to twelve thousand, Barlon thinks it's going to hell, Chester says it's impossible to call and according to Brian, we're in a trading range." There was now more anger than edge in Jon's tone. "They're not only useless, they're downright destructive."

"You'd better keep your views to yourself, Jon boy," Ellen interrupted. "That kind of attitude doesn't exactly promote the one-big-happy-family image we're trying to project to our clients."

"I don't give a shit, and I'm certainly not going to pay attention to any of their nonsense." Jon swiveled his chair toward Ellen. "The markets are noisy enough. Part of our job here is to cut out all this background noise and make our own judgments." Jon was now addressing all three members of his team, each of whom had heard it all before. "That's the difference. We have to act on our views. We live by the sword and die by it. These clowns just run off at the mouth about it."

By now Tony and Gary were pantomiming yawns while Ellen rolled her eyes heavenward. Jon regarded them with affection. His was a tight group. It had to be, since even the slightest misunderstanding could be extremely costly. The speed at which the U.S. treasury market moved did not allow for easily unwound mistakes. His team had to be able to absorb a huge amount of risk, and the rewards they could reap were substantial not only for the bank, but for the team as a whole. Plus, the higher the profitability of the team during the year, the larger their share of the annual bonus pool.

Jon glanced toward the floor entrance and saw Robert Baldwin approaching. Heavyset, but with a chiseled fitness admirable for a man in his mid-forties, Baldwin walked like the college athlete he'd been. Even though he and Jon were no longer as close as when they were coming up together, between blowing off steam late at night in the pool at the club and strategizing and covering each other's back at work, Jon still considered Baldwin a friend. After he'd married Rita and the kids had come along, their paths and priorities became so different that the newer employees at the bank couldn't figure out why they were friends at all. But they noticed how Baldwin could say things to Jon no one else could get away with, and they wondered.

Making a show of ignoring Baldwin, Jon turned toward Ellen and commented loudly, "Have you noticed that every time I pick up the telephone these days, the head of compliance comes trotting over to make sure I'm not in the process of destroying his and the bank's livelihood and reputation?" Turning toward Baldwin, he continued. "And then after I hold his hand and tell him all is okay, his confidence is restored . . . for at least five whole minutes." He smiled.

"If that!" Baldwin nodded.

"It's a wonder you weren't climbing all over me on Friday when I put these bond trades on."

"I was out, otherwise I would have been." Baldwin was not joking.

"Wait a minute. Are you serious? What's the big deal, here?" Jon's tone shifted. "We're talking $500 million worth of U.S. Government bonds, arguably the strongest credit risk in the world. Any risk attached to them is simply price risk, and I have no doubt whatsoever the bank can live with that." Baldwin started to reply, but Jon cut him off as he got up from his desk and shrugged into his coat. "In any case, and not that it really concerns you, these suckers will be gone before you know it. It's just a trade, Robert, the kind of trade I'm paid not to ignore, and I also want to clear my book before the auction."

That brought a look from Baldwin that made Jon laugh out

loud. "Don't say it! Come on, let's get out of here. Where am I taking you to lunch this time?"

Soho, Manhattan

After indulging themselves on pasta and veal chops, they sipped espressos at one of Jon's favorite hangouts, I Tre Merli on West Broadway, off Prince. Whenever he could, Jon took the extra few minutes to grab a cab to Soho rather than patronizing the dark, wood-paneled and leather-furnished establishments preferred by most of the denizens of Wall Street. The streets and shops of Soho seemed to date from a decade later than those in the financial district, and he didn't mind the tourists. Most of the time, he felt more like one of them than a New York native himself.

Reflective after their meal, the two men were discussing a familiar topic, Baldwin summing up his argument. "The simple question is whether the bank needs to incur the risks you take on a daily basis when the income these days is so strong elsewhere. I know you and I will never agree on this. We just see this business from different angles."

It made Baldwin uncomfortable that he did not understand precisely how Jon generated his profits for the bank. Proprietary trading was not a science, and the profits it produced were entirely the result of judgments made by the kind of individual who was notoriously averse to being controlled. Jon's team was still a strong profit center for the bank, so Baldwin had to live with the bank's decision to continue to maintain a large proprietary book.

As always, Jon was quick to defend his position. "That's the problem with you guys, you always gravitate toward the safe and easy buck. May I remind you of how ten years ago, when I first came to New York, the markets were flat, and mine was the only area making any money? Other areas of the bank were sacrificed to concentrate on the game of the moment, which happened to be trading. Now it's the steady, no-risk income of the advisory business — brokerage, mergers and acquisitions, and investment banking.

When that dries up, you'll see, you'll be looking toward proprietary trading again to boost the bank's falling income."

Baldwin started to reply, but Jon quickly cut him off. "The brokers won't be able to get a client to buy any stock, for love nor money, and merger and acquisitions activity will have well and truly died off, as it's already done. At that point, you'll be desperate for a trading team, and all you'll have is a floor full of glorified sales-people who wouldn't know a real market if they fell on it. Your competition will be doing the same. You'll see. You'll all be desperate to set up a proprietary team again so you aren't left behind by your competition."

Baldwin smiled broadly. "It's interesting to note that you don't include yourself in this scenario of the future."

"Damn right I don't. At least I'm smart enough to realize I've got a limited shelf life. That what's I'm saying, it's cyclical. There will be a time when my type of business is completely out of favor before it turns around again."

Baldwin interrupted. "And that time may be now. Inevitably there will be more crash-and-burns, like Enron, WorldCom, LTCM, and the others. Are we just expected to ignore that fact, or be trying to prevent them?"

"Come on, Robert, you of all people should know where the real problems come from. It's not from risk-taking. It's lack of experience and control that create them every time."

Baldwin was quick to counter. "You couldn't possibly describe John Merriwether and the team at LTCM as inexperienced. They built Long Term Capital Management into the largest and most successful hedge fund ever. And then led it to ruin."

"I agree. LTCM is a modern classic, a prime example of over-confidence, not incompetence. They had the experience, but the leverage they were using, nearly fifty times their capital at the time of their collapse, was downright reckless. Not to mention, they were also unlucky. They might have pulled it off, but they just plain got unlucky."

"So what's your point?"

"My point is, Robert, that LTCM was raped. As you know very well, their downfall was used as an opportunity for certain members of the fourteen banks they owed to simply steal the money back. And steal it they did. Come on, the Chapter 11 bankruptcy process normally takes between three and five years, and the largest financial collapse in the history of America was completed in five days. The whole thing was just outrageous. But the LTCM experience was unique."

Baldwin distractedly acknowledged Jon's point while fumbling in his pockets for his vibrating cell phone. It was his daughter calling, and while Baldwin questioned her about the ballet class she'd just taken, Jon signed for the check, thinking back on his own peripheral, though fortuitous, involvement with the LTCM failure.

Early in August of 1998, rumblings in the futures market had suggested that a massive spread trade was being unwound. Jon believed it to be LTCM. As it happened, he had been following LTCM closely, even regarding its CEO, John Merriwether, as his role model. He figured that if the rumors were true, the prices of the thirty-year U.S. government bond futures market would rise sharply, as these spread trades were sold into an increasingly tough market. Although still a young and relatively green trader at the time, Jon managed to wrest permission from the bank to buy large quantities of the thirty-year government bond futures on its proprietary account. He was also quick to advise other departments in the bank that he thought a storm was brewing with LTCM right in the middle of it. A number of the senior traders within the bank listened to what Jon was saying, subsequently selling large quantities of corporate bonds only days before their prices collapsed.

Jon had second-guessed the largest financial collapse in American's history, and had gotten it spectacularly right. Not only did the government bond futures rally strongly, making Jon's position very profitable, but the early warning he had given his colleagues was both greatly appreciated and widely recognized. In nailing it, he had become something of a local hero. Nonetheless, he was one of the few who didn't openly delight in the misfortunes of the

LTCM team. He saw it as the end of a very short, though important, era. Wall Street would be unlikely to again support such financial leverage.

Baldwin assured his daughter he was very, very proud of her, then hung up and turned to Jon. "But what about the others? Less complex and more relevant to where this discussion started."

Again Jon was quick to respond. "Yes. Totally different. Take Barings, for example. An idiot kid from south London, based in Singapore and in over his head trading in the Nikkei Index futures, gets into a giant hole and panics. So what does he do? He starts selling index puts, thereby exacerbating the problem in a desperate attempt to cover his margin calls. And nobody picks up on it. No one. Although Barings is happy to send five hundred million dollars cash across to Singapore with no questions asked. Meanwhile, the board is sitting around in London, the other side of the world, marbles firmly lodged in their mouths, fretting about what claret they are going to order for lunch. Who's to blame? What did they think that five hundred million dollars was buying them?"

Baldwin cut in. "Exactly. That's exactly the kind of trouble I'm paid to keep us out of and to ensure that no wayward individual," Robert shot Jon a meaningful look, "can put together a position that could threaten the well-being of the bank."

Jon was undeterred. "You know, it's not that easy to lose one billion dollars, and it's virtually impossible to do it all by yourself. Look at the guy at Daiwa: he drops $1.1 billion plus over ten years. Ten years, for goodness sake! And what about the guy at Allied Irish who got whacked in the dollar-yen market? That one took two years! Who's running the accounts, for Christ's sake? Fiduciary responsibility? These senior administrators have proven themselves simply incapable of running the very businesses that they have helped create. And when the going gets tough, they're never willing to step up to the responsibilities that go with their position. So what do they do? They immediately search for a fall guy, it doesn't matter who it is as long as it's someone as far removed from the board room as possible."

Jon paused briefly to take a breath. This was something he felt strongly about. "If an operation is properly managed, there is only so much damage a rogue trader can do. Look at Sumitomo, there's another fine example. A 'one-off' disaster in the copper market that took over five years to unfold and cost the Japanese Bank over two billion dollars. How can something so isolated take over five years to be noticed? The simple answer is that without a chain of complete incompetence throughout the senior management, it can't."

Baldwin had had enough. "All that may well be true, but don't think you're diverting me from my determination to make sure that a few years from now, some other traders aren't sitting over lunch discussing how *your* big move went wrong."

"You've made your point, Robert, but I've gotta go. Gotta get back to the desk."

Wall Street, Manhattan

Friday afternoon, and the week was drawing to a close. For those involved in global markets, or in instruments like the U.S. government bond markets, which traded across Asia and Europe each day before the U.S. market opened, there was a point on Friday afternoon when it came time for the week to end. Most U.S. financial market participants could operate within the civilized East Coast time frame of nine to three. Jon's week, however, began with the opening of Tokyo on Sunday night, and ended as the bonds closed shortly after 3:00 P.M. on Friday afternoon. Only those who actively traded the foreign exchange markets had to put in more hours.

The week had continued uneventfully for Jon. Baldwin had taken him aside to brief him on the upcoming bond auction. Keeping his voice low, he'd again pointed out what Jon was well aware of. By taking control of all the government's bonds in order to manipulate the market for a substantial profit, the bank would be in technical breach of SEC rules. Despite this, Johnston had confirmed to Baldwin that the Bank of Manhattan's Board of Directors was not only approving Jon's intended maneuver, but was providing a U.K.

institution to take another thirty-five percent of the auction so Jon could double his position while at least appearing to stay within the rules, even though he wouldn't actually be doing so. Jon had asked Baldwin the name of the company.

"It's a new institutional client of Johnston's called the U.K. Trading Company. I don't know much more than that," Baldwin had responded.

"Is the documentation in order?" Jon had asked perceptively.

"We're putting it all in place now, and Johnston has already organized the funding with them. They have already remitted thirty-five million dollars into their new margin account here at the bank."

"That's more than enough for them to buy a ticket into the game isn't it?"

"It is."

"Well, then, relax. The idea to take the auction out may have been mine, but it's the board that's making it possible, so you're in the clear. We have authority at the highest level."

"I suppose you're right," Baldwin had acknowledged hesitantly. "But this is my direct responsibility, and unfortunately, I have little choice. If Johnston says it's okay, then it's okay with compliance. Who am I to question the word of a senior director representing the board?"

Jon had smiled at his friend's discomfiture. "Exactly. This has been approved at the very top, so on Tuesday we'll be ready to go."

"Yes, it looks that way," Baldwin had reluctantly agreed.

Jon was always ready to tease Baldwin about being scared of his own shadow, but he understood where Baldwin was coming from. Throughout the 1990s, banks were increasingly expected to know what and who their clients were in order to protect themselves against different types of risks. The problem of money laundering was growing, however. The more traditional centers had largely been closed down over the past twenty years, as sanitizing dirty money became a globally monitored activity, and any financial institution found assisting it was harshly dealt with.

Although global financial institutions such as the World Bank and the Bank of International Settlements had vast powers to monitor the international flow of funds, they could not possibly monitor each and every transaction. Because of this, they required the compliance of all regulated banks. Any bank that failed to fully comply ran the risk of losing its banking license, effectively putting it out of business. Enforced compliance also meant any prospective client of the Bank of Manhattan would have to withstand the increasingly rigorous due diligence process imposed by Baldwin and his team.

Wall Street, Manhattan

Traders were beginning to gather in small groups scattered around the trading floor to discuss the upcoming weekend. Although they were predominantly young and male, there were a lot more women scattered among them than when Jon had first come to New York. The trading floor was both managed and monitored, but this did not prevent the pursuit of sexual conquests, especially at the end of the week, when letting off steam would be the chosen activity for most of them. They all had plenty of disposable income and were itching to spend it.

One of the brashest young traders approached Jon. "Hey, Jonny, why not join us for a few beers?" He was smartly dressed, and if he had any trepidation in approaching his senior, he wasn't letting on. "Should be a laugh and plenty of chicks to go around. Perhaps an old guy like you could pick up a few pointers from us young bucks. What d'ya say, man?"

There was a time when Jon would have joined them. Now he smiled and shook his head. "I'm sure you guys party too hard and too fast for an old guy like me. Maybe next time." It wasn't just an excuse, he realized. He really wasn't interested. His partying was better done in private. He had nothing to prove to them anymore.

The trader was disappointed. "If we can't tempt you, you must have something better lined up."

"Not me. My idea of a wild time is a few beers and a video. I get enough action in here every day. I don't have the energy for anything else. You youngsters go out and have a wild time on my behalf."

"You guys are getting old before your time." The young brokers included Delboy, who had wandered over and was listening to their exchange, in his comment. "Ah, well, can't say we didn't try to improve the quality of your dull existence, Jonny. Catch you later, old man." And he moved away from the desk to rejoin his friends.

Delboy stood, coat in hand, caught in a rare moment of reflection. "I guess maybe we are getting old."

"And why do you think that?"

"We're a different breed from these new boys and girlies."

"That's true. Handsome, street-smart, and fun to be with. Now that you need an MBA or a PhD just to get onto a desk, we're getting people who've had no real experience outside a classroom. They never have a chance to learn what's really important."

Delboy immediately cheered up. "Exactly. Experiences like running gambling rackets and abusing alcohol and drugs while they are still young and carefree enough to enjoy it. It's true; these Harvard types are pure textbook. Wouldn't know a workable scam if they fell on it."

Jon smiled broadly. "Never a truer word said. But I tell you what; they sure know how to beat a path to Brooks Brothers and Barneys." Delboy laughed in agreement. "And they are also PhD's in knowing how to steal your job, your girlfriend, or anything else of value that's not nailed down."

The two became aware of a small group centered on one of the more aggressive young over-the-counter option traders. He was excitedly boasting about acquiring a brand-new Porsche 911. All day he'd been telling anyone who would listen, describing every detail of his S4. Jon had made no comment during the day, but now, with a wink at Delboy, he called over to the trader, who was preparing to leave. "Hey, Charlie, I hear you're about to pick up a new sports car."

Delighted to have attracted Jon's attention, the trader turned, beaming. "Sure am, Jonny."

Jon continued. "You must be very excited. A 911, huh? Terrific. But let me ask you, do you know the difference between a Porsche 911 and a porcupine?"

The trader shook his head. "No, what's the difference?"

Jon's voice rose, for all to hear. "With a porcupine, the pricks are on the outside."

Midtown Manhattan

Jon gulped down his long, tall glass of beer as Delboy leaned forward to poke a folded ten-dollar bill underneath the garter of the dancer who spun professionally around her pole. The bar was full of suits enjoying their first drink of the weekend as they happily ogled the wide variety of strippers who came and went in the midtown girlie bar.

Delboy reached into his pocket for yet another ten-dollar bill from his seemingly inexhaustible supply. "I'm considering going back to London."

It wasn't the first time Jon had heard this from Delboy. "I suppose it happens to all of us at some point," he commented, as he gave the roaming waitress in the dangerously low-cut bunnyesque outfit the high sign for two more beers.

"Well, it's happening to me now," said Delboy, thoughtfully. "Do you know how New York and London are different?"

"I think so, but please tell me, oh wise one."

"It's simple, really. In this city, everybody is from somewhere else. That's what makes it easier for guys like you and I. We can just slip into a place like this because everyone else here is a foreigner as well. They may not sound like we do, but they're the same as us."

"So what?" Jon asked, knowing what the answer was going to be.

"That's why this place will never be home. There is no sense of belonging. This city recycles everything, including its people." Delboy took his new beer off the waitress's tray and tipped her generously. "In London, that's not true, and that's what makes it home.

This place is full of predators just waiting to be recycled. London is full of Londoners, real ones, born and bred."

"Perhaps, but in London, someone with an accent like mine will always be a foreigner and looked down upon. Here, not only do they not hold it against you, they love it." Jon took a gulp of his beer. "They are just different, that's all. But it's true; New Yorkers have forgotten you within moments of your exit. The Brits don't forget you quite so quickly. Once you've established yourself in London, you can always go back."

But this time, as he repeated, almost by rote, the words he'd offered so often before when Delboy turned nostalgic and needed cheering up, Jon wasn't so sure. Still, he continued to make his argument. "So what's your hurry to leave? You can make loads more money here, and home will always be there for you. London, my friend, is not going anywhere." Jon paused, considering. "You know, maybe it *is* our age, at that."

Delboy laughed. "Well, it can't be that either of us is going through any kind of mid-life crisis . . ."

"Shit, no," Jon interrupted. "We've both been going through that for years." He was silent, taking stock. "But I think you are right, pal."

"About what?"

"It's time for a change." Jon drained his glass. "I'm sick to death of the politics and nonsense of working in a bank like ours. I'm not sure I like what this place is turning me into. It's time to move on."

Delboy nodded. "Any thoughts on how to do that?"

Jon reflected for a moment. Then, his voice hushed, he said, "As a matter of fact . . . Delboy, there are certain things that can't be repeated. I mean, seriously can't be repeated."

Intrigued, Delboy moved closer to Jon, all ears. "Now, this sounds a little more interesting than my plan of heading back to Oxfordshire."

"If I leave, I want some additional capital before I split. And as you know, the only place you and I can earn real money in this business is through our bonuses, so that's where I'm taking my shot."

"That's the edge you've got over me. I'm stuck with bonuses that can only come out of the whole damn institutional sales trading pool. The way they figure yours, you have a whole lot more control over what you get. I've always envied you on that score."

"Del, we all know there's nothing equitable about the distribution of the bonus pool in this business, but there's fuck-all you can do about it."

"And that's meant to make me feel a whole lot better? But you are quite right. Back to the issue at hand. What's the score?"

"Well, I'm thinking of a 'last hurrah,' of sorts. Given the bank just had its best year out of the last three or four, the profit pools should be in pretty good shape. My department's profit-and-loss is fair, but I'm not exactly setting the world on fire. The truth is, I've had a pretty ordinary six months. Everything I've done has been too damn Mickey Mouse." Jon paused, before continuing. "You know, the bonds have been falling for the last couple of months, and they look very good value at the moment. I doubt they can fall much lower, and it wouldn't take much to push them sharply higher if they got the right news. The timing looks fabulous."

"You're right. The market is very bearish and the recent weakness has pushed most of the momentum players short," Delboy concurred.

"Exactly. The setup for the big but sharp long trade is close to ideal, but I need something with real size attached to it and there's only one place I can get that kind of immediate action in the government sector . . ."

"The auction," Delboy interrupted.

"Boom," Jon nodded. "There'll be around fifteen billion dollars worth of ten-year bonds being issued, and the bottom line is that I want to get as many of them as I can."

"But you know as well as I do that thanks to that mess involving Joseph Jett a few years ago, no one's allowed to take more than thirty-five percent, tops, of what's offered."

"I'm aware of the rules of the game. I'm going to get control of that auction anyway."

"And how are you going to manage that?" asked Delboy, with genuine curiosity. "They won't let you have them all, Wallaby. If they did, the traders at the other majors would all be scrambling to do the same thing. He who controls the stock controls the market."

"Bingo. All I want is to control the process for a couple of days . . ."

"And that 'process' would be the United States Government funding its own massive operational deficit?" Delboy was trying to take in the enormity of Jon's scheme.

"That's the one." Jon chuckled, also imagining the scale of what he was proposing. "There's a way around some of the regulatory problems, starting with a large discreet client to take a piece, allowing me to double my position."

"Wal, I get it, but that's still around three to four billion dollars of ten-years, and that'll require a very risk-tolerant client. That's real money, old cock."

"No, Del. You don't get it. The bank is going to guarantee losses for a U.K. client they've come up with who's apparently willing to play the game. All I really need is their name. The process will be over in less than two days, and with no major economic figures due out next week, I should have a firm, tight market to ease the bonds into."

"Yes, but even with ten billion dollars worth of bonds, there'll be another five billion dollars out there for the overall market to take, so you still won't control it."

"This is where you come in, since my plan isn't strictly kosher."

Delboy grinned. "This just gets better and better. Tell me what you've got in mind."

"Okay. The bonds look weak, as if they couldn't fall much further. So I'll just need to give them a little push-up right after the auction."

"And how do you intend to do that?"

"Remember the LTCM thing in September of '98?"

"Don't be a wanker, of course I do. That trade put you on the map."

"Exactly. The rumors of LTCM's demise were all over the place, days before the actual announcement, and the moment the rumors hit, the government market rallied and the long bond went through the roof."

Delboy nodded. "I see what you're about to say, and it's very, very out-there. Where do I fit in?"

"I'm getting to that. The movements in the foreign exchange markets have fucked up a lot of hedge funds recently. The volatility in the dollar has been a killer."

"Yes, that's all over the papers. Everyone knows that."

"Which supports my plan. What's the biggest hedge fund in the world at the moment?"

"Well, we lost Tiger and Soros in 2000 to the volatility of the markets, so they're gone. I'd say the most aggressive in the foreign exchange markets right now would be Connecticut Capital. It's a monster."

"It is. So I intend to get seventy percent of the auction with the help of this other company. That's just over ten billion dollars. Immediately after I have confirmation from the Fed that I've purchased the bonds, I want you and me to simultaneously call our most influential contacts in the major markets. I'll call Dan in Moscow and deal with New York. You deal with London. We'll start a solid rumor of a major hedge fund teetering on the brink. They will believe it if they hear it from us. They're players; they'll spread it all over the place, and right away."

Jon spoke with confidence, his enthusiasm growing as he pictured what he was describing. "No names at first. We'll only drop in Connecticut's name if we have to. Even if they deny it, the market won't believe them, just like they didn't believe Merriweather at LTCM when he tried telling everyone things were fine when they weren't. By then, I'll be out. The bonds will have been sold."

Delboy laughed out loud, lifting his beer and finishing it in one long gulp. "Well, I can certainly handle London. Those Foreign

Exchange guys will make a meal out of any scrap. But hold on a minute. I don't exactly fancy being taped on the bank's phone trying to artificially manipulate the financial markets." He smiled at the mere thought of such stupidity.

"We'll use our mobile phones, Delboy," Jon said, somewhat dismissively. "There's no crime associated with passing on a rumor, and no one will be able to prove we're the source. Plus, I plan to fix you up nicely for your part in all this, don't you worry about that."

"This is outrageous, but it's your neck, son, not mine. What's next, after we get the rumors going?"

"At that point, I will very aggressively purchase up to another five billion dollars worth of ten-years, via the futures market. The rumors should push the bonds half a point higher very quickly, and the jump will give my P&L a substantial and immediate boost. Then all I'll have to do is sell them into the rumor, which shouldn't be hard, since the rumor should nudge up volumes as well."

Delboy was nodding. "The funny thing is, the market will want to believe it. There's plenty of chat around about the damage done by the recent dollar moves within the hedge fund community, and Warren Buffet is always reminding the market about systemic risk. The timing is good. It's a cracking idea and a fast way of making some real money."

Jon smiled, appreciating Delboy's reaction. "That, Delboy, is exactly the point."

Delboy was clearly savoring the enormity of Jon's plan. "Let's just say you're able to nail this one. Where do you go from there? My guess would be that the very hedge fund market you're trying to use to push the bonds up could be an obvious port-of-call for a handsome, successful lad such as yourself."

"It's always an option. There seems to be a new hedge fund starting up on every street corner at the moment. There could be a few offers out there, but what I'd really like to do is be on my own. I just want enough dough to chill out for a while and consider all my options. I feel burnout looming, and like you, I'm really feeling the need for a change. But first things first."

"Wal, as you know, the bold ideas are the ones I like best.

That's what we were taught all those years ago on the old floor in Threadneedle Street. Have a go, develop your bottle. But this one is not without some pretty serious risk. You could run up against the SEC, and they've got almost as much power as the IRS."

"Nothing ventured, nothing gained." Jon shrugged. "It has all the makings of a great trade. Plus, it's breaking new ground, and I really like the idea of that. The 'go where no man has gone before' thing appeals to me. Mate, if I don't do this now, I never will, and I may end up being stuck on that desk amongst that lot for the rest of my livelong days. You're right Del. It's time to live a little. Change."

Chapter Five

Central London

James Remini had worked for the Central Intelligence Agency for a long time, and accruing very little benefit from his efforts became a state of affairs he resented. In the early 1980s, the swashbuckling figures so glamorously portrayed in novels and Hollywood movies could not have been further removed from the sort of people who actually worked for the CIA. They looked for bright individuals who were discreet and without attachments, people who could move swiftly from one assignment to the next without making waves or leaving tracks. Remini fit the description. He was neither handsome nor ugly, neither short nor tall, an individual who in no way stood out in a crowd. His ability to be unnoticed was one of his great strengths. It had served him well throughout years spent in Latin America and Central Asia, during which he had slipped identities on and off with the greatest of ease.

Under the first Reagan administration, Remini had been involved with securing the heroin trade out of Pakistan and Southeast Asia. As a cash-earning product, heroin was second only to oil. With the Cold War in full flight, Russia and the U.S. were slogging out a bitter battle to bring under control the lucrative illegal businesses associated with the drug. Some of the dirty money inevitably stuck to the fingers of those charged with stemming the exportation of the drug.

An assassin by training, Remini had been assigned the task of taking out the man in charge of local Russian intelligence, one Boris Posarnov. Remini had been operating in the area long enough to realize that the way for each party to maximize profits was to join forces. This was his chance to cash in on those thankless years of anonymous and unremunerative service. So when he put a knife to the throat of the Russian lieutenant, instead of slicing his jugular, he made him an offer. Posarnov could trade his life for a small percentage of everything earned on all the drug trades he discreetly but effectively controlled, and they would split the profits between them. If the Russian didn't agree to this proposal, Remini would promptly carry out his mission, as ordered.

The lieutenant, not a stupid fellow, gave his wholehearted consent, and an unlikely partnership was born. Posarnov was a brute of a man, his viciousness notorious even among his hardened colleagues in Russian Intelligence. He and Remini were an incongruous pair. One in his mid-fifties, big, brutish, and always in search of the spotlight; the other in his forties, quiet, calculating, and almost comically desperate to blend in with his surroundings. It was because of these differences that they complemented each other so well, and they developed a strong bond based on a curious mutual trust, devoid of any personal affection.

By the early 1990s, Remini and Posarnov had managed to accumulate close to seventy-five million tax-free and largely anonymous dollars. Posarnov decided to retire to England, and once there, he set about transforming himself into a businessman of sound reputation — a private investor. With the dawn of Glasnost and the fall of the Soviet Union, Posarnov also wanted to escape the turmoil of Eastern Europe. To do so, he needed a legitimate western identity, so he applied for residency in England.

Remini, on the other hand, saw no need to abandon the shadows that had always suited him so well, although he did permit himself one personal indulgence by growing his thinning hair long and pulling it back into a pony tail. He quietly moved to New Jersey and applied for early retirement, filing tax returns there as an exempt Services veteran. He was only too happy to let Posarnov divide his time between Moscow and London while attempting to legitimize their funds in various black market ventures in Russia and Eastern Europe.

This proved to be a mistake. Posarnov turned out to be a poor businessman, his judgment easily influenced by promoters who were not what they seemed. By the time it had become clear the Yeltsin regime was a disastrous one for investors in the region, and the collapse of the local foreign currencies making an already terrible financial situation even worse, he'd managed to lose almost half of their money. Remini was, needless to say, unhappy with these results and put considerable pressure on his partner to make up his losses.

Liquidating their remaining investments, Posarnov and Remini converted all their foreign currency into U.S. dollars and stashed it in offshore banks, where the money then sat. They desperately needed to gain access to the publicly listed U.S. and European financial markets, that being the fastest and most efficient way to achieve what Posarnov, at least, craved most, beyond making them whole again — recognition and legitimacy, along with solid investment opportunities. However, access was near impossible. So when Posarnov found himself being romanced at a party in London by a New York banker who made it clear he didn't care where his clients' money came from, so long as they had plenty of it, Posarnov was only too eager to respond to his overtures. He very quickly realized that Ernest Johnston might be able to provide the sort of mechanism they'd been searching for to legitimize their money.

Initially, the contact between the two and their new, reputable banker friend involved buying and selling small amounts of publicly traded U.S. securities through a variety of different accounts at the Bank of Manhattan, set up for them under several company names by Johnston and his associates. Because they made sure to deal in small increments and used semi-legitimate banks in Europe to transfer the funds to and from the Bank of Manhattan, their transactions attracted little attention. By the end of a year, the Bank of Manhattan, through Johnston, had unwittingly washed nearly ten million dollars through the U.S. financial markets for Posarnov and Remini. Pleased, they made sure Johnston was separately and generously remunerated for his compliance and contributions to their efforts.

But as attitudes toward banking jurisdictions changed, the team of Johnston, Posarnov, and Remini could see their window of opportunity closing. Developments such as the Patriot Act in the aftermath of 9/11 were making legitimizing dirty money in the U.S. increasingly difficult. Also, the global banking industry was slowly shutting off the already limited avenues to laundering funds internationally. Consequently, the black market value of unwashed money was shrinking almost daily. What the partners needed was a large transaction to complete their exercise, so that they could then move forward with legitimate U.S. dollars, and they had been pressing Johnston to find such a transaction for them.

When Robert Baldwin first approached Johnston regarding Jon's ambitious plan to corner the U.S. government bond market, Johnston had been dismissive. Baldwin had tried his best to represent Jon's interests when discussing the transaction with Johnston, but was quick to volunteer his own disapproval of the plan, so much so that he felt Johnston would likely dismiss it out of hand. Privately, Baldwin worried that Jon might even be risking a formal reprimand for suggesting such a reckless and inappropriate transaction.

Instead, Johnston surprised Baldwin by almost immediately reversing himself, switching from disinterest to wholehearted approval. When they met again to discuss the issue further, Johnston had come right to the point. He had gone over Jon's plan with the board, and given the role the U.K. client was willing to play, they, and more importantly, the bank's lawyers, felt the transaction could be attempted. Baldwin was assured that the client in question was a sophisticated investor who well understood the risks of buying and selling large quantities of U.S. government securities. That the bank would cover any losses was the board's decision and one of no concern to the SEC. Johnston was emphatic. He saw no SEC issues and felt that the transaction proposed by Jon was within Jon's mandate, and within the scope of the bank's existing trading activity.

Although stunned at this turn of events, Baldwin had to defer to him. As soon as Ernest Johnston, a senior figure within the board structure, had given him explicit authorization for Jon to proceed, all systems were go.

Wall Street, Manhattan

Monday mornings could be quiet, the recovery from the weekend a slow and painful one for the many occupants of the trading floor who had indulged themselves over the previous couple of days and nights. With no major economic figures out, the trading in bonds was subdued. This was not unusual on the day before a government bond auction. These auctions were conducted on a regular, quarterly basis and were designed to allow the U.S. government to finance its spending deficits. The size of the auction was dependent upon the amount of money the U.S. government needed to borrow at the time. The bonds would be issued in two-, five-, and ten-year durations.

In recent days, the U.S. government bond market had been relatively inactive, after reacting to the strong economic data reported on Friday. But the bond price had risen marginally above the level at which Jon had purchased five hundred million dollars worth, so he was about to unload them.

Jon swiveled his chair. "Tony, could you get a price in the long bond? I'm looking for the bid."

Tony picked up the receiver as usual to ask the market maker, although he was sitting only thirty feet away. He yelled the price back at Jon. "They are 109 and 21/32 bid in 250 and 109 and 19/32 bid in 500."

Jon gestured with his right hand to sell them. "Knock out all the bonds I bought last week. I need to clean up my book before the auction."

A moment later, Tony put down the receiver. "Confirmed. You sold $500 million of the Feb. 2031s at 109 and 19/32. That's a yield of just under 4.72%."

Jon turned to Ellen. "Ellen, what's the profit on that?"

Ellen began punching the transaction into her computer. Logging the transaction into the bank's mainframe computer system enabled it to be paid for and physically delivered to the new buyer. It also allowed various authorized senior members of the bank to review every aspect of the deal, including its risk and profit-and-loss profile.

Ellen completed punching in the details of the latest trade. "The profit on that 500 is just under $895,000."

Jon was only half-listening. He looked up, distractedly. "It's small, but I suppose it's better than losing it. Thanks."

Jon was by now completely preoccupied with tomorrow's auction. Curious about Johnston, over the past few days he'd asked some of his colleagues about him, since their only prior contact had been across a room at an occasional crowded office party. It seemed Johnston was a born-and-bred WASP, whose rise to prominence at the bank was attributable more to his Ivy League background and social contacts than to his banking acumen. His profile within the bank was unusually low for an individual of his position. Rarely involved in day-to-day operations, he concentrated on client liaison, where he used to advantage his years as a public relations man while wining and dining important clients, making sure their every whim, both personal and commercial, was catered to.

His function within the bank was integral to the kind of relationship banking that had been successfully developed in the early 1980s by one of the most dynamic investment banking operations in U.S. corporate history, Drexel Burnham Lambert. And it was as head of Drexel's public relations and new business departments in the anything-goes environment of the 1980s that Johnston had learned and honed his trade. Up until then, the banking industry had been a conservative and somewhat dull business. Drexel changed all that, doing whatever was necessary to attract bold entrepreneurs to their new and aggressive style of banking.

Drexel's charismatic head, Michael Milken, pioneered high-yield, junk bond financing, lending large amounts of money to companies run, more often than not, by aggressive, ambitious individuals who were unable to obtain credit from the more traditional banking sector. These loans were pricey, partly because of what it cost Drexel to raise the financing, and partly because of the steep interest rates associated with such loans. By the mid-1980s, Michael Milken had become the highest paid executive in America, and Drexel's Los Angeles operation was the first port-of-call for any enterprising executive keen to take advantage of the increasingly deregulated Reagan economy. However, Drexel's phenomenal rise had also created a good deal of envy.

Key to Milken's success was the extraordinary relationships that he had built with his clients, which included many publicly listed companies. He wanted his firm to be involved with these companies at every level. One form this took was his insistence that his clients provide financial support for other Drexel deals, thereby intricately intertwining them with one another. Over time, this highly unusual practice would help to bring down the House of Milken.

Somewhere along the way, Drexel's lavish, annual party in Los Angeles earned the dubious sobriquet of "The Predators' Ball," and became emblematic of the company's allure. America's top industrialists and investors attended, many using the event as an opportunity to drum up interest in the companies they ran or, in Drexel's case, the financial products they were promoting. Johnston coordinated the event, and at his direction no expense was spared. It was quite a party, but it couldn't last forever.

In October of 1986, one of Drexel's biggest clients, the infamous corporate arbitrager, Ivan Boesky, stunned the financial community by announcing to the world that he would plead guilty to a variety of securities violations, agreeing to pay a staggering one hundred million dollar fine to the SEC. This was the beginning of the end for Drexel Burnham Lambert. With that one defection, the tightly bound associations and alliances Milken had engineered began to fall apart. Boesky was soon joined by a number of high-profile witnesses, many of whom had formed an important part of the Milken network. Driven by a young and highly ambitious New York-based prosecutor by the name of Rudy Giuliani, the case against both Milken and Drexel gathered steam. By the end of what became the biggest financial scandal in America's history, Drexel Burnham Lambert was closed down, Michael Milken was imprisoned, and a whole group of what had been the country's most admired businessmen saw their credibility destroyed, and in many cases, their fortunes lost.

Johnston managed to exit the train wreck of Drexel unscathed, quietly slipping out the back door. Since he was only a bit player and had escaped the attention of Giuliani and his team, he was not implicated in the scandal. His reputation had remained intact, as had his list of commercial contacts. Moving to New York, he was quickly absorbed into the Bank of Manhattan, to play, though more discreetly, a role similar to the one he had played at Drexel; to attract many of the same clients that had hastily deserted his old employer, and bring in as much business as he could.

Jon still knew very little about the obliging U.K. Trading Company. It didn't matter. He knew all he needed to know. The U.K. Trading Company was to receive a hefty fee for its cooperation, but it was subject to neither the risk nor the anticipated profits that were expected from the transaction. It was clearly understood that the bank was to take one hundred percent of the risk and one hundred percent of the profits.

Almost no one in the bank was aware of this highly unusual and in fact illegal arrangement. People knew, of course, that the proprietary desk usually played a substantial role in the quarterly auction processes. Jon had already discussed the upcoming auction with one member of his team, Tony, after Tony had remarked on the treasury's announcement of the details of its tender. "Seems like they're issuing a stack of new paper. We're looking at ten billion dollars worth of five-years today, and thirteen billion dollars worth of ten-years tomorrow."

Jon agreed. "That's right. As you know, they gave up issuing thirty-year bonds back in August of 2001. Everybody wants cheaper interest rates, even the mighty U.S. government."

"When do you think they'll start issuing thirty-year bonds again?"

"The market's looking at the first quarter of next year."

Tony nodded as he punched at his Bloomberg keyboard. "So are you squaring up for the ten-years tomorrow?" Tony was always trying to understand the logic behind Jon's trading. He was eager to learn.

"Yep, that's exactly what I'm doing."

Jon had no objection to letting his team know of his interest. But only up to a point. Beyond that point, no one needed to know. If the market became aware of what was happening, the maneuver was likely to fail, thereby subjecting the Bank to unwanted scrutiny at the highest regulatory levels. Confidentiality was key.

Upper East Side, Manhattan

Since he needed to keep his head clear for the auction, Jon didn't want to go out drinking to calm his nerves the night before it took place. So he turned to his other opiate. He left the office early and when he got home, he was met by the familiar sight of Danielle lying seductively on his sleek, contemporary bed, dressed only in her *agent provocateur* underwear. To Danielle, underwear mattered, and the underwear she had on was so sheer that Jon could easily make out the round, protruding nipples on her large, upturned breasts, and the outline of her virtually hairless vagina between her casually spread legs. She kept her pubic hair neatly trimmed, often varying the design for her own amusement. Gratefully, Jon felt his cock stirring almost immediately. He needed to be distracted, and this girl was pure, unadulterated sex, always ready, her pussy sweet, wet, and tasty. He moved toward her, silently taking the Vogue magazine she'd been reading out of her hands and tossing it onto the floor. Before she could react, he knelt on the bed and began to remove her underpants.

"I want to lick your pussy," he whispered.

"Tell me where you're going to lick it," she demanded.

"I'll start with your clit and work down toward your ass. It's the bit in-between I really like."

Danielle wriggled delightedly, opening her legs as wide as she could and bending her knees upward to offer herself to him. Like someone starved, Jon began to devour her. He was unusually good at cunnilingus and he knew it. As he greedily licked her clitoris, he lifted his right hand up and placed it just above her pubic bone. He knew from experience that the gentle pressure on her stomach would immediately heighten her pleasure. He began to feel her stomach muscles contract, a sure indication of the very early stages of orgasm. His cock stiffened.

He lifted his mouth momentarily from her flooded pussy. "My cock is already hard; your sweet taste does it every time."

She acknowledged the interruption by shoving his head back down toward her groin. "Stop talking and lick my pussy. You can talk all you want when you're fucking me from behind later on."

He needed no encouragement to return to the job at hand, inserting his tongue deep inside her and varying his licks to heighten the sensation. He moved lower toward the perineum, the much neglected area between her pussy and her anus. This was one of his specialties. One or two well placed licks there and she opened her mouth wide with pleasure and began moving her hips with added vigor.

"I want you inside me *now*," she demanded. As he slid his steel-hard cock inside her, she moaned loudly. "Oh, fuck, I'm coming," she exclaimed, but she didn't need to tell him, he already knew.

He could now concentrate on his own pleasure, knowing that Danielle had been satisfied. He moved his body across her, lying at almost right angles and facing toward the darkening sky outside his window. "I'm about to come," he warned, quickening his rhythm. After unloading into her, he was still, staying inside her. But she quickly rolled herself out from underneath him and was in the bathroom before he had a chance to catch his breath.

Great sex, he thought dispassionately, as he lay alone on the bed, the shower now running behind the closed bathroom door. It generally was with Danielle, but when the lust had passed, there was nothing to keep them connected in its place. Tonight, however, he was grateful to her for taking his mind off tomorrow, however briefly. He would no doubt sleep well.

Wall Street, Manhattan

The next morning, Jon rose early and dressed with unusual attention to detail, even for him. He had a heightened awareness of every act he performed, conscious that it could be one of the last times he would be going through his familiar routine. Once at his desk, he'd forced himself to interact with his colleagues as he normally did, but he was functioning on automatic. Baldwin stopped by and gave him thumbs up and a shrug, indicating ambivalent good wishes, and Delboy caught Jon's eye every now and then and grinned. Otherwise, it was business as usual for the first few hours of the day.

Jon bided his time. At 1:00 P.M., after poring over his screens until he had completed strategizing all of his moves, he was finally ready to place his bids with the U.S. Treasury Department. The results of the auction process would be announced soon afterwards, with the treasury advising each of the participants of the degree to which they had been successful. Jon had placed aggressive bids for almost ten billion dollars worth of the total thirteen billion dollars of the new November 2015 ten-year government bonds being issued. For window-dressing purposes, the bonds they received in the process would be split on a fifty-fifty basis between the two accounts; the bank's and the U.K. Trading Company's. In reality, they were all Jon's.

Immediately prior to the auction announcement, Jon stood to address the trading floor as usual. The noise level fell as he began. He was brief. "We remain constructive toward the bonds and, for that reason, we have an interest in the upcoming auction. We may have an interest in the bond futures, but it'll depend on how many we get in the auction. If we are in a position to sell some of the bonds, we intend to wait for reasonable levels before selling. But if you have any buying interest in the bonds issued in the auction for your clients, please let us know. Thank you."

The trading floor quickly settled back to work. Jon had been particularly low-key. His nerves weren't obvious, but behind his calm exterior, he was now terrified. He had just played his trump card and there was no going back.

As the auction announcement approached, Jon and his team sat quietly. Jon had pitched his bid at a yield of 4.50%, just slightly better than the current yield of 4.52% on the existing 4.25% August 2015 ten-year government bond. This gave him an excellent chance of getting a large portion of the bonds he needed. What he didn't need was any unanticipated surprises. Surprises were unlikely, however, as there were no major economic releases due in the following two days, and two days would give him enough time to unwind the position.

Jon was speaking on the telephone when Tony looked up from his screen. "The announcement is out and it looks like 4.50% on these new Nov 2015's was a pretty good bid. Chances are you've got a chunk of stock."

Jon was not listening; his attention was focused on his telephone call. He was hearing confirmation from the U.S. Treasury Department that the Bank of Manhattan and the U.K. Trading Company had together received an allocation of just under $10 billion of the new November 2015 4.50% U.S. government ten-year bonds, out of a total of the $13 billion being issued in the auction. The balance, just over three billion dollars, had gone to other institutional bidders. At this stage, Jon was the only member of his team who knew how massive his position was. He hung up and walked over to Ellen. Since she would have to input the information into the system and monitor it's every move, he couldn't avoid telling her. He had no intention of telling anyone else, though, and she knew better than to say anything. Access to the computer system was highly restricted; his position would still remain largely his secret.

Jon leaned down and whispered into Ellen's ear. She gasped. "That's one hell of a position, Jon!" she hissed. "What the fuck are you doing?"

Chapter Six

Although Ellen was clearly shocked by the size of Jon's position, she wasn't about to question him. Realizing something unusual was in the offing, she turned her full attention to monitoring every sale and maintaining the profit-and-loss account for Jon, her expression giving away nothing.

Tony was still concentrating on the benchmark thirty-year bond futures furiously blinking on his monitor. "As you can see, Jon, we are steady at about a quarter of a point above the auction level. The price action is behaving well." It was normal practice to use the price level of the futures contract as a guide to the physical bond's performance; one was a reflection of the other.

Jon signaled to Delboy that now was the time to inject some rumor mongering into the program. Walking away from his desk, he punched a Moscow telephone number into his mobile phone. "Dan, its Jon Phillips. I'm hearing one of the major U.S. hedge funds is on the brink of collapse. Have you heard anything through your sources?"

Jon paused, listening before responding. "Well, there are major rumors coming out of the U.K. foreign exchange market, and the suggestion is that they've been caught up in the Russian equity market." That was enough for the first round, he thought. "Thanks, pal. If you hear of anything, please let me know. This could be a market-mover."

Jon quickly dialed another number. "Mate, I'm hearing one of your largest competitors has a major U.S. dollar problem and is about to collapse. Have you heard anything?"

Again, Jon just listened, and then added, "This could be a big deal, we all remember LTCM, so let me know if you hear anything." He hung up, knowing that phone lines would already be humming with traders gleefully attempting to figure out which fund might be in trouble.

Returning to his desk, he geared up for action. "Tony, I want you to buy me twenty thousand of the ten-year futures contracts and I want you to be aggressive about it. I want them all in ten minutes."

Tony looked at Jon with a slightly puzzled expression. "That's over one hour's volume. It's not going to be easy, Jon."

The look on Jon's face was enough to silence him, and within moments, Tony was scooping up ten-year futures in the market, still having no idea of the size of Jon's position in the auction.

Jon sat staring intently at the ten- and thirty-year futures prices on his screen. Both were ticking higher.

"Jon," Tony shouted. "I'm having trouble getting set. There's a rumor out there that a hedge fund is in trouble."

"Which one?" Jon inquired, innocently.

"Not sure, but the bonds are moving away from us. You'll have to pay at least another four ticks to get set." Tony informed him.

"Tony, I want those futures. Pay up." With that, Tony got back on the telephone to bump up the price he'd be willing to pay, as the bond prices continued moving upward.

Fifteen minutes later, Jon had purchased his twenty thousand futures contracts, the equivalent of another two billion dollars worth of ten-year government bonds via the highly efficient futures market. He notified Ellen.

She blanched, shocked by the shear size of his position. "Jon, I don't get it! You are now long twelve billion dollars worth of ten-year bonds!" She knew she was out of line, but she couldn't help herself. Jon didn't reply.

The bonds had settled a full half point above the auction prices and remained well bid, as the rumor of a hedge fund collapse spread. Jon was ready to move again.

"Tony, call the market-makers and start selling these in clips of $250 million, without putting any pressure on the price. Start with the futures. Gary, speak to the Institutional Desk and let them know we may have some small selling interest at these levels and remind them that any buying should be directed specifically to this desk and nowhere else."

He nervously rubbed his favorite kangaroo cufflinks, which he'd worn for luck. He was feeling the pressure.

Now that he'd acquired as much of the bond market as he was going to, he needed to go into the selling process gently, and without alerting anyone on the trading floor to the size of his position. If the market got wind of an anxious holder with a lot of bonds to sell, the chances were they'd try to force down the price.

"Tony?" Jon prompted. "What's with this rumor?"

"Other than some general market speculation, there's nothing of any substance to report. It's probably just another beat-up from a jealous rival. No one's paying much attention to it now."

Already comfortably in profit, with the selling process begun, Jon decided to let the rumor sit quietly in the market. It looked as if it wouldn't be necessary to add Connecticut's name to it.

The proprietary desk remained extremely busy as the afternoon progressed. Tony and Gary coordinated the sales, and Ellen entered each transaction. Jon monitored the price action. The higher the bond and futures prices moved, the greater the profit Jon would generate for the bank, not to mention for himself and his team.

Jon was feeling quite pleased with himself when Baldwin appeared beside his desk. "What the hell are you doing buying these additional futures?" he demanded.

"The auction is over, so I'm no longer restricted under the SEC guidelines," Jon replied, calmly.

"Jon, you are way overstepping the mark. We never discussed this."

"It's a necessary part of the trade and I didn't feel as though it needed to be discussed." Jon didn't like lying to his friend but he knew he'd never have gotten a green light from Baldwin's department.

Baldwin was furious but impotent. The trades had already been made and there was nothing he could do. "We will discuss this later," he said as he left, shaking his head in anger and disbelief.

Jon turned back to the Bloomberg monitor. On the bottom of the screen, a constant stream of news items from every corner of the world ran through a scroll bar. Most of the information was irrelevant, occasionally appearing in a foreign language, but sometimes even a seemingly innocuous scrap of news could be devastating in its impact. Jon was on the lookout for any such scrap that could cause the bond market to fluctuate unexpectedly. So far, so good. He was starting to breathe more easily; the bonds were up nearly half a point or 16/32nds from where he'd purchased them. The market was holding up nicely at the levels Jon and Delboy had pushed them to after the auction. The rumors had worked well.

A little after 2:00 P.M., Jon turned to Ellen. "Where are we, Ellen?" Jon asked confidently.

Her reply was discreetly hushed, just above a whisper. "Of the total of $12, we have sold $2.2, leaving us with just over $9.5 to unload. So far, we're up about fifty-eight million dollars on our total position based on the sales and current prices."

The day's trading environment had turned out to be ideal for this particular exercise. The markets were quiet, and demand for the bonds was solid and consistent; the lack of supply available in the auction had, predictably, forced the institutional buyers into the marketplace. Interest in Jon's rumor had largely evaporated. In effect, at this point in time, Jon *was* the market and he had reasonable control over it. Tony and Gary coordinated the large institutional orders through their trading desk. Things were going smoothly, according to plan.

Confident that the market was now capable of absorbing more bonds, Jon turned to Tony and Gary. "The market's going to be closing in about an hour. Can you gently pick up the pace without it doing too much damage? Sit on it, but do it softly. I want to reduce the position."

Tony and Gary acknowledged his instruction and were moving to act on it when suddenly Delboy yelled over to Jon. "You're not going to like this, Jon. We're hearing there's a young-girl-with-a-senior-government-official story about to break."

Jon said nothing, having no idea what this story could be. His pulse quickened. Just then, the bonds started to weaken. He shook his head, trying to clear it. "Jesus. Not the President again?" Start at the top and work down, he thought.

"Worse," Delboy responded, despondency washed across his face.

Jon knew there was only one person more important to the financial markets than the President. "Oh, fuck." His heart began pounding, the blood throbbing in his ears.

Delboy nodded. "Yep. I'm hearing the Chairman of the Fed."

"Oh, Christ." And with that, a headline unspooled across the bottom of Jon's Bloomberg screen. "The Treasury Department confirms that the Chairman of the Federal Reserve Bank of America, Mr. Owen Taber, has taken ill. No other details are available at this time."

Jon tried to reassure himself that, after some initial uncertainty, the market would hold steady. But the bonds were continuing their downward drift, pushing Jon's position into losses.

Attempting to keep calm and focused, Jon continued to reduce his position at an even pace, trying not to put any further pressure on prices. By two-thirty, he was at $8.2 billion, with only half an hour to go before the market closed for the day. Then, liquidity would effectively dry up until Tokyo opened later that night. The Asian and European markets might provide some movement for the U.S. government bonds throughout the night, but trading volumes were low, so not much could be expected from those regions.

And then, without any discernible cause, the gradually softening bonds began to weaken quickly. Jon's cool had evaporated with his profits; his losses were now building at an alarming rate. He hadn't expected such a strong reaction. His once freshly starched shirt was becoming drenched with large sweat stains under each armpit, his panic was now evident.

His tone reflected his growing anxiety. "Why are those things falling so sharply? Can anybody give me a reason?"

Tony read off his information terminal. "Here it is. There's more on that story involving the Chairman's health . . ."

Jon turned toward Delboy, his brow furrowed. "Del, what's going on?" he pleaded.

Delboy shook his head. "Nothing more, mate, same story about the Guv'ner having taken a nasty turn, nothing about any girlies just yet."

"We saw that forty minutes ago. Isn't there anything new?" Jon looked around the dealing room, searching for answers. "I can't believe this." The bonds continued to tick steadily lower.

Tony piped up. "Jon, a story's coming out on the wire now." He paused briefly, then read aloud from the screen. "The Chairman has had a mild heart attack, but it's not serious."

Jon momentarily relaxed. "That's . . . not too bad. We knew he'd been ill, and at seventy-four, he's no spring chicken."

Nonetheless, the still weakening stock and bond prices suggested the news was worse than the wire showed. This was often the case; the market had a habit of knowing the truth before it was made public.

Tony, glued to the screen, suddenly blurted out, "Wait a minute, there's a new twist. CNN is reporting that there is a girl involved. She's claiming they were having sex at the time and wants to sell the story to the highest bidder."

Jon was expressionless. "Jesus." Jon looked toward Delboy,

knowing that his friend was well aware of what this could do to Jon's plans. "Here it is, Del, looks like your information was right."

If true, this would mean the Chairman would have to resign. Such a high-profile departure would have an unsettling effect on the market. And a new Chairman would almost certainly raise short-term interest rates. The market's immediate response would be to kick the hell out of ten-year bond prices. Never mind the rumors about Taber planning to retire anyway. Gossip trumped facts every time.

Tony turned away from the screen and glanced at Jon. He, too, was worried now, his voice remorseful at delivering bad news. "There's more. It appears she's only seventeen."

Jon's eyes remained fixed to his screen, watching in fascinated resignation as the bonds he had thought of as his ticket out maintained their downward direction. "Not good. That's definitely not good."

Tony was not quite finished. "There's one last item. Apparently, she's got proof."

"What proof?" Jon wanted to know.

Tony gave Jon a look. "They say she kept the condom."

Jon almost smiled. "Oh, nice touch. Bad for Taber, bad for us, never mind tacky." His half-smile faded quickly. He was finding it hard to suppress a wave of nausea.

Jon's position was now losing serious money. He instructed his team to continue to sell into the weakness, to lighten the position. The price of the bond future was a full point off its high, and falling. His position was worsening by the minute.

Jon turned as calmly as he could toward Ellen. "What's the damage?"

Ellen whispered back. "The book is currently long $6.3 billion. The overall P&L, including realized gains, is down roughly seventy-eight million dollars. It's looking like a really bad hair day."

"Even Don King doesn't have days like this." Jon's attempt at a joke fell flat. "You know, it's always what you least expect in this damn business that causes the greatest aggravation." Ellen simply nodded in response. "I suppose it goes with the territory. I'll just have to try and minimize the damage. As they say, if you can't stand the heat . . ."

They both smiled weakly. Tony and Gary were privy to neither the existing position nor the profit-and-loss account, but at this point they both realized something was seriously wrong. They searched Jon's face for clues, and found only confirmation that all was not well.

At 3:00 P.M., the main session of the trading day in the U.S. bond market was over. Jon had access to the after-hours sessions, dominated by the Globex futures market in Asia and Europe. He was already calculating how he could continue to reduce his position. But in truth, other than maybe off-loading a small number of the bonds, he would have to wait and see what the new day in New York City would bring.

Wall Street, Manhattan

When Ellen arrived at 7:00 A.M. the following morning, Jon was sitting at his desk. She noted without comment that he was wearing the same suit and tie from the previous day, not something Jon was likely to do. For someone who had not been home, he was surprisingly relaxed, though, acknowledging her with a friendly nod.

She wondered if this meant things had improved. "Did you manage to sell any bonds in Tokyo?" she asked, as she switched on her monitor.

"Only small. I sold $250 mil at 4.64% to one Japanese institution. The market held up okay, but there was no sign of the Bank of Japan. They'll want to see Taber jogging around Capitol Hill, scandal-free, before they start buying treasuries again."

Once his losses were known by the compliance department, Jon would be under substantial pressure to justify how he'd handled the auction. Time was not on his side. He had no option now but to close down his position.

"The Chairman is being described as 'comfortable'," he commented. "And I'll bet he's a damn sight more comfortable than I am right now."

"I'm not so sure. What about the girl?" asked Ellen. "There was nothing new on the news this morning."

"He'll have to quit, no question. But in the long run, it won't matter. Our immediate problem is the damaged market and over six billion dollars worth of bonds on our book we need to unwind, hopefully before they start climbing all over me."

Ellen wasn't persuaded this was possible. "I dunno. They've got eighty-three . . ." she paused, and looked at the screen, "Nope; it's now eighty-four million reasons to not be thrilled."

"Thanks for reminding me. One thing at a time. First, I have to fix up the position. Medium-term, these bonds look pretty good value around 4.65%. Ordinarily, I'd much prefer to be buying the bloody things than selling them, but I just can't carry a position of this size. The problem is it's too big, and too much damage has already been done." Jon was silent. "The bottom line, Ellen, is that I'm fucked."

Ellen shrugged, at a loss as to how to deal with a side of her boss she'd never seen. His anxiety was communicating itself to her, and she didn't like the feeling. In an effort to restore order to her world, she busied herself at her desk and avoided looking at Jon.

As 8:00 A.M. approached, almost everyone had arrived, and the time was coming for Jon to be candid with Tony and Gary. The idea of maintaining complete silence was no longer feasible, since now they had to help him reduce his position as speedily as possible without causing a panic sell-off. He cautioned them not to let anyone else on the trading floor know what they were up against, although he knew most of them would guess soon enough.

Their meeting was followed by Jon's regular morning briefing to the floor. He made it short and upbeat. Briskly, he outlined the constructive medium-term outlook for the U.S. government bonds, making no mention of his proprietary position other than to suggest he might be a seller into strength, while maintaining a long position. He reiterated that the sales staff should continue to direct their buying orders toward the proprietary desk.

Throughout the morning, the market remained generally weak. Jon knew that, ironically, were it not for his own unrelenting selling pressure, the market would probably have been drifting higher, but he had no choice.

He leaned back in his chair and rubbed his eyes, the strain beginning to tell on him. "Ellen, what's the position now?"

She glanced up. "We are down to the last 1.3 billion."

"Shock me. What does the P&L look like?"

"Holding the bonds steady at the current prices, the all-up loss is . . . ." She paused as she typed in the latest price of the government bonds that Jon still owned. "Its one hundred twenty-one million dollars, give or take a nickel or two. The good news is that we've sold almost all the bonds, so it can't get too much worse from now on." She smiled weakly.

Jon was relieved to have addressed the immediate problem by cutting his losses. By themselves, these losses were not large enough to jeopardize the safety of the bank. If his contravention of the SEC rules became public, however, the breach would give the SEC the right to suspend the bank's banking license. Its license was its lifeblood; without it, the bank could no longer function.

The problem now was to deal with the internal procedural issues. The starting point was the compliance department. As the link between Jon and the authority at board level, Robert Baldwin, had to be consulted immediately.

Wall Street, Manhattan

The views from Johnston's office spread south, over the Statue of Liberty and out toward the open sea. The office's dark mahogany paneling, large leather-topped desk and brown tweed-covered sofas presented an image of another, more conservative era. A detailed model of an old, two-masted wooden sailing ketch dominated the front of his desk, which was otherwise immaculate. A visitor would certainly be forgiven for thinking that he or she was well outside the throbbing and often chaotic heart of Wall Street.

Johnston sat motionless and silent, staring at his computer

screen. Given his overall responsibility for compliance, he had unrestricted access to the bank's profit-and-loss system, and that's what he was looking at.

He placed both his elbows on his desk and buried his head deep into his hands. He was watching the fallen U.S. government bond futures and the effect they were having on Jon's proprietary profit-and-loss account. Jon was being killed and so was Johnston's client — never mind Johnston himself. Things were definitely not going as anticipated.

Suddenly, he picked up a crystal ashtray and hurled it at the wall, accompanied by a string of expletives. It fell onto a sofa, ungratifyingly intact. Johnston shrugged, then lifted the telephone receiver to his ear, dialing a number with his other hand. Sitting absolutely still, he waited while the telephone rang several times, half wishing there would be no answer.

When someone finally picked up, Johnston did not bother with even the most basic telephone greeting. "Johnston here. I need to see you," he said abruptly. "We may have a problem."

Chapter Seven

Robert Baldwin sat alone in his eighteenth-floor office, overwhelmed by the issues Jon's losses had created. Searching for some form of consolation, if not inspiration, he glanced out of his large office window and across the skyline of lower Manhattan, depleted by the loss of the World Trade Center, but still impressive. In all his years at the bank, he had never tired of the spectacle of the magnificent skyline spread out below him. It was a view to which he dedicated a few minutes of each day, to look upon in silent contemplation. He found it to be somehow evocative of his success, a reminder of his achievement in a world where the odds had been stacked against him. Today, though, when he looked at all the steel-and-glass towers, those emblems of commercial aspirations glinting in the sunlight, his mind was elsewhere.

He had just put down the telephone after informing Jon of what Jon already knew — his proprietary losses had broad and potentially serious implications. He had no desire to tell Jon "I told you so." Rather, he was concerned for his friend, a friend who right now might not even realize just how much trouble he was in. Friend or not, though, Baldwin's first priority had to be to protect the bank from outside forces. He knew he needed to move quickly. He also knew the situation was going to get worse before it got any better.

At Jon's knock, Baldwin turned around to greet his visitor. Jon acknowledged Baldwin in a courteous but rather formal manner, as if intentionally setting up a space between them in which Baldwin could more easily say what he had to say. Their personal relationship would have to be put aside for the time being.

Jon plunged right in, with no preamble. "We have a number of problems to address. First, you are by now aware that the proprietary desk has realized a loss of just over one hundred twenty-one million dollars on positions taken in the U.S. treasury auction. Technically, the U.K. Trading Company is liable for about forty million dollars of these losses. This leads us to the second problem. As I understand the situation, the U.K. Trading Company provided funds on the condition that the bank would cover any losses. I believe you initially had about thirty-five million dollars in their margin account. Is that correct?"

Baldwin nodded. "Yes, that's correct." He picked up a series of documents from his desk and handed them to Jon. "This is strictly confidential, but here are the details regarding those funds. All in order but incomplete, which could be a real problem now."

"What's missing?"

"Some additional information on the client to meet money laundering and Patriot Act regulations; I should be receiving it from Johnston shortly. To put this deal to bed in time, we had to shortcut some of our usual compliance procedures. Another reason to keep the SEC out of this."

"It is." Jon looked at the document. It was too detailed for him to do more than scan it. "Can I keep this to look over later on? I see it's a file copy."

Baldwin shook his head. "No, I'm sorry. It's highly confidential as it contains, amongst other things, the company's full banking details."

Jon tried not to show his surprise at Baldwin's uncharacteristic skirting of the rules; he was not the type to tolerate incomplete documentation. He held onto the document, scanning it. "Robert, given the circumstances, I really need to know more about who I'm dealing with. You have my word that I will treat this information with the utmost confidentiality."

"Look Jon, you know I trust you, but you will understand I can't just toss this type of client information around." Baldwin hesitated, considering his position thoughtfully. "Take it, but make sure you keep it in a very safe place."

Jon folded the document carefully and placed it in the inside pocket of his suit. Baldwin continued. "There is another problem. With the losses amounting to forty million dollars, their account now requires a cash top-up of almost five million dollars. We will need to deal with this immediately, since this additional loss is above and beyond their original thirty-five million dollar commitment and will need to be covered somehow within forty-eight hours. This is a standard procedure under our existing margin agreement."

Jon understood. "Yes, and if you and Johnston can settle this within the bank, the most serious problem, the violation of the SEC rules and regulations, may not arise." Jon spoke in a monotone. "Let's hope that can happen. The last thing we want is for the SEC to revoke the bank's license. It would probably not be able to survive that, so it's obviously in its own best interest to suppress the details of the agreement between the two parties."

Baldwin nodded. "We really need to address the complexities of this situation."

Jon was heartened that Baldwin appeared to be on board. "By which you mean, how to go about covering our partners' losses, since this particular situation hasn't occurred before? How does the process ordinarily work?"

"If we were dealing with profits, the process would be quite simple — routine, in fact. But losses covered by the bank are a whole new ball game. The problem is that if the bank were to make a payment as large as this directly into the client's margin account, it would be such an unusual transaction that it would be bound to attract attention. The bank's auditors would pick it up immediately, and we would have to come up with some sort of credible explanation for it."

The kind of surveillance Baldwin was describing was a relatively new development, new enough to be strictly enforced. During the 1990's, companies in the U.S. had come under increasing pressure to report ever more favorable earnings. Shareholders had insisted on it. The extremely strong economy brought with it genuine increases in corporate earnings, but as the decade drew to a close, the economy had begun to weaken and, consequently, pressure on earnings escalated. Books got "cooked" to paint a far rosier picture than actually existed.

It was such highly creative accounting practices that caused the collapse of companies like the Enron Corporation in 2002, setting off alarm bells across the breadth of the U.S. economy and its financial markets. Suddenly, any inconsistencies within a company's balance sheet or on its profit-and-loss account required detailed explanations. No longer was it possible to use a combination of smoke and mirrors to gloss over financial irregularities. It was in this environment that Baldwin would have to find a credible way to explain the losses associated with the relationship between the Bank of Manhattan and the U.K. Trading Company.

Jon realized he was out of his depth. "Well, in any case, the bank's losses are my responsibility and I'll have to wear 'em. At the end of the day, the bank will have no trouble absorbing them, provided you can sort out some way to make it work with the U.K. Trading Company and camouflage the payment. But how you offset it . . . that's not my issue."

Baldwin nodded. "Agreed, that's up to Johnston. It is his client and the arrangement was made entirely on his and the board's authority."

"Then you and I agree the ball's in Johnston's court. I know what the bank's reaction will be, as far as I'm concerned. They'll find an excuse to bury me, along with the whole damn incident. But the last thing Johnston and the rest of the board want is any noise, so you should be all right."

Jon started to leave, and then turned back. "Robert, I'm really sorry about all this, I . . ."

Baldwin gently cut him off. "What's done is done. Let's just do the best we can to fix it now."

Jon gave him a grateful smile and said no more.

Within minutes of Jon leaving, Johnston arrived at Baldwin's office. Baldwin greeted him. "I was just about to call you, sir."

Johnston extended his hand, then quickly settled into the chair facing Baldwin. "This whole bond auction has rather blown up in our faces, hasn't it?"

Baldwin responded without hesitation. "Yes, sir."

Johnston changed tack to test the water. "Tricky thing betting on the whims of the Chairman of the Fed, don't you think? I wonder if Phillips really understood that."

Baldwin was not to be manipulated. "With all due respect, sir, he was acting under the authority of the board."

There followed an awkward silence. Then Johnston said, slowly, "Was he, now? Are you quite sure of that?"

Baldwin was immediately on guard. He measured his words carefully. "Yes, sir. My understanding is that you personally gave the authorization for Jon to undertake the auction transaction, just as you gave authority to me to process it. As a matter of fact, I have it fully documented here, sir."

Johnston smiled, but shifted uneasily in his chair. "Quite right. Compliance has an important job to do in this day and age. Things have certainly changed over the last few years, haven't they? Every 't' has to be crossed, every 'i' dotted."

Baldwin wanted to bypass the generalities. "That's correct, sir. Obviously, this will need to be dealt with very discreetly, and I will require the board's specific guidance as to exactly how we are going to off-set these losses incurred by the U.K. Trading Company, from an audit perspective."

Baldwin paused, yet Johnston remained silent. "As you know, since Enron, our auditors have become impossible, so we will need to be extremely circumspect as to how we deal with this, um, adjustment." When there was still no response, Baldwin continued. "I'd like to remind you, sir, that we still have one or two outstanding compliance issues to complete, relating to your client, and I would appreciate it if you could ask them to deal with these issues with absolute priority."

Johnston looked thoughtfully at Baldwin. "Are you suggesting that the basic documentation is still incomplete?"

"Yes, sir. I have in the file all the standard account documentation on your client, but since we accelerated the process, I still require certain standard confirmations relating to client credibility and money laundering regulations. Perhaps I could ask you to ensure those documents are sent to me as soon as possible." Baldwin had barely paused for breath.

"Ah, yes. I'll see what I can do," Johnston replied. "Given the circumstances, a little extra housekeeping seems in order."

Baldwin was feeling increasing regret for having relied so heavily on Johnston, but it was too late now. There was nothing for it but to project a confidence he no longer felt, and move forward. "Yes, sir. We also have the more short-term issue of the additional five million dollars immediately required to top off the margin account, given that the losses are that much greater than the cash we were holding in the account. As I'm sure you realize, I require the margin funds immediately from the U.K. Trading Company."

"Can't we use the bank's capital to finance this additional amount?"

Baldwin's tone was firm. "No, sir. We cannot operate outside the mandate. There is no room for flexibility on this aspect of the problem."

Johnston paused, staring directly at Baldwin. Another silence fell between them. "Let me see what I can do."

Baldwin drew a deep breath. "Just to remind you, technically I require these funds to be deposited within two working days. Let me get the exact amount for you." He transferred his attention to his computer screen as he went through the complicated security processes to access the restricted details of the banks' clients' accounts. "Here it is, sir, an additional $4.87 million." Looking up, he added, "I also have here all the details of the account, including your authorization to open it."

Johnston craned his neck to inspect the screen. "Of course. As always, you seem to have everything meticulously documented. Good job, Robert. I'll deal with U.K. Trading." He offered one last flinty smile, and left the room.

Baldwin wiped a bead of sweat from his lip, turned off his computer and strode briskly out of the office. He needed some air.

Wall Street, Manhattan

When Jon returned to his desk, Ellen allowed him a moment to gather his thoughts before asking, tentatively, "What's the scoop?"

As first, Jon attempted to make light of the situation. "Too early to tell. Compliance is dealing with the immediate issues. Obviously, they're not going to like it. A one hundred twenty million dollar problem is . . ."

"Ah . . . a one hundred twenty-three million dollar problem," Ellen interrupted.

"Fair enough." Jon slumped into his chair as Tony and Gary arrived back at the desk. They were still unaware of Jon's situation, although they could see he continued to be upset about something.

Tony reached into his desk drawer. "Jonny, I almost forgot . . ." He removed an envelope and handed it to Jon. "Robert came to see you while you were at lunch. He left this for you."

Jon opened the handwritten note and scanned it.

Jon:

I met with Ernest Johnston today and he assured me he would personally settle the issue, as he regards U.K. Trading as his responsibility. He said we should keep this between ourselves for the time being, to allow him time to smooth things over with both the board and his client. Should be okay.

Regards, Robert

Jon folded the note and placed it back in its envelope, which he then slipped into his inside suit coat pocket. He was touched that his friend had made a point of getting this reassuring information to him as soon as he possibly could. Glancing at his monitor's screen, he then realized there was little point in doing so. Whatever happened from now on would have no impact on his fate at the bank. He stood and meandered toward the large, floor-to-ceiling windows of the trading floor. The view had changed dramatically after the World Trade Center complex came down, now looking directly north across lower Manhattan, and up toward Central Park.

Like all other New Yorkers, Jon had been forced to soldier on during the difficult days after September 11. Looking back, he felt some embarrassment remembering how successfully he'd worked the crisis to his and the bank's financial advantage. It wasn't that he'd been untouched by what had happened; on the contrary, he still felt great sadness every time he passed by Ground Zero, and was reminded of the shock and chaos of the days and months following the attack. His was a competitive environment, and it was second nature for him to immediately start figuring the angles. He'd learned early on that those determined to climb the corporate ladder must look beyond the headlines and position their firms to take advantage of the next, unpredicted wave of commercial prosperity.

Jon had recognized that the U.S. economy could recover from the downturn following the attack, and he'd wanted to profit from it when it did. After assessing the situation, he built a substantial short position in the thirty-year U.S. bond futures, selling bond futures he did not own. Jon figured their prices would fall, and when they did, he would buy them back for less than he had sold them. Within days, the bonds did, in fact, begin to fall, allowing him to clear a nice profit, just as he'd planned. Once again, he had nailed an opportunity by taking advantage of a crisis. Right now, it wasn't something he felt proud of.

The same confidence bordering on arrogance that had propelled him to success now undermined him. It is generally under-

stood that nothing and no one is bigger than the market. Jon belat-
edly realized that in taking out the bond auction, he had hugely
overstepped the mark, just as Baldwin had warned him. He had
convinced himself that he had the market's measure, and this had
proven to be his downfall.

Chapter Eight

It did not take Johnston long to track down Boris Posarnov. He found him in New York City, in a private Westside screening room, sprawled across a plush, padded armchair, a huge Cuban cigar protruding from his mouth. His smoke spiraled blue-gray into a single stream of intermittent light in the otherwise darkened room. A movie projector whirred somewhere behind him and groaning noises dominated the foreground. Posarnov stared dispassionately at the screen, where a man and a woman, or two men or two women, it was difficult to tell, participated in various forms of sex. He made no attempt at concealing his disinterest as he exhaled, adding to the growing cloud above his head. He turned and spoke into the blackness. "What do you think?"

Johnston leaned closer. "It's, um, very arousing."

Posarnov grunted. "It's filth." Soft laughter from an unseen man could be heard somewhere in the background. "But filth sells, right? At least it does in the Ukraine." He turned to Johnston and fixed him with a look that referenced another matter.

Johnston was quick to respond. "The bank stands guarantor for all your losses."

Posarnov returned his gaze to the screen. "I should hope so. Our commitment was thirty-five million dollars, and I want it back immediately."

"There's a problem. Not to put too fine a point on it, Boris, but it's dirty money." He stumbled. "The bank is certainly good for it, but replacing it will attract some attention, which could be problematic on several levels. However . . ."

Posarnov interrupted. "Are you suggesting that an enquiry could put my money at risk?"

"Well . . . yes, possibly," Johnston stammered. "With both the SEC and the bank, I'm afraid, if things cannot be contained." He paused uncomfortably. "The bank is unaware of this transaction, so the losses on this deal pose a serious complication. The U.K. Trading Company will now be scrutinized at board level, and unfortunately, it will not stand up from a compliance perspective. This could put us in a very difficult situation."

Posarnov reacted immediately and violently, his rage growing. "How dare you allow this to happen with my money?" he shouted, reaching forward and grabbing Johnston's lapels.

Johnston pulled away, terrified. Posarnov backed off, but a hand provocatively brushed Johnston's shoulder, causing him to jump. It belonged to someone behind him, virtually invisible in the darkness.

"In that case, it must be contained," Posarnov continued, his tone now icy. "We cannot tolerate such scrutiny. We must remove any obstacles that could prevent us from getting our money back. This is your responsibility." There was no doubting his resolve.

Johnston had to take several deep breaths before he could answer. Then, reluctantly, he ventured, "There is another issue. Our losses have technically exceeded the thirty-five million dollar cash margin we lodged with the bank. They want an additional $4.9 million U.S. dollars within the next 48 hours."

Posarnov stared at him in disbelief, his anger still palpable. "This is out of the question. Intolerable!" He said, his wide-eyed fury building to the point of implosion.

The unseen figure leaned toward the two men and spoke quietly but clearly, in an American drawl. "Perhaps we can make the transaction look like something else."

Johnston paused. "There is nothing I can do," he stuttered impotently.

His words were left hanging in the darkness. The unseen man continued calmly. "We need a distraction. Someone to blame and someone to tidy up behind us."

Johnston squirmed in his chair. "I mean, I'll do everything I can, but this was meant to be a routine laundry run."

Posarnov was swift to respond. "Nothing is routine in our business, Mr. Johnston," he spat. "You should know this."

When Johnston answered, his words tumbled out too quickly. "It's not that I don't want to help, but you must understand my position here. If there's even a whiff of scandal, I'm finished. Then, I'll be of no help to anyone, and it'll be even more difficult to get your money back." His weakness infuriated Posarnov.

Johnston could feel the unseen man's warm breath uncomfortably near him. The hairs on the back of his neck rose. "Then let's hope there is no whiff of scandal. As I was saying, what we need is a fall guy."

Johnston turned toward the voice; he could not make out the figure behind him. "Maybe we could, uh, maybe we could make it look like another rogue trader scandal," he stumbled. "Perhaps we could base it around the idea of unauthorized trading losses. When the bank finds out we acted in breach of the SEC rules, they certainly won't want to draw any attention to it. This contravention of the rules may in fact help us, as it could cost them their banking license." He paused in a more considered, thoughtful fashion. "If we get someone to take all the heat, well, no one is likely to look any further and you will get your money back. This is our only option."

Both men listened intently. Finally, Posarnov nodded. "That would be a comfort. Do you have anyone in mind?"

Johnston did not hesitate. "Yes."

Posarnov blew a noxious cloud toward him. "And how does one go about bringing down this fall guy?"

The unseen man began to laugh. "This is America. Put him on TV."

Posarnov gazed into the darkness toward the unseen man. "Then do it quickly and make him fall hard." Silence fell between them, before he added sternly, "Is there anyone else who can connect us?"

Johnston hesitated. "Yes. There is one other person. Only one."

Wall Street, Manhattan

Jon was increasingly distracted, his lack of concentration becoming obvious to those around him. In a trading floor environment, it was difficult to keep anything a secret. The floor was beginning to suspect something was very wrong.

So Jon wasn't surprised to see Tom Edwards, a thirty-three-year-old, Harvard-educated rival, approaching his desk. He had recently been promoted to head the Derivatives Department. Since both men had reached the top of their respective departments, opportunities for each to move to the next stage had become limited. Both were recognized as potential 'director material', so if a position were to open, each would have to mobilize his own support within the bank to pursue it. In such situations, the loser often forfeited more than just the position he vied for, as reputations could be destroyed in the intensity of the fight.

"Hey, Tom, what's up?" Jon asked, without enthusiasm.

"I was just wondering if you got caught up in the crazy story that upset the treasuries after the auction yesterday," Tom said, grinning smugly. As usual, he was dressed casually in an Armani shirt, chinos, and Gucci loafers.

"Now, what would give you that idea?"

"I appreciate that your positions are your business, but I couldn't help but notice the size of your selling into the weakness.

Do I smell trouble?" Tom didn't bother to hide his delight at the prospect.

"Given the nature of the derivative business and the state of your department's P&L, I'm sure there are all sorts of unpleasant smells floating around. There is only so much an expensive after-shave can hide, Tommy boy. But thanks for your concern. I'm touched."

Tom wasn't going to give up so easily. "At the end of the day, pal, our fortunes tend to become linked, so naturally I like to keep an eye on your fortunes, as you, no doubt, do on mine."

"Don't flatter yourself. Anyway, I wasn't aware your department made enough money to take note of."

Now it was Tom's turn to become annoyed. "Derivatives are the future, even if it takes a while for them to become profitable. But I'm not sure that you'd understand the complexities of any but the simplest of economic theories. After all, what can one expect from someone from a colonial outpost?"

"A colonial outpost?" Jon took the bait. "What would you know about Australia? And it's fair to say that some of the stupidest and most impractical people I've ever worked with have been prod-ucts of the Harvard Business School. MBA's are a dime a dozen these days. You'll need something more than that to succeed, and from where I'm sitting, you just don't have it."

Tom drew breath. "Yeah, I almost forgot how clever you are. In fact, you must be Harry Houdini himself to be making money selling treasuries into this weak market. Too clever for me, us MBA's just aren't smart enough to make money that way. Unlike some damn foreigner lucky enough to somehow obtain a green card."

"Which I'd be happy to give back," Jon retorted.

"You may be giving it back sooner rather than later. And when you do, I'm sure you'll have no trouble settling back in among the aborigines. Anyway, I just wandered over in the hope that I'd find you hiding under a rock from a position that looks to be in a whole lot of trouble. Rumor has it you've got a major problem, and after this little outburst of yours, I'm convinced of it."

He turned to leave, but couldn't resist another jibe. "Watch your back, Jonny. If the rumors are true, they'll get rid of you in a second. Of course, for me that's a dream scenario. In fact, it's a sure-fire career move. Let's hope the treasury continues to fall, just to keep the pressure on."

"Tom, I don't want to be rude but don't you think it's time you went back to your department? If you spent a little more time with your team, you might learn how these markets work," Jon offered lamely.

Tom shrugged. "Remember what they said about the Titanic?"

Jon had had enough. He didn't respond, and Tom left.

The main line for the proprietary desk had rung while they were speaking. Tony picked up. Jon, still fuming at Tom's taunts, only half-listened to Tony's end of the conversation at first.

"Who?" said Tony. There was a pause. "Hey, man, this isn't a nightclub. This is a bank and all our telephone conversations are taped so that kind of talk isn't going to get you anywhere."

Tony put a hand over the receiver and swiveled around to face Jon.

"Who is it, Tony?"

"I've got some guy asking for you, talking some trash. He wants to know whether we've got someone called George McWilliam on our payroll, says he's your drug dealer."

The color left Jon's face. "It must be some mistake. Just get rid of him."

Tony went back to the phone. "Mr. Phillips isn't here," he said firmly. "I don't know when he'll be back. I have to go." And he hung up, shaking his head.

Jon looked around, to quickly averted gazes. "What are you looking at?" he snarled. He then turned his wrath on Tony. "And what the hell are you doing talking about me to a stranger?"

Realizing that he was only drawing more attention to himself, Jon got up and slowly backed away, holding up his hands apologetically. Gary and Ellen pretended not to notice as Jon headed for the door, muttering about getting a sandwich. His behavior had thoroughly unsettled them.

On the sidewalk, Jon furiously punched numbers into his mobile telephone. Putting the telephone next to his ear, he waited for an answer.

"And why am I getting calls for your drug dealer at work, darling?" Jon snarled into the telephone, when his call was picked up.

"I don't know. Did you page him?" replied Danielle.

"Of course I didn't page him," Jon snapped, as he strode along Broad Street and turned right, into Exchange Place. "Somebody just called my office and asked if George McWilliam was on the payroll."

"Georgie?" replied Danielle, laughing. "He's so funny! What did he want?"

"He didn't want anything," an exasperated Jon shot back. "Would you have had him or anyone else call my office, for any reason?"

"Sweetie, why would I do that?"

"Well, somebody's trying to connect him to me. Do you have any idea who that might be, Danielle?"

"Do you have these in a size seven?" Danielle asked, in an aside. "No idea, Jon. Am I going to see you tonight? It's just that I've got a yoga class from seven to nine and I can't not go. I have to be in shape for my Florida shoot."

"I don't know," said Jon. "I'll call you." And he hung up.

Wall Street, Manhattan

Later that evening, as Robert Baldwin walked through the bank's dimly lit parking lot, his head began to clear of the day's events. He was looking forward to seeing his family. Jenise, the younger of his two children, had been excited last night about another ballet performance, and the dinner table would be full of their chatter. Baldwin smiled, recalling his daughter proudly showing off her new outfit, complete with brand-new tutu and ballet slippers dyed to match. Such a contrast to her younger sister, who was still a tomboy. He climbed into his car, a lovingly restored 1966 Ford Mustang.

As he started the engine, he might not have noticed the man rising from the rear seat in his mirror right away. But he definitely felt the strong hands grab his head, viselike, and twist it so forcefully that his neck snapped on the first rotation.

As Baldwin collapsed, the man unfastened his seat belt and lifted his already lifeless body forward, positioning his head strategically onto the steering wheel. Moving methodically, the man wedged himself behind Baldwin's body, reaching down to press Baldwin's knee so that his foot pumped on the gas pedal, causing the engine to accelerate and the car to lurch forward. As it built up speed on the down ramp, the man used his left hand to steer directly toward one of the concrete pillars. Approaching impact, the man braced himself behind Baldwin so when the car crashed into the pillar, crumpling the engine, it was Baldwin's head that took the brunt of the collision.

It was late, so the garage was quiet prior to the crash. The brief cacophony it created was now replaced by the muted sounds of various fluids leaking onto the stained asphalt, and the creak of metal adjusting to the new shapes into which it had been twisted. The car horn had been become disconnected, so unlike the movie cliché, it did not emit a monotonous blare under the weight of Robert's torso. Satisfied, the man, who wore a baseball hat with a ponytail protruding from it, slipped silently from the wreck. He stood, waiting, looking in all directions, but there was no one around to witness him leave.

East Side, Manhattan

Johnston received two telephone calls that evening. The first came in on his cell phone during a client dinner at Sparks Steakhouse on E. 46th St., near Dag Hammarskjöld Plaza. The conversation was short.

"Mr. Johnston?" a voice had asked in a familiar American drawl.

"Yes."

"The matter has been taken care of. You must now take control of the process." There was no doubting the clarity of his instruction.

Before Johnston could speak, the line went dead. He was left frozen, holding his cell phone to his ear, as he began to grasp the implications of what he had just been told. He feared the severity of their actions in their determination to restore their fortune.

Confirmation came in the second call, this one from another senior member of the bank's board. Johnston took the call in the den of his Park Avenue co-op later that night, a call informing him that the head of the Compliance Department, a dedicated bank employee of twenty-two years, Robert Baldwin, had somehow lost control of his car in the company's garage and succumbed to injuries sustained in the accident. Due to its age, the vehicle had not been equipped with modern safety equipment and Baldwin had died upon impact. Mechanical failure was suspected. Mr. Johnston replaced the receiver and settled back into his leather club chair.

He sat quietly for only a few moments before rising to cross the room to a collection of crystal decanters. While he poured himself a large glass of bourbon, a photograph from his college days caught his eye. The black-and-white picture portrayed a young and enthusiastic version of himself in a football uniform. He was grinning, confident and carefree in those long-ago days. Everything had seemed so simple then.

Johnston was only now realizing with whom he had associated himself. Also, only now, did he understand the extent of his own involvement in the unfolding drama. To these people, patience and attempts at persuasion were not options. To them, it was open-and-shut. Aside from Phillips, Robert Baldwin was the only link between Johnston and the Russian money deposited in the U.K. Trading Company's margin account. If the link was uncovered, they would all lose their money, and along with the bank and Johnston, be subjected to the kind of scrutiny that could land them all in prison. And so they had acted.

Chapter Nine

At home that night, Jon sat in front of an impressive array of state-of-the-art monitors, a complete home office communication system. Dark circles smudged the skin under his reddening eyes. Danielle was positioned elegantly on the sofa, absorbed in a magazine; she was sober and looked astonishingly beautiful, had Jon been noticing.

Unable to tear his gaze away from his once-beloved data streams, Jon was unaware that she was not even pretending to listen to his rambling monologue. He was, in fact, just thinking out loud, trying to get a grasp on the situation in which he unexpectedly found himself.

"You know, maybe it's better to be pushed than jump. This job is an obsession, not an occupation. It's never possible to get away from it, now that the markets no longer ever close." Danielle hadn't looked up from her magazine. "A long weekend is all you ever get. Well, what does it matter? I'm going to be canned anyway. I'll no doubt be described by the press as some sort of rogue trader, so the bank can cover their ass. It looks like I've come to the end of my run in this town."

Finally noticing Danielle's lack of response even to the prospect of his leaving New York, Jon spun his chair around to look at her. Generally, she did not have a great deal to say unless the conversation was about her. Jon found this self-absorption relaxing. So much on guard at the office, he liked being able to say whatever came into his head around her and know that it would hardly register. Taking in her slim, well-toned limbs, which she'd unconsciously arranged into graceful curves, it occurred to him that she was rather like an exotic pet, an Afghan, perhaps, or a saluki. A creature of which one knew not to expect anything more than a visual feast.

Now that he thought about it, though, Danielle did perform an invaluable function in his life. As an up-and-coming young model, she had an access-to-all-areas pass to New York's trendiest social scene. Working as hard as he did, Jon didn't have the time to keep up. Filling in the gaps was where a fashionable girlfriend could come in very handy. She definitely delivered on that score.

Later, as Danielle slept, Jon lay awake, his thoughts returning again and again to the U.K. Trading Company. He still knew virtually nothing about it, even though it had played such a critical role in the auction process. Now that his relationship to the company promised to be closer than either had anticipated, he wanted to find out all he could.

On impulse, Jon decided to contact Penny Jordan, an old girlfriend from his postgraduate days at Cambridge University. Although Jon had not kept in touch with her, he was familiar with her work as a journalist with a London tabloid newspaper. The British papers were available in New York and Jon often picked them up to keep abreast of the London gossip. He had followed Penny's career with interest. She had progressed from ambulance chasing to features. She might not be on the cutting edge, but she knew her way around.

Sliding noiselessly out of bed, he padded out to his computer, pausing only to consider how long it had been since the messy end to their brief relationship. What he had regarded as nothing more than a university fling, she had apparently taken more seriously. It hadn't helped that he'd left her for her prettier best friend. But now, twelve years later, surely she wouldn't be holding a grudge. He began to type an email to her.

Penny:

It's been a long time, but I've enjoyed reading your work here in New York. I trust all is well in Fleet Street, although I imagine there can't be many of you journalists left now that Mr. Murdoch got his way all those years ago.

I was wondering if you could do me a favor? I don't know whom else to ask. Could you please see what you can find out about a company called the U.K. Trading Company? I'd appreciate any information you can dig up about them, as there isn't much available over here. Thanks, I owe you.

Regards,

Jon

When the alarm clock sounded as usual the following morning at five-fifteen, Jon rose and began going through his morning motions. His monitors still illuminated the den, and he went over to see if Penny had responded. He wasn't surprised to find that she had, but he was taken aback by her reply.

Jon:

Go to Hell.

Penny

Leaving Danielle to forage for breakfast and find her way out when she woke up hours later, Jon met his driver downstairs in front of his building. Today he was in no hurry to get to work, so he sent the driver away and set out walking. Wandering aimlessly, he found himself drawn to the place that most closely resembled nature amid the steel, glass, and concrete environment that was New York City.

Entering Central Park at 59th Street, he rounded the pond,

crossed the Gapstow Bridge and headed north. It wasn't until he reached the Ramble, a large area of open woodland between 74th and 79th Streets, that he felt some of the tension of the last days lessening. The area was known for homosexual assignations at night, but at this hour he was more likely to run across birdwatchers than cruisers.

He climbed the hill up beyond Belvedere Castle and the Great Lawn and sat down on a bench. Watching the armies of joggers making their 1.5-mile laps around the reservoir, he was suddenly struck by the absurdity of it all. All these people, sweating, straining, huffing and puffing, running as fast as they could only to bring themselves back to exactly where they had started. Breaking their necks to get nowhere, just as they'd break each other's necks if they thought it would put them ahead of the pack. Exactly as he had been doing all these years. He chuckled. The chuckle became a laugh, and he sat there, alone, roaring with laughter. No one passing by paid any attention to him. It was not unusual to find a man conversing with himself in the city. To everyone else, he would be just another crazy. Jon, however, was convinced he'd had an epiphany. He had perceived a truth no one would want to hear. In fact, they would cover their ears and run faster, specifically in order to avoid hearing it.

Wall Street, Manhattan

Standing out in his bespoke suit among the secretaries and administrators, Ernest Johnston approached the unattended reception desk on the Compliance Department's floor. He glanced around impatiently until a woman hurried over, balancing a container of coffee as she approached him.

"Yes, sir, can I help you?"

Johnston spoke with a forceful authority intended to be intimidating. "My name is Ernest Johnston. Could I please speak with Mr. Baldwin?"

The woman recognized Johnston's name and was clearly impressed by his presence. "I'm terribly sorry, sir, but Mr. Baldwin has not come in yet. Can I have him contact you as soon as he arrives?"

Johnston showed signs of irritation. "This *is* inconvenient. Robert and I had a meeting organized at 8:00 A.M." He turned as if to leave, then turned back. "Could I please speak with Mr. Baldwin's assistant?"

Relieved, the woman was glad to accommodate his request. "Yes, sir, I will ask Peter Smith to join you immediately. Would you care to wait in Conference Room Two, and perhaps I could get you some coffee while you wait?"

"If you would be so kind."

Peter Smith felt a slight chill run through his body as he entered the conference room a few minutes later. It wasn't that there was any temperature change; every room in the building was climate-controlled. Nor was he intimidated by the prospect of meeting such a senior board member, but something about the man unsettled him.

"I'm sorry to keep you waiting. I'm afraid Mr. Baldwin's secretary neglected to enter the meeting into his diary, and I haven't been able to reach him on his cell phone. Can I be of any help?" Peter was, as yet, unaware of Robert Baldwin's tragic death the night before.

Johnston nodded slightly. "Mr. Baldwin was going to familiarize me with certain compliance procedures. I won't be able to reschedule our meeting today. Perhaps you could fill Mr. Baldwin's shoes for fifteen minutes or so and take me through your procedures."

"I'd be delighted to, sir. Where would you like to begin?"

"Let's begin with credit checking."

"No problem, sir. If you'll come with me to my office, we can access the system there."

"Perhaps it would be easier to do this in Robert's office. Then, if he arrives, he can join us."

"Certainly."

Johnston allowed himself to be led to Baldwin's office, where Smith pulled up a second chair in front of Baldwin's computer terminal. He logged on to the highly secure system. Paper files were virtually obsolete; all the information in the department was computerized.

Smith walked Johnston through the various systems and procedures he knew so well. While he was pleased to have an opportunity to impress such a senior executive at the bank, he could not quite shake the feeling of discomfort he had in Johnston's presence.

After about an hour, Smith had gone through just about every procedure and the time had come, he thought, to start wrapping things up. "Well, sir, that's about it. Is there anything else I can help you with?"

Johnston's smile was noncommittal.

Smith continued. "If not, I'd just like to let you know how much I've enjoyed the opportunity to present our system to you. I don't want to rush, but I have a prearranged meeting down the hall."

"No, that's it." Johnston broke in to assure him. "Thank you for your help at such short notice. I look forward to telling Mr. Baldwin what an asset you are to the department. There are a couple of details I'd like to run through again, but I wouldn't want to keep you from your meeting, so you just go on ahead."

"Certainly, sir." And with that, Smith stood, extended his hand and left.

As the door closed behind him, Johnston sat down at Robert Baldwin's computer and keyed in the client name "U.K. Trading Company" to open the file. This gave him complete access to the account. He scrolled down the file, carefully reading each section as it appeared. There were a number of references to himself as holding the ultimate authority for the account, references that he carefully deleted and replaced with "Jon Phillips." Once all the changes were complete, he saved the new version of the file. Next, he reviewed the Account Opening Authorization for U.K. Trading, which indicated that "R. Baldwin" had now authorized it. Leaving this unchanged, Johnston exited the file. Last, he accessed and deleted all relevant email exchanges between Baldwin and himself. As a final check, he opened the file again, to confirm that the changes he'd made were still in place. After ascertaining that they were, he leaned back and smiled. In just a few minutes, he had secured his future and reputation within the bank, at the expense of both Jon Phillips and the recently deceased Robert Baldwin.

Wall Street, Manhattan

Ellen, Tony, and Gary had been marking time for nearly two hours. It was after ten and their leader was nowhere to be seen. The phone rang, and looking hopeful, Gary picked it up.

"Proprietary Trading." There was a pause. "I'm sorry, he isn't here right now . . . I know you've called before, sir, but he hasn't come in yet . . . Yes, I'll be sure to tell him right away. Goodbye."

"Be sure to tell me what?" The voice came from behind them. "As if I can't guess. I've been summoned upstairs, right?"

Gary nodded. "They are waiting for you in the boardroom."

Jon smiled at his team. "It was inevitable. You know by now what went down, so there it is."

He shook each one by the hand. "It was pleasure working with you all," Jon said, with genuine feeling.

Without waiting for a response from his stunned team, he turned and headed toward the elevators. He had walked no more than halfway across the trading floor when he passed a small cluster of traders. Tom Edwards stood among them, watching Jon. As Jon passed, a comment Edwards made caused the group to burst into suppressed laughter. Jon whirled around to look Edwards directly in the eyes.

"What was that, Tom?" he asked, nonchalantly.

"Nothing, Jon. Just team talk."

"I see," said Jon, letting it go.

"Something you won't be having from now on," Edwards added. His cronies exchanged smug looks.

Jon stopped. "Now that I *did* hear."

"Well, its true, isn't it? You're finished here and everyone knows it."

Jon turned around. "Yes, it's true. But you know what else is true, Tom?" He took a few steps closer.

"What?" asked Edwards, turning cautious.

"You should never bait a man with nothing to lose."

Jon swung, his fist connecting squarely with the bridge of Edwards' nose. Edwards was knocked backward with such force that he fell sprawling in the aisle between the work stations, a bewildered expression on his face.

Jon stood where he was. He eyed the others, as if daring them to have a go. They all looked away. Jon glanced down at Edwards, who lay still, in shock. "It's been a pleasure." He smiled and left the trading room for the last time.

Although within the same building, the executive offices existed, for all intents and purposes, in another world. As the elevator doors parted, Jon felt uneasy away from familiar territory. He was now entering an environment reserved exclusively for the upper echelons of the bank's management team. This was strictly invitation only, and Jon was there for all the wrong reasons.

Jon walked into the boardroom to find three senior directors seated with the Chief Executive. Jon was familiar with each — one had recently negotiated his employment contract — but he was disappointed to see that Johnston was not among them. He obeyed the instruction to sit, and waited.

The Chief Executive spoke. "It is our intention for this meeting to be a brief one. First, are you willing to admit that your recent dealings on the bank's proprietary account have resulted in substantial losses for the bank, losses exceeding one hundred twenty-three million dollars?"

"Yes," Jon acknowledged.

The Chief Executive continued. "And are you aware that during the course of these dealings, you breached both the bank's internal exposure limits and trading mandates, and you may even have breached SEC regulations?"

Jon chose his words carefully. "Under certain circumstances, I may have."

The Chief Executive looked annoyed. "What on earth do you mean by 'under certain circumstances'? Did you, or did you not, contravene these rules and regulations? I want a straight answer."

Jon was not rattled. "Well, I may have."

"I will regard that as a 'yes'. Do you know that the bank has been aware of your increasingly erratic behavior for some time now?" Observing Jon's puzzled look, he paused momentarily. "I would guess not. Robert Baldwin approached a board member recently with his concerns about your behavior and the manner in which you have been conducting business on behalf of the bank."

This was nonsense and Jon knew it. "That's not true. That is simply not true," he said, heatedly.

"Mr. Johnston, who, as you know, sits on the main board of the bank and works closely with our Compliance Department, advises me that Baldwin was concerned enough to begin conducting an internal investigation into your behavior."

"That is not correct," insisted Jon. "I suggest you speak with Mr. Baldwin. He'll tell you otherwise."

"I'm afraid that won't be possible, Mr. Phillips."

"May I ask why not?"

The Chief Executive looked at the other board members and momentarily hesitated. "Mr. Baldwin was killed in an automobile accident last night."

"*What*?" Jon was shocked by the news. "Robert's *dead*?"

"I'm sorry you had to learn of it in these circumstances, Mr. Phillips. We recommend you consult a lawyer if you wish to take issue with any of these allegations."

Jon was too overwhelmed to comprehend what was being said. "Lawyer? An automobile accident? Where?"

The Chief Executive nodded. "In the bank's garage. Mechanical failure, apparently." He was keen to cut straight back to the chase. "You should know that a separate internal investigation into your recent trading will begin immediately. Mr. Johnston has offered to assume responsibility for this."

"I'm sorry, but I don't know what you're implying. What allegations are you talking about?" Jon was still trying to make sense of what he was being told.

"Mr. Baldwin and Mr. Johnston were concerned not only with your behavior in conducting trades on behalf of the bank, but that you had exposed one of our clients to enormous risks, and had even given them some sort of assurance that the bank would indemnify any losses."

Jon could feel the pressure building. "No. That's just not right." He was trying to keep calm. "Mr. Johnston was the one who indemnified the client. He was the one who sanctioned this." Jon looked desperately around at each of the four unfriendly faces. "Don't you see?" He pleaded.

The Chief Executive's manner became brusque. "There will be an appropriate forum to conduct a defense, but this is not it. Furthermore, such were the concerns of Mr. Johnston that the bank thought it appropriate to investigate not only your dealings within the bank, but also your activities outside the bank." The other board members nodded. "This has apparently revealed a lifestyle exhibiting a sorry list of vices, the very antithesis of everything this bank stands for. The most distressing aspect of all is that it took us such a long time to discover the truth, almost allowing you to drag the bank down with you."

"This is bullshit!" Jon had known the bank would do whatever it deemed necessary to protect its own interests, and that he would be required to assume the role of the fall guy, but he was nonetheless unprepared for this kind of assault.

The Chief Executive forged on. "In fact, had it not been for the responsible action of Mr. Baldwin and the swift response of Mr. Johnston, you might have done so. Our position is clear. You are dismissed. As we speak, your desk is being cleared by security. The bank will issue a statement outlining your dismissal on the grounds of breaches of internal mandates. Gentlemen . . ." he turned to the other men at the table. "Unless you have any further comments to add, I would like to terminate this meeting." He looked back at Jon, sternly. "You may leave."

Jon was speechless. It was all too much to comprehend. He had no option but to regroup in private. He stood and allowed himself to be escorted by two security guards through the doors and toward the elevator. The doors slid open and the three men stepped inside.

A man already in the elevator put his hand helpfully to the panel of buttons and looked questioningly at Jon. "Going down?" he asked.

"It certainly looks that way," Jon answered, unsmiling.

Chapter Ten

Left on the street by the guards, Jon stood on the sidewalk in a state of bewildered humiliation. To make matters even worse, two large plastic garbage bags filled with his personal belongings had been unceremoniously dumped at his feet. New York rushed past, oblivious to his predicament. The truth was, who cared? Jon was just another of the city's casualties. The worst of it was that he was directly responsible for his own misfortune. He'd walked straight into this mess, like a lamb to slaughter.

Jon slung the bags over his shoulder, hailed a cab and directed the driver to his apartment. There was nowhere else to go. All the way home, his thoughts were occupied with Baldwin's wife and his two children. The Bank had wasted no time in disconnecting his cell phone so he would have to wait to call Rita on his landline.

Once back at his apartment, he threw the garbage bags under the kitchen counter and went straight to his desk. He hit the speed dial and, after a few rings, a woman picked up.

"Rita?"

"No," the woman replied, "this is Joanie, Rita's sister."

"May I talk to Rita, please?"

"I'm sorry. She isn't able to speak to anyone right now. She's too upset."

"I understand. Please, would you offer her my condolences? My name is Jon Phillips."

"Okay, Mr. Phillips, I'll be sure to . . ." and at that point, he could hear a muffled voice in the background. Then the phone was passed over to someone else and another voice spoke into the receiver.

"Jon? This is Rita." Her whisper was hardly audible.

"Hello, Rita," said Jon. "I just heard."

Rita started to sob. "Oh, Jon, it's just so terrible. I don't know what to do."

"I know," soothed Jon. "I know. It's dreadful. Robert was a great man."

"Thank you, Jon. He was, wasn't he?"

"Is there anything I can do for you, Rita? Would you like me to come over?"

"That's very kind of you. But if you don't mind, I need to be on my own with the kids. I only came to the phone because it was you."

"Of course," said Jon. "You'll let me know if you need anything. I mean *anything*."

"Thank you, Jon, I will. Thank you." And she hung up.

As Jon replaced the receiver, his eyes filled with tears. An overwhelming sense of responsibility consumed him and he buried his head in his hands. For the first time in years, he was able to feel some of the emotions he usually kept buried. And as he let out the pain, his sadness at the loss of his friend overshadowed the concerns he had about himself. An accident in the garage? It was difficult to believe. Eventually he managed to compose himself and go to his computer. Maybe there would be a message there that would throw some light on what had happened.

Scrolling through his messages, one email in particular caught his eye. He clicked on it.

Jon:

You caught me at a bad moment before. Sorry. Here's what I found. Maybe you can return the favor someday.

The U.K. Trading Company turns out to be quite intriguing, a shell with no hard assets and no real business, owned by an obscure Cayman Islands company. But, one of its directors, a London-based Russian named Boris Posarnov, is a real villain and, oddly, is linked to Victoria's father; he's a regular at Stanford Hall during the shooting season. There's another link; he's also a sailing buddy of one of your Bank's directors, Ernest Johnston. I gather he's someone to steer clear of. Big Russian money, big trouble.

Penny

Jon stared at the screen, rereading the message over and over again. He was stunned at the prospect of being caught in an elaborate setup. Or, if not exactly caught, he'd at least allowed himself to be put in a position where he could be highly compromised, which was just as bad. But how did it all fit together? As he contemplated possible scenarios, the doorbell rang. Even through his fog, Jon noted that this was unusual. He lived in a doorman-controlled building and normally visitors were announced before being let up. Maybe Danielle had lost her key. He went to the door.

"Who is it?" Through the peephole, he saw two men dressed in overalls. The one nearest the door spoke.

"Maintenance."

Jon opened the door. "What's the problem?

"We're here about the mess," said the first man.

"What mess?" asked Jon, confused.

"Yours," said the same man. As he spoke, the man laid a body punch into Jon with such force that Jon thought his ribcage had collapsed. He fell heavily to the floor, winded and fighting for air. The two men stepped casually over him and into the apartment, closing the door behind them.

They clearly knew what they were doing. The younger of the two knelt down and bound Jon's hands behind his back with a belt.

He dragged Jon into the den and left him on the floor in the middle of the room. The older man surveyed the apartment. Jon wondered if he was being robbed.

"What do you want?" he rasped.

The older man stared down at him, as if sizing him up. He took off his cap to reveal a head of gray, stringy hair pulled back in a ponytail. He was wearing a pair of tight, black leather gloves.

"We'll assume this is your first professional beating," the man said, calmly. He began looking around the room once more, occasionally stopping to pick up items and weigh them with both hands, as if evaluating them.

The younger of the two men adjusted Jon's position on the floor to make sure he was lying on his back, his bound arms under him.

"It's free-form, really," the pony tailed man continued, conversationally. "There are some rules, just in case you didn't know. This is just a warning; we are not here to really hurt you. Well, that's not exactly true." He chuckled, looking conspiratorially over at his assistant. "In fact, we're going to hurt you a lot."

The assistant picked up a large steel table lamp and swung it around, pantomiming whacking an imaginary victim before putting it down and heading for the bedroom.

"It's just that no one will notice what we've done to you."

"What the fuck is this all about?" asked Jon.

"I'll get to that," smiled the man, as he put down the lamp. "Nice apartment. Obviously, you were very successful." Jon noted the past tense.

The assistant came back from the bedroom with a golf club. "Perfect," approved his boss, as he caught it in mid-flight. He walked over to Jon and swaggered above him, like a pro warming up to tee off. Jon saw the first blow coming, and cowered.

"Yes, if I said we didn't want to hurt you, that would be untrue . . ." And the man struck Jon with the full force of the club. The blow knocked any remaining wind out of him. "But we don't really want to hurt your lovely girlfriend, if we don't have to."

"Danielle?"

"Don't worry, she's not hurt, at least, not yet," the man reassured Jon, as he swung the club for a second time, with a force so strong that Jon felt his spleen slam against his liver.

And as the man continued the slow, methodical process of beating every available part of Jon's body — back, arms, chest and legs — he explained his purpose. "We share the same interests. Provided you are smart enough to leave things as they currently stand, neither you nor we will have anything to worry about. If you get clever and start making a noise about the U.K. Trading Company, things are bound to turn sour. Next time, I may not show such restraint toward your pretty little girlfriend. Lord only knows what I could do to her. And to you. You don't even want to think about it."

Careful just to bruise, not break, any of Jon's ribs, the younger man took over, pummeling his kidneys.

"I'm a man of many talents, and pretty good with my hands, practical, in a mechanical sense, fixing cars, that sort of thing. We will do whatever is necessary to protect our position, and the money, of course. Now, provided the details of our arrangement are kept quiet, you and I can say goodbye to one another."

Jon had caught the sly reference to Robert's accident. It left him in no doubt as to whether Baldwin had been murdered.

The pony tailed man kicked Jon in the stomach one last time, for good measure. Jon did not even reel back in pain. He was spent. After the man knelt to remove the restraints from Jon's wrists, he and his assistant sauntered out of his apartment without another word.

Thoughts of Danielle forced Jon to drag himself up from the floor. As he struggled to stand, he felt as though every bone in his body was shattered. But he managed to make his way to the telephone and dial her number. Relief washed over him as he heard her answer.

"Danielle! Are you alright?"

"What do you mean?"

"Are you okay?"

"I'm fine . . . I mean, apart from the fact that I pulled a muscle doing Pilates this morning."

"Did anyone try to hurt you today?"

"Don't be ridiculous."

"No one approached you, or tried to make contact with you in any way?" Jon persisted.

"No. What are you going on about?" Her irritation rising.

"You're sure? You're absolutely positive?"

"Well, come to think of it, and I didn't really take much notice of it when it happened," she paused.

"What? When *what* happened?" Jon pressed her.

"Why are you being so dramatic?" Danielle said, angered by his persistence.

"Never mind, just tell me what happened."

"Well, I was having lunch with Tilly upstairs at Barneys this afternoon and a man came up to me. I thought he was just hitting on me at first. But then he said the strangest thing. He said you better behave yourself or I would be sorry. I didn't take him seriously, though."

"That's all he said?"

"He said you would understand, and then he left. Is something going on?" Jon had finally managed to pique her curiosity.

"I'll explain everything later. The important thing at the moment is that you're okay." Then, wanting to reassure her, he added, "Don't worry, you're not in any danger."

The intercom buzzed but Jon was oblivious.

"What do you mean, Jon? Of course, I'm not in any danger. But if you don't tell me right this minute what's going on, I'm going to hang up. In fact, I'm busy, I'll call you later."

"No, wait, Danielle. You don't understand. You aren't at your apartment, are you? Where are you?"

"I said, I'll call you later. And stop being so possessive, it's so uncool." She hung up.

Frustrated and angry, Jon replaced the receiver. He shouldn't be angry, knowing Danielle's concentration span had merely expired, as it tended to do. Nonetheless, he was contemplating calling her back when he heard someone at the unlocked front door. Barely able to move, his body aching all over, he looked around for something with which to protect himself. The footsteps continued. The men were coming back. Jon grabbed the only heavy object he could reach, the Yellow Pages. He lifted it above his head, and waited. A man walked into the room.

"David!" Jon exclaimed, relief flooding his entire body.

"G'day, mate." A broad smile washed over his brother's face.

Then, stopping in his tracks, David looked Jon up and down, quizzically taking note of the phone book Jon still held in mid-air. "What the fuck are you doing? Are you going to hit me with that, or call me a pizza?"

"You're a pizza," Jon just managed to get out, before collapsing onto the floor.

Chapter Eleven

Upper East Side, Manhattan

The alarm clock glowed 7:42. Light crept around the edges of the blinds Jon rarely closed. Was it morning or evening? Jon tried to get up, forgetting why he might still be in bed at this hour, day or night. The sharp pain immediately electrifying every part of his body was a searing reminder. Easing himself to his feet, he noticed he was dressed in pajamas, which he rarely wore, preferring to sleep in the nude. Somebody must have put him to bed. He looked around for Danielle, but she was nowhere to be seen, and her space beside him in the bed had not been slept in. Then he remembered that she'd left for a week-long modeling assignment in the Florida Keys. He picked up an unfamiliar bottle of Vicodin from the nightstand, reading on the label that it had been prescribed in his name. The pain was not receding so he tapped out a couple of the large white pills into his palm and headed to the bathroom.

The vast living room was clean and quiet. After opening the blinds and seeing it was morning, Jon slowly made his way across the stripped wooden floor to the answering machine. He was surprised to see he'd received no messages. His first assumption was that he'd become such a pariah after what had happened that nobody wanted anything to do with him. But then he noticed the machine had been unplugged. He checked the phones. Sure enough, their jacks also lay disconnected. Someone had made very sure he wouldn't be disturbed. David. Suddenly Jon remembered his brother's arrival. The door to the guest room was closed; he must still be sleeping.

Not wishing to wake him, Jon avoided putting on the television and shuffled over to his faithful computer screens. There were 117 new messages in his e-mail in-box. Jon scanned the list of subjects and names. Among financial newsletters, notes of commiseration and messages of good cheer, he fastened on one in particular. It was from Penny.

> *Jonny:*
>
> One minute you're asking me about some shady company, the next you're making the news. Do I smell a story even bigger than the one that's being reported? I read in today's Wall Street Journal that you've been dismissed for "gross misconduct" and that the bank is investigating "trading irregularities." I also hear from my sources in New York that News/Copy is running an interview with someone who's going to expose "the lifestyle behind the rogue trader," as they're promo-ing it. It looks as though someone is doing a real job on you. So what's the scoop? Please give me a call so that I can help explain your side of the story. You get a chance to set the record straight and I get a hot story with an American angle.
>
> Are you ever in London? If so, do give me a ring.
>
> *Penny*

Jon realized immediately that he'd better respond before Penny concocted a story and made things worse. He needed to at least stall her. As the Vicodin kicked in, he typed out a reply he hoped would deflect her.

Penny:

Off the record, the "gross misconduct" relates to some substantial trading losses on the bank's proprietary book. They were my responsibility, and consequently, I've got some pretty big fires to put out. The timing of my inquiry about the U.K. Trading Company was purely coincidental. Sorry to disappoint. I'm being told to lay low by my learned legal counsel. I'll ring you if I'm in a position to give you a story. Thanks for your interest.

Jon

"Jeez, mate, it's first thing in the morning and already you're logging onto one of those porn sites." David's broad Australian accent was noticeable even to Jon, a reminder of how long it had been since he'd been home.

He smiled, grimacing as he stood. The two men embraced warmly, if gingerly on Jon's part.

"Am I glad to see you!" Jon exclaimed.

"And just in the nick of time, it seems. You had me worried there for a while," David replied.

"Ow, watch it!" Jon winced at his brother's grip. "I'm still a little tender."

"So I see," said David. "You can tell me all about it tonight."

"Tonight? What about today? Now?"

"You can't today, you've got a funeral to go to."

"Already? Robert only died yesterday."

"No, he didn't," replied David, seriously. "You've been asleep for almost two days."

Montclair, New Jersey

A fleet of Lincoln Town Cars and limousines waited patiently for the large, upscale group of mourners in the light drizzle of the Montclair Cemetery. Jon, standing graveside among them, found himself overwhelmed by a now all-too-unfamiliar feeling of guilt and responsibility. He was having difficulty coping with this on-slaught of unfamiliar emotions. In recent years, compassion and consideration for others had not figured largely in his makeup or actions. But as his eyes scanned the faces of Robert's friends and family, he felt a newfound empathy.

On the intermittent occasions when he would hire a car and driver to take him out to Queens for an early dinner with Robert and Rita and their two young daughters, he would be reminded of his own close-knit family. The talk would be not about the office but of family holidays, Robert's coaching prowess, summer camp activities, and gossip about the gym where Jon's and Robert's friendship had been forged by years of sharing the same swimming lane. He'd enjoyed the times he'd had with them, even though he'd always been more than ready to return to his East Side bachelor apartment after just a few hours.

As the service ended, Jon approached Rita Baldwin. They em-braced.

"I'm so sorry, Rita. So sorry."

"I know, Jon. It's too terrible for words."

"Is there anything I can do for you? I mean, will you be okay?"

She sighed heavily. "Thank you. We'll get by."

Jon could sense a weight, an underlying worry. "Rita, you're like me, a survivor. But, you're really all right? I mean, what about money?"

"To tell the truth, Jon, we're a little tight. The insurance set-tlement is barely going to be enough to make the mortgage pay-ments. I'm probably going to have to sell the house and the kids are so young, I'll have to go back to work to get them through school."

"Are you sure? I mean, Robert was so conscientious about his responsibilities."

"He was, but the policies he had will take some time to reach fruition, and after taxes and all, the money doesn't go a long way." She sounded resigned.

"I'm sorry to hear that, Rita. Maybe there's something I can do."

"That's very kind of you, Jon, but you have enough worries of your own right now. Besides, it might even be a good thing for me to get back to work. It will help keep my mind off this nightmare."

"Look, I . . ."

But her attention was being sought by several other mourners who had been waiting to offer their condolences.

"We'll be fine, Jon, really," she reassured him, as she pulled him close for a hug. "Now you take care of yourself," she whispered softly.

"You, too," Jon whispered back. And for a long moment, they embraced.

As they broke apart, he felt the scrutiny of the bank's chief executive, who was standing nearby. "I didn't think you'd have the balls to show your face, Phillips."

"He was my friend," Jon replied. "Anyway, I've been set up and when I prove it, you'll owe me an apology."

As the chief grunted in reply, Baldwin's assistant, Peter Smith, approached them. "Jon, you got a sec?"

The chief glared at each of them in turn, before Jon moved away with Smith.

"Peter," Jon said, grateful to have been interrupted. "Good to see you. What's on your mind?"

"It may be nothing," Smith replied. "But I thought you might like to know. The morning after Mr. Baldwin's accident, that dickhead, Johnston, spent over an hour in his office tampering with his computer."

"Why does that not surprise me?" Jon commented ruefully. "Thanks for the information, Peter."

"There's more," continued Smith. "It's a strange thing, but a couple of days later, a guy comes in and removes Mr. Baldwin's whole system — screen, hard drive, everything. Said he was authorized by Johnston."

"Is that so unusual?" queried Jon.

"Yes. In compliance, we're very security conscious, and this sort of thing doesn't happen without prior discussion and appropriate authorization. If Mr. Baldwin had been planning to replace his system, I would have known about it. Plus, there would be no reason to get rid of it because of his death."

"Thanks for giving me the heads up."

Smith went on, lowering his voice. "I know you and Mr. Baldwin were close and there's just something about Johnston that leaves me cold. I'm sure you'll be discreet with this information. I hope it makes some sense to you. It doesn't to me."

Jon was appreciative. "It does, and I will not breathe a word to anyone. You have my word on that. But do you have any idea where they took the computer?"

"I was curious so I asked the same question. He told me it was going to Sag Harbor." Jon extended his hand to Smith and shook it warmly. He nodded his thanks and left.

Upper East Side, Manhattan

By the time Jon returned to his apartment after paying his respects at the Baldwin home in Queens, he was in a fog, for which the Vicodin was only partly responsible. If Johnston had tampered with the files, then removing the hard drive would merely be a form of insurance for him, in case the old file information hadn't been completely deleted. But why take it to Sag Harbor? Jon wondered whether the hard drive was still in use. His thoughts moved on to Robert Baldwin's young family. Sadness and guilt again engulfed him.

He was relieved to find his brother watching television. Having already helped himself to a glass of Scotch, David poured one for Jon.

"Whew! Thanks, David. You're a rock. I'm sure you're dying for an explanation."

"Too right," his brother responded, "but hang on. There's something you should see first on *News/Copy*. It should be coming on any minute. They've been promoting it like crazy."

"Ah, yes, the rogue trader. Someone e-mailed me about that." Jon sat down next to David and started in on his scotch. "Don't be expecting a puff piece. They're out to get me."

"Who's 'they'?" David began, but Jon shushed him as an attractive anchorwoman began introducing the program's upcoming stories. His was the lead, it seemed.

"Tonight we bring you yet another tale of greed and recklessness on Wall Street: The fall of Jon Phillips, otherwise known as the Wizard — or should I say Lizard — of Oz. This Australian-born rogue trader pushed around vast sums of money in his attempt to gain fame and fortune . . . and apparently, that's not all he pushed. In our lead story, we will be exposing the dark side of this latest casualty of Wall Street. Our second story . . ."

David hit the Mute button. Jon got up to take another Vicodin, then settled carefully back to prepare for whatever new twists his life was about to have invented for it. Once again, the camera zoomed in on the anchor.

"Another tale of careless trading and reckless controls in the unending pursuit of profits? We seem to be hearing this all too often these days . . ."

The screen showed an unflattering picture of Jon in a tuxedo — glass of champagne in one hand, cigar in the other — at a charity dinner. He had a smug smile on his face and Danielle, draped over him, appeared drunk because of the way her eyes had been caught mid-roll. A sterling example of opportunistic photography.

"Jon Phillips was dismissed from his post as head of proprietary trading at the Bank of Manhattan earlier this week, after creating losses estimated at nearly one hundred and twenty three million dollars. An innocent trader brought down by unbearable pressure to create big profits for his bank? Not this time. We meet a man who has known him well, a man who must remain anonymous to protect himself from almost certain prosecution."

The television screen flashed a series of intercut images of drug use re-enactments and stock footage of street hookers before returning to the studio where the silhouette of a man appeared, seated casually in a studio chair. He was shrouded in darkness. "This is Mr. X., drug dealer and occasional pimp to the Wizard of Oz."

Outraged, Jon turned to his brother. "I've no idea who this guy is!" he protested. David held up a hand for quiet.

The anchor continued. "We ask the question: do banks have responsibility for knowing the real, but often hidden, sides of the sort of young men and women who seem so prevalent on Wall Street? Mr. X, please give our viewers an insight into the *real* Jon Phillips."

And as the man started speaking, Jon realized that in fact he did know him, although not well. It was Georgie McWilliam, the bar owner who was Danielle's drug dealer. He was holding forth with the authority of one who had been a long-time close associate of Jon's. "Jonny was always a player; I'm talking a real goodtime Charlie. At first, he was just into the ordinary stuff — coke, pot, that sort of thing."

"He was a regular user?" The anchor prompted.

"Sure, big boozer as well. I'd often see him late at night. He'd be drunk and looking for some action," Georgie offered. "Over time, he got a bit more exotic in his drugs of choice."

"You mean . . . like heroin?" the anchor ventured.

"Yeah, smack, PCP, crank, anything that had a bang to it . . ." Georgie was now on a roll, the truth left far behind. "And then there were the girls; he loved paying for sex and liked 'em young, real young — and kinky. Yeah, he's out there, all right. And he liked to dress up, if you know what I mean . . ."

"Dress up?" The anchor asked, genuinely startled at this unrehearsed revelation. "You mean, like a woman?"

"Yeah, like a girl. Jonny's quite a number — though a very good client, I should add."

The anchor seemed anxious about the direction her primetime interview was taking. She wrapped it up quickly. "Thank you for these disturbing insights into the man who until recently was regarded as one of Wall Street's finest. If nothing else, these shocking revelations may give the rest of the financial world something to think about . . ."

Jon reached for the remote and switched off the television. Up until now, media attention had been limited to speculations about the bank's press release. Fortunately, the release had been short on detail, designed, as it was, to protect the bank's interest. The losses were described as "not material" for the bank, and "outside its normal course of business." The tabloids had not yet picked up the story, but given the *News/Copy* exposure, their treatment of him in the following morning's press would no doubt be savage.

"So, Jon, where would you like to start?" His brother's voice broke into his thoughts.

"Well, it's not true, none of it, if that's what you're thinking."

"Jon," said David quietly. "I'm your brother. You can tell me anything." His tone of voice invited a confessional.

"David, it's not true!" Jon protested. "Really. I don't take heroin, you know that."

"And the rest of it?"

"Not true. Any of it."

"Oh, come on, don't bullshit me. I found dresses and wigs in your closet when I put you to bed. Jesus, Jon! That part's true, you've been dressing up like a girl."

"Well, I . . . No! I did it for a couple of charity events. Me and a pal, we dressed up like The Carpenters to raise money. And, by the way, it worked. We were a big hit. The way they slanted it makes me look like some kind of deviant."

David shook his head. "The only way you could ever get me to dress up like a woman would be over my dead body." He stood up and helped both of them to another drink. "But you can't blame me for being confused, Jon. I show up here and find you half-beaten to death. Then I'm fielding God knows how many phone calls from journalists and all sorts, asking me about things I know nothing about. You have to see how I might wonder what the hell is going on. Now why don't you tell me everything? Who was that guy on television, for a start? You do know who he is, don't you?"

"Alright," Jon admitted. "I've met him a few times. His name's Georgie McWilliam. He's a low-life scumbag who sells drugs to my girlfriend, Danielle. But the truth is that Georgie was stoned half the time and probably wouldn't recognize me if he fell on me. Someone is doing a real job on me."

"Who would want to do that? And why?" David asked, skeptically.

"Oh, I don't know," Jon replied sarcastically. "Maybe it's the Russian mobsters I've been buying government bonds for."

"You've been doing *what*? Just how bad a mess have you gotten yourself into?"

"So bad that I think they killed one of my friends at the bank in order to silence him. Seriously."

David was stunned. "Robert? Fuck! Why don't you start at the beginning."

"It all started when I came up with the idea to corner the U.S. Treasury bond auction market as a way of making a bundle so I could leave and try something else. You're not supposed to do that, so the government limits the amount any one party can buy to thirty-five percent of the total. The only way I could get around this was to have a supposedly independent partner come in for another thirty-five percent. Unfortunately, the partner I wound up with seems to be a U.K.-based front for a very questionable Caribbean "trading" company. In fact, they were really just laundering dirty Russian money. That's why they agreed to come on board."

"Well, that was smart. Why on earth did you get involved with them in the first place?" David asked.

"I had no idea. The company is a client of the bank's, and a senior board member named Ernest Johnston lined the whole thing up. He said the bank's board had sanctioned it. I never questioned the set-up since the bank has very strict compliance controls. But Johnston even managed to get it through Robert's department without the usual checks, because of his seniority."

"So it's not your problem then. This partner was not your client. Surely the bank will realize that this is Johnston's responsibility."

"You'd think. But it looks like he's changed all the account records to make it seem like I'm wholly responsible for it."

"You and Johnston are the only two people who know the truth?"

"Yes," confirmed Jon. "Well, there was one other person who understood the set-up and that was Robert."

"Whose funeral you just attended." David's growing concern was evident.

"Robert died the day after he met with Johnston. Robert was insisting that this situation should be sorted out at the highest level within the bank, which would have exposed this trading company for what it really was. They would have lost all their money and been arrested, along with Johnston."

"So they *murdered* him? Jesus, these guys don't fuck around."

"You said it. They were the ones who paid me that little visit the day you arrived. They want me to agree to take the fall associated with the losses, so the fact that the bank's client is a money launderer will be kept under wraps. The whole thing will blow over. I'll stay out of prison, they'll get all their money back, and the SEC won't get involved, so the bank will be okay. That's what all this is about. They were giving me a warning — keep quiet or else."

"I presume you don't need further convincing," said David.

"I know I don't want to go to prison, and I probably would if the SEC got involved. The truth is, David, I don't know what to do.

"There's no evidence to prove your innocence?"

Jon delved into his briefcase and removed a large file, tossing it to his brother. "This is a copy of the file on U.K. Trading. I had my attorney request it. Johnston has changed everything on the system and recalled hard copies of all the original filing, which nobody else saw anyway. A complete whitewash job."

David leafed through the file. Jon was right; the only names referred to were Jon's and Robert Baldwin's. "And you kept nothing relating to it? Any letters, a note?"

Jon had begun pacing, forgetting the pain in his body; just talking through the situation was causing him to become agitated.

"No, I had no access, nor any reason to . . ." And Jon stopped in his tracks. A realization had just come over him. He hurried to the bedroom. David got up and followed him. Jon was in the closet, rifling through racks of clothing. He spoke without interrupting his frantic search. "What happened to my blue Dolce & Gabbana suit? Did you see it?"

"There was a bunch of clothes over that chair. Maybe it was one of them."

Jon whirled to look at the chair. It was empty. "What clothes? There's nothing there."

"Well, not now, there isn't," replied David. "I sent them to the cleaners."

"What!" Jon was desperate.

"Yeah, some guy came up, said he picks up your dry cleaning every week. I gave him all the stuff."

"I don't believe it," Jon cried. "What about the things in the pockets? Did you even check?"

"I'm not an idiot, Jon. Everything that was in the pockets I put in the dresser drawer."

"Which one?"

"That one over there," David pointed.

Jon dashed over. He jerked the drawer open and scanned its contents urgently. It took only a few moments before he found what he was looking for — Baldwin's handwritten note. He opened it and reread the words that directly implicated Johnston. Another folded document containing the bank account details of the U.K. Trading Company and other account information remained in the drawer.

"What's that?" asked David.

Jon smiled, his first genuine smile in some time. "This, David, is what I needed. Some hard, cold evidence."

Chapter Twelve

Ernest Johnston had not attended Robert Baldwin's funeral. He preferred not to think of him. His week had been busy, and his social schedule kept him from having to devote too much attention to anything so disquieting. He was relieved to have it in the past and to be getting on with life as usual. Tonight was no exception; he was entertaining a couple of investors from Arkansas. Overweight businessmen in town for a couple of days without their wives were generally pretty easy to please. They needed a decent New York steak, first of all, which could be found at any number of expense-account eateries all over Manhattan; tonight it was Smith & Wollensky on Third Avenue. Afterwards, they would move on to enjoy the seamier pleasures offered by any one of the city's many strip joints and fleshpots. Dinner was coming to an end, and as he excused himself, Johnston was debating whether the next port of call should be Scores or the VIP Club.

The one other occupant of the men's room soon departed, leaving Johnston alone. His back turned away from the door, and preoccupied with planning the rest of the evening's entertainment, he paid no attention as someone entered the room behind him. Nor did he hear the newcomer lock the outer door, sealing them in, alone. He became aware of his company when he felt someone's fingers grab the hair on the back of his head and sharply yank it, twisting his head back. The pain was so intense and unexpected that he nearly cried out.

"Need any help finding that thing?" his attacker asked. Then he ordered sharply, "Don't turn around."

"What do you want?" Johnston managed to gasp.

"You think you did a pretty good job setting me up, you and your goons, don't you?"

"Phillips?" Johnston blurted, giving himself away. "What the hell do you think you're playing at?" He struggled to turn around, but Jon kept his grip tight.

"Shut up and face the wall," Jon barked.

"Listen, you shouldn't take any of this personally."

"Oh, okay," replied Jon. "How should I take it, then? Lying down or bending over?"

"The losses and Robert's inflexibility forced their hand. We simply needed a fall guy and you were it. They want their money back."

"Oh, yeah, and the *News/Copy* piece was a nice touch. How did you manage to dig up that scumbag?"

"You don't know who you're dealing with, Phillips. These people have no patience for heroics."

"And I have no patience for being smeared by a bunch of lying gangsters."

"From your point of view, I think a brief period of public humiliation is a small price to pay for staying out of prison," Johnston commented. He was regaining his composure as Jon loosened his grasp.

"Well, maybe I think differently."

"What do you want, then? Let's get this over with, shall we? I have clients to get back to." Johnston's tone was now dismissive.

"Have they killed anyone else I might know? Just curious." Jon reached into his pocket and pulled out a card and a slip of paper. "You have a problem," he said.

"No, Jon," Johnston sighed. "It is you who has the problem.

Anything you do now will only make matters worse. You remember the little warning you received? That was mild compared to the damage you can bring upon yourself and those around you if you don't toe the line."

"I have evidence that clearly links you to the trumped-up deal with U.K. Trading," Jon continued. "If I were to produce this evidence, I fully appreciate that I'd be compromising my own position, and might be buying a ticket to prison. That said, I believe a plea bargain with the SEC would probably keep me out. Under those circumstances, you would have a great deal to lose, as I would do everything in my power to destroy both you and U.K. Trading, which shouldn't be too difficult to do."

"What evidence? You're bluffing, Phillips. You've got nothing." But a hint of anxiety had crept into Johnston's voice.

"Oh, really? If you think that, you might want to give my lawyer a call. This is his card." Jon shoved the business card into Johnston's top breast pocket. "The evidence has been produced in triplicate and is already addressed to the chairman of the SEC, the chief executive of the bank, and the New York head of the FDA. The envelopes are stamped. The instructions relating to its release are crystal clear. If I sustain any form of injury, or there is any threat of injury, my attorney will immediately release the document. The bottom line is, I'm ready to take you and your pals down, no matter what."

"And exactly what evidence do you have that has come to light in the past couple of days?"

"I have the account details of the company, but it's a handwritten note from Robert Baldwin that directly implicates you. A rare stroke of luck that I kept it."

"So why not go straight to the authorities and book your time in jail? Why waste our time?"

"Because bringing everyone down won't put Robert's kids through college, nor will it restore my fortunes, that's why."

Johnston laughed. "I get it. You want money. That's what this is all about."

"As I understand it, U.K. Trading had to deposit thirty-five million dollars cash with the bank in a cash margin account. Even though it's gone now, that's what they're owed by the bank for the trading losses on the account, according to their arrangement. If I start singing, the government authorities will freeze those funds in an instant. And your client can then kiss their dirty money goodbye forever. We all lose, but you and U.K. Trading more than me, given how grateful the SEC is likely to be for my information. For three million dollars, I can be persuaded to tear up my evidence and we all win, no fuss, no bother."

At that moment, the door handle rattled impatiently. Somebody was trying to get in. Jon realized there was little time left. "That's my offer. Tell your clients they can take it or leave it." He shoved the piece of paper into Johnston's pocket. "This is my new cell number. They have twenty-four hours. And remember, if anyone so much as even breathes on me, or anyone else, for that matter, I'll drag us all down, without a second thought. In fact, I would even enjoy it."

Without a further word, Jon unlocked the door and brushed past the man trying to enter, disappearing quickly in the clatter of diners. Johnston took a deep breath and rubbed the back of his head, ignoring the curious stare of the newcomer.

Upper East Side, Manhattan

"I thought you said you didn't like to dress like a girl," teased Jon, on his return to his apartment from Smith & Wollensky's.

"Very funny." David stood in the kitchen over an assortment of bubbling pots and steaming pans. He wore a brand-new apron someone had given Jon, looking very much the accomplished chef he was. He wagged a wooden spoon at his brother. "Like I said, over my dead body. This is a bold move Jon; I've been concerned about you. How did it go?"

"I think he got the message," Jon replied, tossing down his keys. "I guess we'll know soon enough." He walked over to examine the various concoctions simmering on the stove, keen to change the subject. "What are you making?"

"A home-cooked meal, since I can see this kitchen doesn't get much use. These pans still had their labels on."

"What can I say?" Jon shrugged. "This is New York. Everybody eats out all the time and Danielle's hardly a homebody."

"You don't miss it, then?" David asked.

"Home? Sure I do. Mum, Dad, the farm. You can't beat it," Jon said. Until recently, in fact, the idea of living outside New York City had not so much as crossed his mind for years. But suddenly, all options were open, and he had a momentary pang of real homesickness.

"Then why don't you come back with me? You'll be back for the wedding anyway." David was serious.

"Maybe," said Jon. "Maybe not. I just don't know."

"Aren't you tired of working all the time? I know I am. It's been coming for over a year now. I want to settle down, grow roots." David sighed a heavy sigh. "I'm sick of being constantly on the move and Lucy won't wait around forever."

"I can see how all that would be true for you. But I like it here, plus I've got a home." Jon wasn't at all sure he still believed what he was saying. Right now, he felt his words were coming more from habit than conviction.

"This place? Look around you, mate. This isn't a home. It's a cage on a stinking, rat-infested, over-populated island where everyone's scrambling over one another to get a bigger bite of the garbage." David had never been a fan of cities and New York was no exception. "Come with me, Jon. It'll be like the old days. We can run the farm together. You know it's what Dad has always wanted."

"I don't know, my life is so completely different now," said Jon.

David was quick to interrupt. "*Was*, mate. Not any more. It's time for a change."

"I'll think about it," Jon conceded.

"You already have." His brother responded confidently. "It's written all over your face. Look me in the eye and tell me you haven't thought about it."

There was a long pause while the brothers surveyed one

another. David knew he was right. And Jon could see no sense in arguing. If he hadn't contemplated returning to Australia, it was becoming clear that he was going to be leaving New York.

"The fast times are over, Jon. It's time to start living the good life," David said finally. "Now come on, let's eat."

Gramercy Park, Manhattan

The following day passed slowly and without event. Jon did not expect to hear from Johnston until the twenty-four hours were nearly up. He'd instructed his attorney, Andrew Harris, a partner in a small Long Island practice, to inform him immediately should any inquiry be made into the nature of the documents he was holding.

Jon had formed a Bahamian Trust when he'd started his first job in London, taking advantage of the same tax breaks that had brought the Saudi princes and other wealthy foreigners to London in the seventies and continued to attract them. Over the years, he'd squirreled away a tidy sum, despite the relish with which he used his off-shore credit card whenever he was either outside the U.K. in the early days or outside the U.S. over the past ten years. This credit card was a secret, undeclared to the IRS, so he'd intentionally hired a low-profile lawyer, not wishing to draw any inadvertent attention to this arrangement. He was willing to put up with the inconvenience of the location and the limited resources of the office in exchange for what he considered protection for his tax-dodge setup. It had worked out well so far.

Predictably, at midday Andrew called to let him know that persons unknown had dispatched a courier to collect a Xeroxed copy of the note from Robert Baldwin. The fish were biting, thought Jon. He smiled to himself as he imagined the mayhem that must be going on among his enemies. They would see there was no other way out if they wanted their money back. Within a few short hours, he hoped, they would be forced to pay up. It wasn't the perfect solution, but it was a solution he could live with. The money would give him freedom and providing for Rita and the kids would ease his guilt. It crossed his mind that maybe he should have asked for more. He shelved the idea; there had to be honor among thieves. Maybe he would charge a late fee if they failed to pay up within the allotted time frame.

Jon had never seen himself as an extortionist, but he had been thrown into a game where the participants played by a totally different set of rules. Then, too, New York was a city fueled by greed and opportunity, and he was no stranger to either. He was merely holding onto his last chance to make a big score. He felt he deserved it. The bank had discarded him, and Johnston had thrown him to the wolves. This new money, along with the sale of his apartment and his savings, would amount to a solid nest egg. It would give him options he no longer had.

Jon's mind was filled with these thoughts as he sat at a sushi bar near Gramercy Park. Danielle had arrived wearing a sixties-style Gucci mink stole, set off by big gold hoop earrings. She failed to even acknowledge that she was twenty minutes late, much less apologize. Today, Jon hadn't minded waiting. He found himself rather bemused by this new life where time didn't much matter, and nothing pressing waited to be done. He observed details he'd have been too busy or too preoccupied to have noticed — the light bouncing off the fish scales on the ice under the sushi counter, the individual styles of the sushi chefs, the body language of a couple dining together wordlessly.

Besides, tonight was a special occasion, although Danielle did not yet know it. The meal passed quickly with Danielle making her usual show of over-ordering, then under-eating, while delivering a monologue about matters of little or no interest to Jon. It was only once the waiter had brought the check, along with a small pot of green tea, that she fell silent, gazing at him with the hint of a pout clouding her expression.

"Daddy says I shouldn't see you anymore," she suddenly announced, her eyes widening as if she was imparting a daring piece of gossip.

"I think your father is right," Jon said, matter-of-factly.

"What?" She was unprepared for Jon's response. "Don't take me so seriously, Jon. I've never done what Daddy wanted me to do."

"Well, now may be the time to start. Come on. We both know it's over. You and I were in it for a good time, not a long time. So what's the point?"

"The point is, Jon . . ." and she paused, making an effort to express herself as clearly as possible. "You and I are very similar animals, we're mainly interested in ourselves and we admit it. Plus, sweetie, I like having my very own soldier of fortune. It turns me on."

Jon was not swayed. "I'm not that at all. You've never tried to understand what I'm really like. Anyway, Danielle, there's just no point in going over the reasons why this won't work out; it'll just be painful to us both. The bottom line is that when you take the "L" out of Lover, it spells 'over'. And it's definitely over between you and me. Too much has changed." His delivery was very straightforward.

Danielle's demeanor was less certain now. She was caught between disbelief and fear that this time he meant it. "So, is that it? The master has spoken. What about me? Where does this leave me?"

Jon remained stalwart. "You will be fine. This chapter in my life is simply closing. Our relationship, my career, this city, it's all over."

Danielle sought refuge in denial. "You can't leave me, it doesn't work like that. You'll change your mind." She stood up, struggling to put things back on a normal footing. "I've gotta rush, we can talk about this tomorrow. See you later, lover."

"As I said, take the 'L' out of Lover . . ."

"Don't be silly, you know that you'll be begging me to come back, once this all blows over," she said, with a tentative smile.

Jon sat where he was, keeping his tone deliberate. "Don't wait by your phone, honey. As they say, if the phone doesn't ring, it's probably me."

Danielle leaned down as if to kiss him on the cheek and whispered. "You'll ring because I'm one of the few things you've still got going for you."

Jon smiled graciously. "Don't flatter yourself. This is good-bye."

"Nonsense," she said, as she walked toward the door.

She was gone in a designer flash. Jon was left thinking about her youthful dismissal of his words. It had been her beauty and the vast confidence she projected that had drawn him to her in the first place; it was that same youth and confidence that now kept them apart. They were similar animals, she was right about that, but on different tracks. It really was over.

Jon felt the familiar vibration of his cell phone. The number on his caller I.D. was withheld. He answered. The accent was American, but it was not Johnston, as he'd expected.

"Your demands are unreasonable, Mr. Phillips. You are playing a very dangerous game." It took Jon only a few short moments to recognize the speaker as one of the men who so expertly beat him only a few days earlier.

Jon felt his heartbeat quicken, but kept his voice level. "If you're calling to intimidate me into some sort of compromise, I have to warn you that I am simply not flexible. Robert is dead and my professional reputation has been destroyed. I view my demand as pure compensation."

"I can see your logic." The man responded with chilling calmness. "But you really aren't in any position to be making demands of anyone."

"You must understand the situation. I have written evidence. This is check, game's over."

"Checkmate, I think you'll find. But not to you. You have played your hand and been outbid, Mr. Phillips. You gave us no choice."

"What do you mean by that?" Jon found it difficult to mask his concern.

"Why don't you ask your attorney? I'll see you real soon, Mr. Phillips." The man signed off with a faint laugh.

The line went dead. Jon was unnerved by both the tone and the content of the discussion. This was certainly not the result he'd been expecting. He wondered if the man was bluffing. "See you real soon" had clearly been delivered as a threat. Hastily, Jon dialed his attorney's office telephone number. The line on the other end rang and rang, unanswered. He checked the number and redialed, as he stepped out into the street. Still no response. He called Harris's cell phone. This time, he received a reply.

"Andrew, its Jon Phillips. What's going on?"

"Jon, I'm really sorry, it all happened so fast. There's been a fire."

"Where?" Jon already knew the answer.

"The office, the whole building, was burned out. I just got here a little while ago. Thank God, no one was hurt."

"And the documents? Are they safe?" Jon asked.

"Gone, I'm afraid." There was little else Andrew could say. He had failed in his role as Jon's custodian of the evidence and apologizing would change nothing. "I was having copies made and hadn't yet stored them in a safe place and by the time I got here, the building was in flames. The police think it was probably some sort of electrical problem, they said not so unusual in these old buildings."

Jon's stomach had begun to knot. "Are you sure nothing survived?" he pleaded.

"Well, I suppose anything's possible, but the fire was very intense. It's a million to one that there's anything left at all. The police have the building sealed off and we're unlikely to get access for days. I'm going to be working from home."

"Well, you're okay and that's the main thing. I better run."

"Thanks, Jon, for being so understanding. Put a file back together and send it to my home. I'd better go, too. Goodbye." And with that the line went dead.

Jon was dazed; "put a file back together" indeed. Jon had not wanted to keep the originals in his apartment. What next? Maybe David would have an idea. He hailed a cab on Park Avenue and headed uptown toward his apartment. Traffic was heavy and it wasn't until they hit 42nd Street and the Grand Central overpass that he realized, finally, how scared he was. He was now the likely target. They knew where he lived. Time was now against him. And David was alone in the apartment. He had to get home, fast.

Jon had never found New York's midtown traffic logjam more agonizing. It seemed as if the entire state had driven into the city. He buried his fingernails into his legs and wiped the sweat from his palms regularly, as they inched their way north. After what seemed like an eternity, the cab drew up outside his building and Jon leapt out without waiting for his change. Not wishing to alert the doorman to anything untoward, he managed to curb his pace as he entered the building and affect a casual manner. The doorman nodded politely.

"Evening, Mr. Phillips."

"Evening, Gerry. Is my brother upstairs?"

"I think so, sir. I haven't seen him leave." This was not in itself a comfort. But what Gerry said next had Jon's heart practically thumping out of his chest. "Besides, he had takeout delivered."

"Really?" Jon could barely disguise the tremor in his voice. As someone who took pride in his own cooking, David objected to ordering in simply on principle. "When was that?"

"Oh, about half an hour ago."

Jon's mouth was dry as the elevator swished up to the sixtieth floor. He had never felt such dread.

Chapter Thirteen

Upper East Side, Manhattan

Everything seemed normal. Jon gingerly inserted his key into the lock and turned it slowly. At first he stayed outside, in the hallway, hanging back and pushing the door ajar to catch a warning glimpse should anything be out of the ordinary. There was nothing. The television was on rather loudly, its sounds echoing past him and down the corridor. Jon edged farther inside; there was nothing to suggest any mischief had taken place. The den appeared as neat and well ordered as always.

"David!" he called out. The only noise was that of the television, which continued to blare. Jon slowly made his way down the hall toward the living room.

"David!" he said again, louder this time. Still no answer. By now, Jon's heart was beating so hard he could feel it in his throat and he was finding it difficult to get words out. "David, are you there?" Rounding the corner, he could see the living room in its entirety for the first time.

Incongruously, the television was tuned to a fitness program, an infomercial featuring a group of hard-bodied Californians performing aerobics in fetchingly inadequate Lycra outfits on some anonymous beach. But Jon's attention was elsewhere.

There was a woman sitting on the sofa. She did not turn around as Jon entered the room, but continued to stare at the television. Only the back of her head was visible to Jon. His eyes quickly scanned the rest of the living room to see if anyone might be hiding there. The doors to both bedrooms were open, but nothing seemed out of place. His attention returned to the woman, her long dark hair falling in a tangle over the back of the sofa.

"Hello?" Jon croaked, his throat now completely closed. He swallowed and tried again. "Hello. Can I help you?" Still, the woman did not turn around or acknowledge his presence in any way. Jon moved closer to her. "Hello!" he said louder. She remained where she sat, the infomercial blaring aggressively. As he drew closer, Jon saw she wore a scarf of some kind. It was made of a material he did not recognize, black nylon possibly. It trailed out from under her hair and spilled several inches over the back of the sofa. Moving closer, Jon could see over her shoulder her thick, stocking-clad legs spread wide apart and planted on the floor. Beyond her, on the coffee table, he spotted the TV remote. As he moved around to pick it up and confront his mystery guest at the same time, the sight that greeting him caused Jon to streak out of the apartment in absolute horror.

He reached the elevator and sank down against the wall. He could feel an unwelcome heave rising but forced himself not to throw up. He closed his eyes, trying to blank out the image, but it was emblazoned in his head, no doubt forever. He remained crouched against the wall while desperately trying to compose himself.

The person on the sofa was not a woman at all. It was David. For a split second, Jon had not recognized his brother. His features were smeared with makeup and contorted in death. The blue of his lips blended with the red of the lipstick he wore, giving them an almost maroon hue. His eyes were rolled back, staring blankly. The scarf was not a scarf, but a tourniquet, a woman's black nylon stocking tied so tightly around David's neck that the blood vessels had burst, creating a macabre scarlet necklace. His brother had been strangled, dressed up in clothes from Jon's Karen Carpenter cos-

tume, complete with one of his Karen wigs, and placed there like
some kind of perverted *memento mori*. Jon could suppress his horror
no longer. He retched onto the corridor carpet, unable to shake
from his mind the vision of the hideously contorted face he loved so
much.

It took him some time to fight the urge to run, to simply get in
the elevator and leave the building in the irrational hope that what
had happened might simply undo itself. Jon knew in his logical
mind that this was not an option, but he couldn't bring himself to
re-renter the apartment. Eventually he opened his cell phone and
called the police.

He was still crouching in the hallway when they arrived a short
time later. They acknowledged his presence, prompting him to
point out his apartment door to them. Initially, they were far more
interested in David than in him, so he remained where he was, trying to rein in his emotions enough to think coherently. More police
officers arrived, bringing in their wake forensics experts, photogra-
phers, crime scene experts, and toxicologists. Within a short time,
the ordinarily hushed penthouse floor had been transformed from a
haven for the privileged few into a swarming feeding ground for the
law enforcement community. Those who ventured out were told
politely but firmly by the police that they would be interviewed in
due course; those who did not squinted at the show through their
peepholes. And in the middle of this maelstrom sat Jon.

There was no doubt in his mind that he had been the target.
David's death was a case of mistaken identity, and when the killers
discovered their mistake, Jon would still be targeted. As he watched
the professionals at work around him, men and women yelling conflicting instructions to one another, the persistent squawk of their
radios intermittent in the background, Jon began to feel on familiar
ground. He had experienced this before. This was the trading floor.
Sure, these were cops, not Wall Street brokers, and the circumstances were radically different. But the underlying zeitgeist was the
same. He knew how to function in this kind of environment. With
only an hour or two to decide what to present to the police, a deci-

sion that could affect the rest of his life, he felt confident he could pull off whatever he chose to do, given the set of variables he had been dealt. By the time the detective in charge of the investigation approached him, Jon was able to maintain a calm and centered façade, although inside he was shaking.

"Mr. Phillips?" the detective asked, gently. "We'd like a statement."

Jon looked up at the tough, lined face. "Yes," he replied, rising shakily from the floor. He now knew what had to be done, unpleasant as it might be. Often enough, he'd done what he had to do on the trading floor, regardless of the consequences in human terms, and it had paid off. This was no different.

Autoerotic asphyxiation. That was the most likely cause of death, according to the police. David had dressed in women's clothes, tied the stocking around his neck and strangled himself in order to achieve the ultimate orgasm but had either pushed it too far or had blacked out before he could loosen the noose he'd improvised. Jon nodded, in seeming acceptance of this bizarre theory. He described in precise detail his gruesome discovery upon returning from his early dinner with his now ex-girlfriend. They took Danielle's contact information, but said they might not even need to speak to her. Regardless, Jon knew they'd have no difficulty in corroborating his story, if need be. Events had occurred just as he had outlined them. He had not lied, just omitted mentioning some very relevant information.

It hadn't taken the police long to figure out he was the cross-dressing rogue trader currently being demonized in the tabloids, following the *News/Copy* exposé. The only connection they made between him and his brother was one that conveniently served their theory. If one brother was a depraved cross-dresser, why not the other? Still, police protocol dictated they follow certain procedures. David's body was to be held for autopsy and toxicology tests. The results of those might not be ready for weeks. Until then, his body would be held at the 17th precinct morgue.

"The only way you could get me to dress up like a woman is

over my dead body." The irony of David's casually jocular words haunted Jon. He could not yet begin to deal with the responsibility he bore for causing David's death, however inadvertently, so he dwelt instead on the shame he felt in allowing his brother to be perceived in the eyes of the world as dying a pervert's death. In no way did his brother deserve this.

His adversaries would no doubt be looking for him, and if he stuck around, he too would soon enough meet with some form of untimely accident. His time in New York was very rapidly coming to an end. The police seemed unconcerned when he told them he planned to get out of the city for a while, that he needed a change of scene. They arranged to be in touch with him by telephone and to contact him when his brother's body was cleared for its return to Australia.

Jon reckoned that his enemies would not attempt anything with the police around. Once David had been removed from the scene, but before the place had been entirely vacated, Jon was allowed to re-enter the apartment and pack some suitcases and a large duffel bag with as many belongings as he thought he might need to take with him during his getaway. When he was led toward the elevator and down to a waiting squad car, Jon had no idea when he would next return, if at all.

Night had fallen over the city by the time he eventually emerged from the Police Department building on 51st Street. He'd spoken to a succession of officers, to make, check and recheck statements, fill out forms, and wait for all the red tape to be unwound. Finally, he stepped out into the street, tired but alert. He didn't know when his hunters might choose to strike, so he had to assume that even now he was being stalked.

He took a cab to Times Square, the busiest intersection he could think of. There he went underground into the subway but instead of taking a train, he re-surfaced on the other side of the street, then re-submerged through another entrance. His journey wound up at a fleabag hotel on 2nd Street and Avenue A on the Lower East Side. He paid for a room in cash, and lugged his duffel bag up three flights, since the elevator wasn't working and probably never had. The room was filthy, carrying a heavy aroma of sweat, grime, and depravity, masked ineffectively by a thin layer of Lysol.

His thoughts turned to the impossible task of contacting his parents with the horrific news. And Lucy, what about Lucy, planning their wedding, only weeks away? He sat on the edge of his bed, engulfed in sorrow and regret as the truth hit home. His head dropped into his hands and he began to sob uncontrollably. He had never felt so alone. Time passed, and finally he composed himself. There was much to do. He hoisted the duffel on the stained and cigarette-burned bedspread and opened it up.

Alphabet City, Manhattan

The large yellow 1970 Cadillac Eldorado convertible was one of Georgie McWilliams's three great loves. The car was an integral part of his lifestyle and it played an important role in his growing, if checkered, business career. More than a mere companion, it assisted him in the pursuit of his two other great loves, money and drugs. This was because hidden beneath it, safely welded to its chassis away from the prying eyes of law enforcement agencies, was a secret compartment. This was the means by which Georgie was able to transport his stash of narcotics around the city without fear of detection.

Although a pimp, pusher, and general lowlife, Georgie was, in some ways, unexpectedly law-abiding. If, for example, he had been drinking or taking drugs, he would use one of his boys to do the driving, handing over the keys to his prized possession quite cavalierly. His boys were generally kids from the local streets whom he'd lured into service with promises of free narcotics, access to plentiful girls, and easy cash.

Georgie had had the car meticulously restored to his exact specifications. It was a masterpiece of engineering, right down to the hydraulic suspension that not only earned him the respect of local gang leaders but also allowed him to lift the chassis a full twelve inches off the ground. This gave him access to the secret compartment without even having to risk getting grease on his threads.

The car sat behind the Easy Bar in Alphabet City, its presence there usually a sure sign Georgie was around. Generally, he didn't like to be more than a few yards from the vehicle. Tonight was no exception.

Nobody paid much attention to the Amazonian figure walking carefully on high heels toward the entrance of the downtown bar. Transvestites had become commonplace in the area since the gentrification of the Meatpacking District had pushed them east. So there was nothing remarkable about seeing a six-foot-two man outfitted in a long brown wig, full makeup and a mauve evening gown. A man wearing a pageboy wig, brown slacks and a dated polo neck sweater greeted the man in drag at the door. At first glance, they looked an unlikely couple.

It was Jon's friend Timmy who met him at the entrance to Georgie McWilliams's Easy Bar. A small chalkboard sign sitting on the pavement announced "Tonight! Amateur Drag Talent Night!" The bar was busy, the crowd's attention focused on a small makeshift wooden stage set into a dark corner of the room. A female Charles Aznavour look-alike was belting out the final strains of the singer's famous hit, "She," accompanied by a bored-looking musician playing an upright piano. The crowd was more amused by Charles than appreciative.

The bar manager and part-time Master of Ceremonies stepped up onto the stage. "And thank you, Charles Aznavour." The crowd applauded politely. He continued. "And now, ladies and gentlemen, it is my great pleasure to introduce the fabulous Carpenters."

As Jon and Timmy walked onto the stage, the crowd began to snicker at the sight of such a towering Karen Carpenter. Timmy quietly took his position as Richard Carpenter at the piano. Jon grabbed the microphone and the stage lights dimmed. Timmy played an introduction and Jon began to sing. "Why do birds suddenly appear, every time you are near . . ?" He was remarkably convincing and the crowd was soon drawn in. Jon's double-handed grip on the microphone, the way in which he leaned forward toward the crowd, his seeming immersion in the lyrics, combined to help put the song across. In fact, Jon actually had immersed himself in his performance, knowing that if he didn't, he'd be in real danger of falling apart on stage. "Close to You" came to an end, and the crowd gave them an enthusiastic response. They took a bow and left the stage.

The Master of Ceremonies stepped back into the spotlight. "Now those two will be a hard act to beat, but our show must go on." An unconvincing but enthusiastic Cyndi Lauper look-alike jumped up on stage and launched predictably into "Girls Just Want to Have Fun."

Jon and Timmy headed for the bar. The revelers voiced their approval as the pair walked by. Jon waved his thanks, but quickly sobered. "I really appreciate your coming, Tim. I know it was very short notice."

"Well, I figure it was the least I could do, what with the papers giving you such a hard time and all. But why were you all of a sudden so keen on us performing tonight in this dinky little contest?"

Jon didn't answer. He hadn't told Timmy about his brother. Not only did he not trust himself to talk about it, but he knew that to discuss it with anyone could compromise not only his position, but theirs as well.

Timmy waited a moment, but didn't push it. "Well, I'm going to head back uptown. Let me know if we win, okay, pal?" And with that, Timmy was gone, lost in the crowd.

Jon, now standing alone at the bar, turned toward the barman, who eyed him appreciatively. "Nice outfit. Haven't I seen you here before?"

Jon's face became expressionless. "I don't think so. Where is your boss, George?"

"In his office, same as always." The barman nodded toward the rear of the bar. He moved away, turning his back on Jon, who began moving gradually toward the closed door indicated.

Behind the door, Georgie was sitting at his desk, two young men standing at attention in front of him. Both shifted nervously as they absorbed a barrage of abuse. "I don't give a flying fuck what she said. I have an important client who wants a seventeen-or-under, and that's what I'm going to deliver to him."

Georgie picked up his car keys and threw them aggressively toward one of the two young men. "Now take my fucking car and bring her here. I don't care if you've got to physically drag her. Just make sure she looks good. No fucking tears. This guy is paying a big premium for an under-ager." Heads bowed, the two young men silently nodded. "Now fuck off," he dismissed them.

It was from this small office that Georgie ran his growing empire. He operated in a cash economy; the margins were high and the taxes negligible. His most recent enterprise, the supplying of girls, was turning out to be very lucrative. Los Angeles might have the film business, but when it came to modeling, New York was Mecca. The city was full of pretty young girls in search of success at any cost, so supplying them to eager clients was a perfect add-on. Georgie had set up a modeling agency as a front and business was booming. Cocaine was his principal tool of trade, for payoffs and as currency. Most of his girls were quick to develop a taste for it, and he knew, given his almost unlimited supply of the drug, he could keep them moving through both his bar and his agency. For the girls who could tolerate the work, the money was good, the hours undemanding, and it provided an opportunity for them to supplement their legitimate, but often-modest, modeling income. Those who couldn't tolerate it, or got hooked, were soon shown the door by Georgie.

Often, if Georgie was busy inside, one of his lieutenants would stand guard outside the office to prevent any unwanted interruptions. Tonight, after the two young men hurried out, there was nobody. Jon arrived at the office door as "Cyndi" finished her song to restrained applause, and slipped in unobtrusively, closing the door behind him.

"You don't know how to knock, sweetheart?" The office was dank and smelled of late nights and liquor.

"Only gentlemen knock," said Jon, approaching Georgie at his desk and pulling up a chair.

"Well, one of *them* you sure ain't," Georgie sneered.

Jon regarded him for a few moments. "You don't recognize me, do you?" he said finally.

"Well, I know I haven't fucked you, if that's what you're implying," Georgie laughed.

"Oh, but you have," replied Jon, without missing a beat. "Just not in the way that you're talking about."

Something about Jon's demeanor caught Georgie's attention. He stopped laughing and reached behind him for a bottle of whisky, without taking his eyes off Jon. "What the fuck are you talking about?"

"I'll give you a hint. *News/Copy*," replied Jon.

Georgie paused at that, but remained unfazed. "I didn't recognize you. You look better in a suit. What do you want?"

"Some information."

Georgie poured two drinks and slid one toward Jon. "Listen, guy, I don't know what you think you're doing here but if I were you, I'd get the fuck back uptown before you get me in trouble, *capiche?*"

"Oh, I *capiche*, all right," said Jon, lifting the shot. "Just tell me who put you up to it. Was it a man called Johnston?"

"Who?" asked Georgie, looking confused. Clearly not Johnston, thought Jon.

"A guy like you wouldn't risk a television appearance for small chips. How much did they pay you? What about if I double it if you tell me?" Jon smiled and threw back his shot. "How about it, Georgie?"

Georgie drank his whisky in one gulp. "No dice, freak. Now get the fuck out of my office."

"Triple, then," Jon continued. "Just give me the name."

"You have no idea who you're dealing with," Georgie sneered, shaking his head.

"How much, Georgie?" insisted Jon. "Name your price."

"You really have no idea, do you? You think this was only about money."

"Isn't everything?" Jon asked. But no sooner had the words left his mouth than he realized, "it isn't just about money, is it? This is about drugs."

"I'm just a hired gun."

Jon was quick to move the conversation forward. "So we are talking about money *and* drugs."

"Congratulations, asshole." Georgie stood up, threateningly. "You're a marked man. No one will go near you, especially not me. Now get out of here and never come back. If I ever see you again, you'll end up in a concrete block at the bottom of the Hudson. Just fuck off!"

"Not yet," said Jon defiantly. "I need a name first." And he too stood, pulling himself up to his full height and moving purposefully toward Georgie.

Alphabet City, Manhattan

As the rear door to the office was smashed open, the relative peace of the alley behind the bar was suddenly shattered, and Georgie tumbled outside. Under most circumstances, the fight between these two would have been no contest. A tough, mean street fighter versus a Wall Street Upper East Sider. A product of the prison system against a Cambridge graduate, albeit an Australian one. However, Jon had not allowed the years of high living to obliterate his roughneck roots in the Australian bush. Motivated by blind rage and pumped full of adrenalin, Jon was a formidable opponent for anyone.

Georgie fell backwards down some steps and onto the trunk of his Cadillac. Jon followed and grabbed him by the throat, punching him in the face. "Give me the name," he shouted. Georgie reacted with a random flurry of kicking and biting. Jon momentarily lost his grip. Georgie seized the opportunity and wriggled free, ducking under Jon's flailing arms to scramble beneath the car. Jon knelt down and reached for him. "Come out of there, you piece of shit," he growled.

"Fuck off, you freak," was Georgie's only response, as he cowered under the car. Jon crouched down to grab him and Georgie scuttled across to the car's far side. Expecting Jon to stand and run around, he waited for an opportunity to make a break for it. Instead, Jon dived under the car and got him by his hair, intending to drag the scumbag out, but as he started to do so, he heard muffled voices. Someone was coming. To avoid detection, Jon rolled back all the way under the car alongside his quarry.

Georgie's two young lieutenants were heading toward the Cadillac. Jon had Georgie pinned to the ground, covering his mouth to silence him, but Georgie wriggled away and sank his teeth into Jon's hand. "What'd you say?" asked Pablo, one of the young men, hearing Jon's muffled cry.

"Nothing," replied the other, Felix. "You must be really fucked up."

"The only one fucked up around here is that fucking McWilliam," snarled Pablo. "I fucking hate him. We shouldn't let him talk to us like that. I'd like to whack the fucker."

Jon pulled off his wig and stuffed it into Georgie's mouth to keep him quiet. Jon expected the two men to walk past the car, but to his surprise, the chassis of the car lowered as they got inside. Jon's surprise turned to panic as the engine started. When the young driver shifted the vehicle into Drive, Jon grabbed Georgie by the wrist. As he flailed and kicked to free himself from Jon's grasp, Georgie somehow managed to get his gold Rolex hooked over the handle of the stash box welded to the chassis.

"Last chance. I want a name," Jon hissed.

Whatever Georgie's reply, if any, Jon didn't hear it. The sub woofer pumped a heavy bass line, causing the whole vehicle to vibrate. As the car began to move, Jon wrenched the wig from Georgie's mouth and watched as he was dragged away screaming into the night, hidden but still firmly attached to the underside of the car by his watch and tangled clothing.

Jon remained where he lay, sprawled on the edge of the road clutching the blood-and-saliva-soaked hairpiece. Jon's evening gown was now in shreds and the heel of one of his stilettos broken. He got up and stood silently, watching the car disappear into the dark of the night, with Georgie pinned to its underside. Jon put the soiled wig back on his head and began to straighten himself up, looking around to see if anyone had noticed the scuffle. They had not. He was alone.

CHAPTER FOURTEEN

Upper East Side, Manhattan

The realtor was an overdone woman in her early fifties. Outfitted in a clashing mélange of designer clothes and accessories intended for teen-age models, she wandered around Jon's apartment waiting for her call to connect, randomly examining items that caught her speculative eye. Except for the large pieces of furniture he was leaving behind, Jon's belongings had been packed by a moving company he'd hired into dozens of large cardboard boxes marked with an address of a storage facility in Queens. Two oversized suitcases sat next to the front door, both addressed to London.

When Jon's cell phone rang, he was heading up Third Avenue on his way to an electronics store. The woman at the other end of the phone spoke with a strong Long Island accent. "I'm at your gorgeous apartment as we speak, Mr. Phillips. Everything seems to be in order here so we're all set to go ahead. I just wanted to know, are there any other numbers we should have in case we need to contact you?"

"No, I'll be in touch with you. I'm sure you'll be able to sell the place without any trouble. But it's essential that the proceeds are handled exactly according to my instructions, even if you can't reach me."

The realtor stopped beside a stack of boxes and surveyed the sweeping view beyond. "Yes, $500,000 to Mrs. Rita Baldwin, the balance minus our fees to your account in the Cayman Islands. We have all the details on file at the office."

"Good," said Jon.

"And will Mrs. Phillips be traveling with you?"

Jon smiled at the obvious ploy. "There is no Mrs. Phillips."

"In that case, I have a knockout of a daughter," the agent promptly responded. "Why don't I give her your telephone number so she can call you when you get back?"

"It's a nice thought, but I'm not coming back for quite a while."

"Can't blame me for trying," she laughed good-naturedly, as they hung up.

Downtown, Manhattan

Jon pushed through the doors of the large electronics store he was now standing in front of and found his way to its software section. He approached one of the salesmen. "Can you help me?" he asked. "I recently deleted some files on my hard disk by mistake and I was wondering if there's any way to retrieve the deleted information."

The salesman nodded and gestured for Jon to follow him through the rows of various software packages. "Hard disks are like elephants, they never forget," he said sagely.

Jon gave him a questioning look.

"What I mean is that it is much more difficult to delete information from a hard disk than people generally think. All you need is a basic "Restore" program and you should be able to retrieve most, if not all, of the lost information." Stopping, the salesman bent down and selected a software package from the shelf. "This is what you need," he said confidently.

Jon was relieved. "It's that simple, then?"

"Just insert the disk into the hard drive and follow the basic instructions. If you know the lost file's name, this software should definitely be able to retrieve it."

"What about emails?" Jon asked.

The man nodded affirmatively. "You'll be amazed what old stuff you'll turn up."

After purchasing the software, Jon went back to the seedy little hotel room that had become his home for the past few days and pored over the instruction manual. Later, he checked his watch, calculated the time in England, then dialed a telephone number.

Gloucestershire, England

A crest, depicting in elaborate detail a knight slaying a dragon, was carved into the hardwood headboard of the massive antique bed on which two figures were actively engaged. Lady Victoria Cheyne, the only daughter of the seventeenth Earl of Colarvon, fixated on it as tears of pain and humiliation welled in her eyes. She scrunched handfuls of silky Frette sheets as she braced herself against the rhythmic pounding against her body. The creaking of the bed's worn springs was punctuated by a succession of heavy grunts.

Boris Posarnov heaved behind Victoria. Yet another bead of sweat meandered down between the wiry gray hairs on his ample breasts and splashed onto the small of her back. His grunts came closer together as he approached his climax. Victoria whimpered quietly into the mattress as his vigor increased. Not long now, she thought, and squeezed her eyes tightly shut.

The bedroom they were in was one of too many to keep track of at Stanford Hall, which had been owned by Victoria's family for generations. Beyond the windows of the magnificent bedchamber, its lushly planted but somewhat overgrown grounds extended for miles. Period furniture was scattered throughout the room that had been Victoria's since childhood.

Boris performed a flurry of final thrusts and groans before letting out a final, long, satisfied sigh as he reached release. He remained crouched behind her for a few seconds, his weighty body expanding and contracting in recovery, before he started to laugh, a deep, triumphant chuckle. He slapped her pale bottom jovially and retreated from between the backs of her legs. She remained where she was, on all fours, until he had risen to his feet and departed for the bathroom. Knowing he would be there for a while, doing whatever it was that he did after sex, she collapsed on the bed, wiping her tears away on the end of a delicately embroidered pillow case.

Just then, the phone rang. Victoria drew a calming breath and answered it. "Hello," she said, weakly.

"Victoria? It's Jon Phillips."

Her expression changed in an instant to one of surprise mixed with delight. "I don't believe it's really you!" she breathed. Untangling the phone cord, she curled up under the covers.

"Have I caught you at a bad time?" Jon asked.

"Not at all! In fact, you can't imagine how happy I am to hear from you at this very moment." She paused to collect herself. "But why are you calling after such a long time?"

"Oh, no reason really. Just checking in."

"After eight years, Jon? Eight long years? I don't think so."

"Good point. Actually, I was thinking of paying you a visit."

"What? You're coming to London?" Victoria exclaimed. "When?"

"Soon. But I thought I might come down to Stanford Hall, if that's okay with you."

"It's marvelous. But when?"

"I don't know exactly. I hear the place is full of bloody foreigners these days. That true?" He asked jokingly.

"Jon," smiled Victoria, "don't forget, *you* are a bloody foreigner."

"Another good point. Well, what if I come the opening weekend of the pheasant season? You'll no doubt have an interesting crowd then and I'm sure brother Andy will be at his brilliant worst. It will be so marvelous to see you all." Surprised at the warmth of his former girlfriend's reception, Jon was finding it difficult to steer the conversation to the real reason he was calling.

"It's always crowded with regulars that weekend, but why not, if that suits you. It will be so good to see you again at any time, Jonny."

Jon decided to cut to the chase. "Who knows, there may even be a few captains of industry for me to hobnob with. I'm going to be looking for a job, maybe moving back to London."

"Really? You really mean it? I'd given up on your ever coming back." Victoria didn't try to conceal her excitement.

"We'll see," Jon said, uncomfortably. Then, "Isn't your father in league with some Ukrainian magnate?"

"If it's who I think you mean, Russian. No doubt he'll be here when you come. He virtually lives here these days." Victoria's tone had abruptly flattened.

"I'm told Eastern Europe is very big these days. When exactly does the season start?" asked Jon.

"The twelfth of August, the first day of the shooting season. That's the day all the bigwigs want to come down to shoot. It's a status thing."

"Fine." Jon smiled to himself. "I'll see you on the eleventh. If there's room," he added.

"There's always been room for you, Jonny. I'll look forward to it."

The phone went dead. Jon was gone. Victoria replaced the receiver. She sighed deeply, smiling to herself. Her reverie was spoiled by Posarnov's reappearance.

"You were fantastic, darling," he commented sarcastically. He sat down heavily and began stroking her shoulder with a moist, ruddy palm. She recoiled.

"Please, Boris, no."

Posarnov kept his hand where it was. "Now why would you say something like that?" He feigned hurt.

"Because I can't do this any more," Victoria blurted. "I'd rather die than do this again. Ever!" She glanced up at him, nervous at having revealed her genuine feelings for the first time.

Posarnov smiled menacingly. "Don't think that can't be arranged, my dear." He tipped her chin up with his forefinger so they were face-to-face. "But I know you don't mean it. You're just saying that."

Victoria gathered her courage. "No, I'm not. You disgust me!" She stared back into his narrowing eyes, knowing she would pay dearly for her honesty.

Whap! Posarnov slapped her across the face with the back of his hand. The intensity of the blow coupled with the impact of the several heavy rings he wore caused Victoria to nearly lose consciousness. She fell back against the pillows. Blood began to collect in her mouth, where the inside of her lip had been split by her teeth.

"Perhaps this will teach you some manners," Posarnov snarled within an inch of her face.

Victoria spat. A glob of bloody saliva sprayed Posarnov's cheek. His expression curled into a sneer. Victoria stared defiantly back at him.

Posarnov got up, sucked in his gut, bent over and picked up his belt from the floor. It was time for this disobedient filly to be broken.

Alphabet City, Manhattan

Jon methodically cleaned his small hotel room and packed his bag. He wanted to leave no trace of his presence. Clothing he wouldn't be needing, such as his Karen Carpenter outfit, he placed in a series of garbage bags. He wiped down every surface, then carted all his bags down to the small reception area and paid the modest bill with cash. After dropping the garbage bags into different dumpsters along the way, he took a cab to his final destination, the 42nd Street Seaport, and settled down to wait at the end of the pier, staring up at the cloudless blue sky.

Sitting there, he felt a momentary sense of peace, though soon shattered by the memory of his conversations with his parents and with Lucy about his brother's death. He had been the one to break the news that David had somehow managed to strangle himself — no one knew quite how — in a terrible accident. He would never forget their stunned disbelief when he told them. Lucy had immediately become hysterical, and remained inconsolable. Once his parents had finally absorbed the awful reality of David's death, their grief had frightened Jon at first in its intensity. But now when he spoke with them, they seemed to have retreated into a kind of forced stoicism, no doubt brought on by the drugs prescribed by their family doctor. Jon had been doing his best to repress all thoughts of David and of the misery that he, Jon, was responsible for causing, fearing he would become immobilized. He was grateful when the faint sound of an approaching aircraft engine distracted him.

The small, single-engine seaplane descended toward the calm waters of the Hudson River. It landed smoothly and slowly taxied toward Jon, perched at the end of the pier. The pilot greeted him with a warm smile. Like most families on cattle stations and farms in Australia, the Phillips family owned and routinely used a small plane to cover the long distances between properties and townships. Jon had flown the plane since he was a teenager, taught by his father. He had never flown a seaplane, though, and was not licensed to do so. But something about them fascinated him, and he had always wanted to own one.

Since he was the only passenger, he climbed into the cockpit and settled next to the pilot. The plane moved quickly out into the middle of the river to prepare for takeoff. The pilot applied full throttle, and as the giant mechanical bird skimmed across the water, south toward the Statue of Liberty, he tugged back on the stick. The plane's nose lifted, and in seconds, they were airborne. As the small aircraft gained altitude, Jon glanced over his shoulder toward the New York skyline. It was a view he had marveled at a thousand times before, but now it held a special significance. He felt a premonition that it might be quite a while before he would again drink in this spectacular sight. When they reached the southern tip of Manhattan and flew over the World Financial Center and the site where the Twin Towers once proudly stood, he turned his head away. There was no point in looking back. The plane banked sharply left, leaving the city behind and heading toward Long Island.

Fifty minutes later, the seaplane landed at the small, manicured East Hampton airport. Jon hopped down onto the tarmac and found a waiting taxi. Sag Harbor was a picturesque old whaling port situated on the northern edge of the southern fork of eastern Long Island. Investment bankers and well-known actors, artists, and writers had slowly replaced the whalers over the years, and while the locals might have resented their new, well-heeled neighbors, they were only too happy to cash in on them. And so Sag Harbor became an exclusive resort for those rich and famous vacationers put off by the social pretension of Southampton and the nouveau riche excesses of East Hampton, preferring instead the historical charm this seaside village had somehow managed to retain.

Jon climbed out of the taxi on Sag Harbor's main street. Selecting a busy but welcoming diner, he ordered lunch and struck up a conversation with his matronly waitress. By the time he paid for his meal, she had offered to store his duffel bag behind the counter while he checked out the several addresses she'd given him of houses in town with rooms to rent. Thanking her both verbally and with a lavish tip, he pocketed the list and headed to the nearby marina. There, he wove his way past an array of formidably expensive and meticulously maintained vessels of different sizes and shapes.

Few people were around, as it was midweek in early summer, before the high season got into gear. This was the time when owners had their boats readied for the approaching vacation months. The work was entrusted either to the local tradesmen who tended to the smaller boats in their owners' absence, or to the skeleton crews responsible for keeping the larger boats fully maintained during the winter months and ready for use in the summer. The larger boats especially required constant attention and care.

Jon was looking for a specific boat. It didn't take him long to find it. The *Southern Star* was a magnificent, 120-foot, wooden-hulled racing ketch built in the 1940s. A true classic. Jon stood on the quay looking up at the magnificent vessel, admiring its graceful lines and gleaming surfaces as he waited to attract the attention of one of the crew.

A young man of about nineteen came into view on the quarter-deck. Jon yelled to him, intentionally broadening his Australian accent. "Excuse me, mate, is the skipper around?"

The crewman acknowledged him but did not pause in his task of lugging a large coil of rope from one deck hatch to another. "Sorry, the captain isn't here at the moment. Can I give him a message, or can I help you with anything?"

"Yes, thanks," Jon smiled disarmingly. "I was wondering if there was any work around for an experienced, hardworking sailor."

"You'll need to speak to the captain. Why don't you come back after six this evening. He should be back by then."

"Thanks, I'll do that." Jon waved to the crewmember, by way of introduction. "Rick Mears, pleased to meet you."

"Fred Huffman," the crewman responded. "Come back at six. I'll let the captain know you're coming. See you then."

Alphabet City, Manhattan

After failing to convince the girl they'd been sent for to come back with them, Georgie McWilliam's two young lieutenants were relieved to find Georgie gone when they returned to the Easy Bar. They'd waited around until the bar closed, then returned the Cadillac to its usual spot in the basement garage of Georgie's apartment building. Now, two days later and with no sign of Georgie, they worried about the loss of their meal ticket and decided to drive his car around the neighborhood to see what they might turn up.

"He can't just have disappeared off the face of the earth," said Felix, as they entered the garage. "Maybe we should file a Missing Persons."

"No way, man, no way, we can't go to the cops. That's Georgie's golden rule, never involve the law," replied Pablo, the younger but wiser of the two. "He'd kill us. When Georgie shows up, he'd never forgive us, we'd be back on the streets."

"I guess you're right," Felix agreed.

As they clambered into the car, they were overwhelmed by an

odor so foul it caused them to grimace and hold their noses. They looked at each other with puzzled expressions.

"Oh, man, what is that God-awful stink?" exclaimed Felix. "For God's sake, open the window."

"Don't look at me, man. You must have stepped in something. Clean your damn shoe, man, that smell is gross."

Felix checked his shoes. "There's nothing there."

Pablo gave his own shoes a once-over. Nothing there, either. "Maybe it will go away if we get some air going through the car." He opened his window.

"Let's just get moving."

Pablo gunned the Caddy. As the car bucked forward, then moved up the ramp toward the exit. Had one known to look, Georgie's body could just be glimpsed under its frame, swaying with the motion of the car. Felix and Pablo drove out of the building and turned right, into the street. After they'd gone just a few blocks, a severed hand suddenly spun out in the wake of the car and into the gutter. An unwitting pedestrian, stepping down from the sidewalk, gasped as she realized that her stiletto heel had pierced the palm of the hand. She began screaming as she tried in vain to shake her shoe free of the appendage. Her increasingly desperate efforts were to no avail; the hand wouldn't budge. A small group of horrified onlookers gathered as the woman fell to the ground, unable to remain upright while hopping on only one leg, reminiscent of the old, Chaplinesque silent comedies. The skewered hand remained stubbornly attached as she tore off her shoe.

The Cadillac moved on, its occupants laughing and joking, oblivious to the chaotic scene they were leaving behind. As they turned a corner, a shoe tumbled out from beneath the car. It landed right side up on the edge of the road, part of Georgie's leg still attached. This too created an almost immediate commotion among the passing pedestrians. As the car continued through the streets toward its destination, Georgie was becoming dislodged, bit by bit. By the time Pablo and Felix arrived at the Easy Bar and parked directly in front, most of the rest of Georgie was clearly visible.

The two men got out and entered the club, re-emerging moments later after a passerby rushed in to report the grisly sight. One glance told Pablo and Felix that Georgie's fate was no longer a mystery.

Sag Harbor, New York

Just before six o'clock, Jon walked over to the marina and threaded his way along a series of walkways to the *Southern Star*. He called out to the several crew members who were still engaged in various tasks on the boat. "Excuse me. I'm looking for the captain."

Before anyone could answer, a weathered and bearded man in his fifties stuck his head up from the hatch to the galley. "You must be Rick."

"That's right," said Jon.

"Davies is the name. Please come aboard."

Jon removed his shoes and stepped up a stripped gangplank. "Hello. Thanks for seeing me."

They shook hands and sat down. Jon continued. "I'm looking for work over the summer and wondered if there are any positions available on your boat. I have pretty good experience in working on boats, both sailing and motorboats," he said confidently.

His claim wasn't all that untrue. At boarding school in Melbourne, a three-hour drive southwest of the family's farm, and later on, at the University of Melbourne, most of his friends were city boys whose parents had houses at the beach. During school holidays, Jon had spent many weeks with these friends, sailing on Port Phillip Bay and becoming proficient enough to be a member in good standing of the Melbourne Grammar School sailing club.

Captain Davies was sizing him up. "As you're probably aware, there's always work to be had at this time of year, but its hard work and long hours, and not everyone is suited to it. A boat with some age on her, like this one, requires a lot more attention than the new boats, all aluminum, fiberglass, and electronics." The tone of his voice betrayed his contempt for these travesties. "It's a different type of sailing, this — teak, canvas, and hard grind. You don't look like you've spent much time outdoors recently. What do you do for the rest of the year?"

"I'm an accountant by training," Jon said smoothly. "But after a while, I tend to get a little restless and take some time off. I was working in the French Alps over the past winter, skiing and working. I'll head back to the real world in the autumn. I'm pretty experienced, very hardworking, and keen for the job."

The captain seemed to like this response. "I'll tell you what I'll do. I'll offer you a couple of days work to check you out. For the time being, you'll have to organize your own accommodation. If things work out, we'll look at something permanent. I'll pay you the going rate. If that sounds good to you, when can you start?"

"I can start right away, I haven't anything else to do. Is six tomorrow morning okay?" Jon asked eagerly.

Davies nodded. The two men shook hands.

Jon was lucky in his timing; almost to the week, this was the easiest time of the year to be hired on as crew. He found a local bar, ate an early supper, and settled in, not wanting to go back to the room he'd rented until the family there had finished their dinner. To kill time, he flipped through a newspaper, hardly listening to the TV mounted on the wall above an array of wines and liquors, when an item on the news caught his attention.

"We lead tonight with the bizarre death of a Manhattan man who appears to have been dragged to death beneath his own car. We have a reporter live at the scene. Jean . . ."

Jean was a slender woman in her thirties, of Asian and Hispanic descent. She stood yards away from the Easy Bar, amid a melee of official activity. "Thanks, Cathy. You see behind me the 1970 Cadillac Eldorado that sealed the fate of a man who has been tentatively identified as bar owner George McWilliam. According to police, it seems that at some time over the past few days the victim climbed underneath the vehicle, perhaps to retrieve drugs that were contained in a compartment welded to the underside of the chassis. Details here are sketchy still, but police are saying that the man somehow got entangled in the compartment's mechanism and the car was then driven off, with the victim pinned underneath."

"Bizarre, indeed," agreed Cathy, from the studio, ". . . and gruesome, Jean. You say he went under the car to retrieve drugs. Was the police department familiar with the victim?"

"Yes, we understand he had a long list of offenses."

The anchor jumped back in. "And the car was driven while the dead man was trapped beneath. There are reports that various appendages of the deceased were found several blocks away from each other. Can you confirm this?"

"Yes, Cathy, parts of the deceased were found in the Bowery and in Alphabet City. Specifically, a foot and a hand, the hand still adorned with gold jewelry."

"I see," Cathy responded, and paused just long enough to allow the image to be imprinted on the imagination of the viewing audience. "So where does the investigation go from here, Jean?"

"It seems that the police are still trying to trace his last movements, but they are having difficulty getting people to come forward."

"So no leads?"

"Not as yet, Cathy, but I might add, the police are telling us that despite the bizarre nature of the incident, they are treating the death as accidental."

"Thanks, Jean. Our next story . . ."

A smile had crept over Jon's face as he watched the news report. When it drew to a close, he picked up his beer and drank the rest of it down in one gulp. A private celebration.

Chapter Fifteen

On his first morning on the boat, Jon busied himself sanding the teak handrail; nearby, the Captain and his first mate labored at their own tasks. There were hundreds of different jobs to be done on a sailing vessel of this size, ranging from menial to highly complex. The *Southern Star* was, in effect, a floating hotel, and as such, needed to create for itself the services generally provided by local utility companies. The electricity it employed was produced by its own generating equipment. Water-making machines turned salt-water into fresh water, utilizing high compression technology that required constant maintenance. Sewage had to be pumped, stored, and dispersed. Communications systems dependent upon compli-cated satellite systems were also in constant use. The cabins had to be heated or cooled to a comfortable, even temperature. All this was in addition to maintaining the diesel-fuelled engines and the basic sailing equipment, not to mention scrubbing and varnishing every nook and cranny of the boat's enormous wooden super-structure, polishing its numerous fittings, and ensuring that all day-to-day guest facilities and services, such as kitchen, laundry, and entertain-ment systems, operated with efficiency.

When something did go wrong, it was up to the captain to make sure the guests and the owner — especially the owner — had no idea anything untoward had happened. The first rule of crewing was that the owner was always the last to be told bad news. Owners of luxury boats such as the *Southern Star* tended to be tolerant of the cost and appreciative of the work involved in maintaining the boat at a high standard, and equally intolerant of any problems arising while they were on board. For a captain, a key part of making sure everything went smoothly was hiring the best crew possible. Jon knew he had to make a strong impression during his trial period.

As the crew broke for lunch, the captain approached him. "So, Rick, how's the sanding going? Had enough yet?"

Jon responded with an enthusiasm he was in fact feeling. "The sun's shining and I've got a view clear across the bay. I have to say I've worked in tougher environments. This is a wonderful old boat. What's its history?"

The captain seemed pleased at Jon's interest. "I was only hired on a couple of years ago, but I know that in the eighties she was owned by a corporate raider who went down in the '87 stock market crash. There was a real estate fellow who also went bust. Then, a Silicon Valley guy who cashed in on the tech boom bought the *Star*, and got rid of her pretty quick after realizing he'd got himself more of a liability than an asset."

Jon laughed. "What is it they say? If it floats, flies, or fucks, rent it?"

"You've got that right," the captain chuckled. "But for all that, she's a fine old vessel. We keep her in tiptop condition, operating with a full crew of six during the summer and between two and three throughout the winter. We're moored here because the facilities are good and the owner lives in the city. He also has a house in East Hampton, not far from here."

"Does the owner use the boat much?" Jon inquired casually.

"He's a keen sailor and it's his great passion, but he's a real city type. He doesn't like it when things don't go his way. Then again, he's got every right to expect the best, he pays all the bills. I've had worse owners." The captain paused for a moment, thinking back on some of the more difficult owners he'd had to endure over the years. "He's not around all that much. We get some good sailing in, though. He likes hanging out at the big regattas along the Northeast coast, so we see our fair share of competitive sailing, and that's when the *Star*'s at her very best." He and Jon finished their sandwiches in companionable silence.

Later that afternoon, Jon wandered into the owner's private quarters to have a look around. It was not unusual for new additions to the crew to familiarize themselves with all aspects of a new boat. During the pre-summer maintenance period, no part of a boat of this size is off limits to a general deckhand. The high season was an entirely different matter. Then, the owner's and his guests' privacy had to be respected at all times.

Jon's interest in this part of the boat went far beyond mere curiosity. The *Southern Star* belonged to Ernest Johnston, which was why Jon planned to make it his home for as long as it took to get what he was after. Off the master bedroom was a small study. After carefully checking outside the room to make sure no one was nearby, Jon moved quickly toward the computer sitting at the center of a built-in desk. It was possible that this was the hard disk missing from Robert's office, but he couldn't be sure. Even if it was, now would not be the right time to use the software he had brought with him, as the crew was constantly wandering throughout the boat. He was prepared to wait for the most propitious moment, even if it took weeks. It was as good a place as any to hide out from his pursuers.

Over his brief trial period, Jon worked hard and effectively, becoming comfortable with both the captain and his first mate. Rather to his own surprise, he was beginning to enjoy the work. His priorities had changed completely and he didn't miss the frantic pace of the financial markets. But now he was free of the distractions and stressors of his former life, he found that not an hour went by without his thoughts turning toward his brother. He continued to make every effort to submerge those thoughts, and the sadness they caused him, in order to concentrate on his day-by-day tasks.

Unused to close living, he sought time alone, spending his evenings drinking at a nondescript bar on Main Street. Without the props he was used to — the $2,000 suits; the expensive accessories; and the beautiful girl on his arm — and the confident swagger the props provided, he faded easily into the background. He drank quietly by himself, passing for one of the locals, and watched whatever happened to be on the television above the bar. He'd always found these televisions annoying, a hindrance to socializing, and only now did he realize what a useful function they served by providing companionship to solitary patrons.

The only person he exchanged words with was the bartender, a friendly if rather plain young woman in her twenties, who had begun flirting with him the first night he'd come in. He hadn't given any woman a second thought since David's death, but he found himself looking forward to her flirtatious remarks and responding in kind, even more so after several rounds of Amstels. One night, as last drinks were called and he'd had quite a few too many, it seemed only natural to accept her invitation to come upstairs to her room for a drink.

Her room was small but clean. It contained little more than a double bed and a spindly bureau. They sat on the bed, but before he could open the bottle of red wine she'd brought up, she had already removed her blouse, revealing large, round beasts constrained by a black, lacy bra. Jon removed her underwear and his jeans almost simultaneously. The sight of her ungroomed pubic hair sent him down between her legs, licking furiously. She leaned back against the pillow with a sigh of pleasure, arching her body toward his eager tongue. He reached up and cupped one generous breast, kneading it none too gently.

"Come inside me," was all she had to say for Jon to move up and slide himself into her. The thought of putting on a condom had not crossed his mind, nor did she suggest it. Opening her legs wide, she lifted her hips off the bed to achieve maximum penetration, crying out. He fucked her rhythmically and with great force, his abdomen slamming noisily against hers. This was purely sex; it had nothing to do with anything else.

Moments after they both came he was dressed, thanking her politely on his way out. As he went down the stairs, he thought with some regret that he would now have to find another place to drink in town. No matter. Soon enough, they would be sailing.

The following evening, when he, the captain, and several of the crew were enjoying a few drinks, the captain took Jon aside. "Rick, the bottom line is that you seem to have worked well over the past few days and you fit in with the rest of the crew. Frankly, your knowledge of sailing looks a little thin, but you aren't being offered the position of skipper, so I guess we can live with that. If you want it, the job's yours, at the same rate, and you can pack up and move onto the boat, which should save you a bit of money. What do you say?"

Jon could not hide his delight, although it was prompted by reasons other than those envisioned by the captain. "Thanks," he grinned. "I'd love to join you for the rest of the season."

Captain Davies extended a friendly hand. "Welcome aboard, Rick."

Long Island Sound, New York

Some days later, the *Southern Star* glided majestically over Long Island Sound in full sail. Jon hung precariously but confidently from the crow's nest atop the main mast, adjusting the main sail's rigging. He realized he was humming "Down Under" by Men at Work, the theme song adopted by the triumphant 1983 American's Cup challenger *Australia II*, and noted what an appropriate choice his subconscious had made. The final preparations for the season were almost complete, the captain had assembled a full crew of six, the winter maintenance was done, and the boat was finishing up its sea trials.

By careful design, Jon's appearance had changed substantially. He had grown a full beard and his hair was now long and untidy.

His pale, New York complexion had been replaced with a deep tan. Always the chameleon, able to blend into any environment in which he found himself, he regarded himself as virtually unrecognizable to almost anyone who had known him in the city. Tomorrow would be the test of that. Ernest Johnston, his wife, and several guests were arriving in the morning. However intimately connected they had become because of recent events, Jon had almost no in-person contact with Johnston while at the bank. Bank directors did not often wander onto the trading floor. Even after Jon's losses, Johnston had made a point of keeping his distance during Jon's few remaining days at the bank. During their bathroom encounter, Jon had positioned himself behind Johnston. Bolstered by the knowledge that crew tended to be invisible to those who pay their wages anyway, Jon felt relatively confident he would remain unrecognized.

The next morning the crew made their final adjustments to the boat in preparation for receiving the Johnston's and their guests. For the first time, they were all turned out in crew uniforms, consisting of a long-sleeved, black-and-white diagonally striped tee-shirt with "Southern Star" embroidered on its top left-hand side, topping off plain white shorts and white deck shoes. Both the boat and the crew looked immaculate.

As a large black Mercedes pulled up to the quay, the captain arranged the crew next to one another. The welcome would be formal, with the crew standing in line to be introduced. This kind of formality reflected the character of the owner; it was he who dictated the style in which his boat should be run. The chauffeur got out of the car and opened the rear passenger door. A tall, noticeably well-groomed man stepped onto the quay and approached the boat, followed by his wife and three guests. It was Johnston.

Waving to the captain, he guided his guests toward the gangplank and onto the boat. Although outfitted from head to toe in high-end boating gear, he carried with him the aura of the painstakingly tailored three-piece suits he favored in the city. His wife was less formal and more outgoing; it was often remarked what an asset she was to him in the socializing critical to advancing his career.

One by one, the captain introduced each member of his crew to the owners. When it was Jon's turn, he stood up straight but tucked his chin down into his beard and didn't risk looking Johnston directly in the eye. As they shook hands, Johnston did not show the faintest hint of recognition, preoccupied as he was with getting his guests on board and comfortably settled. Jon made himself scarce, relieved to have successfully cleared the initial hurdle. He was gradually edging closer to his purpose which was two-fold, to retrieve information from the missing hard disk and to confront Johnston at an opportune time regarding the killers of both his brother and Robert.

The destination for the weekend was Newport, Rhode Island, a long-established wealthy enclave that was still a summer cynosure of the socially ambitious along the eastern coast. Much as Johnston genuinely loved sailing, racing his boat was secondary to taking advantage of the opportunity it provided for him to mingle with, entertain, and impress an elite group of clients and potential clients in places such as Newport. A boat with the elegance and provenance of the *Southern Star* gave him the additional leverage required in a milieu in which it took more than just money to be noticed, much less accepted.

Over the next few days, Jon familiarized himself with the changes in the routine and operation of the *Southern Star* brought about by the presence of the owner and his guests. The competitive sailing was taken very seriously by all, and especially by Johnston, who threw himself into the role of active crewman throughout each race, climbing up and down the rigging, hoisting the sails, and performing a variety of tasks under the watchful eye of the captain. Although reasonably experienced sailors themselves, his guests were gracious enough to seem duly impressed.

Jon kept searching for a time when he would be uninterrupted below, and finally, an opportunity presented itself. With the boat docked in the Newport harbor, Johnston and his guests would be spending the evening on shore, giving the crew a well-earned night off. Jon immediately volunteered to keep watch since a skeleton staff had to be on board at all times for security and safety purposes. After everyone left, there was only one other crewman aboard as Jon slipped below into the owner's cabin. Turning on the computer, he pulled out the restore software disk from his pocket, and quickly began the installation. A series of jumbled half-sentences appeared on the screen. The file names and data on the screen supported his supposition that this computer was indeed the one taken from Robert's office. Jon smiled broadly. He would still be out of a job. But at least two reputations might be salvaged, and Jon would have some leverage over his adversaries.

Jon was jubilant, but prematurely so. After several false starts, he managed to open the file. When he attempted to transfer it onto a series of diskettes he had brought with him, the files would not copy. His mind raced, searching for a solution. There was little point in simply knowing this information still existed if he could not take possession of it.

He quickly concluded he would have to remove the hard drive itself. After a day of racing and an evening of dining and drinking, Johnston would probably retire to bed quite promptly upon returning to the boat. He would be unlikely to notice the missing drive until the following day. At least, that was Jon's hope as he disconnected it and crept up the narrow stairs onto the main deck. There, he carefully stored the hard drive in a rarely used sail locker. Since he was planning to rise before first light and quietly leave the boat for good, he felt it would be temporarily safe there. He would have to confront Johnston about David's killer another time. Jon slept soundly for the first time in several nights.

He opened his eyes the next morning to the sun's rays shining brightly through the porthole to the east. He glanced at his wrist-watch, then did a double-take. It was almost 8:30 A.M. His alarm had not awakened him, nor had the crew. He bolted upright to look out of the porthole. The ocean was moving rapidly past. They were already at sea. He broke out in a cold sweat. He would have no chance to replace the hard drive while they were out at sea. Chances were good that either its absence would be noticed at some point, or it would be found. How could he have allowed this to happen? He quickly threw on his clothes and bounded up to the main deck, where he approached the captain. "Why didn't you wake me, for God's sake?"

The captain was a little taken aback. "Given you offered to keep watch last night while the rest of us went out, we thought we'd let you sleep in. I figured you'd welcome the rest. It appears I was wrong."

Jon was quick to backtrack. "Sorry, I didn't mean to sound ungrateful. Thanks." He was quick to hide his frustration and obvious concern.

The day progressed like any other. Although Jon remained anxious, he went about his business, hanging from a safety bridle high above the deck, but with his attention firmly centered on the sail locker far below. Late in the morning, Jon noticed one of the crew walk toward the locker in which the hard drive was hidden. The crewman had just about passed it by when he hesitated, opened the adjacent locker and searched for something he apparently didn't find; then, as Jon gulped in dismay, he opened the next locker and saw the drive. He picked it up, examined it closely, then returned it to the locker and walked off. Jon remained frozen, watching.

Within minutes, the crewman returned with both Captain Davies and Johnston. Jon could not hear the conversation from his perch high on the mast, but he could easily make out what was happening. While the captain appeared calm, if puzzled, by the hard drive's presence in the locker, Johnston's agitated body language clearly revealed his anger. As the crewman lifted the drive, Johnston gesticulated toward the sea, indicating that it should be thrown overboard. The captain seemed to protest, but apparently Johnston insisted. The crewman finally tossed it over the rail.

Jon was seething with impotent rage as he watched the hard drive sink below the surface of the ocean's waves. He had suffered yet another setback which could have been avoided. Fuck Johnston! Fuck watching Johnston swan around pretending to be someone and something he most definitely was not. Just fuck everything, he thought, overcome with emotion. Feeling himself losing control, he shifted his anger inward, berating himself for all that had gone wrong. He immediately grew desperately sad, thinking back on the long, happy summers he and his brother had spent working on the farm together. Going back even further, he conjured up images of himself and David playing together as very young children, becoming so absorbed in his memories he lost track of the present.

Within moments, he felt himself spinning dizzily, and with a start, came back to reality. He had lost his grip on the mast and was twirling like a ballerina in his bridle, bouncing off the mast with each pirouette. Just as the captain glanced up, Jon regained his hold and with it, control. The captain shifted his attention elsewhere, never seeing the tears the wind whipped from Jon's eyes before they had a chance to roll down his cheeks.

There was a trial to run before the next race, so for the time being, sailing would take priority over all other issues. The stolen hard drive would be dealt with only when they were safely tied up in port at the end of the day. Jon knew he would have to leave the boat before then.

The trial began with all the intensity of a real race. Although there were fewer boats than usual and they were racing close to shore, the *Southern Star* was in full sail, the crew busy at their assigned tasks. Jon was once again secured to the main mast in the detachable bridle, eighty feet above the deck. He dangled just below the crow's nest, making routine adjustments to the rigging.

His frustration was growing. He had to make some move — any move. It was now or never. Since the only remaining proof of his innocence was on its way to the bottom of the sea, all that he could do now was get whatever information he could from Johnston. To do so, he would have to isolate him first. Thinking no further than that, he needed to quickly create such an opportunity.

Noting that he was largely out of view of the rest of the busy crew, he produced a knife from his pocket and began to saw back and forth through a rope attached to the mainsail, stopping before the rope was completely severed.

He bided his time until Johnston was directly below him and

then called out loudly, "Captain, we have a damaged rope on the mainsail and I need a new rope right away. Can you send one up?"

Jon was counting on Johnston to volunteer to climb the mast with the rope he'd requested. Climbing the mast was dangerous, so Johnston would probably opt to do it in his ongoing effort to impress his guests. And indeed, he immediately volunteered as he had done many times before. For a few pounding heartbeats, Jon watched as the captain politely suggested the task be carried out by a crewman, but Johnston was insistent. Draping two thick ropes around his neck, he climbed up the mast and clambered into the safety of the crow's nest, putting him within inches of Phillips, high above the main deck of the boat.

Jon savored the moment; after all the other reversals, it had been almost too easy. But now he had to figure out his next move. He stalled for time. "Mr. Johnston," he screamed above the howling wind. "Could you please hand me that rope?" Johnston complied, and Jon tied it to the mast. The wind picked up, and the mast swayed violently from side to side as the boat rolled with the swells of the ocean.

"Thanks," Jon shouted. Johnston hung onto the rail, waiting for further instructions. Jon realized that not only was he in physical control of Johnston as long as he was in the crow's nest, but that Johnston was, for the moment at least, voluntarily following whatever instructions Jon gave him. It was a perfect setup. "Could you please secure one end of that other rope to the top of the mainsail rigging and hang onto to it while I work on this rope?" Again Johnston did as he was told, tying one end of the second rope securely to the mast, exactly as instructed. The other end of the same rope still hung loosely around his neck. Jon finished replacing the damaged rope. "Now, could you please help me into the crow's nest?" he yelled, looking up and extending his hand.

Johnston reached down from the crow's nest and Jon clasped his sweaty palm. In that moment of contact, rage engulfed him, a cumulative fury at this man who had been the cause of so much pain, and yet continued to live such a charmed life. It was more than

Jon could bear. Moving swiftly, he looped the rope around Johnston's neck, and tightened it. Johnston was uncertain at first as to
what Jon was doing, thinking he might be reaching over his shoulder to untwist or remove the rope. But as he felt it tighten instead,
he realized something was wrong. Alarmed, he began to resist and
to shout at Jon to loosen it. A brief, violent struggle ensued, unnoticed and unheard by anyone below. Jon continued to yank the rope
until it was wound tightly and securely. By now he was unstoppable.
Johnston's distorted, terrified visage conjured up his brother's
bruised and swollen face. Johnston was half-in and half-out of the
crow's nest, his fate entirely in Jon's hands.

Although just inches from Johnston, Jon had to again scream
over the noise of the wind. "Who killed my brother?"

It was only at that instant that Johnston recognized Jon.
His expression registered sheer terror. "I didn't," he protested
desperately.

Jon yelled out over the wind, his anger fueled by the denial.
"Who, then?"

Johnston immediately caved. "Boris Posarnov."

In gaining control of Johnston, Jon had lost control of himself.
All he wanted was to see this man get what he deserved. Running on
pure adrenalin, he used his free arm to haul Johnston over the edge
of the crow's nest. Tightening the rope even more, he hesitated for
a split second. "See you in hell. Think of my brother on your way
down."

"No! Oh, my God . . ." Johnston choked.

Frantically, he attempted to grab onto one of the ropes attached to the mainsail as Jon reached up and pulled him clear of the
crow's nest. The other end of the rope remained firmly tied to the
top of the rigging. Johnston fell heavily toward the deck below. His
head snapped back with a sickening crack and his body jerked upward when the rope reached its limit, halfway to the deck.

Seeing that the captain and some of the guests were looking up
to see what had become of Johnston, Jon began to pantomime calling for help, as if he'd been trying to get their attention but hadn't

been heard. Johnston was still making intermittent attempts to free himself, but after a few moments, his movements stopped. His body relaxed and began swinging gently from side to side in rhythm with the ocean's swells as the boat continued to career through the water under full sail.

Jon now needed to make a choreographed exit. He climbed on top of the mainsail rigging and pretended to try to untie the rope and release the lifeless Johnston.

"For God's sake, be careful, Rick, don't be a hero," the captain shouted. Jon *was* being careful, careful to position himself toward the far right edge of the rigging, so that when he fell, he would drop directly into the water below, narrowly missing the deck and handrail. Having reached his perch, he took a deep breath before allowing himself to slip off the rigging as the mast lurched to the right. Adding a touch of drama for those watching below, Jon clung momentarily from the rigging by one arm, appearing to have lost his grip with the other. Kicking his legs wildly, he let go and plummeted almost one hundred feet from the mainsail into the water below. It was a long and dramatic fall. The captain, some of the crew, and the three guests rushed frantically toward the safety rail to look for Jon in the water. Johnston's wife was below deck and unaware of her husband's plight.

There was a circle of foam where Jon had plunged into the water. Those hanging over the boat's railing watched as the boat slid past the circle and quickly moved on. Two crewmen were frantically trying to release the lifeless owner. Later on, they would attempt the long and arduous task of bringing the vessel around to search for their shipmate, and would radio the Coast Guard to mount a full search, but everyone knew it would be fruitless. One of the disadvantages of old sailing boats such as the *Southern Star* was that they were unstoppable; by the time the sails were down and she had lost all forward momentum, their Ozzie mate would be long gone, lost at sea.

Jon hit the water, feet first. His momentum plunged him deep into the ocean. Swimming quickly up to the surface, he paused just long enough to take a gulp of air and get his bearings. To his left was the wake left by the hull of the *Southern Star* as she plowed through the water. He turned away from her, attempting to swim as far away as possible underwater, with a single breath of air. As he slowly came back up to the surface, he pushed only his face above the waves, careful to keep the rest of his body underwater.

The Southern Star was rapidly fading into the distance, Johnston's lifeless form still swinging as rhythmically as a pendulum from the mast. Jon turned away again and headed toward the shoreline, just visible in the distance, beginning the long and arduous swim back. Once safely on dry land, he breathlessly saluted the ocean and the identity he had just left behind — that of a courageous sailor who'd sacrificed his own life in an attempt to save the life of another. How ironic, he thought, that he'd created for Rick Mears a far better legacy than he had for his own dear brother.

Chapter Sixteen

Penny Jordan sat up straight at her desk in the offices of the *London Globe*. Her antennae had been put on alert by a seemingly innocuous item that had just come across the Reuters wire:

> *U.S. Investment Banker Dies in Yachting Mishap. Bank of Manhattan Chief of Operations Mr. Ernest Johnston died yesterday afternoon in a yachting accident on Long Island Sound. A member of the crew fell overboard in an attempt to save Southern Star owner Johnston and was lost at sea. His body has not been found but he is presumed dead.*

Penny had learned to trust her antennae, so she put in a request for more information, then pulled out a file marked "Phillips, J." The same antennae had prompted her to create the file after Jon's curt reply to her second email, which had seemed to her a blatant attempt to throw her off the track.

Of course, it had done no such thing. Since then, she'd been keeping tabs on anything relating to Jon, and there'd been plenty to keep tabs on. Opening the folder, she flipped through the printouts and clipped accounts of his dismissal, Robert Baldwin's fatal accident, David's bizarre death, gossip column items about Jon's dissolute ways, and financial reports detailing the impact of Jon's trading losses on the bank. Now, here again, was an untimely accidental death connected to the Bank of Manhattan. It was getting harder and harder to believe these were all unrelated incidents.

Penny knew that as a journalist, she had to be careful of her own motives where Jon was concerned. He had no idea — never had — of what an impact he'd had on her life. He'd been her first love, the first boy she'd slept with, and when he'd cavalierly dumped her in favor of her best friend, she'd lost the two people closest to her all at once, and had been humiliated in front of her friends. It had made what was left of her time at Cambridge a miserable experience.

Twelve years later, she was still out of touch with Victoria, but she'd kept track of Jon from a distance. She blamed him for a series of failed romances, telling herself and her friends how she'd never be able to trust a man again. Her career and a long succession of one-night stands had sustained her, but at the moment, her career was at a standstill. Breaking a big story might give her just the push she needed to get to the next level, whatever that might turn out to be. And, she mused, what poetic justice it would be if Jon became the agent for such a change. Nothing would satisfy her more than to turn the tables on him — if not romantically, then professionally would do.

In following the story of Jon's downfall, Penny wondered at the speed with which the assassination of his character had been accomplished. *News/Copy* in particular seemed to have obtained all kinds of dirt on Jon almost immediately, which was odd, considering he wasn't a public figure. She'd wondered at the time if there had been some orchestrated effort to make him a scapegoat beyond the already embarrassing fact of his trading losses, but she'd been waiting for another piece of the puzzle to fall into place before starting to dig in earnest.

She suspected this piece had just turned up. It was time to begin. First she would find out how *News/Copy* got the goods on

Jon, and if their source was credible, which she already doubted. Jon had been a lot of things when she had known him, but a budding heroin-shooting cross-dresser hadn't been among them. She'd never met David, but from the way in which Jon had spoken about him, snuffing himself out like some fading rock star in search of the ultimate sexual thrill didn't sound at all in character.

Now that she'd decided to take a crack at the story, she was eager to get going. She'd need to call her U.S. contact first, but he wouldn't be in his office in New York for another three hours. Impatiently, she accessed her database and found his home number. It rang several times before he picked up.

"Hello." The voice sounded barely awake.

"Hello, is that you, Freddie?" Penny chirped.

"Who's that?" Freddie groaned.

"Your old pal from the *London Globe*. Sorry I woke you."

"Penny, darling, this must mean you want something," he yawned loudly into the phone. "I can't imagine you've called me at this ungodly hour merely to inquire as to my well-being."

"Guilty, as charged," Penny confessed. "You may remember we spoke a little while back regarding a banking friend of mine who got into hot water."

"Yeah, I remember." Freddie was sounding more alert. "It developed into quite a story. Drugs, sex, alcohol abuse, high flyers, and big losses — is there anything we missed? If so, let me have it. We'll see if we can spill some more blood." He yawned again, loudly.

"Nothing just yet, but I'm working on an angle relating to the story. I need some help. Can you get me access to the guys who ran the story on *News/Copy* you tipped me off about? I'd like to find out how they got so much info so quickly, and I'd also like to get access to their source. The story is dead by now, so they shouldn't have too much of a problem with putting me in touch with their source, should they?"

"So what's in it for me?" Freddie asked.

"A New York exclusive, if anything comes of it."

"Fair enough. I can't imagine I'll have much trouble getting you in the door, but you'll have to come over here if you want the lowdown. You won't get anything over the phone. And remember, you'll owe me."

"Sure. I'll have a word with my editor now to see if he'll cover my expenses, and in the meantime, could you check to see if they'll see me?"

Penny hung up. She immediately got to work gathering information regarding the mysterious boating accident, intrigued by the disappearance of Rick Mears and the conflicting reports on what exactly caused Mr. Johnston to fall from the mast. Later on, Freddie called; her *News/Copy* meeting was looking doable. By early afternoon she was at her editor's office door.

"Peter, do you have a minute?"

Her editor looked stressed. Despite a large No Smoking sign hanging over his desk, a cigarette burned between his fingers. "A minute? Right, come on in then, that's all you've got."

"I'm working on a story that I'm just starting to develop, but I think that potentially it has some real punch."

"Give it to me in brief."

Penny did. Rhys-Jones looked skeptical after she'd finished. "So what are you suggesting? That your pal Jon is in some way involved in all this?" The editor's tone was dismissive.

"Maybe. I'd like to take the idea to the next stage, see if I can find out."

"I'm getting the feeling there's something else going on here. Is there a personal angle? How good a friend was this Jon?" Penny looked down at the floor. Rhys-Jones raised his eyebrows, shook his head and continued. "I see. With friends like you . . ." As he started laughing, a long cigarette ash fell onto the papers scattered in front of him.

"What do you mean by a 'personal angle'?" Penny was indignant; never mind that he was correct.

"Still bitter after all these years," he sang, with Paul Simon's phrasing. "Come on, what's the scoop here?"

Penny decided honesty might be the best policy. "Not that I

think it's any of your business, but yes, I am a little bitter. He was my boyfriend at university but dumped me for the daughter of an earl, who until then had been my closest friend."

"And this is your chance to square up?"

"Don't be a wanker, Peter. I think he's a prick and sure, I was a little hurt at the time, but I'm in it for the story."

"You've been around this business long enough to know that people are always using their position to settle old scores. I'm your editor; it's a question I have to ask"

"Hey, I understand, but I've told you straight up why it's potentially a great story, and I believe I've got an inside track to this jerk."

He nodded, allowing a note of enthusiasm into his voice. "So what's the next move?"

"A quick, cheap trip to New York to investigate that *News/Copy* story and to talk with the police officers who've been in charge of the various investigations."

When Rhys-Jones still hesitated, Penny stepped up her sales pitch. "The airfare to New York should only be a couple hundred quid, I shouldn't be gone more than two or three days, and I can bunk up with friends."

"All right, bugger off then. But I don't want you spending too much time on a wild goose chase, and make sure you keep what's personal out of it. You've got two days to convince me you've got a story here. Otherwise, it's dead. Is that quite clear?"

"Crystal. I'll see you in a couple of days then," she beamed enthusiastically.

Within the next few hours, Penny had contacted the various police departments responsible for the investigations into Robert Baldwin's, David Phillips's, and Ernest Johnston's deaths, and had received confirmation from Freddie that all was arranged for her to meet with a producer from *News/Copy*. After making her reservations and calling her friends in New York, she was ready to go.

Lanesborough Hotel, London

Jon stood in his faux eighteenth-century suite in the Lanesborough

Hotel on a corner of Hyde Park, just a stone's throw from Buckingham Palace. He was surrounded by empty boxes, all bearing the same electronics store logo, from which he had unpacked and set up a computer, printer and scanner. He had begun to punch in a number on a telephone, but hesitated, instead pulling out the document he'd persuaded Baldwin to give him after the auction, the document containing all the banking details concerning the U.K. Trading Company. Reading it carefully, he broke into a broad smile. It was only now, given recent developments, that he realized its enormous potential.

Putting down the telephone, he sat to ponder his situation. He had crossed many lines in the past few years, but murder had never even been visible on his horizon. True, Johnston's death had not been a premeditated act on his part, and he was still astonished at the power of the raw rage that had overcome him in that moment, but what was done, was done, and his mission was still incomplete. Posarnov, whom he hoped could provide the answers he so desperately sought, was now in his sights, but before he could get to Posarnov, Jon had other, smaller fires to put out.

Picking up the remote, he flicked on the television. The hotel had web TV, so he logged on to his email. At the moment, it displayed a missive from Penny. Jon walked over to read it.

Dear Jonny:

Sounds like things have been pretty tough for you lately. I was very sorry to hear about your brother's tragic death. I'd love the opportunity to catch up. It's been a very long time. Please give me a call sometime soon.

Love, Penny

He began to punch in the same telephone number again. While doing so, he considered how much had changed since Penny had initially put him on to Posarnov and the U.K. Trading Company. Reluctant as he was to involve her, he needed to know what her real interest in the story was, and how much she knew, or thought she knew.

"Jon!" Penny exclaimed. "It's so nice to hear from you. Thanks for getting in touch."

"That was a pretty feisty first email you sent me. Are you sure you've forgiven me for my lack of tact all those years ago?" he began cautiously.

Penny had been regretting her initial sharpness. It was unlike her to declare her hand so openly. "Forget it. As I explained, you caught me at a bad moment. Anyway, I thought you might want to tell your side of the story at some point. Always happy to help out an old friend."

"Again, I'm sorry to disappoint you, but there's no story to tell."

"Well, in any case, I'm less interested in the story than in what's going on with you, Jon," she lied. "How are you? I'm really sorry about your brother."

"Thanks, Penny. I'm coping. It was a tremendous shock."

"I can imagine. What are your plans? By the way, it's good to hear that you haven't lost your Ozzie twang after all these years. I suppose if Cambridge and your posh friends couldn't rid you of it, New York won't."

"Damn right." Jon replied. "It's been my experience that the only Australians who lose their accents are those who are looking to, and I'm not. Even after all these years, it still feels really good . . . " Jon flirtatiously turned his remark into a double entendre.

"What still feels really good?" Penny responded suggestively in kind.

"It still feels really good to be Australian," Jon laughed. "In fact, the older I get, the better it feels."

"Does that mean you're heading back to Melbourne? Is that where you're calling from?"

Had she not caught him off-guard, he might not have told her his whereabouts. "No, I'm in London."

Interesting, Penny thought. "Then let's get together, just for old times' sake. It's been a long time, and by the sound of it, there's been plenty happening in your life."

"Not so much," said Jon, once more on guard. "Just a bit of enforced retirement."

Penny wasn't to be put off that easily. "Well, let's get together anyway. I'm sure you have an interesting tale to tell, despite what you say. All off the record, of course."

"Of course," he agreed, not believing her. "I tell you what; I'm meeting a few old friends from the Exchange next Tuesday night at Walthamstow. Why don't you join us?" Safety in numbers, he figured. Plus, the fact that it was nearly an hour out of the center of London might put her off.

Good, she thought. Tuesday gave her just enough time to get to New York and back, armed with more information. "Walthamstow?" she repeated. "Interesting choice. It doesn't exactly offer the convenience of Fleet Street or the style of Berkeley Square. You must still be hanging around with your dodgy friends from the old days. Where shall we meet?"

"The dog track, in the Greyhound bar, at about eight."

"The dog track? Of course, where else? Ask a silly question. I'll be there at eight. See you then," she said, hanging up before he could think better of agreeing to see her.

Penny knew if she pressed him over the telephone, Jon would have closed himself off from her completely. Her interests were best served by taking advantage of their previous relationship and whatever residual guilt he might still feel about the way he'd treated her. Meeting him in a crowded, non-threatening environment offering lots of diversions was ideal, now that she thought about it. She wanted to lull him into trusting her, just as she had once trusted him.

Jon put down the telephone. After so much time had passed, he considered Penny more of a friend than a threat, but he was aware her ambition might be enough to turn her into a nuisance. Ignoring her was unlikely to discourage her. She was one of the very few people who knew the U.K. Trading Company might be involved in his rapid change of circumstance. He needed to convince her that there was no story. If he failed, and her paper went ahead and printed whatever she could make of a series of occurrences, he would have to rely on England's stringent libel laws to protect him, which they probably would. Still, it would be far easier to head her off at the pass with whatever diversionary tactics he could muster.

His thoughts were interrupted by a knock at the door. He opened it to an obsequious bellman.

"Mr. Chambers?" the bellman asked.

"Yep," Jon replied. He was handed a large brown envelope.

"Courier brought this."

"Thank you." Jon took the envelope and tipped generously before closing the door.

He tore open the envelope he had requested only that morning. It was addressed to Derek Chambers Esq., and contained a recent tax filing on the U.K. Trading Company Limited, which included details of the company's business dealings and its financial statements. Jon flicked through the list of company directors; Posarnov was one of them, although the other names meant nothing to him. He removed the cover letter, headed with the U.K. Trading Company logo, and placed it onto the bed of the scanner. Within seconds, the computer screen filled with a replica of the letter. Jon deleted the text, leaving only the letterhead.

Jon pulled an envelope from his file, the same envelope Robert had reluctantly given him shortly after his trading losses. It contained highly confidential information regarding the affairs of the U.K. Trading Company as they related to the Bank of Manhattan. He studied the detail carefully and smiled broadly; the documents contained, amongst other things, the full banking details of its account at Bank Cayman. He began to type, frequently referring to the document.

Mr. Ernest Johnston,
Director,
Bank of Manhattan,
72 Broad Street,
New York, New York 10013

Dear Ernest:

As discussed, could you please remit all remaining funds relating to the reimbursement of the unauthorized trading losses that are held in the U.K. Trading Company's cash margin account to our existing bank account. The details, as you are aware, are as follows:

Bank Cayman,
P.O. Box 134983,
Bank House,
Port Street,
Grand Cayman

Account number: 543678598
ABA number: 34598
Account name: U.K. Trading Company
Contact: Gerry Rice

My understanding is that this amount will be 40m usd, less the $5m usd additional margin provided by your bank, the total being approximately $35m usd plus any associated interest.

Please regard this as a standing instruction; any funds that accrue to my account should be remitted to the above account with immediate effect.

Please note that this instruction replaces all previous correspondence.

Kindest Regards,

_____

Boris Posarnov
Director

Jon printed out the letter. It came out looking identical to the U.K. Trading Company original, except for its text. He then carefully forged Posarnov's signature, using the tax filing's signature as a guide. The facsimile was good enough that on cursory examination, it would pass for genuine.

Jon then began to type a second letter on his fake U.K. Trading Company stationery, this time to Gerry Rice, senior account manager at Bank Cayman.

Mr. Gerry Rice,
Senior Account Manager,
Bank Cayman,
P.O. Box 134983,
Bank House,
Port Street,
Grand Cayman

Dear Gerry:

As you are aware, we are anticipating receiving a sum of approximately $35 million usd from our margin account at the Bank of Manhattan into our bank account at Bank Cayman. These funds should be received into our existing bank account imminently.

Could you please open a new bank account under the name of U.K. Trading Charitable Trust. Once this new account is established, please remit all the funds deposited in our existing account, under the name of U.K. Trading Company Limited, into this new account. This should be done immediately once the funds are received from the Bank of Manhattan.

Please fax full details regarding the new account to me at: 001-4471 7379465.

I thank you for your help in this matter.

Kindest Regards,

_____

Boris Posarnov
Director

Once again, Jon printed out the letter and forged Posarnov's signature. He smiled broadly as he put this second, forged letter aside, delighted with the efficiency of his scheme should it unfold as he now anticipated.

He then began to type a third letter, with the same letterhead, also addressed to Gerry Rice at Bank Cayman.

Mr. Gerry Rice,
Senior Account Manager,
Bank Cayman,
P.O. Box 134983,
Bank House,
Port Street,
Grand Cayman

Dear Gerry:

Further to my previous correspondence relating to the setting up of a bank account for the U.K. Trading Charitable Trust, please be advised that, in addition to myself, Mr. Jon Phillips should be a signatory to this account and also a named beneficiary of the Trust. This will give him full access to and control over the account. Please execute the appropriate documentation immediately.

I will have Mr. Phillips call you so that you can arrange for him to sign all the appropriate original signature documentation.

Kindest Regards,

_____

Boris Posarnov
Director

Jon forged Posarnov's signature for the third and last time. Using the computer, he addressed the three envelopes and sealed each letter inside. He then placed all three of them into his small overnight bag. He grinned smugly, feeling that he was finally beginning to gain the upper hand, although a great deal still remained to be done.

Chapter Seventeen

The olive green 1966 Aston Martin Short Chassis Volante convertible powered through the picturesque country lanes of the Gloucestershire countryside. Jon had the top down and was humming along to Tom Jones's "It's Not Unusual," which played loudly on the car stereo, a tune from a similar era as the car. He was relaxed, enjoying putting his classic car through its paces and enjoying a perfect summer day in England. The pastures he passed were a deep, even green, enclosed by walls of carefully layered Cotswold stone. The fields were lush and dotted with blackberry bushes, although it would be another month before their berries would ripen. Summer brought with it a full social calendar. When he'd lived in England, he'd made a point of attending all the prime events — from the Chelsea Flower Show in late May, to Wimbledon, to Royal Ascot, and on to the Henley Regatta and Glyndebourne — but such activities held little interest for him now.

There was much to be said for England's other seasons, too, he mused: winter, offering the camaraderie of the pubs, long evenings around inviting fireplaces, and transforming dustings of snow over the countryside; and spring, marking the end of mid-afternoon darkness and the beginning of the regeneration process signaled by brilliant patches of early daffodils, closely followed by colorful blankets of bluebells and tulips. But it was autumn that Jon always looked forward to the most, the season he believed best suited his character, cool and changeable. As the chameleon shed its skin, so the autumn discarded its unwanted cover. It was a time, Jon felt, when he blended most easily into his environment.

A few miles after passing through the tiny village of Sherston, Jon arrived at an impressive set of wrought-iron gates. He slowed to a more dignified pace as he drove through them and continued down a long, tree-lined driveway toward Stanford Hall, the imposing Gothic residence of the family of the Earl of Colarvon. As he pulled up in front of the stately home, a casually dressed man about Jon's age bounded out of the main entrance, waving enthusiastically. Jon opened his car door as his old friend approached him, a broad smile on his face.

"Amazing, now that you've put on some years, you look slightly less of a prat behind the wheel of that ridiculous machine, but a prat nonetheless," he said, in an unmistakably upper-class English accent. "I would have thought you'd have sold that old banger long ago."

"It's good to see you, too, Andy," Jon retorted, laughing good-naturedly. "Or are they still calling you Scott?"

"Scott?' Andy asked. "I'm sorry?"

"You know, Scott-No-Mates. As in, you were never very popular either at Eton or at Cambridge, or weren't you aware of that?"

"Oh, very funny, what a dazzling wit," Andy smiled. "After all this time, rude as ever."

"Then I'm in very good company here, aren't I, Andy?"

"Mind your tongue! Given that I'm greeting you as Lord of the Manor, I would ask you to address me with a little less informality, if you don't mind."

"Oh, but I do," Jon laughed. "Thank God your father's still alive and well. I can't even begin to imagine how impossible you'll be when you become an earl and this place actually does belong to you."

"One thing's certain, when that day comes, I'll hardly be standing here chatting up some Ozzie ne'er-do-well, so enjoy it while it lasts. And by the way, it's rare that friends just ring up and invite themselves to stay; something about waiting to be asked. How long will we be graced with your presence?"

Jon shrugged. "Unfortunately, I have to go back to London tomorrow afternoon. But in the meantime, it's wonderful to be back at Stanford Hall."

Jon had first caught Andy's attention at Cambridge because, unlike many foreigners in England who change their accents, style of dress, and even their personality in attempting to assimilate, Jon had never made any effort to conceal his Australian origin. He had, in fact, played to the wild colonial lad image, and as a result was taken up, though at first only as a curiosity, by Andy and his insulated circle of young aristocrats who'd known one another from childhood. Jon was not intimidated by the opulent surroundings and blue-blooded lineage of most of the other guests, and because he'd grown up handling both guns and horses, he excelled at their preferred weekend activities. So, after he had proved himself a fine shot at several shooting parties and an all-around jolly decent chap, in Andy's words, he'd become one of the regular weekend guests at Stanford Hall.

Like so many titled proprietors of England's stately mansions, Andy's father, the Earl of Colarvon, was strapped for cash and had come to rely heavily, even in those days, on guests who paid handsomely to spend a weekend at Stanford Hall being wined and dined when not shooting pheasant. Jon's shooting expertise often came in handy, when he was called upon to fill in for missing guests. He was happy to do so despite regarding pheasant shooting, as it was practiced on these weekend parties, as something less than sporting. Where was the challenge in ten double-barreled guns being trained on birds who had just been scared a few feet off the ground by hired beaters? Growing up, Jon had hunted rabbits and foxes, but for necessity, not sport. He much preferred to ride the few horses left at Stanford Hall, and on cold winter mornings he would go off alone on horseback for hours at a time whenever he could tactfully escape the hunting parties.

It was during one of these solitary rides that Andy's sister, Victoria, first took note of him. They had often been part of the same crowd, but Victoria was usually distracted by the many eligible young swains who vied for her attention and affections. Most were products of the best the British class system had to offer, but some from much further afield were among those wrangling weekend invitations for the chance to pursue the Earl's lovely daughter. Among the latter were the titled Euro-trash scions whose depleted financial resources left them with only their title and their charm to rely on. They mistakenly assumed that Victoria's family's wealth could solve their financial problems, if they could but win her hand. In fact, she was in a situation similar to theirs, of having social position without ample financial resources to back it up. Jon had become aware this was the case when they had been together, but he had no idea how dire the family's circumstances had become in the intervening years. All he knew at the time was that Victoria was far beyond his reach — a classic English rose, different from any girl he'd known, beautiful, sophisticated, and aristocratic. Girls like her simply didn't exist in Australia, and not knowing how to begin to approach her, he had taken himself out of the running and virtually ignored her.

Had she noticed, this in itself could have intrigued her. But she was too occupied with her numerous suitors and viewed Jon simply as a new friend of her brother's, a bit rough around the edges, although pleasant enough. Then one day, as she cantered through a forest on the estate's grounds, she noticed a lone figure expertly negotiating his way on horseback through the thickly wooded valley leading to the river dividing the property into two parts. She watched with admiration as the rider jumped his horse confidently over several fallen trees, ducked beneath low-hanging branches, and forded the river as though it were little more than a puddle. Curious, she followed him at a distance until he finally headed back toward the stable, unaware of her presence. This moment marked the beginning of their involvement, since when Victoria subsequently showed an interest in Jon, he immediately reciprocated.

As Jon and Andy walked with Jon's overnight bag toward the main entrance of the house, a tall, dark, strikingly beautiful woman dressed in formal riding gear appeared at the front door. She ran quickly down the stairs and over to Jon. Wrapping her arms around him, she kissed him full on the mouth, then leaned back to gaze affectionately into his eyes.

"Hello, Jonny, it really is terribly good to see you," Victoria said softly, in a mellifluous accent echoing her brother's.

Jon smiled back at her, pleased that her dazzling beauty was undiminished by the years that had passed since he'd last seen her. "And you, too," he said, keeping her close.

Andy raised an eyebrow. "This is starting to look all too familiar. Are we in for a replay?"

"Hey," Jon protested. "We haven't seen each other in years. Give us a break."

Victoria nodded in agreement. "Exactly. We have a lot of catching up to do. Come on, Jon, walk with me. Andy, be a dear and take Jonny's bag up to his room, won't you?"

As Andy rolled his eyes heavenward, she linked her arm in Jon's and led him toward a path winding its way to the back of the house and out into the garden.

Midtown, Manhattan

Penny arrived at the midtown Manhattan office of the *News/Copy* producer she was scheduled to meet. An assistant ushered her into a small room and offered her a welcome cup of coffee. Within minutes, an attractive, well-groomed young woman in her late twenties walked into the room and introduced herself. They greeted each other warmly, almost with a sense of familiarity, despite never having met.

"I'm delighted to meet you," the producer, Fiona Lane, said. "Freddie tells me you are one of Fleet Street's finest."

Penny surprised herself by blushing. "Thanks, but as you know, Freddie will say anything; he has no shame. Thank you for meeting with me on such short notice."

"The pleasure is all mine. Any friend of Freddie's . . ." She paused before continuing, as though other thoughts were overriding her small talk. "I'm not sure I'll be able to be of any help to you, but you do come highly recommended, and you never know, one day you may be able to return the favor. We journalists need to network, and we females especially need to stick together." Her eyes never left Penny's.

"You're absolutely right." Penny smiled, a little unsettled by the openness with which she was being regarded.

"So how can I be of help? Freddie mentioned you were interested in a story we ran on the Wizard of Oz." Fiona smoothed a non-existent crease in her snugly fitting suit jacket.

"That's it. I want to run a follow-up story, but I need a little more background information. Can you tell me, for example, how you got the story so quickly? You seemed to have your sources lined up almost before the story broke."

Fiona shrugged. "The guy's lifestyle tripped him up and we got lucky, in that an acquaintance of mine just happened to know the right person for us to break with story with." She hesitated. Penny felt there was something she was holding back. "And don't forget, it took a while for the Bank of Manhattan to calculate and release the extent of the losses, and to decide what action they were going to take, so we didn't get the story quite as quickly as it might have seemed."

"Would it be possible for me to speak with your friend?"

"He's not really a friend. And I doubt there is much else he can tell you," Fiona shrugged. "The story said it all. His source had all the dirt on the trader's bad habits."

"Indeed," Penny responded, with a hint of irony. "Any chance of getting to his source, then? He might have some background material."

"I'm afraid that to get information out of him, you'd need contacts even we don't have." She laughed. "Although come to think of it, I do know one or two tabloid hacks who've already sold their souls to the devil any number of times. Perhaps they could help."

Penny gave her a puzzled look.

"He's dead," Fiona explained.

Penny sat up. "Seriously? It's unbelievable! Everyone involved in this story seems to die. It's really weird. Do you have any idea how he died?" Penny was excited.

"It was in the papers. Some sort of accident in his car, I think. I'll give you his name. You can check out the coverage at the library. We didn't do a follow-up." She swiveled around to her computer, clicked a few times, then scribbled a name on a slip of paper and handed it to Penny.

"Good luck, and by the way, if you find a story in all this, remember who helped you out. We're always looking for follow-ups." Pausing, she changed tack. "How long are you in New York for?"

"I'm not sure, but not for long," Penny replied. "It depends on how the story develops over the next couple of days. My editor's not convinced there's anything there."

"If you're interested, I'm going to a party tonight with some friends. Why don't you join us?" Fiona asked. "You might meet some interesting contacts," she added, as Penny hesitated.

"Well, I was going to have dinner with the friends I'm staying with but I guess it doesn't have to be tonight." Penny wasn't sure herself what was prompting her to change her plans — the possibility of picking up new contacts or the opportunity to spend more time with this woman whom she found so unexpectedly compelling.

"Good! Let's meet at around nine at Soho House in the Meatpacking District for a couple of drinks beforehand. Can you find your way there?"

Penny didn't need any further prompting. "Yes, I'd like that very much."

"Great," said Fiona, handing Penny her business card. "Here are my numbers, if you need them. I look forward to seeing you later."

As Penny stood to leave the room, the women moved toward each other to say goodbye. Penny extended her hand. Fiona took it, and then pulled Penny forward until she was near enough to kiss Penny on the cheek. They remained suspended in close contact for just a moment, but it was a moment that made Penny slightly breathless.

Gloucestershire, England

Later that day, Jon changed into his breeches and boots, and he and Victoria rode together on the grounds of the estate. On an incline overlooking a breathtaking panorama of the Cotswolds, Victoria pulled up her mount and Jon came to a halt alongside her.

Victoria turned to him. "Jonny, would you say that, despite everything, you've achieved your ambitions? You were always so ambitious."

Jon was wistful. "Interesting question. Strangely enough, I think I have, or am about to, but not in the way I thought. Had I not lost so much of the bank's money, I might have ended up staying there forever, just out of inertia. Having been forced out, I'm realizing it's true what they say, there is more to life. I never believed it before. And right now, I'm in the middle of something that should leave me with a lot of options." He gave her a sidelong glance, then ventured, "Too bad none of those options seem to include you."

She smiled. "Even when we were together, your future never really included me. You were always too busy wanting to be master of the universe of finance."

"Sadly, you're right. But a lot's happened since then, a lot just in the last few weeks. Once I got there, I figured out pretty quickly it wasn't what I really wanted, even though I stuck with it."

"I'm glad of that, Jonny. And you really don't know how glad I am that you're here. Besides, . . ." she hesitated and her voice broke. Jon saw there were tears in her eyes.

"Victoria, what is it? I've been doing all the talking. Tell me," he urged.

She shook her head. "Later. I promise. Right now, why don't

you go for a ride, like you used to, while I head back and do a few things to get ready for the onslaught. I remember how much you used to like riding here."

"Are you sure? I can ride another time."

"When? You're leaving tomorrow. Really, Jon, it's fine. I'll see you back at the house." And before he could object further, she turned her horse around and cantered off.

He paused, watching until she disappeared into the trees. He was thinking of what could have been between them, if only he had not let her slip away. Although she was a year younger than Jon, Victoria had graduated from Cambridge when he did, he from a post-graduate economics course, and she in modern history. In London, Jon had quickly gotten caught up in life as a fast-living de-rivative trader on the floor of the old London Stock Exchange in Threadneedle Street, while Victoria spent the next two years work-ing in Christie's graduate program, with contemporary art as her specialty. She shared a flat on the Old Brompton Road in South Kensington with several close girlfriends, spending weekends out of London, many with Jon, often at Stanford Hall. Once Jon could af-ford it, they traveled abroad, skiing in the winter and sunbathing on the continent in the summertime.

When Jon moved to New York, Victoria considered moving there with him. Instead, they visited back and forth, a few days at a time for the first few months, and then the visits dwindled. She had left Christie's to work in a gallery just off Berkeley Square, in May-fair's fashionable Mount Street. The gallery failed, however, as the art world stalled, and her mother died of cancer around the same time. The death was traumatic for the family. Lady Colarvon was an aristocratic beauty, whose resemblance to her daughter was often described as uncanny. Like many of her generation, she had an un-expectedly frugal, practical side, a direct result of the lean, post-War years in Britain. Strong, intelligent, and independent, it was she who provided the foundation for the family. The shock of her death, coming only a few months after the diagnosis, left her family floundering.

With the help of more alcohol and drugs than were good for

them, Andy and Victoria tried to escape their sadness in the fast lane of London life, while the Earl turned to gambling to distract himself from her loss. He never really recovered. Seeing what was happening, Victoria pulled herself together and began spending most of her time in the country, keeping her father company and helping sustain the property.

Jon had been absent for most of this period, a circumstance he now found himself regretting. He'd noticed that the life-sized portrait the Earl had commissioned right after he heard his wife's illness was terminal was still prominently hung on the wall of the grand staircase, and photographs in sterling frames were scattered throughout the house. Only now did he sense what a difference he might have made had he been around to see Victoria through that unhappy period of her life.

A year had gone by, then two; Jon heard Victoria had gotten engaged, then that it was broken. There was another engagement, also broken. After that, he'd lost track. But never of the memory of their times together.

Jon knew it would be irresponsible to involve anyone else in his current problems, especially someone he cared for, although he was feeling an almost overwhelming urge to confide his deepest thoughts to Victoria. Maybe the time would come when he would be able to, but for now, he could not allow the memories and emotions engulfing him in waves of nostalgia to dull his anger and blur his focus.

He rode for another hour, reacquainting himself with paths and places he and Victoria had explored together, a field in which they'd often picnicked, a fence where she'd taken a tumble and his heart had stopped beating until he'd seen her get up, brushing leaves off herself and laughing. Two unlikely young lovers. Now, a little older, they seemed less unlikely to him. He was starting to think less about what could have been and more about what perhaps could be.

The afternoon sun was beginning to disappear behind the trees when he finally turned back.

Chapter Eighteen

Penny left the *News/Copy* offices hungering for more details. Like all good stories, this one was beginning to develop its own momentum, one thing leading to the next.

Heading straight to the 42nd St. Library, she began sifting through archived copies of local newspapers. Her first find was in a recent *New York Post* story headlined "Pusher Perishes Under Pimpmobile." It outlined George McWilliam's drug-dealing past, his questionable character and the highly unusual way in which he had met his end, a death that, like the others, appeared accidental.

After a fruitful few hours at the library, she returned to her friends' Upper West Side apartment to make some calls. She looked over the list she'd prepared of the various relevant police departments and detectives and started with McWilliam, making her first call to the police precinct on 11th Street. The response she received was cool and disinterested; an assistant explained to her that, as the case had been officially closed, the police would have no further comment to make. Penny got the impression that it had been regarded as a low priority investigation by the NYPD. She decided to move on. She would come back to him later.

Her second call was to the Port Authority Police Department that had investigated Robert's fatal car crash. She was connected to the officer for the investigation, a detective by the name of Roland Rogers.

"I am researching a number of accidental deaths," Penny began, " . . . one of which is an automobile accident involving a man named Robert Baldwin. I'm interested in any possibly suspicious circumstances that might be related to the accident. Can you tell me, is there anything you've uncovered?"

Detective Rogers scratched the side of his neck as he tried to remember the details of the case. "We conducted a thorough investigation into all aspects of the accident and came to the conclusion that, like many other fatal automobile accidents, it was an avoidable tragedy with no one to blame except the driver involved." He might as well have been reading from an all-purpose prepared statement.

"From what I understand, the victim drove into a concrete pillar at twenty-five miles an hour inside a garage. That didn't strike you as unusual?" Penny persisted.

"These things happen. People mistake the accelerator for the brake." Rogers wasn't about to take the bait.

"What if I told you that this just might be one of a series of suspicious accidents that have several things in common?"

"I'd ask you to show me some evidence," he retorted.

"I was rather hoping that you might be able to supply me with some. Are you aware, for example, that three other accident victims connected to Mr. Baldwin through another party at the Bank of Manhattan were . . ."

"Look," Rogers interrupted, impatiently. "I'm sorry, but if you're trying to drum up some kind of elaborate conspiracy here, you're going to have to look elsewhere."

"But . . ."

Again he cut Penny off. "The case is closed. I do not have anything else to add. Goodbye."

Penny had no choice but to let it go. "Thank you for your time." Her voice trailed off as she heard the click of the receiver at the other end. For the moment, this particular avenue of exploration also appeared to be a dead end.

Downtown, Manhattan

People of all descriptions — suspects and their lawyers, relatives and friends, policemen dressed for undercover assignments — mingled in a crowded downtown New York police station, making it almost impossible to tell who was what. Two plainclothes detectives stood chatting next to a fax machine, their conversation turning toward the death of Georgie McWilliam.

"I thought we'd closed that one. Anyway, who gives a shit if some low-life scumbag is found dragged to death under his own car," the first detective, Francis Sciapelli, said dismissively.

His companion, Detective Louis Gennaro, nodded. "We had, but then the coroner's report turned up some long, black strands of hair stuffed down this guy McWilliam's throat."

"Maybe he was into oral sex. Can't we just forget about it? Chances are it's not going to amount to anything, and I've got an "in" box I can't see over."

Detective Gennaro pulled a fax off the machine. "But you may like this. The night of this asshole's death, there were a bunch of female impersonators competing in some contest at his club. A couple of them were wearing long black wigs."

"So? Look, forget about it." Detective Sciapelli tossed the fax on his desk. "I've got a million things to do that are far more important than following some vague lead relating to a scumbag that, in my opinion, is better off dead anyway."

Detective Gennaro shrugged. "Fair enough, you're the boss. But I'm going to keep that report on file anyway. Just in case."

Upper West Side, Manhattan

Penny's next telephone call was to Newport, Rhode Island, to the police officer, one Peter Thompson, who had headed the investigation into Ernest Johnston's yachting death. The press accounts had dwelt far more on Johnston's background and accomplishments than on the circumstances of his untimely death. His death was glossed over, almost as though it had been somehow unseemly. She considered making the trip up there. In person, she was less likely to encounter the kind of treatment she had just received from Detective Rogers. But, aware of her limited time, she picked up the phone and dialed instead, this time prepared to be more assertive. The operator quickly put her through.

"This is Detective Thompson, how can I help you?"

"Thank you for taking my call, Detective," Penny began politely, surprised and encouraged by the speed with which she had been connected to him. "I am a reporter based in London researching the death of a Mr. Ernest Johnston, and I was wondering if you can add any details to the information published in the press regarding his death and the accident in general."

"Well, given who he was, his death attracted considerable attention from the press. I assume you've read the stories."

The detective seemed far more pleasant and relaxed than Detective Rogers. No wonder, thought Penny, since the level of crime in Newport must be only a fraction of what they had to deal with in downtown New York City. "Yes, I have, but I was hoping you could tell me more," she replied.

"There's little I can add that has not already been documented," he continued. "This is a boating community so we are familiar with the dangers of water sports and the wide variety of accidents stemming from them. No two accidents are identical; each has a unique quality, unlike automobile accidents. Even so, this was kind of a freak thing. But we conducted a thorough investigation into the circumstances surrounding the accident and found nothing suspicious."

Having found someone who seemed willing to talk, Penny was reluctant to push things too far for now. She'd keep him primed for when she might need him to fill in more specific details. "Then I have just one question. Could you please tell me where I might be able to locate the captain of the boat?"

"I don't have any specific knowledge as to where he is right now, but the last time I spoke with him he was in Sag Harbor on Long Island, where the boat is permanently moored. Your best bet would be to try and track him down there."

Great, thought Penny. "Thank you very much for your help."

"If we can be of any further assistance, don't hesitate to give us a call." He seemed to mean it.

"Thanks again," she replied. "I really appreciate it."

She put down the receiver. She had the names of two more police officers, both in the city, which meant she could meet with them in person. She again tried to reach the detective responsible for the investigation into the death of Georgie McWilliam. He was unavailable, but Penny arranged a meeting on Monday morning at his downtown precinct. As for the officer in charge of David's investigation, she had so far been unable to contact him, but she had been promised a return call.

Gloucestershire, England

The heavy brocade drapes, rumored to have been stolen from Marie Antoinette's bedchamber during the French Revolution, were drawn. It was early evening. Lady Victoria Cheyne, seated at her dressing table in a low-backed black Valentino cocktail dress, noticed that even the luxuriant thickness of the material did not muffle the grating crunch of tires on gravel, as a succession of high-end vehicles pulled up in front of the house. She put the final touches on her subtly applied makeup, adding a smudge of rouge to set off her hazel eyes. Her hair was loosely pinned up, tendrils artfully arranged at the nape of her neck. She was very aware that her role as hostess at these paying shooting weekends was, if not pivotal, at least a valued bonus to the guests, and she was always careful to dress for the part. She viewed her participation as part of the job she'd had to do since her mother died. But tonight, with Jon as a member of her audience, she was preparing herself with more care than usual.

After trying it out against her dress, she fastened an uncharacteristically showy diamond pendant around her neck. It was too big to be real, but simple enough to keep her affluent guests guessing. Slipping into a pair of black Jimmy Choo stilettos, she gave herself one last appraising look, then, meeting with her own approval, she headed out to hostess the pre-prandial drinks and hors d'oeuvres being served in the palatial drawing room.

Classical music played unobtrusively in the background, barely loud enough to distinguish one piece from another, lending more ambience than substance. As was usual on these occasions, the men were dressed impeccably, the wives and girlfriends formally. Jon was lounging in front of the fireplace in his well-worn Thierry Mugler dinner jacket, marking time until Boris Posarnov made his appearance. He'd surveyed the room and eavesdropped on any man who looked remotely Russian and was disappointed to conclude that no one present filled the bill. He was impatient to confront the man, to see, in this setting where he had to be on good behavior, how much information he could to pick up or extract from him. If not tonight, then perhaps tomorrow during the shoot. Preoccupied as he was, however, he was drawn to his feet when Victoria appeared at the top of the long, curved staircase. She looked regally beautiful as she gracefully descended. Everything about her was simple, yet effortlessly elegant. He felt slightly overwhelmed.

He approached her and took her hand in his, gently kissing her soft cheek in greeting. He wondered if she felt the rough calluses he'd built up during his days on the *Southern Star*, and if they offended or attracted her, or if she even noticed. Whatever hope he'd had of monopolizing her was not to be. She gave him a smile but quickly left him to make the rounds of the other guests, while he tried not to follow her every move with his eyes. Later on, when dinner was announced, he moved to her side to offer her his arm. To his surprise, Victoria ignored it. Instead, she walked alone into the dining room, her eyes taking in every detail, the perfect hostess.

His next disappointment awaited him in the dining room. The grand teak and mahogany banquet table, which spanned three chandeliers, was set for twenty-nine. Jon had expected to be seated at least within chatting distance of Victoria, but he found himself not only sitting at the opposite end of the table from her, but on the same side, making even eye contact a virtual impossibility. Worse still, with fewer women present than men, he found himself placed between a terminally dull internet multi-millionaire from Weston-birt and a local polo player who immediately confided, in a lisp, that he had three broken teeth, having taken a mallet full-force in the mouth at the Beaufort on the previous weekend. Jon sat down with a sigh. There was still no sign of anyone who could be Posarnov, and it was beginning to look like a long evening.

As Victoria engaged the favored regulars seated near her in small talk, it was Andy who dominated the general conversation at the table, standing up to make toast after toast. It did not take long before he turned his attention to Jon. His jocularity was fueled by the extended cocktail hour he'd just presided over.

"Jon," he started, glass on high. "I was thinking about your sleeping arrangement and it occurred to me that perhaps you might be more comfortable downstairs in the dungeon. If you could wrap some chains around you, you might feel a little more at home."

Jon stood up and raised his glass. Heads turned his way, as the polo player slurped noisily through a straw. "Your offer is much appreciated, but I must regretfully decline. I fear any proximity to chains would bring back too many fond memories of my beloved homeland. But I will say that when I arrived this morning, I was hoping that I might be the recipient of just two small favors," he paused for effect, "namely, that I would be provided with a bed and that you would not be in it." Jon held up his hand, as if to silence the ripple of laughter his remark had generated. "It's just that now you are no longer Head Boy in the College, I don't feel as though I should have to kiss and cuddle with you at night any more."

Andy was ready. "Then why in God's name do you think you were invited here this evening? Surely not because of your winning personality. Don't be stupid, man, come here immediately and give me a big one, right on the lips." Andy grinned happily. This school-boy badinage was all part of the entertainment package, and the guests were clearly enjoying their exchange.

"Not right now, Andy, I'm afraid I have a terrible headache."

Victoria broke into the laughter, exclaiming in mock disapproval, "Andy, you are appalling."

"Perhaps. But remember, dear sister, before you condemn me, that I am made of the very same stuff that you are, aren't I, Daddy?" It was rare that these dinners included the whole family, but the Glorious Twelfth dinner was an exception, and the Earl was ensconced at the head of the table.

"Damn right," the Earl nodded. "I'm afraid the two of you share the same genes, my dear, genes that date back to the Roman Conquest, of which you should be very proud."

Jon felt it was time for him to throw in a compliment or two. "Quite. And I'm told, Your Grace, that you and Andy have established one of the great shoots of Europe and that you attract the finest shots from all around the world." He surveyed the guests, including them in his compliment. "You must be very proud of what you have accomplished." The table acknowledged the compliment by raising their glasses to Jon, accompanied by hearty cries of "hear, hear!"

The earl was flattered. "Very nice of you to say so, Jonny. But what choice did we have? After all, we have to keep my family and myself in the lifestyle to which we have become so thoroughly accustomed." His comment elicited polite, if slightly subdued, laughter.

"Quite right, and we're an expensive lot to maintain," Andy agreed. "Now, how about a round of jokes, starting with Jonny?"

It was a long-established rule at such gatherings that each guest must come armed with a set of interesting or amusing anecdotes or jokes for moments such as these. Rudeness, drunkenness, arrogance, ostentation — all were tolerated, but dullness was not. The guest's obligation was to contribute to the entertainment of the host and the other guests, or be damned. Damnation took the form of never being invited back. The only exceptions to this universally understood rule were for those who socially outranked the host or hostess. Those guests could be as dull as they wished, and often seemed to make a point of being so, in Jon's experience.

"If I must," Jon began. "Here goes . . . A zebra walks onto a farm. It goes up to a cow and asks what it does on the farm. The cow answers that she provides the farm with all its milk and dairy products. The zebra then goes up to a chicken. "And what do you do on the farm?" the zebra asks. The chicken answers that she provides the farm with all its eggs. Next, the zebra walks over to a sheep and asks what it does. The sheep replies that it provides the farm with all its wool. Finally, the zebra walks up to a prancing stallion and asks it what it does on the farm. The stallion stands proudly and with purpose in front of the zebra. He looks left, then right, leans toward the zebra and whispers, "Well, good-looking, if you take off those silly pajamas, I'd be delighted to show you."

Amid the laughter that followed, Jon excused himself under the pretext of getting some fresh air. He walked out of the main entrance into the tranquil, clear night air. With Posarnov not yet on the scene, his thoughts throughout the evening had so far centered on Victoria. Fleetingly, he allowed himself to hope that his exit from the party might encourage her to follow him, knowing it was unlikely, given how she'd been ignoring him in favor of playing hostess.

As he gazed down the long driveway, a set of headlights came into view around the curve from the main gates, starkly illuminating the lawns on either side of its path. The night was dark and the headlights so bright that it was not until the car was almost upon him that Jon recognized it as a black Bentley Mulliner. Its only occupant, the driver, pulled up to the portico and strode toward the house. As he passed Jon, he nodded with a grunt, barely glancing his way. Jon, however, knew immediately who he was and smiled to himself. Boris Posarnov had finally arrived at Stanford Hall. Jon spent a few moments considering the implications of his presence, and then walked slowly back to rejoin the party.

The revelers had moved from the dining room back to the drawing room, and Andy was entertaining them with a selection of games in which the main activity seemed to consist of drinking to excess. The music, no longer classical, had been turned up and it blended with sporadic bursts of raucous laughter, echoing through the ancient, cavernous halls. Posarnov had already seated himself next to Victoria on a sofa upholstered in striped satin. He was whispering in her ear. Her expression was one of pained forbearance. Her eyes widened as Jon entered the room, and to his surprise, she abruptly stood up and headed straight toward him, leaving Posarnov in mid-sentence.

"Where have you been?" she asked, as if they had been in close contact all evening. "Please dance with me."

As Jon stood next to Victoria, he felt Posarnov watching him. Had he been recognized? Not wanting to draw any unnecessary attention to himself, he would have preferred to blend into the background just then.

"No one's dancing," he pointed out. "Let's just sit down."

"Nonsense," Victoria protested. "I feel like dancing, and dancing with you. Come on." She pulled at his arm.

She was not to be put off. His refusal was, in fact, attracting notice since wherever Victoria was, she became the center of attention. So without further argument, he folded her into his arms and began to dance with her.

As they moved around the periphery of the room, Jon could feel Posarnov's eyes burning into him. Still anxious about being recognized, he was slow to notice that Victoria was caressing his back. He felt her warm breath on his neck. When she let go of his hand to put both arms up around his neck, Jon saw Posarnov's eyes narrow to slits, as if trying to contain a fury scalding his insides. Only then did Jon realize he was not the object of Posarnov's scrutiny, Victoria was. Posarnov was in a jealous rage.

With the realization came not only relief but also an awareness of an unexpected new weapon in his armory. And what good was a weapon if you did not use it? Especially when, as in this case, the weapon was so appealing in and of itself. Jon pulled Victoria more tightly to him, stroking her hair with an intimacy intended to drive his envious rival into a frenzy.

A well-lubricated Andy had started mischievously encouraging the pair in their romantic pas de deux. As they continued dancing, all eyes now upon them, he moved back to the dining room and recklessly cleared everything still left on the table onto the floor. Wine glasses, dessert plates and an assortment of cutlery clattered all over its mosaic surface. He gestured for them to crank up their act to another level. Hesitant at first, Jon need not have been. Victoria stepped lightly onto a chair, then seductively pulled him with her onto the table. The others gathered round, clapping and calling out encouragement as Jon and Victoria improvised dramatic maneuvers and routines for their audience. To the guests, it was just Andy coming up with yet another form of entertainment to keep them all amused, another country party in full swing. To Posarnov, however, it was an affront, one that he was clearly having a difficult time stomaching.

Finally, the song ended. Posarnov leapt to his feet, clapping loudly. "Bravo," he cried, with forced enthusiasm. "Bravo." And he moved around the table to assist Victoria down. She did not accept his outstretched hand, instead looking to Jon for support. Posarnov, too, turned his attention toward Jon. "Have a drink with me." It was not a question. He turned to a waiter. "Bring us two Cristals," he barked.

"I'm afraid I must decline," Jon said, believing that by now he'd drunk too much to deal effectively with Posarnov.

"A nightcap, then," Posarnov urged.

Jon leaned toward him. Posarnov's nose had been broken and reset more than once and Jon could see the cruelty in the man's iron-gray eyes. "Not possible. But I look forward to seeing you tomorrow. Perhaps we could meet before the shoot gets underway."

Not anxious to lose face in front of Victoria, Posarnov acceded to Jon. "Fine. Tomorrow, then."

Jon turned away to seek out the Earl. "Your Grace, thank you for an excellent evening. I bid you goodnight."

"Goodnight, dear boy," the Earl responded affectionately. Others nearby also said their goodnights, as did Andy. Jon nodded to Posarnov and finally turned to Victoria.

"Thank you for the dance, my Lady, and for a wonderful evening."

Victoria nodded. "It's getting late; I think I will follow your example. Walk me upstairs?"

Under the Russian's gaze, Jon accepted. "It would be my pleasure." And he offered his arm to her. This time she took it, gratefully. As they turned to leave the dining room, Posarnov called out to Jon. "Wait. We haven't been introduced."

Jon turned. "I'm sorry." He looked at Victoria. "It will have to wait until morning. I have to get my hostess to bed." He shot Posarnov an intentionally wicked grin before leaving the room. Posarnov could only remain where he was, fuming.

Jon and Victoria mounted the stairs together in silence. Their show was over, but Jon was still confused by Victoria's changeable behavior toward him. He longed to kiss her, but decided he would let her take the lead. She didn't keep him in suspense for long. At the top of the landing, she reached for his hand and led him down the hall to her bedroom. "Come," she whispered. "We need to spend some time together."

Jon needed no further encouragement. He shut the door behind them and swept her into his arms with all the passion he'd been denying for so long. Breathing in her Chanel Number 5 scent, he felt his heart beat and his stomach churn just as it had when he was a teenager first experiencing sexual arousal. Everything seemed new, and yet familiar. Their clothing virtually fell off. No fuss, no effort, and no awkwardness. Victoria was the epitome of femininity in her skin-colored underwear, her figure slender, but with a curvaceousness inspiring such an intense level of attraction within Jon that he felt almost dizzy.

"Jon, please make love to me," she whispered into his ear. With that, he laid her across the bed. She arched her back and instinctively lifted her hips, inviting him to remove her underwear, which he needed no encouragement to do. As he admired her thick but neat mound of pubic hair, she leaned forward to pull down his underpants, now stretched to the breaking point by his already firm erection.

Their kiss was long and intimate as they lay naked together across her bed. Before either had even considered what might be done next, he found himself slipping inside her. They sighed in unison as he penetrated her, slid deep inside her. His strokes were slow and considered, and there were moments when he would pause just to savor the fullness of her completely enclosing every inch of him. The two flowed together in unison, each sensing the other's next move before it was made. There seemed no need for elaborate sexual positioning, no need for either oral stimulation or anal titillation. It was enough that they were in each other's arms.

Victoria's gasps became shorter and louder, her expression more concentrated as she approached orgasm. Jon, too, felt he was nearing his moment of sexual release. After one final flurry of thrusting, he came long and hard inside her, and they both reached intense and fulfilling climaxes simultaneously. They collapsed, entwined in a full embrace, Jon's now flaccid penis still held tightly inside her by her warm, moist vaginal lips. Neither said anything, as nothing needed to be said. This was love, Jon thought, love with the woman he was meant to be with. He vowed at that moment he would not let her go again.

Chapter Nineteen

Gloucestershire, England

Posarnov knocked on Victoria's door twice during the night. The first time, they did not stop their lovemaking, barely taking notice despite his persistent pounding on the heavy oak door. The second time, they were curled up together, spoon-style, basking in each other's warmth after alternately making love and talking for hour upon hour.

"I had no choice," she said quietly, into the silence after Posarnov finally gave up. So few words had rarely conveyed so much to Jon. He knew enough about the man to guess he had frightened and coerced Victoria to a point where she had indeed been unable to resist his advances.

"I understand," he reassured her calmly. "You don't need to talk about it if you don't want to."

"Oh, but I do want to." She turned him around to face her. "You know, Daddy turned into a real gambler. He's stopped now, but he got into serious trouble a while back. He was on the verge of bankruptcy after my grandfather died. The inheritance taxes pushed him over the edge, and when he first met Boris at Ascot, Boris agreed to help Daddy out with a loan to keep the house going and even upgrade it to make the hunting weekends more profitable."

"So that's when the shoots became more business than sport?" asked Jon.

"Yes. But Daddy's no businessman. Boris got him to sign over the deed to the house as collateral on the loans. It did keep the property together, and the business has been doing brilliantly and growing every year. But it seems that the way it's set up, the better it does, the more Daddy ends up owing."

"And Boris had been using the threat of taking away your family's property as a means of getting to you?"

She nodded, avoiding his eyes. "He threatens to foreclose the minute I don't do everything he says, and he's vile, Jonny, just vile. I can't bear for him to touch me ever again and now he knows it. I couldn't help rubbing his nose in it tonight, so it'll be even worse . . ." She shuddered, hugging herself. "But it would absolutely kill Daddy — I mean, literally kill him, his heart would give out — if his gambling debts caused us to lose the house," she whispered. "He already blames himself so much." And she began to cry. "I don't know . . . I'm so afraid of what he'll do to us."

"It's alright," soothed Jon, holding her to his chest. "Everything's going to be alright." He kept holding her until she stopped crying and dropped off to sleep.

Jon slept fitfully and rose before dawn. He left Victoria sleeping and slipped quietly down to his own room, dressing in his riding gear. No one stirred in the house as he went down the stairs and across the dew-laden grass to the deserted stables. He walked past stall after stall until he found the bay gelding he'd ridden the previous day. Saddling up, he mounted and trotted past the riding ring set with its course of jumps, heading away from the buildings. He was hoping his familiarity with Stanford Hall's grounds would compensate for the variables he wouldn't be able to control during the day's shoot.

The pheasant shoot was divided into five drives, or locations, at which the parties would gather in sequence to shoot the birds.

Each participant, or 'gun', would have his own prearranged place to stand. Once the position of each gun was established on the first drive, his position would move two positions forward at every subsequent drive. Jon would have to know Posarnov's position on the first drive in order to predict where he would be standing on the third, but he couldn't determine that until the shoot actually began, later in the morning, leaving him very little time to prepare.

Arriving at the third drive, Jon dismounted, tied his horse to a tree, and walked through the woods, looking for appropriate cover. This drive was best suited to his purposes, in that it was heavily wooded on one side and open on the other. The beaters would be on the open side, scaring the birds into flight and toward the guns. The guns would be positioned with their backs to the edge of the woods, which was an important factor in Jon's selection process. He paced the length and breadth of all five drives, realizing as he did so how much luck he would need for his plan to succeed. He had still not completely determined his course of action. But now, at least, he had done all he could to prepare for the most extreme scenario.

He untied, mounted, and cantered his horse back, handing him over to a stable boy. He returned to his room just after seven-thirty, where he changed into slacks and a sport coat before packing his suitcase. Only then did he return to Victoria's room. She was dressed and ready to go down for breakfast. He explained to her that business had called him back to London early and he wouldn't be able to stay for the shoot after all. She protested, but since this was the Jon she'd always known, putting work before her or anything else in his life, she soon gave in and accompanied him downstairs to his car to say goodbye, her arm curled around his. The soft, gray light accentuated her pallor and fragility. They stopped and clung together silently in the morning dampness. Finally Jon spoke, choosing his words carefully. He'd faced some hard truths before falling asleep.

"I've loved you for a long time, Victoria, and I love you now. But I can't be sure that you wouldn't be better off without me. In fact, I'm quite sure you would be."

"Why don't you let me decide that, Jonny?" Victoria asked. "We're no longer twenty-one." Sadness crept into her voice. "I've learned to look after myself, if not all that well." She paused. There seemed little to add. "It appears it's goodbye for now." She paused again, and for a moment, they stood together in silence. Then she burst out, "Why is it, Jonny, that what we do best is saying good-bye?" As she kissed him hard on the lips, tears spilled onto her cheeks.

He wiped them away. Her question was rhetorical and they both knew there was no answer to it.

As he held Victoria in one last embrace, over her shoulder Jon's eye was drawn to the main entrance of the house as Boris Posarnov strode out and headed straight for them. He looked tired and haggard but seemed to be trying to put up a good front.

"You're leaving us already? Before the shoot?" he asked, nodding toward Jon's car. "I thought we were going to get together this morning."

"I'm afraid something has come up, but I was planning to catch up with you before I left," Jon replied.

"Such a pity. Victoria seems to hold you in such high regard, and I was looking forward to spending some time with you during the shoot. You never know, perhaps there's some business we could do together."

Jon turned to Victoria and pushed her gently toward the house. "I'll see you when I can, sweetheart," he murmured.

As she reluctantly left, he turned back to confront Posarnov, waiting until she was out of earshot to speak. "We've already done business together, don't you remember?"

Posarnov frowned. "I think you must be mistaken, I . . ."

"You don't remember?" Jon interrupted. "Well, maybe I can prompt your memory. I helped turn thirty-five million dollars of your dirty drug money into squeaky clean trading revenue, and in return, you had my friend and my brother murdered."

"You . . .?" Posarnov exclaimed. "But what are you doing here in England?"

"Not much, really. I just came to take every penny of cash you have in your margin account, that's all."

Posarnov laughed uneasily. "What are you talking about? My money is in New York and it is safe."

Jon let it go. "I want the name of the man who killed my brother."

"I am sure, Mr. Phillips, that you want many things you cannot have." Posarnov had already regained his confidence.

Jon remained calm. "This is your last chance to tell me."

Posarnov shrugged. "Is that so? Well, you might want to watch your own back, Mr. Phillips. You are bolder than I imagined, but that will not save you. Goodbye. We shall not see each other again." Dismissively, he walked away from Jon to retrieve his gun from his car, in anticipation of the day's pursuit.

Jon was determined to have the last word. "You're right, we won't. But if I have my way, you'll burn in Hell." And with that, Posarnov stopped and turned toward Jon. The two men stood momentarily frozen in place, their eyes fixed on each other. It was now kill or be killed.

Posarnov's grip tightened on his shotgun before he broke the uncomfortable silence. "You can't threaten me. No one can threaten me. You will regret it."

Jon shrugged, then stepped into his car without taking his eyes away from his adversary's cold stare. He turned the key and the powerful Aston engine roared into life. As he drove off, he continued to watch the Russian standing defiantly on the circular driveway until he was gone from his rear view mirror.

Posarnov turned and looked back toward the house in time to glimpse Victoria moving away from the window where she too had been watching Jon's departure. His anger settled into a cold, quiet fury. She would pay for last night's humiliations, oh, how she would pay.

Jon drove quickly to Cirencester, a town about half an hour away from Stanford Hall. He now knew what had to be done. He parked in a large indoor parking structure, removed from the Aston's trunk a pair of binoculars and a long, thin case wrapped carefully in a field umbrella, and walked toward the exit. Making his way to a local car rental agency, he rented a small car and headed back toward Stanford Hall.

Gloucestershire, England

By nine-thirty in the morning, the guns had gathered in front of the house for the day's shoot around the estate's several Land Rovers. All the men were dressed appropriately in plus fours and a jacket and tie, and each carried his gun in a cocked or open position. Most of them were accompanied by a gun dog, and a noisy pack of English Pointers, Labradors, American and French Brittany Spaniels, and Vizslas ran about barking in anticipation. As hosts, both the Earl and Andy circulated among their guests, making sure each had what he needed. Andy noticed one individual in particular who looked like he could do with a dose of good cheer, and approached him.

"Boris, it's always a pleasure to have you at Stanford Hall," he lied. "I hope that today's shoot will be as successful as your previous visits. You seem to have developed a very keen eye over the years."

"Yes, indeed, Lord Colarvon, what was a casual sporting interest has developed into a passion bordering on obsession. And this day is always one of the highlights of the season. The very fact that this is where I choose to be attests to the fact that Stanford Hall is the finest shoot in Europe, and I say that as a sportsman, rather than an investor."

"Yes . . . quite," said Andy, hurriedly. He did not enjoy being reminded, in public or in private, of Posarnov's vested interest in his inheritance.

"I also do some shooting in South America," Posarnov continued. "Have you ever shot game there?"

"I don't believe I have, but I would like to." This was not the only time this conversation had been had, but Andy answered as though the prospect had never occurred to him.

"At my property in Argentina, it takes me forty minutes to

drive from the front gate to the main residence," Boris announced, as if for the first time.

"Yes, I once had a car like that also, and a damn nuisance it was," Andy retorted with a smile. Several guests laughed, but Posarnov remained unamused, not fully understanding the joke but sensing it had been at his expense. Andy was quick to note his discomfort and dispel it. "That is a most kind invitation, and if I travel to Argentina, I will hold you to it." To Andy's relief, Posarnov nodded, placated.

The men were called to the Land Rovers; they climbed in and were seen off by Andy, his father joining the shooting party.

Jon, perched high on an overlooking hill, watched the vehicles approach the first drive. He had positioned himself carefully so as not to be seen by either the beaters, who had arrived earlier to position themselves for scaring the pheasants into flight, or the guns, who were now pulling to a stop. He focused his binoculars on Posarnov as he stepped down from his Land Rover and followed his movements closely until he was able to determine what Posarnov's shooting position would be for the rest of the day. Having established that, Jon lowered his binoculars and moved quietly away.

Meatpacking District, Manhattan

The first things Penny was aware of as she began to stir were the casually but artfully draped sections of soft white chiffon enclosing the four-poster king bed. The early light streamed through large, arched industrial windows at the far end of the room, creating moving patterns on the bedspread. The hardwood floor was broken up only by several painted steel columns and the occasional piece of furniture. Penny climbed quietly out of bed so as not to disturb her sleeping companion, who was only partially covered by the bed linen. But as Penny crept over to where her clothes lay scattered around an original Knoll recliner, Fiona opened her eyes. She smiled languorously at Penny and stretched out into the newly vacated, still warm area of her bed with a contented sigh.

"Hello, there."

"Hello, good morning," Penny ventured.

"Have a safe trip to Long Island. And good luck with the story. Call me when you get back into town and we'll get together," Fiona yawned.

"Sorry to wake you. I was hoping not to disturb you," Penny was still whispering.

"I'm glad you did."

"I'll call you this afternoon. Thanks for a great evening." Penny meant it. Really meant it.

"My pleasure. Now come here and kiss me goodbye." Penny happily did as Fiona suggested. Fiona wrinkled her nose and turned over, snuggling back into the sheets with a smile.

Long Island Expressway, New York

The drive from New York City to Sag Harbor took just over three hours in the rented car. Penny had left early enough to avoid the logjam of escapees to the relative peace of the Hamptons. She welcomed the enforced downtime in the car. The directions were easy to follow, so she allowed her thoughts to dwell on the night before, reliving every nuance of her time with Fiona.

They'd met as scheduled at Soho House. Fiona had the martini of the moment, one infused with fresh passion fruit, waiting for her. After some conversation, many martinis, and a certain amount of unmistakable, accidental touching, Fiona had suggested that instead of going on to meet her friends, they order in at her loft. After only a moment's hesitation, Penny agreed.

As Fiona led Penny to her Meatpacking District apartment, Penny's heart was racing. She didn't know how to react or where to turn, so she decided to simply follow Fiona's lead. The loft was effectively one very large room, an enormous space without so much as a single internal wall. As Fiona moved toward the kitchen area to mix another couple of drinks, Penny wandered over to the CD player and selected some music, then stood in the living area, awaiting her cue.

Fiona approached Penny and placed two martinis on the sideboard next to the CD player. She moved to within inches of her guest. Penny could feel the warmth of her breath. Fiona embraced her. Her kiss was leisurely, intimate. It took no effort on Penny's part to reciprocate. Fiona touched Penny's erect nipple, brushing past it rather than rubbing it, as men always did. Penny felt herself becoming moist in anticipation of what she was fantasizing.

Fiona led her to the king-size bed and gently pushed her down on it. Penny's short dress rode up high, revealing the pale blue Victoria's Secret G-string she had worn especially for the occasion. Removing her blouse in one swift motion, Fiona joined Penny on the bed. They embraced, kissing passionately, and Penny opened her legs in invitation to Fiona. Fiona slid her hand under Penny's underwear, stroking her thick pubic hair rhythmically while varying the pressure. Penny had been fingered hundreds of times, but this time felt different. There was sureness in Fiona's touch. She knew exactly what buttons to push, and how best to push them.

As they slowly removed each other's clothing, Penny's inhibitions began to disappear. Fiona's breasts were small but nicely rounded, her body sleek and buff. Penny tentatively began to suck her large, dark nipples, but Fiona pushed her back down onto the bed. As she moved toward Penny's crotch, Penny again opened her legs, inviting Fiona to go down on her. Fiona licked and stroked, and Penny found it impossible to differentiate between her tongue and fingers. After a while, Fiona lifted her head and invited Penny to do the same to her. Moving into position, Penny eagerly buried her head in Fiona's neatly shaved Brazilian-cut pussy. She was stunned at the sweetness of her juices, lapping up every last drop. Fiona moaned loudly, as Penny used her tongue and fingers on Fiona's slick wetness. Fiona's moans excited Penny even more and when Fiona climaxed, lurching back and forth held down only by Penny's head firmly wedged between her legs, nothing could possibly have distracted Penny, such was the overwhelming intensity of her sexual engagement.

The sex lasted for what felt like hours to Penny. The intensity of her orgasm, when it finally came, was staggering both in its depth and duration, sending electrifying ripples throughout her whole body. This time she felt no need to run away. She could not remember falling asleep in Fiona's arms but when she awoke, she felt no regret or embarrassment. Everything about Fiona fascinated and attracted her. It just seemed right.

Penny parked in town and found a coffee shop that wasn't already packed with tourists. A hangover was kicking in, so she ordered strong coffee, tomato juice, and dry toast, and made an effort to collect her thoughts. She must not allow this amazing new experience to get her off track.

Later, walking toward the marina, she found the *Southern Star* with remarkable ease for someone with virtually no nautical experience. Even from the far end of the port, where she was berthed in an area reserved exclusively for the larger boats, the ketch was an imposing sight. Penny walked up to it, saw that the deck was deserted, and called out to attract the attention of anyone who might be below. Receiving no reply, she looked around, then reached out for the nearest mooring rope. She had no idea what a formidable task it was to board a vessel as large as this without a gangplank. Carefully placing one foot firmly near the edge of the dock, she gripped the rope and stepped out toward the boat with her other leg. But as her foot made contact with the smooth hull, the boat responded by drifting further away, causing her to lose her balance as her legs locked in an ever-widening split between the dock and the retreating ship. She was about to fall into the water when a pair of strong hands grasped her around the waist and lifted her back to the safety of the dock. Penny turned around to thank her savior and was confronted by the stern, if kindly, face of Captain Davies.

"Can I help you, miss?"

"I was, uh, trying to locate the captain. I couldn't see anyone on the boat."

"So you thought you'd just go ahead and climb on up?" He was half-amused, half-annoyed by her effrontery.

"Well, I . . ." Penny blushed, embarrassed. "I just wanted to see if anybody was on board."

"Well, that was no way to do it. I can tell by the way you're dressed that you're no sailor. If I hadn't come along, you'd be in the drink. Why are you looking for him, anyway?"

"I need to ask him a few questions, that's all. Would you have any idea where I could find him?"

"Maybe," Davies responded. "Who's looking?"

"I'm a reporter from London working on a story that has to do with the accidental death of the boat's owner."

"He's not the owner any more," the Captain pointed out, dryly.

Not to be diverted, Penny pressed on. "The Newport police suggested that I might be able to track him down here in Sag Harbor. Do you have any idea at all where I could find him?"

"Sort of."

"What do you mean, 'sort of'?"

"You're speaking to him. I suppose it won't do any harm to talk to you." Captain Davies looked her up and down. "Are you sure you're a journalist?"

"Yes, why?"

"You look too pretty for a journalist."

Penny blushed at the compliment, however sexist. "Well, I appreciate your time."

"Time is something I have plenty of at the moment. So, how can I help you?"

"I wanted to hear your version of events."

"Well, it all happened very quickly, but the details are fairly straightforward. The owner slipped from the crow's nest and became tangled in some ropes while assisting a member of the crew. The crewman tried to save him, but fell into the water and was lost at sea. It was a tragic and unnecessary accident." Unconsciously, he looked up at the mast, to the place where Johnston had perished.

Penny followed his gaze. "Would you say there was anything at all suspicious about the accident?"

"Suspicious?" He seemed taken aback by the question. "I've never thought of the accident in those terms. If you're looking for someone to blame, you don't have to look very far. As captain of the boat, I was responsible for everything that happened on board, including both deaths, and don't think that doesn't haunt me."

"I understand how you feel. That isn't what I meant. But why did Mr. Johnston go up there in the first place?"

"One of the ropes securing the mainsail sheared, and the crewman up top needed another. Mr. Johnston volunteered. He had a habit of showing off like that, and I stupidly let him go. The next minute, he was swinging from a rope."

"Why didn't the crewman climb down and get the rope himself?"

"You've never seen a sail that's come loose from its rigging. It can capsize the boat if you let it get out of control. It wasn't his fault. Rick was a perfectly competent crewman."

"What will you do now? Will you be staying on as captain?"

"Sadly, no. I'll miss the old girl, but she's going to be sold off."

"Can you tell me anything about the crewman, Rick? The news accounts didn't say much."

"I didn't know him for very long. He was Australian, kind of a rolling stone, seemed like . . ."

Penny's heart skipped as she interrupted him. "Australian? Could you describe him for me, please?"

"Tall, about six two, dark hair, and a beard."

Penny continued for him "Blue eyes, athletic, well-educated, good company, that sort of thing?"

"Is there something I should know?"

"No, no," Penny replied. "It's just routine research, that's all."

"Look," he said firmly. "I hardly see how these questions are relevant to Mr. Johnston's tragic accident. Now if you don't mind, I really must get going."

"Yes, of course. I'm sorry," said Penny. Naturally, the captain would want to put this incident behind him, before he became too identified with misfortune in the superstitious sailing community.

"You've been very kind to answer my questions. Just one last thing. Would it be possible for me to take a look at the sheared rope? You know, the one which caused Mr. Johnston to go up there in the first place?"

The captain looked perplexed. "Not possible," he said firmly. "We don't have it on the boat any longer."

"Well, thanks again, you've been most helpful." Penny smiled. And she turned as if to walk away but instead, affecting an air of casual forgetfulness, she removed something from her handbag. "I nearly forgot," she said, holding out a photograph. "Could you confirm that the man in this picture is Rick Mears?"

It was a photo of Jon. Captain Davies looked at it for some time. He was obviously on guard now. "I couldn't be sure," he finally replied. "It's been a while and this man has no beard and very short hair. I couldn't say with any degree of accuracy. I'm sorry."

He handed the picture back.

"But it could be him?" Penny pushed.

"I'm sorry," said Davies firmly. "I just can't be sure."

He nodded a curt goodbye and turned away from her. The conversation was over. What was done was done and he saw no point in raising issues that were now a part of history. He strode off without a backward glance.

Penny, on the other hand, felt a rising excitement. It wasn't enough, but it was a link, and yet another remarkable coincidence. She was convinced the captain had been lying; she'd seen recognition in his eyes when she handed him the photograph. But it was frustrating that he'd decided not to play ball. Once again, Penny had found reason to believe she was on the right track, but had again failed to turn up any hard evidence. Since the police had closed their respective investigations, it was up to her, and her alone, to unmask her cunning long-lost friend and one-time tormentor, Mr. Jon Phillips.

Chapter Twenty

A sharp burst of sound and a blurred explosion of feathers signaled yet another pheasant's fall. Boris Posarnov's aim was near perfect. He had managed to hit some forty-three birds in just over two hours, picking them off in rapid succession as they were flushed from their ground cover in startled clouds of brown and white. He was tired from a night of little sleep and still angry with Victoria, but had already dismissed Jon from his thoughts. He did not see Jon Phillips as a serious threat, except perhaps where Victoria was concerned, and he had ways to deal with that, ways that he was certain would bring her around. Phillips was nothing but a pampered, overpaid city type whose life up until a few weeks ago had consisted of making a few trades, talking into the telephone, and posturing as a know-it-all. Such a man was no match for Boris Posarnov. Squinting along his barrels, he waited for the next covey of birds to come into view.

Jon had arrived at the third drive well ahead of the shooting party. He paced out the exact spot where he believed Posarnov would stand, and mentally marked a place in the adjacent woods where he could position himself to see and be unseen. Careful to break as few branches as possible so the area would offer no subsequent trace of his presence, he collected twigs from the ground to serve as camouflage. Once satisfied with the position he'd chosen, a small clearing probably used as a rough shoot for wood pigeons, he opened the long, thin case and removed the twelve-bore, single-barreled, side-loading shotgun he'd brought for the shoot. He placed a cartridge into the breach and lay facedown on the ground behind and to the side of a large tree. Then, covering himself with the branches he'd gathered, he made himself invisible to even the closest passerby, and settled in to wait.

It took about two hours for the shooting party to arrive, and by then Jon had fallen into a light sleep. Jolted back to consciousness by the sound of shouting, he was relieved to find that it had come from the beaters, who were moving over to the far side of the drive. The shooting party could be heard ambling through the forest, then adjourning briefly for elevenses, a ritual that involved a traditional drink of sloe gin, although it could also include whisky or brandy. What had started as a practical means of warming the body and stirring the senses on cold winter mornings had become a standard part of the event in all seasons.

Once the elevenses were over, the shooting party broke up, and the guns moved off toward their pre-assigned positions. As each of them took his place, Jon was disturbed to find that his calculations had not been altogether accurate. Posarnov was standing some five feet to the left of where he'd envisioned he would be. This meant that the large tree that he'd planned to use as his cover was instead blocking his sight line. He would have to move forward and risk being seen in order to get a clear shot. He lay where he was and waited. After a few minutes, the signal was given for the beaters to begin. The dozen or so gamekeepers and young men started noisily thrashing through the underbrush and beating sticks together. As the frightened birds became airborne and fluttered westward toward the waiting guns, a volley of shots was fired at them. Individual pops at first, then whole series of explosive bangs. The gunfire could be heard for miles around the surrounding countryside.

Waiting until all eyes were on the birds and the noise level was so high he couldn't possibly be heard shifting his position in the undergrowth, Jon reached his elbows forward and dragged himself around the tree, wriggling into a place where he had a direct view of Posarnov. The sturdy Russian was oblivious to any danger as he reached into his cartridge bag for ammunition and pointed his weapon skyward. His mood was lifting in direct proportion to the number of birds he was bringing down.

Jon knew he had to choose his moment with great care. Ideally, it would be when a large number of birds were airborne and flying low, so there could be at least the chance of his shot being an accidental shot from one of the shooting party's guns, however unlikely. So when, soon enough, an unusually large number of birds did appear, low on the horizon, Jon lifted his gun and took aim. Unlike the others, he would have only one shot, one opportunity. He steadied himself and his gun and controlled his breathing.

Posarnov stood straight on his mark, both barrels of his shotgun loaded and ready. All the other guns were firing, but he was too seasoned a sportsman to discharge early. Instead, he bided his time and took careful aim, waiting for his quarry to reach the optimum distance for his shot to hit its mark. His discipline paid off. With his first shot, a bird plunged to the ground with a thud.

Jon, too, had been patient, and now his target was perfectly positioned; the moment to act was upon him. He began to squeeze the trigger, but to his horror, another man — the Earl — suddenly stepped into his line of fire. Jon immediately released the trigger; he didn't want to think how close he'd just come to prematurely transforming Andy into Lord of the Manor. His relief soon turned into irritation, however, as the Earl stood motionless, blocking Jon's view. Within moments, the last of the birds would fly away and his opportunity would be gone. There was nowhere else on the shoot that offered nearly enough cover for the job to be done.

Jon was on the verge of giving up and retreating into the woods when fate once again intervened. One of the party — the inept internet mogul — was a terrible shot. Every year he paid a small fortune to show up, dressed immaculately, and carried only the most expensive equipment. Last year he had gone away with only four birds, and this year, with only two birds down so far, he was on his way to outdoing his own embarrassing record.

Having stood obediently at his master's side with almost no call for action for nearly three hours, his gun dog, an English pointer, decided to undertake an adventure on his own. With his keen sense of smell, he had picked up Jon's scent and was making a beeline toward the wood where Jon was hiding when the Earl reached down and managed to grab the dog by his collar in passing. He thereby not only prevented Jon from being discovered but also, in bending over, created a clear line of sight for him. Jon did not hesitate. He pulled the trigger. The butt of his gun slammed back into his shoulder, but he held his aim.

As the spent cartridge expelled itself from Jon's gun, Posarnov began to waver. Jon had expected him to go flying on impact. Eerily, he remained standing for a few moments. Then stubbornness lost to gravity and his legs gave way. Posarnov's body crumpled to the ground beside his own still smoking shotgun, his agitated and whining gun dog back at his side.

The hunters near Posarnov stared in horror and disbelief at the bloody mess that seconds ago was a man. The more distant guns, whose attention was still on the birds fluttering overhead, had to be waved and shouted into ceasing their firing.

Jon was discreetly but urgently searching for his gun's spent cartridge as the others in the party began to gather around Posarnov's corpse. Recovering from their initial shock, some members of the party were already looking around, trying to determine the trajectory of the bullet. Even though they could not begin to guess it had been fired by a silent assassin lying in wait in the woods, Jon knew all eyes would now be far more alert to their surroundings. He decided that leaving the cartridge was preferable to being discovered, and crawled away out of the woods, taking great care not to be seen or heard.

Once he was well beyond anyone's line of vision, Jon stood,

shook himself free of leaves and twigs, and casually walked back toward his carefully hidden rental car. He threw his gun, umbrella, and binoculars onto the front seat, slid inside, and then without so much as a backward glance, drove off.

Chapter Twenty-one

Upper East Side, Manhattan

As Penny drove back to Manhattan via the Long Island Expressway, she alternated between daydreaming about the Sunday she'd spend with Fiona and going back and forth over her partially completed jigsaw puzzle of a story, trying to fill in the missing pieces.

When she arrived at Fiona's loft, they headed to Central Park. It was a hot summer day, and the Park was part street festival and part grassy beach. Watching the seals at the zoo, Penny laughed aloud, out of sheer happiness. "I love this city!" she exclaimed. "I wonder if I could ever find a job here. I'm just so happy right now."

Fiona smiled. "I hope that has something to do with me," she flirted.

Penny giggled. "Of course it does. It has everything to do with you."

Later, over mussels and salads at Le Bilbouquet on 63rd and Madison, they talked seriously about the possibility of Penny finding work in the city. They agreed that if she could break a story implicating someone as high-profile as Jon Phillips had been, it would certainly help. Her resolve renewed by this additional reason to nail the story, Penny relaxed into enjoying the rest of the afternoon over several glasses of pinot noir and a sinful dessert. By the time they left the restaurant, it felt to Penny as if she'd just experienced a transplanted version of "Sunday lunch with all the trimmings," a veritable institution in England. Walking down Madison Avenue, she didn't think twice when Fiona took her hand. It seemed the most natural thing in the world.

Monday morning, Penny arrived at the busy, almost colorfully squalid downtown precinct where Georgie McWilliam's death had been investigated, sleepy but alert after staying up most of the night with Fiona. She noticed she was attracting an unusual amount of attention from the predominantly male staff, and wondered how they'd react if they knew why she was radiating so much sexuality. A uniformed officer escorted her through a large, crowded office area and introduced her to Detective Anthony Sciapelli, who sat with his feet up on an untidy desk, piled indiscriminately with papers and litter. He wore a cheap brown shirt with a nondescript tie and acknowledged the officer, while taking no notice of Penny.

"You know, Sergeant, I thought the day we buried that no-good, two-bit, hustling scumbag, that would be the last we heard of him. But now out of nowhere, some broad with a fancy English accent pops up wanting to know all about Georgie's final scrape with the law."

The two officers laughed. Sciapelli turned to Penny. "And what can I do for you, madam? I hope you're not going to take up too much of my time."

"Scrape?" said Penny. "I get it. Very funny. Thank you for seeing me, Detective. And don't worry, this broad wouldn't dream of wasting your valuable time. Especially since I see you have a considerable amount of paperwork on your desk that I'm sure you're anxious to get back to."

Sciapelli was disarmed; he glanced ruefully at the morass of papers before him. "Let me assure you I am a great deal more organized than this desk would suggest." He smiled at her. "About the 'broad' crack, it's something I picked up from watching too many Bob, Bing, and Frank movies."

"Think nothing of it, detective. I've seen a few of those old movies myself, on the late-night classics channel."

"Okay, okay, let's start again." Sciapelli was now grinning. "How can I be of help to you? Oh, yeah, that dead scumbag, McWilliam. Just what do you want to know?"

"At the moment, I'm not sure. That's why I'm here. Could you tell me if, in your opinion, there was anything at all suspicious about his death?"

Detective Sciapelli snorted. "Let me start by saying I've seen some unusual things in my time, but McWilliam's death takes the cake. It was the craziest thing I ever saw. Here's a hardened dealer, pimp, and general scumbag who has spent the bulk of his life outsmarting law enforcement agencies, dodging bullets from fellow criminals, and staying on top of the vice game, only to be undone by his own car." He leaned back in his reclining chair and put both hands behind his head.

"Do you know exactly how it happened? I can't quite picture it."

"There was a compartment he'd rigged under his car to hide all his contraband, kind of like a mobile safe. From what we can make out, he was trying to open it when two of his gofers decided to take the car for a ride without realizing he was underneath. It was pretty late at night. Chances are he was stoned out of his mind."

"But how did he become so firmly attached to the vehicle that he could be dragged for literally miles around the city and not come loose?"

"It seems his watch band became tangled in the locking mechanism, and in trying to get free of it, he somehow got his clothes caught up under there. So I guess you'd have to say it was his nice new Roly that killed him, along with his fancy car." He laughed.

"Does this all really stack up?" Penny thought not.

"Only just, but nobody has come up with any better explanation, including me," confessed Sciapelli.

"Was there anyone in particular who might have wanted him dead?" Penny immediately realized how stupid her question sounded and wished she could take it back.

Sure enough, Sciapelli gave her a look. "Are you sure you're an investigative journalist? This is . . . was . . . a man who stole, cheated, trafficked in drugs and prostitutes, and hustled whatever contraband he could get his filthy hands on." Penny sat silently, chastened. "With the possible exception of Osama bin Laden, it's hard to imagine a man who had more people wanting him dead. There are just too many folks with legitimate motives to even begin preparing a suspect list. Death by misadventure, let's leave it at that. Anything else?"

"Do you know who he was with at the time of his death?"

"The last time he was seen alive, he was alone in his office at the bar." He rolled his eyes. "Now there's a place that's frequented by a real classy clientele — addicts, perverts, deadbeats, and drunks. Believe me, the customers we managed to track down weren't exactly stepping forward to help us out."

"Are you aware that McWilliam went on the TV program *News/Copy* right before he died and smeared a bond trader who'd lost a lot of money? And that others with connections to the same trader have also died recently in freak accidents?"

"I can see what you're getting at, but unless you've got more than that one connection in common, proving anything would be near impossible."

Detective Sciapelli could see that Penny was unconvinced. "I'll give you an example, just so you'll maybe get my point. A guy walks into a drugstore to find a kid robbing the place; he plays the hero and ends up copping a couple of caps in the head. There are witnesses everywhere and I start putting the case together, thinking it's pretty open and shut. Then the witnesses all decide they don't want to testify, except for one, who proves to be unreliable and useless. Turns out the kid was smart enough to have worn gloves, which he got rid of, along with the gun, before we collared him. We found the gun but it was stolen. So there you are. No case, the kid gets away with it, and the dead guy's relatives are blaming us."

He stood up, to indicate their time together was drawing to a close. "Look, Ms. Jordan, by all means pursue any crazy idea you care to, but understand how difficult it is to turn some loosely linked circumstances into a case. If you come up with any hard evidence, then let us have it, but until then, as far as we're concerned, the case is closed."

"Thanks for your honesty," Penny sighed. "I'll do that. But before I go, can you tell me anything at all that wasn't in the press accounts?"

"No . . . Well, maybe." Seeing how disappointed she was, he didn't want to let her go away completely empty-handed. "There were some hairs that were found lodged in the victim's throat," he offered, somewhat reluctantly.

"What kind of hairs? Human?"

"Synthetic. They were from a brunette wig."

"What kind of wig?"

"Expensive. High-quality, man-made fiber."

"Any idea how they got there?"

"None. That's it, that's all I know."

Penny realized she had outstayed her welcome. "Well, thanks anyway, Detective Sciapelli."

"Sure. Anytime."

That afternoon, Penny made her way to the 57th St. precinct in midtown Manhattan, where the detective in charge of David Phillips' death, Eugene Sandler, had agreed to see her. She had been pressing him, knowing she had to hurry if she wanted to make the nine o'clock Virgin Atlantic flight from JFK. But her shortage of time was momentarily forgotten as she tried to take in what the detective had just told her.

"Yes, the clothing definitely belonged to the deceased's brother, Jon Phillips," Sandler repeated.

"You're absolutely sure it didn't belong to the deceased?"

"Yes, Phillips admitted the outfit was one he'd bought as part of a stage act he and another guy were doing for some charity events. The Carpenters. He was Karen. Go figure."

"So there was just the one set of women's clothes, then?"

The detective shook his head. "There was another outfit in the closet."

"Jesus!" This was a side to Jon she was totally unfamiliar with. She hadn't believed the reference to cross-dressing Georgie McWilliam had made on *News/Copy*. "Were there other wigs, too?"

"One, other than the one on the body. Both brown, shoulder-length, bangs."

Like the hairs found in the throat of a certain dead drug dealer in Alphabet City, Penny thought. But the case was closed. And perhaps for the purposes of the story she was gathering, it was best that she start keeping her suspicions to herself. She was now certain she was on the right track.

"Thank you for your time, detective," was all she said.

"No problem," he replied, as he accompanied her to the front desk. He watched her hurry out of the station, thinking that this might not be the last he'd be hearing of this case after all.

Chapter Twenty-two

When Peter Smith received a letter from Boris Posarnov instructing the bank to transfer the funds from the U.K. Trading Company's margin account into the company's Bahamian account, he immediately flagged it. It wasn't that the letter was addressed to Ernest Johnston. Companies were often slow to update their databases when there was a change in personnel. Nor was it that the letter, mailed from London, bore a stamp rather than the customary mark of a franking machine; or even that Posarnov's signature lacked its usual loop above the 'v'. These details escaped Smith's notice because he was concentrating on the fact that although such a transaction would not be generally be considered all that unusual, it did involve an exceptionally large amount, and it had come without any advance notice. He also knew that this was the money the bank had replenished to compensate for Jon Phillips' huge unauthorized trading losses, and that the person who had authorized it, Ernest Johnston, was now dead, so he wanted to be sure of what he was doing before he made a move.

Smith checked the relevant information, then went in to see his boss. He found Tom Edwards looking out of the window, admiring either the view or his reflection in the glass, it was impossible to tell which, although Smith would have laid odds. Edwards had no interest in compliance; in fact, he found it dull. But his derivative department had been downsized — Phillips had been right about that — and he viewed compliance as a perfect place to retreat to. Now, ensconced in Robert Baldwin's office, he found he had plenty of time to pore over real estate listings and L.L. Bean catalogues, and even though he was missing the faster pace of the market, he had had little choice in his reassignment.

"Ah, Peter, come in," he smiled. He didn't like Peter Smith, finding him conscientious to a fault.

"Sorry to bother you, sir," said Smith. Dismissive under his politeness, Smith was aware that Edwards lacked the interest and knowledge to do the job. It didn't help that had he himself been a few years older, he might have had a chance at the position. Meanwhile, he kept his distance from his new boss as much as he could. "We've had a request from this margin account for a remittance of funds into its offshore account."

"And?"

"Well, it's a lot of money." Smith handed over the letter from U.K. Trading that Jon had written in Posarnov's name.

Edwards barely glanced at it. "How much?"

"Thirty-five million dollars and change. Internal documentation authorized by Robert Baldwin when he was alive supports it."

"You call that a lot?" Edwards scoffed. "I used to trade more than that on a daily basis." Not precisely true, but true enough, he thought.

"Yes, but you're not in trading now, are you, sir?" Smith replied, failing to keep the edge out of his voice.

Edwards picked up on it. He frowned. "Are the authorization procedures correct?"

"Yes, sir, all the banking details match with those we already have on our system. It all appears in order."

"Then I don't see that there's a problem."

"No, sir. I was just going to suggest we put in a call to them, just to confirm."

"To confirm what?" Edwards asked irritably.

"The transaction."

"What do you think that letter is for? A call won't establish any more authority than the letter does, as you should know, Peter." Edwards was right.

"No, it won't. It's just that this is the same company Jon Phillips was trading on behalf of when he was fired."

"I am aware of that," said Edwards, reminded that his nose had still not fully recovered from Jon's punch. "Even more reason to authorize the transfer."

"But . . ."

"Look, Peter," Edwards interrupted. "Jon Phillips did not act professionally and he cost the bank a great deal of money. The bank is better off distancing itself from anyone associated with him. You should be aware by now that the board's position toward this whole mess is crystal clear. Deal with it and put the whole thing behind us. Go ahead with the transfer and close the account."

"Yes Sir." The bank's position was clear, yet Smith felt he was still right to flag it. He held out another piece of paper. "I'll need you to sign this release, sir."

Edwards was already unscrewing his Mont Blanc. "Give it here."

East End, London

In the heart of London's East End, Jon leaned against a wooden bar at the Walthamstow Dog Track, surrounded by a group of men dressed in expensive business suits, ostentatiously accessorized with a variety of status symbols. He'd known these men since the 1980s, when they'd all come up together on the floor of the London Stock Exchange. Those days of the old-fashioned open outcry system of buying and selling financial products off the market floor were gone forever. In that rough-and-tumble, politically incorrect environment, only the fittest survived. Young female trainees were the objects of lurid comments and worse, minorities were taunted, and bad habits were celebrated, even encouraged.

Things had certainly changed since then. The old school network, the club-like environment that had worked for centuries within the City of London, had long since succumbed to the growing influence of foreign financial institutions. Threadneedle Street continued to have strong traditions, but the institutions within it were now likely to be controlled from Frankfurt, Zurich, or New York. The markets had moved off the trading floors and into offices and trading rooms, where prices were only traded off screens.

An apprenticeship completed in the City of London continued to produce a very different trader than someone trained in New York, and these men were shining examples of the former. Jon found himself missing his old friend, Delboy, who, had he been in London, would have been the life of this party. Having already covered football and greyhounds, the men were turning their attention to their old friend.

"So, Wal," said one of them, gesturing to show to advantage his diamond-encrusted Breitling wristwatch and huge sovereign ring. "I hear you got into a spot of bother on the Street, over a hundred million bucks' worth." Like Delboy, these men would always know Jon by his old trading nickname, Wallaby. "That makes you a real player. Hell, a hundred bars makes you a bloody minor legend. You may have to wait a few months for the dust to settle, but once it does, you'll be able to write your own ticket."

A man in a bright yellow silk Hermes tie nodded. "One thing we all know is that to lose that kind of money on one position requires serious bottle, and that's not easy to find in this day and age. These young traders nowadays spend half their morning debating what sandwich they're going to order for lunch. No, Wal, you'll be in very good shape, have no fear."

Jon smiled, appreciating but not believing their support. "I'll drink to that. But I think you'll find the press did a pretty good job on me. There isn't much left of the old reputation."

"Don't be clever, Wal," said one of the younger men, whose adornment of choice consisted of a large chunky gold bracelet worn next to an elegant silver Rolex Oyster. "Do you think you've got a monopoly on booze and drug abuse? Have you been down to the futures markets lately? There's more powder down there than in Michael Jackson's compact." The men all laughed.

"No, Wallaby," the man continued. "When you want a new job, all you'll have to do is make a song and dance about the wonders of the rehab program you went to. Whether you did or not doesn't really matter. You may even come out of it as a source of inspiration. We all know it's bollocks, but the Americans love that sort of crap. You know I'm right."

"Yes," the Hermes tie agreed. "If you want to get back in the market over here, give me a bell. We need traders that know how to put on a decent position. See what I mean, you're not even looking for a job and already you're getting offers tossed at you."

Jon laughed. "The only decision I've got to make in the foreseeable future is what doggy I'm going to back in the next race."

"Quite right, that is a decision we all have to make. By the way, don't back doggy number four in this race coming up. My bookie tells me that he's just been given about three tins of dog food to slow him down. If you look closely, you'll probably see it blowing out in the betting. See you later, Wal."

And with friendly nods, slaps on the back and handshakes, the men headed toward the betting windows as a pack.

Penny had been watching the scene from an inconspicuous spot nearby. Now that Jon was alone, she approached him casually, as if she'd just arrived, and greeted him with an embrace. She could feel him appraising her, and was confident that she didn't disappoint.

"Hello, Jonny. You look as handsome as ever. What have you been up to?" she asked.

"Not a lot. Enjoying my temporary retirement; it's one of the perks of being fired," Jon replied.

Penny smiled. "A little bit of bad press in the States is almost a career move here, isn't it?"

"Maybe here, but not in the U.S. It's all changed. The Americans have gotten more and more intolerant of bad behavior in this brave new post-9/11 world."

"I figured you would have hung around New York long enough to defend yourself against those allegations."

"Why?" Jon asked. "I think that, given the situation, I was lucky to get out of New York in one piece."

"Well, maybe." She paused. "I really was sorry to hear about your brother. I remember how close you were."

"Thanks, Pen. I appreciate that."

"Did you get home for the funeral?" Penny asked.

Jon shook his head. "It hasn't happened yet. We've had trouble getting clearance to ship David's body back home, although it's about to be released." His tone was troubled.

"I'm sorry to hear that."

"It has been distressing, on top of everything else. We're planning a funeral for next week, and I'm going back for it." Jon was keen to move off the agonizing topic of his brother's death.

"Look, I've never been to Australia. If you think you might need some support from an old friend . . ."

Jon quickly interrupted. "Thanks, that's very sweet of you, but I'm sure I'll be okay."

Penny was afraid she'd seemed too eager. "No regrets, no bitterness toward the bank?"

"It wasn't their fault," he replied. "I got greedy and the market caught me out. Fair cop. The bank behaved in a perfectly proper manner, truth be known."

"It's just that, well, from a distance it doesn't all look quite as black and white."

"The older we get, the less black and white anything looks."

"Maybe. But what about these accidents that seem in some curious way connected to your dismissal?" Penny asked.

"What accidents?"

"The two senior executives at the bank."

"Two?" Jon feigned surprise. "I was around when Robert Baldwin had a car accident. Who was the second?"

"You didn't hear about Ernest Johnston?" Penny found that hard to believe. "He was killed recently in a sailing accident."

"Really? I hardly knew him. How did it happen?"

"He was a senior executive at the Bank of Manhattan and you hardly knew him?"

"We met maybe once or twice. The bank is a very big place; I knew very few people there, mostly just the ones who worked in my department. What happened?"

Penny indulged him. "He fell from the mainsail of his boat and accidentally hung himself."

"Whew, nasty . . ." Jon offered, a bit lamely.

"And did you hear about Posarnov?"

"Who?"

"Come on, Jon, he's the one you asked me about — the U.K. Trading Company, remember?"

"Oh, yeah, I remember." Jon decided that too much ignorance might be suspect. "You checked it out for me. What happened to him? You said he was a bit dodgy, didn't you?"

"He was killed in a shooting accident last weekend. At Stanford Hall." She looked for a change in Jon's expression, but found none.

"Is that right." Jon wanted to get off this subject.

"So what exactly was your interest in U.K. Trading?"

"Oh, yeah," said Jon. "Thanks for that, you saved a mate of mine some serious aggravation. He was looking at U.K. Trading as a potential client on a deal. The information you came up with killed the idea stone dead. I owe you one for that."

"And that was the extent of your involvement with Posarnov and company?"

"What are you, some kind of journalist?" joked Jon. "That was it. Why, is there something else I should know?"

"No, I just thought your inquiry about U.K. Trading might have been linked in some way to the accidents, the losses, and your dismissal."

"I don't want to disappoint you, but if that's the story you're chasing, I don't think you're in very good shape. There's nothing in it." Jon wanted a circuit-breaker. "And now, Penny, if that wraps up the interrogation, let's go try and back a winner. Are you still having dinner with me or are you going to suddenly decide to tell me off again?"

"You break my heart, I don't hear from you for years, and then when I finally do, it's only because you want something from me. That sort of treatment can put a girl off."

"I was young and selfish. So much has changed since then."

Sure, Penny thought. "Jon, you'll never change. You are a typical scorpion, there'll always be a sting in your tail."

"Penny, you're wrong. I'm a regular pussycat these days. My sting is long gone."

"I find that very hard to believe." And she did.

Later on, at dinner, each nervous for different reasons, they drank far more than either was used to. Quickly falling into nostalgic reminiscing, they were both careful to avoid any mention of Victoria's name or the history associated with it. Penny wanted to maneuver Jon into letting down his guard and Jon was indulging Penny in order to throw her off his track. He hoped her memories of Stanford Hall would continue to be painful enough to keep her off the subject and away from the place itself. It would not be helpful for her to discover Jon had been there when Posarnov was shot.

As they finished dinner with a round of flaming sambuca shots, Penny was hazily plotting how to get something out of Jon before the evening was over, having failed thus far to do so. When he offered to put her into a taxi, she insisted on prolonging their reunion with a nightcap at his hotel. Hiding his reluctance, he agreed. By the time they got to his suite at the Lanesborough, they were both unsteady and light-headed.

Jon stepped back to allow Penny to enter. "Welcome to my not-so-grand abode. Please, make yourself comfortable," Jon was slurring and Penny giggling.

Penny threw her handbag on the couch as she turned to face him, hands on hips. "I'd like to do a little more than that, Jonny."

"What do you mean?" Jon feigned ignorance.

"For old times' sake." Penny purred, walking over and rubbing herself seductively against him. "You used to be pretty good in the sack, as I remember, and I thought we might have at it, for old times' sake."

She found herself wanting him to agree for more reasons than she had bargained for. She was curious to see how he would compare with Fiona. And she wondered if manipulating him into bed for ulterior motives would finally exorcise him from her life, thinking that perhaps Fiona had already done that. She wasn't yet sure, but she was determined not to lose this opportunity to find out.

Jon pushed her away, gently but firmly. The evening was taking a turn he hadn't anticipated. "Is this really a good idea? I don't want to be painted as the bad guy again."

"No, Jonny, no expectations this time. Just a great way to end a really nice evening, nothing more."

"Why not?" thought Jon. If they parted on good terms, she'd be that much less likely to make trouble for him. "Then, by all means, come over here."

They began to kiss passionately. All thoughts of Fiona left Penny as she pulled Jon onto the couch and began to unzip his trousers. He had once been able to give her pleasure no man had given her since. She bit his ear and when he winced in pain, she whispered, "I like it rough now."

Jon obligingly grabbed her hair and yanked her head back sharply. She moaned with pleasure as she reached for his erection. They fell to the floor, their agendas temporarily identical.

When they had last been together, Penny had been wrapped up in Jon to the point of obsession. Just the thought of his finger inside her could bring her to the brink of orgasm. She was pleasantly surprised to feel her body once again beginning to respond to him. Times had changed, though, and she was no longer content to be only subservient.

"Fuck me from behind," she demanded. Within moments, he had rolled her over and she was on all fours, with him behind her and firmly inside her. He toyed with her ass, initially with his thumb. As Penny made no complaint, he began penetrating her with his finger, hoping to progress to anal sex. But before he could withdraw from her vagina to penetrate her ass, she spoke up.

"Don't get any ideas. I'm not interested," she said firmly. She had wanted to push some limits with him, to see if he still held such sway over her sexually, but it wasn't happening for her. "Go ahead and come," she urged him. She was enjoying herself, but thoughts of Fiona had reentered her head, and she knew that nothing Jon could do to her would bring her anywhere near the satisfaction she'd experienced with Fiona. Besides, she was tired and drunk and wanted to go home. Experiment over. "Dump your load inside me now," she ordered.

At that, with his cock firmly wedged inside her and his finger buried in her ass, Jon began to come. Head thrown back and groaning loudly, he was all animal. Once spent, Jon lay back on his pillows, huffing and puffing, the room spinning. Penny feigned satisfaction but rose almost immediately from the bed and headed for the bathroom. By the time she returned, Jon was fast asleep, out cold.

Chapter Twenty-three

After waiting to make sure Jon was sleeping soundly, Penny left the bedroom, easing the door shut behind her. She gathered the clothes that were scattered about the living room, hurriedly put them on, then moved over to Jon's desk and turned on the reading lamp. Glancing over her shoulder at the still-closed bedroom door, she switched on the computer. As it began to boot up, she rummaged through the desk's drawers in search of any clue that might tie Jon to one of the accidents. Her head was throbbing and she was longing for some orange juice or even just some water, but she didn't pause in her search.

She was puzzled to discover a copy of the U.K. Trading Company's accounts in Jon's desk drawer, especially since it had been addressed to one Derek Chambers at the hotel. She was unable to draw any significance from it, however, other than the fact that it was yet another link between Jon and the mysterious company. Penny turned back to the computer and accessed the few documents and files unprotected by a password, but found nothing of interest.

Then, taking one last look in his drawers, she came across a folded piece of paper she'd overlooked. Unfolding it, she scanned its contents. It was a record of the U.K. Trading Company's transfer of thirty-five million dollars to the Bank of Manhattan, dated shortly before Jon's trading losses. She didn't know what it meant, but again she noted the connection between U.K. Trading and Jon's bank.

Thinking she heard Jon stir and not wanting to push her luck any further, she refolded and replaced the document, then picked up a pen, wrote a brief message and left, largely empty-handed.

Jon was awakened by the sound of a door closing. He found himself lying alone in bed, covered only by a sheet. His head ached and he was parched. He was reaching over to turn on the bedside lamp when he noticed a sliver of light coming from underneath the door to the living room. He got up, wincing, and made his way across the room to throw open the bedroom door. The living room was empty, but the desk light was on. He went over to his desk where he found Penny's note, written neatly on hotel stationery. He picked it up.

Jonny,

I don't think you've changed a bit. Sorry I couldn't stay. I'll be in touch.

Penny

Jon was sure that she had a good look around before leaving. He had let his guard down, he should have known better. Having sobered up, he realized how reckless it had been to invite Penny to his suite. What most concerned him was that when he'd been going through her handbag while she was in the bathroom the previous evening, he'd found the ticket stub from her trip to New York. What had she been doing there, and how much had she managed to find out? Penny was a journalist, first and foremost. Chances were, last night hadn't completely cleared the decks of her long-harbored resentment against him. He re-read her words, then looked around to see how far her snooping might have gone. He was not surprised to find that nothing seemed out of place. Then he felt the top of his computer. It was warm. He had no idea what conclusions she might have drawn from whatever files she might have been clever enough to get into. Laying down the cryptic note, he made for the bedroom to start packing. Once again it was time for him to leave.

Gloucestershire, England

It was still early morning when Penny steered her Alfa Spider through the impressive gates of Stanford Hall. Wood pigeons cooed soothingly somewhere in the distance, and the manicured lawn wore a concealing mist of dew. She pulled up outside the house and rang the doorbell. The door was eventually answered, and by the time Victoria had been summoned and entered the living room, Penny was seated in the same chair where Jon had lounged by the fire only days before.

"Penny. This *is* a surprise." Victoria was dressed casually in jeans and a t-shirt, her face slightly puffy. She had just gotten up.

"Hello, Victoria. It's been a long time."

"Are you here socially or on a professional basis?" Victoria asked coolly.

"A combination of both, I suppose," Penny lied. "Actually, I bumped into Jon Phillips in London last night and it made me think of you."

"So much so that you felt the urge to get up at the crack of dawn and turn up at my door unannounced?" Victoria asked skeptically. "And how is Jonny?" Mistrustful, she wasn't going to give anything away.

"Oh, you know, same old Jonny. When was the last time you saw him?"

"What is your interest in Jon? You're not still upset about what happened, I hope."

"So long as I know I can still have him whenever I like, it doesn't bother me."

"Really?"

"Yes. In fact, last night he and I made up for the twelve-year gap like a couple of barnyard animals. He's still the best, I have to say."

"Really?" This time, Victoria's voice wavered. She wondered if Penny was telling the truth or just being spiteful. "You mean you made love?"

"That's not exactly what I would call it. But yes, we fucked for most of the night."

"Penny, why are you telling me this? Why are you being so mean?" Victoria couldn't keep up the pretense, envisioning the man she'd just been fantasizing her future with in bed with Penny.

Penny gave her a look. "Victoria, have you any idea how long it took me to get over the fact that Jonny left me for someone who I thought was my best friend?" Penny laughed mirthlessly. "Now *I'm* being mean to *you*? That's turning the tables, I'd say."

"You're squaring things up? Is that what this visit is all about?"

"No, actually, it isn't."

"So why are you here, Penny?" Victoria wanted nothing more than to go back upstairs to bed, to hide under the covers and sob her disappointment. Their time together had obviously meant nothing to Jon, despite what he'd said as he was leaving. She'd been nothing more than a conquest, a cheap thrill, the same as Penny had been only a few hours earlier.

"I need to know when you last saw Jonny."

"Why? It's really none of your business."

"Boris Posarnov. The man who was killed here last weekend. There may have been a link between him and Jonny."

"Boris and Jonny? No!" Victoria shook her head. "They'd never even met before. Not possible." She was certain. She was quick to stop herself, conscious that she'd already said too much.

"Yes, Victoria. And there have been other deaths, all made to look like accidents."

"And you think Jon has been involved in some way?" Victoria was incredulous.

"I do. From what you just said, I figure he was here last weekend."

"Why didn't you ask him when you slept with him?" Victoria responded bitterly.

"Because I didn't want him to know how much I knew. Look, Victoria, Jon is a selfish bastard. He's good at disguising it and he can be very charming and all that, but at the end of the day, he doesn't give a damn about you, me, or anybody but himself. So, please . . ."

Victoria was quiet for a few moments. She pictured Jon the other night. So dashing in his tuxedo, so tender in her arms. Then the image was replaced by one of him and Penny entwined. The thought was unbearable; it made her physically queasy. "Alright," she murmured. "You'll find out anyway. It's no secret. He was here last weekend. But he left early in the morning, before the accident."

Jackpot! Thought Penny. "But he was here?"

"Yes," Victoria said, her voice quavering.

Becoming aware of the depth of Victoria's pain, Penny experienced an unexpected pang of compassion. "Are you alright?"

Fighting tears, Victoria was unable to answer.

"For Christ's sake, don't tell me you're still carrying a torch for him?" Penny exclaimed.

Victoria nodded miserably.

"You can't seriously be in love with him?" Victoria dissolved into tears. Penny moved forward to hug her former best friend for the first time in over a decade, stroking Victoria's hair gently as she sobbed into her shoulder.

During breakfast together in the conservatory overlooking the summer garden, Victoria began to recover her equilibrium and even, to some extent, her belief in Jon. At least she would give him a chance to tell her his side of the story, she decided. Penny had generously explained how she had been the one to seduce Jon, as payback for the old hurt she'd been carrying for so many years. She omitted that she had also wanted access to his belongings so she could search them for clues. As sympathetic as she was now beginning to feel toward Victoria, she nonetheless told her no more than she already had about what she'd uncovered to back up her suspicions about Jon, knowing that a woman in love cannot be expected to keep confidences from the one she loves. And in Penny's estimation, Victoria was, unfortunately for her, clearly in love and already making excuses for Jon's behavior, rationalizing away her hurt. Penny could empathize all too well, however, and therefore was gentle with her old friend.

Victoria, in turn, was able to forgive Penny for her initial cruelty, understanding only now, for the first time, the impact she and Jon had had on her over the intervening years. Soon becoming comfortable again in one another's company, they talked for hours about their lives since they'd been in contact. And throughout, Victoria apologized repeatedly for the cavalier way in which she and Jon had behaved all those years ago, while trying to convince Penny — and herself — that the Jon she'd known could not be capable of the heinous deeds in which Penny suspected him of somehow being involved.

For her part, Penny mostly just let Victoria talk, realizing as she listened that meeting Fiona had enabled her to release long-suppressed feelings, lifting what she'd sometimes thought of as The Curse of Jon. Perhaps what she'd attributed to Jon had just provided her with an excuse for her inability to make an intimate connection with a man. In any case, her long-held bitterness toward Victoria seemed to have evaporated, and she now felt nothing but sympathy, even tenderness toward her. Not toward Jon, however. Although she might have attributed too much to him in terms of the pain she had suffered, she was still able to separate her conceivably misdirected personal anger at him from her reluctant suspicions about him.

After breakfast, Penny suggested they go for a ride, wanting to have a look around the grounds of the estate. As they were walking their horses through the woods, she casually asked Victoria to show her where Posarnov had been shot.

The area where Boris had fallen was not hard to locate. It seemed clear from how the ground was trampled that the search had been limited to where the guns were normally positioned. To everyone involved, including the local constabulary, the shooting was assumed to have been an accident. Hunting accidents were not unusual during the season, and they were always dealt with as quietly and discreetly as possible. The Colarvon family, anxious about the impact of such an event on their livelihood, was also keen to have any enquiry proceed with all possible haste and a minimum of publicity and complications.

Penny stood in the place where she estimated Boris had fallen and then paced toward the wood, walking in among the trees. She searched fruitlessly for some time among the shaded roots and underbrush. Victoria was urging that they leave when at last Penny spotted something. She called to Victoria.

"What is it?" Victoria asked, joining her.

"There, in the brush. Do you see that? What is it?"

"Where?" asked Victoria, peering where Penny indicated.

"Right there." Penny leaned in closer.

"It's just an old shotgun cartridge," said Victoria, bending down toward it.

"Don't touch it!" cried Penny, grabbing Victoria's arm. "It could have Jon's fingerprints on it."

"Don't be ridiculous. What are you suggesting?" Much to Penny's dismay, Victoria snatched it up. "This is a shooting drive. There must be hundreds of spent cartridges lying around. Even if your preposterous story was true, the chances that this is the one that killed Boris must be a million to one."

She rolled the green plastic cylinder between her forefinger and thumb, obliterating any prints that might have been there. "Look, there's another, and another." She pointed to several spent cartridges scattered on the ground in the nearby area where the guns were normally positioned.

"Yes, but not here, where it's hidden and off by itself." Penny tried not to show her annoyance. The damage was already done.

"I suppose you want to collect them all," Victoria said, sarcasm in her tone.

"Never mind," said Penny, heading back toward her horse.

"Where are you going?" Victoria called after her.

"I should get back to London," Penny replied over her shoulder, while mounting.

"Wait for me," Victoria said, placing the cartridge in her pocket. And as she did so, she smiled a little smile, unseen by Penny.

Chapter Twenty-Four

Melbourne, Victoria, Australia

Qantas Flight 10 from London's Heathrow Airport to Melbourne was a familiar one to Jon. Twenty-two hours long, it allowed him time to reflect on what might await him when he arrived. He found each trip home to be different in myriad subtle, and sometimes not so subtle, ways. This particular visit promised to be a most painful one.

The short stopover in Singapore was just long enough for him to take a welcome shower in the luxurious first-class lounge, and to buy his mother some outrageously expensive La Prairie cosmetics from one of the duty-free shops in Changi Airport. He had been trying his best to imagine himself living again in Australia, either in Melbourne or on the farm, but the minute he landed in Melbourne, he felt somewhat displaced. It was the little things — the relentlessly unchanged drive from Tullamarine Airport, the brash, raw accents blasting from the radio, the obsessive interest in sports in general, and Australian Rules football in particular, bespeaking the insular nature of most of his fellow countrymen. On the one hand, the country would always be home to him; on the other, he no longer felt a part of it when he was there.

As Jon's taxi made its way past the outskirts of Melbourne, he remembered the city as he'd last seen it, two years earlier. He thought of the trams rattling across its streets on into the suburbs, the four seasons coming and going in their disparate glories, and the people getting older but never really changing. Australia was an affluent country, its population happy and contented, and it had no need to change. But, for better or worse, and perhaps sadly, Jon had become used to functioning in more dynamic environments.

Now, his options seemed limitless. The past few days away from Victoria had convinced him even more that his future lay with her, and the prospect of being with her again — this time for good — was what he was counting on to help him get through the agony of David's funeral. Even the money — his new fortune — was secondary to that.

He'd received confirmation that a little over thirty-five million, tax-free dollars had been deposited into U.K. Trading's Cayman Island bank account. It had then subsequently been transferred to the new account at Bank Cayman, just as he'd directed in the forged documents. The money was now under his control and effectively untraceable. He could use the funds in any way he thought appropriate. The inescapable fact that his new-found fortune came from blood money troubled him. For the time being, he would just leave it where it was. There would be plenty of time to decide how to deal with it. Or so he thought.

After a long, two-hour journey from the airport, the taxi eased to a dusty halt outside Baroonga, his parents' property. The cattle farm was situated on six thousand acres, consisting of a series of starkly dramatic rock-and-timber-bordered valleys set beneath the vast Australian Alps. Koala bears thrived in the native Australian gum trees dominating the thick woods on the sides of the mountains. The Phillips family's large, single-storied homestead was surrounded by a wide, open veranda. A classic local Victorian, it dated from the late nineteenth century and managed somehow to be simultaneously elegant and functional, in a particularly rural Australian way.

Jon took it all in for a moment before hoisting his bags, carrying them up the steps, and moving across the veranda, the old boards creaking under his feet. He tapped lightly on the screen door. His mother was sitting in the kitchen. She had been expecting him, but still seemed startled by his entrance. She stood and held out her arms, inviting him into a warm hug. Her lips caught his cheek with a kiss as she held him close, unwilling to let him go. Jon was happy to be back in her arms and did not pull back right away, as he often did.

"Hey," he said, softly. "I'm here now."

She looked up, on the verge of tears. "I'm sorry, Jon, it's just that . . ." She buried her face in his chest.

"I know," he said, soothingly. "I know. We'll all miss him."

After a few moments, she managed to compose herself. She leaned back and stared into his eyes, smiling tremulously as she stroked the hair from his face. "You look well, Jon. A little younger, perhaps, with your long hair. It's so good to have you home."

"It's great to be here, mum."

"We have so much to catch up on, but first, let's go find your father. He's out working in the yard."

She took Jon's hand and led him out behind the house, where they could see Jon's father giving instructions to a farm hand. Jon left his mother and approached his father alone. As he did so, his father turned, a smile breaking out on his face. He cut short his conversation, and walked back toward Jon with his arms extended.

Silently, the two men exchanged a warm embrace. "What's with the hippie hairdo?" The attempt at levity was in character for Jon's father, who did not easily express emotion.

Jon smiled, knowing his father's question needed no answer. "G'day, dad, you're looking great. It's been too long."

"You're right about that. Let's go inside so your mother can put the kettle on and make us all a nice hot cuppa."

Back in the house, Jon knew that the only approach he could take was to be completely honest. The three of them sat at the familiar kitchen table, drinking out of mugs he remembered from childhood, as he haltingly outlined his brother's unconventional, gruesome murder. He chose his words carefully and left out as much detail as he possibly could. For the first time, he told them that David had been killed by mistake, and that the murder, which had been intended for him, had been staged in such a way as to smear Jon's, not David's, reputation. But this kind of violence and decadence were so far outside the realm of their experience, they were still grappling with how it could have invaded their sons' worlds.

Jon explained to them that he'd unwittingly laundered and lost a huge amount of money that turned out to have belonged to Russian gangsters. He explained how they had targeted him, and how he hadn't been completely forthcoming with the police because he'd feared for his life and felt he had to sort things out on his own. He assured them he was no longer in danger and that he hoped he could put this nightmare behind him once David was buried, knowing he would not be able to. Again and again, he said how sorry he was that David had become an innocent victim of the mess he'd gotten himself into, and each time, they reassured him that it wasn't his fault.

Distraught at what he was hearing, his father seemed anxious to change the subject to something less painful. His mother took her cue from his father, so it wasn't long before his father took the lead in speaking of other, more mundane things. "It's nice that you can afford to take some time off, but a man can't be idle for too long. Have you got any plans?"

"Nothing concrete. I haven't had a real break for about twelve years, so it's a luxury to be able to take it easy for a while."

"Well, son, do you think now that you've had your chance to travel and make your mark in the financial markets, it might be time to settle down?"

Jon's mother gave her husband a disapproving look. "Easy, Ted, he's just come home. Give him a bit of time." She turned to Jon. "This is the price you pay for being your father's son."

Jon smiled at them both, affectionately. "Actually, there's a girl in England — remember Victoria, from Cambridge? I'm pretty serious about her. The problem is, our future would probably be over there." Seeing the expression on their faces, he added hurriedly, "I need to consider what is best for her and for me, along with what my responsibilities are, here. It's complicated, but I'm giving it plenty of thought, believe me. Anyway, how are the girls?"

"They're bearing up, under the circumstances. You'll see Alice tomorrow," said his mother. "Now that they're living in Melbourne, we don't see nearly enough of her and Fred and the kids, but there you are. They have their own life to lead. Although we do see a little more of them in winter. They often pop in on their way up to the snow."

"And Elaine?"

"You can ask her yourself. She's driven into town but she should be back any minute now."

"She's here already?"

"Unlike her brothers, who couldn't wait to get away," his father said, giving Jon a pointed look, "she moved back home after graduation."

"You mean she's been living here?" Somehow this news had escaped Jon. How boring it must be on the farm for a young university graduate, he thought, but did not say. Then again, Elaine, the baby of the family, had always been more like her father than any of the other children.

"And settling down like she should," nodded his father.

"Now, then, Ted . . ." his mother intervened once again.

"Settling down? She's got a boyfriend, then?" Jon was certain he hadn't heard about a serious boyfriend either.

"She'll tell you herself. And you'll have to tell us all about your special young lady, once you've had a chance to freshen up," said his mother. Jon nodded, pushed back his chair and picked up his bags.

Entering his old bedroom was like walking into a time warp. Everything was as it had been when he was living in it. The walls were still adorned with his sporting heroes from an era long gone, the closet still full of clothes from his college years, and his framed university degree was still hanging on the wall above his bed.

His father was calling to him from the hall outside his bedroom. "Would you like me to saddle up a couple of horses so we can go for a ride around the property? I'll show you the changes we've made over the last few years."

Tired as he was, Jon gladly accepted the distraction. "I'd love to."

"Give me half an hour. I'll get the horses ready and meet you at the stables," his father responded, sounding pleased.

"Great, I'll be ready," said Jon. He began to rifle through his closet in search of his old riding gear, wondering if it would still fit. Gratifyingly, it did.

As he walked out of the house a short time later, his mother stopped him. "Don't be too hard on your father, dear. He's put his life into this place, as did his father before him. Now that he's lost Davey, he's terrified that you'll go, too." She gave him a quick peck on the cheek.

Jon nodded and smiled reassuringly, but her comment troubled him. The almost unbearable responsibility he felt toward David had not been alleviated, as he'd hoped, by the deaths of either Johnston or Posarnov. Would he have to go so far as to live his brother's life in order to validate his own?

At the stables, he and his father mounted their horses and rode off onto a trail. Both were outfitted in traditional stockman attire — moleskin trousers, long waterproof coat, RM Williams riding boots, and an Akubra stockman's hat. This Snowy Mountain area of Victoria was home to some legendary Australian horsemen. Jon's father was one of them, and Jon had always been able to hold his own amongst them, too.

"We've added to the property since you were last here, son." His father spoke over his shoulder, as Jon followed him along the trail. "As you know, I bought Maninga, next door, about a year ago, nearly 1,200 acres. Small, but some good grazing land. It's been a good spell for graziers over the past twelve months; this place and our other interests have done well. I was thinking that there are some wonderful sites on Maninga to build a home on. If you thought you might be spending a bit more time here, we could build a house for you."

"As I said, dad, I'll give it some thought, but please don't be too disappointed if I don't come back here to live. You know I've never seen managing the property as something that I'd want to do."

"I understand that, son, but I'm not getting any younger, and I have to plan for the family's future, especially given Davey's passing. If your future doesn't include the property, then I must allow for that and plan accordingly. I won't say I'm not disappointed, but then again, I can't say I'm surprised, either."

"Look, dad, I haven't said I won't . . ."

"It's okay," the old man interjected. "I'm sure Elaine will be happy either way."

"Elaine? What's it got to do with her?" asked Jon.

"She wanted to tell you herself, but I was never one for women's secrets," his father said. "She's going to be married. And her husband-to-be is quite capable of running things here."

"Really?" asked Jon, surprised to find himself feeling hurt instead of relieved. "And what makes you think that?"

"Why don't you ask him yourself? Here he comes." In the distance, a horseman was approaching, in a small cloud of dust.

Jon looked confused. "She's marrying Brian?" Brian Alquist was the young property manager who'd been working at Baroonga since he was a boy. He and Elaine had a brief flirtation during their teens, but Jon had never thought of it as serious.

"That's right, Brian. He's a qualified estate manager with a university degree, and it's not like we don't know him. For the time being, it's probably best if you don't let on that I told you." Jon nodded. The old man changed tack. "Anyway, first things first. Brian tells me one of the colts got out of the west paddock. He's coming to help us bring him in. It's pretty rough country up there. I hope you can still ride a horse after all those years in the city."

Alquist rode up and extended his large, tanned hand to Jon.

Brian Alquist was a good man, Jon thought, relief now overtaking his hurt feelings once the initial shock of being replaced had passed. Looking on the bright side, this would make his decision much easier for his parents to accept.

"Are you two ready to retrieve this young fella?" Alquist asked, gesturing toward the wild mountain scrub.

"Don't tell me it's the colt from old Regret," Jon said with a laugh, referring to a line from one of his father's favorite poems, "The Man from Snowy River."

His father was quick to respond. "You may laugh, but that poem is one of the greatest poems ever written, and it's about tough old horsemen just like your grandfather. He was the very type of man Banjo had in mind when he wrote it. Like it or not, Jon, you're a man from Snowy River, too, have no bloody fear, no matter how damn long you've spent in the city."

As the three men rode along the treacherous trail, Jon's father began loudly and enthusiastically to recite the first stanza of the classic Australian poem:

There was a movement at the station, for the word had
     passed around
That the colt from old Regret had got away,
And had joined the wild bush horses— he was worth a
     thousand pound,
So all the cracks had gathered to the fray.
All the tried and noted riders from the stations near and far
Had mustered at the homestead overnight,
For the Bushmen love hard riding where the wild
     horses are,
And the stock-horse snuffs the battle with delight

Jon had managed to keep pace with the other two throughout his father's emotive recital of A. B. "Banjo" Paterson's poem. He had been hearing it since he was a child. It was almost a family anthem to his father, who felt it captured the spirit that had driven the

Phillips family over the generations to achieve the success they now enjoyed.

They had reached the top of a steep ridge from where they could see the young, black colt quietly grazing on the edge of a clearing below them. Spotting them, he began to gallop in the other direction, deeper into the bush.

"Damn it," said Jon's father. "This may be more difficult than I thought. Follow me, son, and remember, try and keep up."

Brian and Jon's father galloped down the steep path toward the clearing, following the colt into the thick mountain scrub. Jon hung back, watching his father's easy interaction with his future son-in-law. He felt as if a heavy burden had been lifted from his shoulders. He was confident that no one would ever replace him in his father's affections, but he could see that his replacement as property manager was a good one.

By the time Jon caught up with the other two, they had cornered the tired and fractious colt in a narrow gully. Jon joined them in the difficult task of attaching a lead to the colt's bridle in order to bring him in. The sun had begun to set over the Great Divide as they made their way home. Exhausted, but feeling a sense of contentment from the hours spent in physical activity, Jon smiled to himself, the words of the poem once again ringing in his ears. Yes, it was good to be home.

Chapter Twenty-five

"Where's my money?"

Peter Smith found the man with the long gray hair pulled into a ponytail unsettling. He wasn't impolite and he hadn't raised his voice. It was something about the way he'd just barged into Tom Edwards's office ahead of Smith that conveyed a readiness to break through conventions to get what he wanted. He was staring accusingly at the startled Edwards, whom Smith had not had a chance to brief.

"What money?" Edwards asked cautiously.

"The money from the margin account of the U.K. Trading Company."

"I'm sorry," said Edwards. "Who exactly are you, and what is your connection with that account?"

"My name is James Remini. I'm a major shareholder in the U.K. Trading Company."

"Is this true, Peter?" Edwards asked.

Smith nodded. "I've checked our records and our attorneys have confirmed this."

"So," Remini repeated, "what happened to my money?"

"The transfer was authorized according to correct procedures," said Smith, looking nervously over at Edwards.

"On whose authority?" Remini demanded.

"As I recall, one of the directors signed off on it. What was his name again, Peter?" Edwards could not remember the details of the transaction.

Smith was quick to supply the name. "Boris Posarnov. I have the authorization right here." Smith offered him a copy of the letter. Snatching it from Smith's hand, Remini glanced at it, then stared incredulously at them, trying to suppress his fury.

"Have you verified this signature?" he asked.

Smith nodded as Edwards added, "Mr. Posarnov was the authorized signatory. If you contact him, no doubt he'll be able explain the reason for the transfer."

"I'll be sure to do that," said Remini dryly, "the next time I visit a psychic."

"What do you mean?" Edwards asked. Smith swallowed.

"Boris Posarnov is dead." Remini snapped.

"When did this happen?" asked Edwards, real concern finally registering. "Are you suggesting this is a fraud? Because if you are, we will need to look into it immediately."

Remini leaned forward toward Edwards. "That is what I'm suggesting. This is a posthumous letter to and from two very dead men regarding an amount of over thirty-five million fucking dollars. And I want to know where my fucking money has gone." His voice had risen and the threat in his demeanor was now palpable.

Edwards was immediately on the defensive. "If you were found to be correct, and I should say at this point that I am not suggesting for a minute that you are, I can assure you the bank is insured against these situations."

"It is?" Remini's tone changed. "What does that mean?"

Edwards explained. "It means that if the money was removed from the account fraudulently, you'll be compensated fully for any loss caused by the bank. The question is, has there been a fraud? We will of course look into it right away but it will ultimately be determined by the insurance company's independent investigation."

"And just what does *that* mean, bottom line?" Remini asked.

"Frankly, what it means is that the insurance company will do everything within its power to find a reason why they shouldn't pay. If this is an outright fraud, however, with no other implications or ramifications involved, they will have no choice but to pay." Edwards paused. "Do you have any idea who could be responsible for doing this, if you are in fact correct?"

Remini sat quietly for a moment, considering. "Will such an investigation open up to further scrutiny the trading losses your trader incurred in our account?"

"No," Edwards replied thoughtfully. "It shouldn't. This transfer of funds happened well after those losses were incurred. And let me remind you that it's not in the bank's interest either to draw attention to those losses and the way they were incurred. That has been dealt with, and the whole incident has been put to bed."

"So they'll concentrate exclusively on this paper trail?" Remini queried.

"That's right," Edwards nodded, then added, "provided that there are not any other issues that we are not yet aware of, of course."

Remini nodded. He had heard enough. He stood to leave, extending his hand to Edwards. "I will leave these details in your hands. Please contact me on my mobile phone if you need to. I'll call you in about a week to see what's happening with the investigation. But be aware that I expect the full amount to be returned to that account sooner rather than later. Thank you."

Edwards and Smith nodded in agreement, relieved that he was taking his leave. They needed to get to the bottom of this, to protect their own interests.

Remini walked out of the Bank of Manhattan, knowing he had to track down Jon Phillips. There was no doubt in his mind that Jon was responsible for the money's disappearance. He wasn't about to wait around for months, or more likely years, for some insurance company to figure out a way to weasel out of paying up. He wanted that money now, and he would get it from the person who stole it from him not once, but twice. Jon needed to be dealt with immediately. Any interference from Jon, one call to the SEC, one unexpected move, and the insurance payoff would be killed off in a heartbeat. Yes, Phillips had to go.

He pulled out his cell phone and dialed a number, leaning on a pillar at the bank's entrance, as he waited for his call to be answered.

"Hello, baby doll," he said.

"Hello, Jimmy," Fiona responded, with a sigh. The sounds of the newsroom in which sat made it hard to hear. "Got another story for me?"

"Not this time, sweet stuff. I need some information."

"Oh, yeah?"

"Jon Phillips. You know where he is?"

"Actually, I do. But if I tell you, I want something in return."

"You owe me, remember? I gave you the Phillips story in the first place. Anyway, if it's me you want, just say the word and I'll come right over."

"No, Jimmy, that's over. I've met someone."

"So what? What's that got to do with anything?"

"Look, I'm not going to discuss it. Let's just keep it professional. We'll do better as sources than lovers, anyway."

"Have it your way. Just tell me where Phillips is."

"Do we have a deal, then?"

"We have a deal." What the hell did he care? She'd already served her purpose.

For whatever that's worth, thought Fiona. "He just left for his brother's funeral."

"Where's that?"

"His parent's place. A village called Mansfield. It's in Australia, near Melbourne, I think."

That's all he needed to know. "Thanks, doll. You're very good. I owe you one."

"Remember that, Jimmy. A deal's a deal. And if you don't mind my asking, what's your interest in him?"

"Come on, toots, you know better than that. See you around."

Chapter Twenty-six

Over the course of the following day, other family members began to gather. Jon enjoyed being around his sisters. He spent his time helping his father and Elaine's fiancé, Brian, with the physical tasks of running the farm, while the women rallied around their mother in preparation for the funeral and the wake. Although always friends, the sisters hadn't been close since early adolescence, and it pleased Jon to see them together again.

Alice had enjoyed her boarding school days in Melbourne more than her younger sister. She had quickly shed her rural ways, wanting to blend into city life and find a husband who would keep her there. So it had come as no surprise when she married Fred, a bright young banker from an affluent Melbourne family. With her two children, attractive suburban home, skiing holidays in the winter months, and trips to Noosa Heads in Queensland for summer resort vacations, she seemed content.

Elaine, on the other hand, wanted to keep her life as simple as possible, aspiring to nothing more than a happy, healthy, and stable family life lived on the farm, preferably with a soul mate. In Brian, it seemed she had found this.

Jon observed Brian in particular, noting the caring way he looked after Elaine and the property, his friendly warm demeanor, and his genuine desire to be a part of the family that Jon had abandoned in favor of wealth and excitement. Jon almost began to dread being in his presence, but not because he disliked him; on the contrary, he saw Brian as the man he himself should have been. It gnawed at him, but there was no going back.

On the morning of the funeral, the sun rose early, the sky a bright azure. The clear skies were deceptive, however, as a chilly winter's wind blew in from the north across snow-covered Mount Sterling, the highest peak in Victoria. Next to it sat Mount Buller, Melbourne's winter playground. Jon's childhood memories were full of wonderful times skiing on Mount Buller's slopes with David. It was only an hour's drive from the farm, but right now it might as well have been a world away.

Jon stood silently at graveside, looking over at the old, sandstone Anglican Church as his brother's body was slowly lowered into the freshly dug grave. White lilies — Christmas lilies, as they were known in Australia — covered the coffin. They had been David's favorite flower, a happy reminder to him of Christmases past wherever he'd come across them in his travels.

Jon felt comatose, physically and emotionally frozen, as his mother held tightly to his arm and sobbed, Jon's father on her other side. Like Jon, he remained tearless, concentrating on supporting his devastated wife. Jon was just focusing on getting through the burial without collapsing. His sense of responsibility was overwhelming.

Once the service ended, Jon watched his father lead his mother out of the churchyard toward the warmth of the car. Slowly, he followed them, at a distance.

After the wake began at the family home, the mood lightened as guests began to share stories of David's adventures. Tales of wild nights in Ulaanbaatar, wild weather in Borneo, wild animals in Tanzania, and wild girls in Moscow were told in celebration of his life. Jon kept busy helping his parents host the gathering and talking privately with Lucy, David's devastated fiancée. By the time the last of the guests had left, the family wanted nothing more than to rest and spend some time alone. Jon wished them all good night, and escaped to his boyhood bedroom with a couple of Magodon sleeping pills. He knew that once he awoke, he would need to give both himself and his parents room to mourn in private.

He and Victoria had been text messaging rather than speaking on the telephone. He needed to be in touch but he also needed to keep his distance, for the time being. Before he turned out the light, he typed, "*V. A sad day. My heart is broken into a thousand pieces. No one here to talk to. Missing you. Jon*".

Almost immediately, she responded: "*Darling Jonny. I wish I could be there to put it back together again. Thinking of you. Love, V.*"

The next morning, Jon drove into the nearby town of Mansfield. As he wandered down the main street, absorbing the appealingly quaint atmosphere created by the town's colorful past as a mountain cattle community, an attractive woman in her thirties approached him.

"Aren't you Jon Phillips?" she asked, tentatively.

Jon immediately recognized her. "Rosemary? Rosemary Watson? You look fantastic. What has it been, ten years?"

"I was very sorry to hear about David, the whole town was shocked."

There was little else that Jon could do but to acknowledge her kind words with a sad shrug. He was quick to move on. "How are you?" He asked.

"I'm very well, thank you, but believe it or not, it's been more like fifteen. It was a long time ago, but I remember it as if it were yesterday."

Jon smiled at her fondly. "We were so young and carefree then, weren't we? It's wonderful to see you, you haven't changed at all. You look fabulous. Perhaps we can catch up while I'm back." His enthusiasm was genuine and nostalgic as, to Jon, their brief time together felt like a lifetime ago.

"We were young," she replied. "But you were the one who was

carefree. You took off to study in England and I'm sure you barely gave me another thought. One minute you were here, the next minute you were gone. It took me a very long time to get you out of my system."

He quickly realized that she wasn't all that pleased to see him, but she was right. He hadn't given her a second thought. "I'm sorry I didn't keep in touch, but I've never been much of a letter writer," Jon said, smiling disarmingly.

"I gathered that. I stopped writing after my third letter wasn't answered."

"I'm sorry. But let's get together, what harm could it do?"

"No harm, but I think not. I'm very happily married now, with two young children. I married Billy Jones about five years ago."

"Great, Billy was always a terrific guy. I understand, and I'm delighted you're so happy. Please say hello to Billy for me. Take care."

As he watched her walk away, Jon's mind drifted back to the time when he and Rosemary were teenaged boyfriend-and-girlfriend. He remembered them as happy, simple days. That her feelings for him had been so strong that she would resent him even now surprised and hurt him. He'd viewed his romance with her as a passing interlude, nothing more, and yet here she was, like Penny, still angry at the way she'd been treated. Penny he could better understand; she'd been put in an embarrassing situation and rejected by the two people closest to her at the time. But a hometown childhood sweetheart, to whom he couldn't remember making any promises whatsoever? He found it hard to fathom. It seemed he'd lived a careless, selfish life that was only now catching up with him. He could only hope that Victoria, at least, could be salvaged out of the damage he'd done.

Right now, he needed to be alone for a while. He had to get some perspective, regain control of himself and his life, and that couldn't be done at his parents' home. He had already determined his destination. He headed directly to the local bank and withdrew twenty thousand dollars in cash from his old schoolboy bank account. Before he had left London, he had replenished the long dormant account with funds from his off-shore bank account. Managing to avoid any further encounters with scorned lovers or envious schoolmates, some of whom he had run into at the wake, Jon walked briskly back to his father's car, a Holden utility he'd parked in an angled parking space in the town's main street, and drove back to his family's property. He turned into the yard and pulled up next to his father, who was inspecting a delivery of fence wire that had arrived that morning.

"Morning, dad," he smiled.

"Good morning, son, did you find what you needed?"

"I did. I thought I might go to Wye River for a few days to clear my head."

His father smiled. "Just like the old days."

"That's right. Do a little surfing and maybe even try my hand at hang gliding again. Mind if I borrow the plane for a couple of days?"

"Have you kept up your hours?" His father asked sternly.

"Yes, dad." Jon felt suddenly childlike. He had in fact kept up his hours, despite the demands of his job. August was generally a slow month in New York. As the sun beat down on the gritty streets, Jon would join the city dwellers escaping to the Hamptons. There he made a point of taking time from his vacation pursuits to rent planes by the hour at the East Hampton and Quogue airports, occasionally even driving to the larger airport at Islip to practice landing and taking off with more air traffic. That way, he'd managed to cobble together the minimum hours he'd needed to keep his license, and he was now itching to get into a cockpit again.

"Okay, if you're sure, I can't see why not. I suppose you haven't lost any of your old flying skills. Remember that you still aren't allowed to fly at night," his father cautiously pointed out.

"Dad, I haven't forgotten that I'm technically color-blind, but thanks for reminding me."

"You'll need to fuel it. It's recently been serviced so the oil should be okay, but check it anyway. Hopefully, you won't need them, but the parachutes are still behind each of the front seats and I had them repacked by the local parachuting club about six months ago." Jon's father left nothing to chance, a trait that had firmly rubbed off on his eldest son.

Jon smiled affectionately at his father. "I'll do all the pre-flight checks, and if it's okay, I'll leave later on this morning. I expect to be back in about a week."

"No hurry, I don't need it." He paused momentarily before continuing. "Take care, son, and give plenty of thought to what I've said. I know your life has been a long way away from here over the past fifteen years, but here is where you belong. There is nothing more important to a man than his roots, and you now have a wonderful opportunity to re-establish them."

"Dad, I'll give it plenty of thought, but I can't promise anything," was all Jon said, just as he'd been saying since he'd arrived, even with the added responsibility he felt since David's death. No matter how hard he tried, Jon could not realistically see his future back on the farm. He knew that home was where he felt happiest, and Country Victoria was not it, irrespective of the strong associations he felt for it. He felt some comfort knowing his youngest sister and her husband-to-be were about to assume that important family responsibility.

Jon packed his bag at the house and bid his mother goodbye. She was reluctant to see him leave again. Meaning it, he assured her he'd be back in a week and would stay with them at least for a little while longer after that.

He walked briskly over to the hangar, which was actually a small barn located on the edge of a long grass strip. A windsock was the only hint that it was something more than just another field. He opened the large creaking doors and began to circle the small, single-engine aircraft. It seemed in pretty good shape. He made the pre-flight checks and filled the aircraft with fuel from a large, forty-four-gallon drum, pumping it manually into tanks located in each of the wings.

Jon climbed into the aircraft and continued to complete his

checks. He turned the ignition and pressed the "start" button. The engine fired and he carefully maneuvered the aircraft forward out of the barn, taxiing toward a windsock positioned at the far end of the strip. He moved the throttle to its "full" position and accelerated down the grass strip. At the suitable speed of about eighty miles per hour, he gently tugged on the stick and the wheels lifted from the grass.

Shortly after Jon's plane had climbed beyond the mountain range, the phone rang in the large colonial kitchen. Jon's mother answered it.

"Is Jon there, please?" an American voice asked.

"I'm sorry," said his mother. "You've just missed him."

"What a pity. I'm an old friend from the States. Do you have any idea where I might find him?" the deep-voiced caller asked politely.

Jon's mother was eager to help Jon's well-spoken foreign friend. "He flew to Lorne in his father's plane about half an hour ago. He's gone surfing for a few days."

"I'm in Australia and I'd love to catch up with him," the American voice continued. "Do you know where he's staying?" he queried.

Jon's mother had no reason to question this polite stranger's interest in looking up her son, and so she told him.

Chapter Twenty-seven

Lorne, Victoria, Australia

Jon's destination was indeed the small, coastal town of Lorne, in southwestern Victoria. He had mapped out a route that was a little further south from the most direct flight path so that he could fly above the Great Ocean Road, a long, snaking highway running from outside Geelong to Apollo Bay, following the magnificent but rugged coastline of the Southern Ocean. Flying low above the jagged coastal cliffs, Jon watched huge sets of swells roll into the shore, with the bravest of surfers jostling for position on the crests of the biggest waves. As his eyes followed the shadow of his own aircraft sweeping along the wide, golden beach below, he felt himself finally begin to relax. His tasks had been completed. David was now buried, Robert's widow was financially secure, Posarnov was dead, and Jon was now, somewhat unexpectedly, a wealthy man. He looked forward to enjoying some of his favorite old pastimes in this wildly beautiful and familiar part of the world as a way of canceling out the events of the past few months.

He landed outside the town of Lorne, registering and locking the plane at the small provincial Geelong Airport. From there he took a taxi to the local car rental agency, where he rented a station wagon. The drive to the Breakers Hotel was short and pleasant, and it wasn't long before he'd checked into the small oceanfront hotel. Winter was just ending in Australia, so the place was nearly empty. Jon was glad it was off-season. He didn't mind the cold water, and was relieved he wouldn't have to contend with hordes of other surfers on the beaches. He ordered supper in his room and settled back to unwind. On his own at last, he felt an urge to call Victoria. He checked his watch. Too early in England. He typed in a text message to her on his phone, *"V. Wye is beautiful. Head clearing and heart mending with the thought of you. Wish you were here, J."*

An hour or so later, he read her response: *"Darling, delighted to hear. Boris's death a huge relief to family, a great weight lifted. I love you, Jonny. V."* Her reference to Boris's death seemed pointed and made him wonder how much she knew or suspected, but he decided not to think about it.

Fleet Street, London

The phone rang, and Penny, back at her desk at the *London Globe* newsroom, was quick to pick it up.

"Fiona?" she asked excitedly, in response to the "hello" on the other end.

"How's London?" Fiona asked.

"Rainy, what else," Penny replied. "I was going to call you this afternoon. How are you?"

"I've got some news that might be of interest to you. It's about Jon Phillips."

"Do tell. I could do with a break on the story about now."

"You asked about my original source for it."

"Someone you knew had an inside track, you said."

"I know I did," Fiona acknowledged. "That wasn't entirely accurate."

"So what's the real version?"

"The story was given to me by a man named James Remini. He was the one who told me about Georgie. He introduced us and set up the whole interview." Penny caught a sheepish tone in Fiona's voice, as she wrote down the name.

"Thanks for telling me. I really appreciate it. Any background on him?"

"He's an investor of sorts, although he hangs out with a bad crowd, so who knows. He seems very well connected. And he wanted Phillips to take a fall, big-time. I don't know why."

"How do you know him?"

Fiona hesitated for just a moment. "He was my lover. For some inexplicable reason I found him intriguing, for a brief moment in time. Gangster glam, or some such. Anyway, that's over, but he's still a good contact to have. I knew he was playing me for his own purposes, but it was a juicy story so I went along with it."

"Well, we've all done some version of that, Fiona. Don't worry about it."

"Thanks, Penny. But you can't tell anyone."

"I promise." Penny was, in fact, flattered Fiona was confiding in her. "But why are you telling me this now?"

"Because I just heard from him. He wanted to know where Jon Phillips was. I thought you'd like to know."

"Did you tell him?"

"Yes. I figured it didn't matter to either of us, and it would keep me on his good side."

"What did he say?"

"Nothing, really. But he did seem very interested in finding out his whereabouts. From what I know of him, he's probably on his way to Australia right now. There was something urgent in his tone, and he's a guy who doesn't mess around."

Penny was thinking rapidly, her mind buzzing with questions and hypotheses. She wondered who James Remini was, and why he had wanted to publicly destroy Jon. Penny had always suspected that the original news story was a hatchet job. If his connection to Jon had to do with a deal gone wrong, it must have gone spectacularly wrong for him to have followed Jon all the way to Australia, an assumption that both Penny and Fiona were willing to make. It had to be linked to Jon's trading losses for the Bank of Manhattan.

Fiona had been listening to the silence on the other end. "You still there, Penny?"

"Uh, yeah, I was just thinking."

"About what?"

"About how I'm going to get to Australia."

"Are you serious?" Fiona hadn't expected this reaction. "You're going to fly all that way just to chase this? Maybe I'm wrong. Maybe Remini's not going there."

"Of course he is." Penny had a strong hunch that this wild card would provide the answers she'd been looking for. Besides, she had no other leads. "I have to go. I'd never forgive myself if I just let it drop at this point. Besides, I can stop over in New York on my way back, take some vacation days. What do you say?"

"I say come, by all means, but try to make it in one piece. This guy could be dangerous if you get in his way. Seriously. You'll need to be very careful." She cautioned.

"I will, I promise. I just don't want to give up on this story without tracking down every possible lead. You can understand that, can't you?"

Fiona sighed. "Yes, unfortunately I can. But I'm almost sorry I told you about Remini. If anything happened, I'd feel totally responsible."

Penny laughed. "Wait a minute, here. It's entirely my decision to go. I'll be careful. And best of all, I'll see you soon. Thanks, Fiona. I'll be in touch." There was now urgency in her tone, a spring in her step.

As she made her way to her editor's office, Penny knew it wouldn't be easy to persuade him to send her to Australia, but she was determined to go, one way or another. She tapped loudly on the smoky-glassed office door and entered before he had a chance to invite her in.

"Peter, I've got another lead on the Phillips story and I need to go to Melbourne to follow it up," she said, all in a rush.

"What story would that be, Penny?" He began dismissively.

"You came back from New York with more to add to your theories but nothing we could print, and now you're asking me to send you to the other side of the world to follow some new lead? I'm sorry, but no. If you're determined to pursue it, take a week off, but it's on your time and you'll have to pick up the tab for the trip." There was no doubting that his decision was final.

Penny was not surprised by his response. She knew there was no point in pushing it further. "If you won't send me, then I'll take that week off and leave as soon as possible. I'm still convinced I'm onto something," she finished, wanting to prove her determination.

His attitude softened. He remembered a time when he, too, would have chased a story he believed in, no matter where it took him. "Don't take this personally, Penny. Money's tight right now and I'm under a lot of pressure to cut expenses. I just can't do it."

She nodded in acquiescence, then left to organize her trip.

Lorne, Victoria, Australia

Wearing his trademark ponytail tucked up into a cap, James Remini entered the empty hangar of the Geelong Airport dressed in a pair of dirty, worn mechanic's overalls. He carried a large toolbox with the words "Geelong Aircraft Maintenance" written across it. In the reception area, he had checked the aircraft registration log, quickly ascertaining that Bravo Tango Oscar was registered under the name of Jon Phillips. There were virtually no security provisions at small provincial Australian airstrips such as this one.

"Can I help you, mate?" asked an airport official who had approached, startling Remini.

"Yes," Remini said, quickly recovering his equilibrium. "Jon Phillips asked me to make a few minor adjustments to Bravo Tango Oscar. I wanted to register the work with you but I couldn't find anyone in the office."

"Fair enough, mate, but it's unusual that Mr. Phillips didn't mention it to me when he arrived. Normally, they at least leave a note, if I'm not around." There was no reason for the official to be suspicious so his manner was relaxed.

Remini had a ready answer. "That's why I wanted to register with you. Jon mentioned to me that he hadn't told you guys about it. It was a bit of an afterthought once he realized he was going to be in Lorne a few days longer than he originally intended."

"No worries, then," said the smiling official. "Go right ahead."

"Right-o," said Remini, and walked purposefully toward Jon's aircraft. Upon reaching it, he opened the engine cowling. He knew exactly what he was looking for and it took him only a moment to locate the fuel system.

Within an hour, his task was completed. As he closed the engine cover, he was careful to wipe off any evidence of his handiwork. Striding away from the aircraft, he allowed himself a smile. Now he was free to take down Jon Phillips at his leisure, with the knowledge that, whatever else might happen, Phillips would have nowhere to run but straight back into trouble.

Chapter Twenty-eight

Night passed peacefully over the Breakers Hotel. Remini had parked discreetly down the road, in a spot where he was hidden but could still see both the hotel entrance and the parking lot. He settled in for a sleepless night, clutching a pair of binoculars. It didn't matter to him that, despite his initial assessment of Jon as a pencil-pushing wimp, he now suspected he'd killed at least two people; what mattered to Remini was that Jon was the only person left who could jeopardize his financial windfall, doubled now that Posarnov was dead. Remini was taking no chances. He'd been wrong about Jon once, and he wasn't going to risk being wrong about him again.

As the first light of day began to appear on the horizon, the front door of the hotel swung open. Remini immediately sprang to attention. He was surprised to see his quarry had developed the look of a surf bum, a very different image from the one Remini remembered from New York. Jon walked over to a station wagon with a large, bound bundle strapped to its roof, which Remini figured was an unassembled hang glider. Two surfboards were visible inside. Remini stayed on the alert as Jon opened the door and moved the boards to the roof as well, where he secured them before driving out of the lot. As he made a right turn past Remini, Remini ducked down to hide from view, then cautiously started up his engine and followed at a distance.

The two vehicles snaked along the picturesque, nearly deserted Great Ocean Road. As the sun began to rise, spectacular waves were rolling in toward the coast, one of the finest surfing regions in the world, and host to the internationally renowned Bell's Classic at Bell's Beach, about half an hour's drive east of Lorne. Jon, however, headed west to Apollo Bay, passing Shark Bay on his way to Wye River. Once there, he pulled into the beach parking lot.

Remini drove on. A few hundred yards further down the road, he slowed his green Land Cruiser to a halt at a viewpoint next to a closed hamburger stand. Remini took his binoculars from the glove compartment and began his surveillance of the beach. Jon had already pulled on a full-length wet suit, removed a surfboard from the roof of the car, and was walking toward the water. Wye River was regarded as a good, but gentle, "break," compared with larger and wilder waves at Bell's and its neighbor, Winkypop. This was exactly why Jon had chosen it. It had been a while since he'd been up on a board, and he was no longer a fearless teenager.

The hours passed. Remini walked over to a small surfing and food store across the road when it opened its doors. There he bought a book called "Know Your Hang Glider" and ordered a sandwich to go, which he took back to his car. With one eye on Jon, he passed the time studying the book. In addition to being known for its surfing, the region offered challenging hang gliding off the huge cliffs rising dramatically above the wide, golden beaches, due to the strong and nearly constant on-shore winds blowing directly up from the South Pole.

Jon had initially been alone in the water, except for some small fishing boats that appeared to be trawling well beyond the break. After a while, other surfers, sixteen-year-old kids mostly, joined him. Jon had had enough by that time, and not wishing to fight for space on every wave, he paddled back toward shore, where he pulled off his wet suit, toweled himself dry, and packed up his surf-board.

In a few minutes the two-car convoy was on the move again, Remini following Jon back to the hotel. Remini stayed in his car while Jon ate an early lunch inside. When he re-emerged, he re-moved the bound bundle from the roof of his car, balanced it ex-pertly on his shoulder, and headed on foot across the Great Ocean Road toward the cliffs above an ocean dotted with surfers. As Jon began climbing the long and narrow pathway to the top of the cliffs, Remini could see that the bundle he carried was, indeed, a hang glider.

A few moments later, Remini got out of his Land Cruiser. In a thin windbreaker and leather-soled loafers, he was not dressed for hiking, but he followed Jon all the same. The path up to the top of the cliff was steep and rugged, and he was out of breath by the time he reached the top. Once there, he spotted Jon immediately. He was hunched over, assembling his hang glider while being observed by several onlookers. Remini moved over to stand behind them for cover, but Jon was too absorbed in his task to notice anything.

Finally strapped to his glider, Jon waited for the breeze to pick up so that he could launch himself off the edge of the cliff. As soon as the wind shifted, he ran down the hill. The wind lifted the sail of his glider, and he stepped off the side of the cliff and out into flight. After at first plummeting to within five hundred feet of the ground below, he picked up a thermal and soared sharply upward. The on-lookers let out a small cheer, then turned their attention to the next glider ready to launch. Not wanting to be noticed by them, Remini quickly descended back to the parking lot below.

Wye River, Victoria, Australia

A half-moon hung over the pitch-black ocean that night, highlight-ing the ripples with its glow, though casting very little other light. Jon's station wagon sat once again in the hotel's small lot. It was 2 A.M. and all was quiet. Remini opened the door of his car and walked over toward Jon's. Free from prying eyes, Remini silently removed the hang glider from the car's roof. Careful not to make any noise and moving stealthily to avoid attracting any attention, he carefully carried the apparatus into a field next to the hotel. Once there, after making sure he was alone, he switched on the powerful beam of a Magnalight torch and took out a number of tools from a small bag he carried. Shining the torch onto the glider, he began to unpack it as though he were about to assemble it. Reading from the book he'd bought, he examined the safety harness that connected the pilot to the glider, paying particular attention to places where it joined the frame. Next, he spent a few moments studying various points in its construction before selecting a single, crucial spot.

Using one of the specialized tools from his bag, he set to work stressing the fabric until it was weakened to the point of tearing, careful to make the stress appear to have been caused by normal wear and tear. Having completed his work, Remini painstakingly repacked the glider exactly as he'd found it, and moving quietly with frequent pauses to look around, he returned it to the top of Jon's car. Remini considered what he had just accomplished; never had he gone to such lengths to dispose of a mark, but to secure his fortune, it was essential to make Phillips' death appear accidental. Besides, he had to admit he was rather enjoying this leisurely stalking of his prey.

The following morning, Jon left the hotel slightly later than before, but his routine was identical to that of the previous day. Wye River to surf, then back to the hotel for lunch. Again he hiked up the cliff, and again he kneeled at the same spot to assemble his glider, this time alone. Remini sat at a distance, hidden behind a large rock on the side of the cliff and keeping an unobtrusive eye on Jon.

Jon completed the assembly and stood up, extending the canopy overhead while he waited for the appropriate moment to launch himself. Feeling the wind hit the right speed and direction, he began to run downhill toward the edge of the cliff. With each stride, his motion jerked the frame laterally, placing increasing pressure on the stressed joint. Remini squinted through the power-ful lenses of his binoculars, concentrating his attention on the weak point, conscious of the pressure being placed on the frame even be-fore Jon was airborne, and hoping it didn't give prematurely.

But in fact, as Jon built up speed approaching the edge of the cliff, the pressure on the frame became too great for it to hold. A sound like the cracking of a whip shattered the silence of the hill-side. Jon fell hard against the rocky ground. His glider crashed down just in front of him. The momentum of his run carried him forward with it until both were precariously close to the edge of the cliff. Jon remained attached to the harness as the wind grabbed at the large area of open canvas, whipping it outward and downward. Jon screamed for help as he continued to be dragged even closer to the precipice. One gust of wind, and the glider would be out over the edge, Jon with it. Remini stood up, but remained motionless in the background, watching intently.

Jon kicked furiously, his feet stabbing at the loose gravel in a futile attempt to gain a purchase on the unstable dirt surface. A handful of stones rained down the face of the cliff. He was now al-most at the edge. He could hear the distant smashing of waves against the jagged rocks at the base of the cliff, so far below.

At that moment, the sound of children's voices mingled with the whistling of the wind. Remini swung around to see a family walking up the path toward them. He had only a split second to re-act. If he were seen by these people doing nothing to help, he might become implicated in Jon's death, certainly so if the glider were then found to have been tampered with. Yet he remained frozen in place.

The family had just realized Jon was in difficulty and needed help. The father began to run toward Jon, grabbing Remini as-sertively to assist him as he sprinted past. He physically dragged Remini with him, this stranger realizing he would need the added help to save the stricken hang glider. Fortunately, they'd been too preoccupied once they'd become aware of Jon's dilemma to notice Remini's paralysis. Remini was pushed toward Jon and in moments, the two men were almost within reach of Jon, still struggling with his harness and calling out for help.

The stranger reached Jon first but was unable on his own to get a firm hold on him. Remini was again pushed forward by the stranger's wife and children, yelling at him to do something. He had no choice. He took hold of a corner of the hang glider and stabilized it so the stranger could grab Jon's harness and release him from it, just as it was about to tumble over the edge. Reluctantly, Remini helped drag Jon from the edge of the cliff and away from danger. The straps that had been released from Jon's harness fell slack as the glider disappeared down the side of the cliff. Jon, the stranger, and Remini were left lying on the ground panting, each contemplating what could have been.

Remini was the first to stand, but before he could make his escape, the stranger stopped him and turned to Jon. "You should be very grateful to this man. Without his help, we would have lost you. Another second and you would have been history." Remini immediately turned away, lowering his head in apparent modesty.

Jon smiled weakly as he studied his rescuers, still in shock from his brush with death. Remini tried to avoid Jon's gaze as he moved to leave, but Jon caught his eye. He recognized him immediately. The blood drained from his face.

Chapter Twenty-nine

Mansfield, Victoria, Australia

A small white car pulled up at the gates of Baroonga. Penny squinted at the signpost to reassure herself that she had arrived at the right place. In the yard, a man was moving bales of fencing wire into the back of a pickup truck. He hadn't noticed her so she decided to head for the house. It felt good to walk even the short distance from her car to the front door. She'd flown economy via Singapore. After a layover there, she'd finally arrived in Melbourne, immediately rented a car, and driven the two hours northeast to Mansfield. She was feeling the effects of the long journey, but there was no time to yield to jet lag.

She tapped on the screen door. It was opened by a young woman in her twenties, Elaine. "I'm sorry to bother you," Penny began, tentatively, "but I'm looking for Jon Phillips. Is he here, by any chance?"

"Oh, I'm afraid you just missed him," said a voice from within. Elaine stepped to one side and motioned to Penny to come in. Jon's mother stood smiling by the kitchen table. She'd picked up on the English accent from the other side of the door. "Do come in," she continued. "I'm sure you must be exhausted."

"Thank you," Penny said slightly confused, but gratified by the friendliness of the welcome.

"Did Jon know you were coming?" asked Jon's mother, becoming flustered. "He'll be so disappointed he missed you. We've been hearing a great deal about you."

"Really?" Now Penny was totally bemused.

"But in any case, we're so happy to finally meet you, Victoria."

Penny tried to mask her surprise. "Uh . . ." she began.

"It's just that we weren't expecting you," Jon's mother continued. "Why didn't Jon say something?"

"Oh, he didn't know. I was planning to surprise him." Thinking fast, Penny decided she might as well play along with their mistake. "Will he be away for long?"

"He said he'd be gone about a week, I'm afraid. And he just left. What a mix-up," Jon's mother replied.

Penny could feel Elaine eyeing her. It made her uncomfortable. Best to get away from here as quickly as possible, she thought.

"A week. That's a shame. But maybe I can catch up with him. Do you have an address?"

"He flew to Lorne this morning in his father's plane," said Jon's mother, nodding.

"Lorne?"

"It's southwest of here. A resort town. He wanted some time on his own, but I'm sure he wouldn't mind being joined by you, Victoria. Shall I try to call him?"

"No!" Penny blurted, then caught herself. "No, I mean, I'd like to surprise him."

Jon's mother smiled conspiratorially. "Very well, dear. I understand. He's staying at the Breakers Hotel there."

"Thanks. Perhaps you could give me the number, just in case. But I really have my heart set on surprising him. How long do you think it will take me to drive there?"

"Five hours. Six, maybe."

Penny looked at her watch. She didn't have the energy to drive half that distance, but she was convinced that a speedy exit was imperative. "I'd better get going, then. It was very nice to meet you both."

Jon's mother was taken aback. "You aren't leaving already?"

"I have to if I want to get there by tonight."

"But at least let us give you something to eat before you leave."

"Really, I should be going." Penny was already backing toward the door.

"So this is Jon's young lady!"

Penny spun around to see the man from the yard standing in the doorway, blocking her exit.

"Yes, Ted, this is Victoria. She's on her way down to Lorne to surprise Jon."

"Really?" Jon's father responded. "Not before we share a nice cup of tea. Why don't you stay the night?"

"A cup of tea would be wonderful. You are so very kind, thank you." Penny didn't see any graceful way out.

"Super." Jon's mother smiled at her. "I'll just put the kettle on and round up a bite to eat."

Wye River, Victoria, Australia

Remini knew immediately that he'd been recognized. He gave a cursory smile to the family, then beat a swift retreat. As he ran downhill, Remini cursed the timing of their arrival. Only a minute or two later and Jon would have been neatly dispensed with. Remini had had enough of these cat-and-mouse games. He resolved to simply take Jon out as expediently as possible and dispose of the body wherever he could. He would deal with the money separately. This was not New York; here there were massive stretches of untouched land and very few people. Dumping a body would be a cinch, he thought.

He was halfway down the deserted path when he heard running footsteps behind him. He turned, and to his surprise he saw Jon, a look of grim determination on his face. Remini raised both his hands, palms outward, as if greeting an old friend, and grinned.

"What do you think you're doing, Phillips?" He laughed out loud. "This is gonna be easier than I thought."

Jon merely increased his pace, as Remini stood his ground. When Jon had come within a few feet of Remini, he unexpectedly threw himself into the air, landing squarely on top of Remini in a flying rugby tackle. Remini was knocked off-balance and, unable to maintain his footing on the rough terrain, he fell to one knee. Jon had landed hard, and lay sprawled on the ground nearby. Younger and stronger and in good physical shape, he was all power but no technique as he began flailing and punching at Remini. Remini, on the other hand, had the experience and training Jon lacked, making them fairly evenly matched. Grabbing a handful of hair, he yanked Jon's head backwards while simultaneously slamming his elbow into the back of Jon's neck. It was a well-executed strike. Stunned, Jon came close to losing consciousness.

Remini was in control. "What do you think you're doing, ass-hole? You're a fucking amateur. Do you really think you can take me down? You should have stuck to wearing dresses like your darling brother." He began to drag Jon off the path toward the cliff's edge. The family might appear at any moment; it was time to get this over with, he thought.

Seeing the precipice rapidly approaching, Jon desperately sank his nails into the fleshy backs of Remini's hands, drawing blood. Remini lost his grip and his patience. He let go and kicked Jon hard in the stomach, then lifted his foot again to stamp on his face. But as Remini brought his foot down, Jon spun out of the way, whipping his arm out to catch Remini's other ankle and knocked him off his feet. Remini fell heavily to the ground, where both men continued to wrestle, just inches from the precipitous drop.

Once again, technique won out and Remini gained the upper hand. He knew it would be difficult to push Jon over without being dragged over himself so he wrapped his hands around Jon's neck and began to squeeze. As Remini's grip tightened, Jon reached up to try to tear at his opponent's most vulnerable spot, his eyes, but Remini expertly leaned back out of reach, while maintaining his grasp on Jon's throat. Switching tactics, Jon scrabbled at the ground around him in search of something, anything, to grab, but his body was fast giving out.

As Remini felt Jon go limp beneath him, he loosened his grip on his throat and fell back panting at his side. The fight had been hard, Jon had been an unexpectedly worthy opponent, and Remini was reminded that he was not as young and fit as he had once been. And he was keenly aware that his task was not yet over. As long as he lay here, he ran the risk of being discovered. He had to get Jon off the cliff. Remini raised himself to his knees and began to push Jon's limp body toward the edge, but he found the effort greater than expected. Struggling with the dead weight, he turned away from Jon to lean down and use his shoulder as leverage to roll the body over. As he did so, a heavy, thumping crack, followed by a sharp pain in the side of his head, stunned him. A rivulet of dark liquid trickled from under his hairline and into his eyebrow. He reached up and touched it and smelled it. It was blood. As he tried to comprehend what had taken place, darkness descended upon him and he fell backwards, inert.

Jon remained where he was for more than a few moments, regaining his breath. On the verge of losing consciousness, he had managed to grab a rock and swing it at Remini with all the strength he could muster, fueled by pure adrenalin. It had been enough. The older man now lay beside him. He was out cold.

Mansfield, Victoria, Australia

Penny had managed to parry questions regarding subjects ranging from the current social climate in England to life at Stanford Hall and Victoria's family. She was thankful that she and Victoria had once been close enough for her to be able to come up with, or at least improvise convincingly about, answers to their questions. After a while she even found herself rather enjoying playing the role of Lady Victoria, potential bride of Jon Phillips, and was touched by the genuine warmth and interest Jon's family showed. Victoria was luckier than she knew, she thought.

"That was a delicious lunch. And this was the best cup of tea I've had in years, Mrs. Phillips. To think I had to leave England to be given it," Penny said, setting down her cup, her third.

"From you that's a great compliment, Victoria. I imagine you were brought up with the finest of blends."

"I like Earl Grey," Elaine offered, a little defensively, Penny thought.

"So do I. But Darjeeling is my favorite. I have a friend, Penny Jordan, who loves Earl Grey, too." Penny had become confident enough in her subterfuge to risk taking a chance. "She went to university with Jon and I," she added.

The three Phillips's exchanged looks. There was an awkward silence until Jon's father answered Penny's questioning look. "Jon spoke about her. She's apparently got some sort of vendetta going against him and has been after him recently, stirring up trouble about his problems at the Bank of Manhattan. From what I've heard, you'd be well advised to steer clear of her, she's not your sort," he said.

Before Penny could answer, Elaine changed the subject. "If you don't mind me asking," she said, "where did you get your shoes?"

Penny had noticed Elaine surreptitiously sizing her up ever since she'd arrived. "Oh, you know," she floundered, looking down at her cheap, scuffed Saxone loafers, "just some place on High Street." She felt herself blushing, as all eyes focused on her feet.

"Oh," Elaine said, "it's just that I would have expected . . ."

"Elaine," her mother interjected, disapprovingly.

"No, it's alright," blurted Penny. "I like to be comfortable when I travel, that's all." When there was no response, she laughed, weakly. "It's not all diamonds and scepters, you know."

Jon's mother smiled politely, and, with a meaningful look at Elaine, indicated that the subject of shoes was closed.

Chapter Thirty

Wye River, Victoria, Australia

Remini opened his eyes. His vision was watery, out of focus. He thought it might be raining on him. A dark figure loomed above him, contrasting with the whiteness of his surroundings. It reached over his head and the rain stopped. Remini's sight became less blurred and he was able to look around, concluding that the source of the water had been a showerhead. He was laying in a bathtub, fully clothed, a gag stuffed in his mouth. He tried to move but found that his hands and feet were tightly bound.

"Good. You're awake," Jon said, grabbing him by the lapels and lifting him up. "Let's talk."

He hauled Remini out of the tub, stood him up, and walked him to an adjoining bedroom. They were in Jon's hotel, and Jon was still recovering from the effort it had taken to get Remini there, dragging him, half-conscious, down the rest of the trail and sneaking him into the hotel through a seldom-used back door. Once inside the room, Remini had passed out and couldn't be roused until Jon put him in the bathtub and drenched him. Jon left him lying in the middle of the bedroom floor and picked up a remote. The television flickered to life. Jon raised the volume. Only then did he release his captive's gag. He did not want to risk him calling out for help.

Picking up a golf club from a set he'd taken from the hotel, Jon walked back over to Remini and looked down into his face. "So how did you find me?"

"Go fuck yourself," Remini snarled. His head ached where he'd been hit by the rock.

"Right. I suppose I should thank you, in a way. You taught me a lot. Remember this?" Jon held up the golf club.

"You're gonna get caught, you know," Remini said, defiantly.

"Why d'you say that?" Jon tapped the club head into his palm menacingly, as Remini once had done.

"Because this isn't your game. You might have got lucky with Johnston and Posarnov, but you're too high-profile. Your motives are too obvious. Someone will put it all together and you'll spend the rest of your life in jail."

"And you're so sure you've gotten away with killing Robert Baldwin and my brother?"

Remini peered around the room. "I want you to know that if you're recording this conversation as some kind of confession, it's worthless. I'm under duress."

"I guarantee that is not the case," Jon said. "But I don't get it. What have you got to gain by coming after me? Your bosses are dead."

Remini was annoyed. "My bosses? Nobody's my boss. It was my money that you stole."

"*Yours*?" Jon's surprise quickly turned to delight. "So *you're* the silent partner behind the U.K. Trading Company? Fantastic."

"Give the monkey a banana. Yeah, and what's more, I'm now the only partner."

"Isn't that the truth," Jon mused. "Yes, after you, there's no one else left. That's nice to know." He paused. "But I still don't get it. Why did you do it? Why did you kill my brother?"

Jon waited for an answer. Remini gazed up at him, reflecting. "It was you we wanted dead. We just happened to kill the wrong guy."

"That much I figured out. But you could have just paid me the fucking money and I would have gone away."

Remini suddenly lashed out at Jon. "Greedy fuckers like you never just go away. Types like you make me sick." Sitting up, he goaded himself on. "You sit in your fucking fancy offices, talking down to people because you happened to have learned a bunch of clever words that nobody else understands, to cover up for the fact that you're robbing them blind. And you don't give a shit so long as you get a new Ferrari every year and you can jerk off into some model's face once a week. You don't know what work is. Well, you picked the wrong fucking guy to rip off this time." He lay back, having exhausted himself.

"Which wrong guy? Would that be the guy who's tied up on the floor of my hotel room? The guy who killed my brother?" And with that, Jon slammed the golf club into Remini's ribs. "So I don't know what work is? You think you know me, you arrogant piece of shit?" Jon could hardly control his rage. He swung and hit Remini again. Remini reeled back in pain, but didn't cry out. Jon stopped himself, abruptly. "I don't owe you an explanation." He straightened up, shaking his head. "It's funny, isn't it? I was supposed to be your unwitting passport to financial legitimacy but, instead, I end up with all your money. And you're meant to be the clever one. That's fucking rich."

Remini contemplated Jon. "There's still a way we can both be rich."

"You don't get it. This is not about the money. I've already got the money. This is about my brother," said Jon, raising the golf club high over his head. "You better get some shut-eye now. We've got an early start tomorrow."

And he slammed the club down with such force that Remini was instantly knocked unconscious again. Had Jon hit him any harder, he might well have killed him, then and there.

Mansfield, Victoria, Australia

As Penny watched the Phillips' farm recede in her rear view mirror, she heaved a sigh of relief. She had made her escape soon after fin-

ishing her third cup of tea, immediately after Jon's mother mentioned another foreign friend of Jon's had called long-distance that
very morning. Jon's unflattering description of her to his family had
brought back the pain she'd felt at Cambridge. Even though she no
longer wanted what Victoria had, she somehow felt that, once
again, Victoria had ended up with everything while she, always the
outsider, had been given unfairly short shrift. Yet it had only served
to strengthen her determination. Her excitement at the prospect of
her gain being Jon's loss was growing with every passing moment.
There was no time to waste. She could not bear the thought of
missing out on a confrontation between Jon and James Remini.

Apollo Bay, Victoria, Australia

Jon drove to Apollo Bay alone. Upon reaching the small fishing
port, he slowed his car to cruise the rows of small commercial fishing boats until he found what he was looking for. He parked near a
fishing boat sign-posted for hire or rent. An old fisherman scrubbed
the deck of the battered, forty-foot converted commercial trawler.

"Hey, mate, I wonder if you can help me." Jon called to him.
"I'm looking to rent a fishing boat for a few days."

"How long for?" the fisherman asked, dropping his brush into
a pail and standing up to take Jon's measure as a prospective client.

"A few days," Jon repeated. "I've got a group of businessmen
from Melbourne coming to the West Coast. We had a boat lined up,
but it cracked its block yesterday, and I've been caught high and dry."

"Do you need a skipper or any other help?" the fisherman
asked, hoping to ring up as many fees as possible.

"No, I've got everything lined up, except for the boat. Is this
one available?"

"I've got it booked for later on this week. It's available for tomorrow, if that's of interest. You may find it a bit tricky renting a
boat at such short notice. There aren't many around this area."

Jon nodded in acknowledgement. "I've got some cash to
spend, if I can find the right boat."

"Cash?" The fisherman immediately became more interested. "Exactly how much do you have to splash on a boat?"

"What's your daily rate?"

"The basic daily rate is five hundred dollars, plus costs, including fuel and crew." The fisherman was exaggerating by two hundred dollars a day.

Jon was unfazed. "I tell you what. If you can give me the boat for up to three days and if you deliver it to me full of fuel and ready to go, I'll pay you two thousand dollars cash."

"Done," agreed the fisherman. "But I'll need the cash up front."

"That won't be a problem, but any trouble with the boat, and I hand it straight back and you refund me my money for the days I haven't used it. Understood?" Jon pretended to be concerned about negotiating a businesslike deal.

"Fair enough," the fisherman agreed. "She won't give you any trouble, but the sea could. The waters here can be tricky, not for the inexperienced. I've got the boat insured, but you're going to have to cover the guests yourself if I'm not in charge. Is that all right?"

"Fine. I'll need the boat ready tonight, and I want to have a good look around, particularly in the engine room, before I leave."

"No problem. In fact, it's always a good idea to have a look at her before you take her out. Come aboard."

Jon stepped on deck, pulling out a wad of fifty-dollar bills. As they made their way toward the cabin, he peeled off two thousand dollars and handed it over.

Wye River, Victoria, Australia

The first thing Remini was aware of when he slowly surfaced to consciousness again was the smell — noxious but unidentifiable — and then the cold. The smell contained the familiar odor of diesel fumes but overriding the diesel was a pungent stench that he couldn't quite figure out. His head felt as though someone had driven a nail through the top of his skull, and his teeth were chattering. He was also nauseated, from a combination of the smell, the concussion his body was no doubt dealing with, and the constantly undulating motion he was experiencing. Gradually he became aware of a low, rumbling whine. He deduced that it was an engine, presumably the source of the diesel fumes. He could also make out the sound of fluids sloshing around in containers through his dreamlike state of semi-consciousness.

He was drifting off again when he felt himself splashed with liquid. The caustic smell grew so much stronger that it seemed to burn his sinuses. He opened his eyes.

"Morning," Jon greeted him loudly, almost boisterously, before disappearing from view.

Seconds later, he appeared again. Remini gingerly tried to move and was surprised to find his arms unbound. He propped himself up shakily on one arm and through his fog, tried to make sense of his surroundings. The low rumbling was indeed the engine of a boat, and the undulating he'd been feeling was the rise and fall of the calm ocean's waves. Remini wiped his eyes and shook his head, trying to clear his mind as he took in the fact that although Jon was on the boat, he himself was lying, face-down, on a large, long, and old-fashioned surfboard, now covered in the sticky, foul liquid he'd been smelling. He was finding it impossible to fathom just what he was doing on a surfboard attached to a rope secured to a small fishing boat in the middle of the ocean.

The first rays of dawn were just appearing over the horizon beyond the boat. Remini could see that they were not far from shore, just marginally beyond the breaking waves.

"It's going to be a beautiful day," Jon called out. He looked around, as if admiring the view. "I'm not surprised you decided to go surfing so early. The swell is good and you've got the whole break to yourself. I'm just sorry I won't be able to join you."

The sea remained calm around them, the only disturbance the gentle white turmoil of the boat's wake. Jon vanished once again, reappearing after a moment lugging a heavy oil drum to the back of the boat. And as he carefully peeled back the cover to reveal the contents of the drum, Remini suddenly recognized the smell.

Jon tipped the drum over the scarred wooden ledge at the back of the old boat and began to pour its red liquid contents into the water. "Cow's blood," he commented, glancing up to observe Remini's reaction. A red plume of fresh blood was now following the wake, trailing both sides of the surfboard on which Remini lay.

After emptying the container of blood, Jon tossed the contents of a large plastic tray filled with fish heads and scraps into the water in Remini's direction. "Here, catch this, mate," he laughed. Remini looked frantically around in all directions. The surfboard was in the center of a widening circle stained an ugly shade of deep sienna. He was gagging from the stench.

"The interesting thing is," Jon declaimed, in mock lecture mode, "that the Southern Ocean is known as the world's largest breeding ground for the White Pointer Shark, known to most as the Great White. This area is riddled with them." He paused, needing all his strength to haul another forty-four-gallon drum of cow's blood onto the rear ledge of the boat and pour it carefully into the water. "It's the cold water they like so much. The water here comes straight from the South Pole. I suppose you can feel how cold it is," Jon laughed. "They can't see much, but they can smell fresh blood for miles and miles. They should be turning up any minute now." The boat's engine continued to provide the only interruption of the silence of the sea at dawn.

A small, angular black object suddenly protruded from the water off to the rear of the boat. It was unmistakably a fin. Remini's panic turned again to nausea. "Look, over there," said Jon, excitedly, pointing in another direction. "A shark." And with that, another fin appeared only a few yards from its mate. Jon continued laying the gruesome trail, with added vigor.

Large gray shadows were racing around just under the surface. Jon lifted several big chunks of fish and tossed them overboard. The first piece had hardly hit the water when, with great speed and precision, the huge jaws of a large White Pointer shark clamped down on the bait. As Jon threw more pieces after those, the thrashing shapes rose to the surface and the predators of the deep began a feeding frenzy.

James Remini frantically attempted to paddle toward the boat. He was now screaming in terror. Jon adjusted the boat's speed so that it stayed tantalizingly just beyond Remini's desperate reach. The roiling water around the surfboard was reeking of fish and blood and rotting flesh. "I wouldn't put my hands in there if I were you," Jon solicitously advised.

"Fuck you!" Remini shouted in a final act of defiance. But he stopped paddling, realizing that his efforts were futile, that Jon would make sure he never caught up to the boat.

"Oh yeah?" Jon crowed. "Let's see what you're made of now, tough guy." He laughed loudly.

The sharks wasted no time. Their appetite for flesh reached a fever point as they fought one another for Remini's warm flesh, whipping the water into peaks of red-and-white foam created by thrashing, silvery, slick gray tails churning remnants of what the powerful jaws tore apart. It was only a matter of seconds, not minutes, before the sharks had ripped Remini's carcass to unidentifiable shreds.

Jon gathered in and untied the rope that remained attached to the remnants of what had been, moments ago, a large surfboard. He then crossed to the boat's wheelhouse and leaned forward on the throttles to begin the journey back to dry land. Calmly, he looked around. He was all alone in the early morning light. Behind him, the blood had already begun to disperse into the blue fathoms of water. Finally, he felt a sense of freedom.

Chapter Thirty-one

Wye River, Victoria, Australia

Heading west out of Lorne, Penny found the landscape she was
driving through unexpectedly beautiful. Before coming, she'd had a
vague impression of Australia as being largely made up of miles of
arid bush, and so wasn't prepared for the lush abundance of the area
in which she found herself.

As she wound her way around the Great Ocean Road on the
approach to the town of Wye River, the road, which had been virtually deserted for miles, was suddenly filled with activity. She
slowed behind a line of cars and observed a policeman directing
traffic, his squad car blocking the highway in both directions.

As she approached the policeman, Penny leaned out of her
open window. "What's the hold-up, Officer?" she asked.

"There's been an accident. The road's been closed temporarily
to allow the emergency vehicles access to the beach area."

"Can you tell me how else to get to the Breakers Hotel?"

"You staying there?" he inquired.

"Yes," Penny lied.

"That's it down there." He motioned toward a group of unas-
suming buildings just beyond the roadblock. "This is the only way.

We'll be clearing traffic as soon as we can. Then you'll be on your way."

"Thank you," said Penny. Her curiosity was piqued by the news that there had been an accident in such close proximity to the hotel in which Jon was supposedly staying. She noticed a group of surfers who'd parked their camper at the side of the road and were making their way on foot down a beachside track, carrying their surfboards. She decided to follow suit and, pulling her car onto the grass verge, she set off walking.

Emergency vehicles were gathered around the entrance to the beach and several search-and-rescue, four-wheel drive vehicles were parked by the water's edge. A small crowd was dispersing from around an ambulance, which was beginning to move slowly away from the scene. Penny noticed a second group of people gathered at the water's edge. They were staring at an object in the sand. Weaving her way through them, Penny discovered that the object of their curiosity was a large white surfboard, or rather, what was left of one. Two large bite marks formed an exaggerated "M" on one side, and the whole surface was heavily scored, as if scraped by several sets of sharp teeth. The conversation among the crowd centered not on whether it had been a shark that had inflicted the damage, but how big it was.

"By the look of that, mate, I'd reckon we're talkin' sixteen-to-twenty-foot. Not that unusual for these waters," commented one man.

"Yeah, at least," agreed another. "Probably mistook the poor bastard for a seal."

Penny ventured a question, her English accent immediately setting her apart from this group of Australian locals. "Has someone been injured in a shark attack?"

"Blimey, is that what happened? I thought he'd been taken by a seagull," joked one of the men. They all laughed.

Penny stared at them, put off by their response.

An approaching policeman took pity on her. "Come on, fellas, you all know this is no laughing matter." He pushed through the crowd to collect the fractured board. "Yes, madam, you are correct. A surfer was taken by a shark earlier this morning."

"Is the man okay?" Penny persisted, naively, too focused on finding a way to make this event somehow relate to Jon to draw the obvious conclusion. The men nudged one another and rolled their eyes but remained silent, smirking.

"I'm afraid there wasn't much left of him when he was discovered. It was a ferocious attack," the policeman replied.

"Do you know his name?" She asked.

"Not yet."

"Or do you have any idea what he looked like?"

"All we know at this stage, miss, is that we believe we've located the victim's rental car and he does not appear to have been a local. Please excuse me."

As he moved away, carrying what was left of the surfboard, Penny began to consider the implications if the dead man proved to be James Remini. Again, nothing seemed to fit. Penny's exhaustion and her isolation from her own environment seemed to accentuate the implausibility of the theory she'd been trying to prove. She felt overwhelmingly alone and out of place.

As she walked back toward the road, two young men in wet suits passed her, going towards the water. Both were carrying surfboards. Placing their boards face-up on the sand, they began to apply wax to the top surface of each one. The crowd by the water lingered, idly chatting and watching the policeman do his paperwork, using the hood of his four-wheel drive vehicle as a desk. Penny watched in disbelief as the two men picked up their boards and entered the water.

"Wait!" she shouted. "Wait! Don't go in the water!"

The men turned and stared at her without expression, already ankle-deep in the water.

"You can't go in there. A man was just killed by a shark," Penny yelled.

One of the surfers spoke up. "Yeah, but from what I hear of what's left of the bloke, I doubt if it will still be hungry," he grinned.

"Please don't go in," Penny implored. She didn't know what had come over her, but she had a sense of general foreboding that made it seem imperative that she at least try to prevent another accident from happening. "It's dangerous." What was the matter with these people? She thought.

"Maybe this pommie bird is right. We could always go to the pub instead." As the other surfer spoke, he fixed his leg-rope to his ankle.

"Too dangerous driving home, given the state we'd be in after getting pissed all afternoon," his friend replied.

The other nodded sagely. "Fair enough." He paused to ponder. "What about drugs, then?"

"We don't have any." The first surfer looked back at Penny. "Thanks anyway, but we'll just take our chances with the Great Whites."

And with that, both men turned and continued to walk into the water, moving toward the breaking waves. Penny was left speechless. If these men were typical Australians, then given that Jon was Australian, perhaps her mistake with him had always been that she had tried to understand him through British eyes.

Chapter Thirty-two

Wye River, Victoria, Australia

The police had reopened the road, and there was a long line of cars proceeding toward the various beach communities along the Great Ocean Road. In no hurry now, Jon slid the station wagon into gear and joined the clearing line of traffic. He parked outside the hotel and went in to collect his belongings and check out. As he walked out of the front door, carrying his bags, he thought he saw a familiar figure just outside. He hesitated, but before he could retreat, he realized he'd been spotted. He walked toward the figure.

"Penny?" he said, trying not to let alarm override surprise. "Of all the people I might have expected to see here, you are about the last. What brings you to the West Coast?"

"You do," she said, triumphantly.

"And how is that?" Jon was anxious to know, but feigned only polite curiosity.

"Well, now, let me see. It appears that a couple of pretty unlikely accidents have befallen two buddies of yours." Penny paused, hoping that Jon would react. When he didn't, she continued. "Being a journalist, I'm always in search of a good story, right? And it seems I've arrived in time to catch yet another bizarre accident, the kind that just seems to happen when you're around, and, oddly enough, only to people who are somehow connected to you. I'm still thinking I might be onto something, wouldn't you agree?"

"No, I wouldn't," Jon replied, more sharply than he'd intended. "Look, Penny, tying together a bunch of random accidents would be a challenge for the most seasoned of investigative journalists. It's just not that easy to make something out of a few circumstantial happenings."

"You're absolutely right. But what if I was able to connect them by the very fact of your presence at all of them?"

"You'd have to prove I was there, number one, which, incidentally, I wasn't, so you couldn't. But even if you could prove it, I doubt that it would be enough," he said in a very matter-of-fact fashion.

"You know, you may be right. But then, how's this? What if I could get a positive ID from someone who was indirectly involved in one, if not all, of the accidents?" Penny asked, her confidence unsettling Jon.

"I'd say that you were maybe getting somewhat closer to having a story to write, but that it would still depend on the quality of the ID and the credibility of the witness."

"Would you think the captain of the sailing boat on which one of the accidents took place might be credible enough?" Penny wasn't above taking a few liberties with the truth to get a rise out of Jon.

"It might be a start. But mere presence is one thing, proving involvement or guilt is quite another. It still doesn't sound like any kind of a story to me."

Ignoring his response, she continued. "Look, Jon, there's Robert's and David's deaths, and I believe I can put you at Georgie's, Johnston's, and Posarnov's as well." She paused, a hint of concern developing in her expression. "There's one thing that troubles me. The one major weakness in this whole scenario is that I can't come up with a motive. Frankly, you don't strike me as a serial killer, but I know you're involved somehow. You may not be responsible for all of the so-called accidents, but I'm convinced you're responsible for some of them." She gave a little laugh, reflecting. "The funny thing is that if you hadn't inquired about the U.K. Trading Company, I never would have started putting all these seemingly unrelated incidents together."

Jon did not need reminding. "Penny, I greatly admire your powers of imagination, and I am relieved to hear you don't regard me as a serial killer, but you're way off. Your imagination has gotten away from you, and this kind of talk is starting to border on slander."

"Well, if I'm way off, I will now have the added resources of the NYPD to get me on track," Penny lied.

Jon tried not to look troubled at this news. "What has the New York Police Department got to do with this ridiculous story of yours?"

Penny was on a roll and she didn't intend to spoil it by telling the truth. She could see that she'd gotten to Jon. "I believe they're reopening the file on the McWilliam incident, though you'll probably tell me you don't know what I'm talking about. In fact, I'm told they have some wig hairs that are now the centerpiece of the new investigation. It will only be a matter of time before the files are reopened on these other 'accidents.' And then, of course, there's also the rope."

"What rope?" Jon took the bait.

"The one that was severed, the one they found hanging from your old boss's neck," she lied, once again. "Plus, Victoria mentioned there was some sort of a mystery around Posarnov's death. The police are looking into that, too." By now, Penny was just tossing out hunches. "It's out of my hands at this point. You know, part of me actually hopes that I'm wrong, but the other part of me knows that I'm right."

Jon's concern was showing. He had no way of knowing how much of what she was saying was guesswork but even if guesswork was all it was, it was getting uncomfortably close to the truth.

"Look, let's suppose, for the sake of argument that you were right about everything you're saying. What good would it do to make it public? It would just cause pain to a lot of people who want to put all this behind them. And why are you so hell-bent on making me out to be a villain, anyway? Didn't we get past those old bad feelings the other night?"

Penny laughed out loud at that. "What is it with you guys? It may surprise you but having sex for ulterior motives is not the exclusive bailiwick of men. I was simply using you to get closer to the story, my friend."

"You had sex with me only because of this absurd notion that I'm in some way involved with all these unrelated deaths?" Although aware that she'd snooped while he slept, Jon was truly surprised that being with him had meant nothing more to her than that.

"Not only that, but when you were asleep, I searched your hotel room," Penny announced proudly.

Jon simulated shock. "You did *what*?"

"I've changed a lot from my days as a virginal university student. It took me years to get over you. Now it's my turn."

"But all that happened over a decade ago."

"Still, you getting in touch after so long, but only because you wanted something from me, stirred up a lot of old emotions. Don't forget, Jon, Hell hath no fury . . ."

"So this is about settling an old score."

"No, not at all. That's simply where it started. It's more a question of opportunity, a springboard out of the tabloids, as it were. This could be a really big story, Jon. Sorry. But as I see it, in a way, you owe it to me. You may have become my ticket into the mainstream."

"Penny, that's really twisted. You've clearly allowed your emotions to affect your judgment. There just is no story. The truth is that I have done absolutely nothing wrong — except to lose a lot of money — and I do not have to explain anything to anybody. I'm afraid you've wasted your time in coming to Australia."

"Not at all. I've only been here for a day and already I've come across yet another remarkable twist to this story."

"And what might that be?"

"James Remini, late of the U.K. Trading Company. It is my belief that half of him is lying in the local morgue and the other half was some shark's breakfast. And surprise, surprise, Jon Phillips just happens to be in the neighborhood." She had no way of knowing that this, in fact, had been the case, but it seemed a good bet. "Good luck, Jon, I've got a feeling you may need it."

"All these twists and turns are making me dizzy. I suppose I should be flattered by your fascination with me, but I'm not. In fact, I think it's pathetic that you would go to such lengths simply to avenge being jilted all those years ago." Signaling an end to the conversation, he tossed his bags into the car and got in. He closed the car door firmly, but his window was still open, so he could hear her parting shot.

"Really, Jon? Or is it Rick Mears, or Derek Chambers, or perhaps Karen Carpenter? I know all about you, you'd be surprised how much I know, and I'm going to do whatever I have to do to get this story out there. Who knows, I may even turn it into a book."

Jon stared back at her in disbelief. There was nothing left for him to say.

"Goodbye, Penny." He leaned forward to start the car.

"See you around," she said flippantly delighting in the extent to which she had ruffled Jon's feathers.

"No, you won't." And he drove off.

Penny shivered. Overhead, a mass of dark clouds had begun to gather. It momentarily crossed her mind that if Jon had somehow metamorphosized into a killer, she could be putting herself in harm's way. She shook off the thought immediately. She was tired from the effort it had taken to try to get a reaction out of Jon, never mind the jet lag. And now she was alone, she wondered what to do next. She was looking around, aimlessly, when she spotted a single car in the hotel's parking lot, surrounded by police. She picked her way carefully across the gravel, to the tow truck they'd brought in to haul the Toyota Land Cruiser away.

"Is this the dead man's car?" she asked the most approachable policeman.

"You're going to have to step out of the area," he responded flatly and began to usher her out of the way. She flashed her light green press pass. He looked at it, dispassionately. "I can't confirm or deny it at this stage. Move along now, please." He continued to gently push her away from the car.

"I'll rephrase the question, then," Penny said, undaunted. "Was this car rented by a man named Remini?"

"Can't confirm or deny. Please step away." Another officer, an older lieutenant, spoke up. He approached them.

"Wait a minute, Constable." He turned to Penny. "Did you say 'Remini'?"

"Yes, James Remini," confirmed Penny.

"Let her through," said the lieutenant. The younger policeman reluctantly obeyed.

"Thank you, lieutenant." She stepped over and showed her credentials. "Penny Jordan, *London Globe.*"

"What do you know about Mr. Remini?" the lieutenant asked.

"Not a lot. He's an investor from New Jersey. Was he the man killed in the shark attack?"

He ignored her question. "An investor, you say? Know any more?"

"Not really," responded Penny, grateful to finally be taken seriously by someone, "but I suspect that he may have ties to organized crime." She moved closer to the Land Cruiser and peeked inside. Nothing out of the ordinary on the front seats.

"It seems your suspicions may be correct. We ran a check on Mr. Remini through Interpol a few minutes ago . . ."

Penny interrupted. "So it was him. The dead man was Remini?"

Again, he did not respond. "How do you know this man?"

"I've been working on a story that he's a peripheral part of. I didn't know him personally."

"Do you have any further information?"

Penny paused. She was reluctant to show her hand. "No, but if I hear of anything more, I'll be sure to let you know."

"Please leave your contact details, Miss Jordan. We might want to talk with you some more."

But Penny had been distracted by some objects she had just

spotted on the rear sear of the Land Cruiser. At first, they seemed innocuous — a greasy set of overalls and a toolbox. But suddenly she realized their significance.

"Thank you for your help, lieutenant." As she spoke, she was already backing toward the parking lot's exit.

"Wait a minute," the lieutenant called out. "I haven't finished yet."

Penny continued to back away, responding over her shoulder. "I'll be happy to answer any questions you have but I have something urgent to do. I'm staying at the Breakers. Or I'll call you." As she reached the exit, she broke into a run.

By the time she got to her car, which was still parked on the side of the road, she was out of breath. Panting, she climbed in, grabbed a handful of maps from the pocket in the door and, selecting one, pored over it, tracing place names with her finger until she found what she was looking for. She memorized the route and fumbled for the keys, then frantically started the engine and flipped the car into drive. She was in such a hurry to pull out that she nearly hit a group of young surfers, sending them scurrying to the side of the road in a cloud of dust and obscenities. Mouthing apologies, she drove off, tires spraying gravel up against the bottom of the car.

Unfamiliar with the roads and the terrain, she twice made wrong turns, wasting valuable time. The words written on the side of the toolbox resonated endlessly in her head. "Geelong Aircraft Maintenance." As soon as their significance had hit her, she knew she had to prevent Jon from taking off in his father's plane — to save his life, certainly, but almost more importantly, she reluctantly had to admit to herself, to save her story. She could not allow either one to go down in flames.

It was well over an hour before she finally tore into the Geelong Airstrip, scanning it in search of Jon's plane. Several light aircraft were parked neatly in bays and in one of the open hangars she could see two or three more. Penny knew she had no time to waste. She screeched to a stop outside the small open hangar and raced inside. A couple of men were pumping grease into the wheel bearings of a small, single-engine Cessna; they looked up, startled by her dramatic entrance.

"Do either of you know Jon Phillips?" she yelled as she ran toward them.

The men looked at one another and back at her, blankly. "Jon Phillips?"

"He's a pilot. He would have flown into here a couple of days ago."

One of the men shrugged, the other ignored her.

"Who's in charge?" she demanded. "How can I find out if somebody has taken off yet?"

"You'll have to go to the tower. They keep a log of all takeoffs and landings," the same man said, off-handedly.

"Where is it?" Penny asked, her tone urgent.

"It's not available to the public."

"Where is it?" she screamed.

"I'm telling you, you won't . . ."

"Just tell me where it is!"

"End of the strip. Small building on its own," volunteered the second man, intimidated into answering.

"Thanks," Penny shouted over her shoulder, as she ran back out the door.

It was more of a squat, circular shed than a tower, but as Penny sped the little white car toward it, she saw something of greater interest out of her passenger-side window. A small, single-engine aircraft had taxied to the runway and looked as though it was making the final checks before take-off. She squinted through the mid-afternoon sunlight and made out the figure of a lone man at the controls. Her intuition told her it must be Jon. There wasn't a moment to lose. The plane's propeller roared into life and the plane slowly began to move forward down the runway where it had been sitting waiting for final clearance from the tower.

Penny had no more time for detours. Without removing her foot from the gas, she yanked the steering wheel sharply to the right. The little car bounced onto the grass median that ran between the gravel roadway and the airstrip. Ahead of her, she could see the ailerons lower into place, in preparation for take-off. Through the sound of her car's racing engine and the banging of its squeaking suspension on the rough surface of the ground, she thought she could detect a rise in the pitch of the airplane. Sure enough, the engine began to scream. He was revving up to take off.

The small aircraft quickly gathered speed. Penny drove directly toward the end of the runway in one last wild attempt to stop the plane from taking off, reaching it only moments before the plane. Recklessly, she stopped her car in the middle of the runway, directly in the path of the speeding aircraft. She looked into the cockpit; it was Jon at the controls, as she had known it would be.

It was not clear to Penny whether he recognized her. She jumped out of the car and waved both her arms in wide circles, signaling him to stop. What she had not taken into account was just how hard it might be to stop a plane in its final stages of take-off. And as she stared at the glittering blades of the front propeller bearing down on her, only then did it cross her mind that she might be in danger, so intent had she been on her mission to stop him.

No one else in the airport was near enough to do anything. The two men from the hangar had come outside to watch. The man in the tower also watched, powerlessly, astonished at the stupidity of the woman. An airport security guard jumped into his vehicle and raced toward the scene, knowing he wouldn't get there in time.

Penny backed up and pressed herself hard against the car; cringing, she turned her head to one side, and felt her hair being sucked toward the shimmering rotors. At the speed at which he was going, not only was it impossible for Jon to stop, he could not turn off the runway onto the grass without risking losing control of the aircraft. He had no choice but to keep going. He pulled down hard on the control column and the nose of the small aircraft lifted into the air. Penny froze and closed her eyes, accepting her fate, waiting for the huge, steel, razor-sharp blades to rip her to shreds.

Somewhere distant, a man, then another man, began shouting. The aircraft left the ground, its wheels grazing the roof of the car,

clearing it by only inches. The deafening noise of the engine immediately began to fade as Jon gained both altitude and distance from
Penny. It took some moments for Penny to register what had happened and to open her eyes. She swung around and watched the aircraft fly east, hugely relieved that she had narrowly escaped death,
but concerned that Jon had managed to take off, unaware that his
fate was now sealed.

"What the hell do you think you're doing?" shouted a male
voice.

"Crazy bitch must be trying to kill herself," said another.

The security guard had stopped his car a few feet away from
Penny and he and several other men were running toward her.

"That plane shouldn't have been allowed to take off!" Penny
exclaimed.

"And why not, you stupid bloody woman?" the security guard
asked.

"It's been sabotaged. It's going to go down."

Jon's plane was now out of sight. The guard grabbed Penny's
wrist. "You've got some explaining to do. You almost killed both
yourself and the pilot. You better come with me," he demanded.

"No!" Penny tried to release herself. "You have to notify the
pilot immediately! Jon Phillips. Right away!"

"Yeah, yeah," said the guard, dismissively. His grip held firm.

"You don't understand," she pleaded. "That plane belongs to
Jon Phillips. It's been sabotaged. That's why I tried to stop him
from taking off. To keep him from crashing."

The guard tightened his grip as he dragged Penny toward his
car. "You can explain all this to the bloody police."

Despite the few dark clouds still hanging over the coast, the
weather conditions inland remained clear as the small aircraft flew
effortlessly above the mountainous terrain of the Victorian Alps.
Jon flipped on the autopilot. He was shaken by how close he'd come
to crashing into Penny on the runway, and was trying to clear images away from his mind of what would have happened to her had

he done so. How had his life become so filled with life-and-death drama? And what had Penny been so urgently trying to communicate to him? He wasn't sure he would have stopped even if he'd been able to. Chances are, it was something else he didn't want to hear. He was troubled enough by what Penny had said back at the hotel. Her determination to bring him down was an unanticipated and potentially devastating twist of fate. If the cases were reopened and she wrote the story she'd described, chances were he would eventually be arrested. He had not anticipated the prospect of anyone putting all the apparently unrelated deaths together. The thought tormented him, and he was unclear as to how to react to it.

He glanced out over the world below him and marveled momentarily at the sheer size and beauty of the terrain, the heavily wooded ranges bordered by deep blue water stretching as far as the eye could see.

At that moment, he thought he heard the engine lose a beat. He quickly turned his attention back to his instruments. All seemed in order, although he noticed that the oil pressure was marginally lower than usual. He tapped the gauge. The needle didn't move. Again the engine skipped a beat, this time there was no mistake. Once more, he checked all the instruments. Suddenly, the oil pressure gauge started falling rapidly. The engine's missing beat turned into a pronounced splutter. Jon broke out in a cold sweat. He was in trouble. He picked up the hand-held microphone attached to the radio transmitter and spoke into it, trying to keep the panic he felt out of his voice.

"This is Bravo Tango Oscar. I am experiencing some engine difficulties and . . ." He noticed engine oil running down the outside of the engine's cowling. The plane began bucking violently.

Air Traffic Control responded, in a calm Australian drawl. "This is Mansfield Control, Bravo Tango Oscar, what is your location? Over."

Jon no longer made any effort not to sound panicked. "This is Bravo Tango Oscar . . ." And at that moment, his engine stopped. Its whine was replaced by a deafening silence. All that could now be heard was the whistling of the wind. The nose of the aircraft dipped abruptly.

Jon tugged on the control column in an attempt to get the nose of the aircraft up, but the plane kept dropping. He leaned forward and pushed the ignition switch. Nothing.

"Mayday, Mayday! I have lost all power. I am roughly one hundred miles . . ." The microphone seemed not to be transmitting out. He continued to press down on the ignition switch, but to no avail. "I have to ditch!" he shouted futilely into the dead microphone.

He did not attempt further contact, dropping the microphone on the passenger seat so that he could control the steering column with both hands. The plane was going down fast.

"Bravo Tango Oscar can you read me? Bravo Tango Oscar can you read me?" Mansfield Control was repeating, over and over, with increasing urgency.

Jon frantically kicked the inside of the door to his left. It was jammed shut. The aircraft was gaining speed as it rapidly continued losing altitude. Jon began to curse while continuing to kick out furiously.

"Bravo Tango Oscar. Bravo Tango Oscar . . ."

Jon spun around, struggled into a parachute, and lying prone, he stretched his body across the two seats. He hammered the passenger door with both feet, screaming wildly, willing it to open. The aircraft's angle of descent had steepened to almost vertical. The rocky, thickly timbered landscape loomed in the window. He pulled both feet back until his knees touched his chin and kicked out in one last, double-legged action. This time, the door buckled and swung open.

He wriggled across the passenger seat, grabbed his backpack and flung himself out of the plane, clawing at the release cord on his parachute. It filled out above him in a rush of canvas and air, slowing his descent. The plane exploded into flames as it crashed nearby, sending Jon's parachute back up into the air on a powerful draft, and he sailed out over the treetops into a narrow clearing. There he landed, the billowing parachute settling slowly around and over him in a makeshift shroud. As plumes of white smoke rose above the tree-covered mountainside at the point of the aircraft's impact, the figure under the parachute began to move. Jon was alive.

Epilogue

The tall palms lining the shore swayed in the gentle, early winter Bahamian breeze. Long afternoon shadows reached deep into the large, single-storied private residence perched high above the glowing golden beaches of the Caribbean Sea. A tropical garden encircled the house, its brilliant colors muted in the fading sunlight.

An open living room looked out onto an enormous swimming pool. Beyond it, the unrestricted views extended across the Caribbean as far as the eye could see. In the far recesses of the room, a man sat slumped in a brown leather chair, staring out at the idyllic scene in front of him. Moving slowly, almost deliberately, he raised his tall highball glass, elaborately garnished with tropical fruits, and drained it. Before he had put down the empty glass, a young Bahamian valet dressed formally in a starched white shirt and black trousers approached him, offering a replacement from an intricately wrought silver tray. Without turning, the man reached out and took the glass from the tray.

Picking up a remote with his other hand, he flicked on a widescreen plasma television and rotated his chair so he could focus on the wall on which it was installed. *News/Copy* was coming on via his cable feed from the United States, and Jon never missed it. It had become the high point of his day, a ritual he looked forward to more than he wanted to admit.

Penny Jordan had recently been hired on as a part-time correspondent, and although he knew there would be no more stories about Jon Phillips — given that Phillips had died in a plane crash in Australia some time ago — Penny, even as nothing more than an image on a screen, was the only link he had to the life he'd left behind.

Soon after she had first appeared on the show, she'd done a brief follow-up to News/Copy's "Wizard of Oz" story about him. As he'd watched the segment, he'd wondered whether she would include her suspicions about him in her report, but she had reported nothing more than that his plane had gone down in an unsettled region near Melbourne, and that although his body had not been found, he was presumed dead. With his death, her story had evidently died. He supposed that this was a good thing for his family and even for Victoria, but it probably wouldn't have mattered all that much if Penny had painted him as a serial murderer. Jon Phillips no longer existed; he had been left to perish in the Australian bush.

In the chaos and shock following his crash, Jon, after considering briefly how unbelievably lucky he was to be alive, immediately flashed on how convenient it would be for him to be thought dead. It took a while for him to collect himself and gather his strength. After extracting only the essentials from his backpack and throwing the remainder, along with his parachute and a few other identifiable articles of his clothing, into the flaming wreck, he then managed to hike out of the mountains with relative ease, due to having spent his childhood hiking and riding in similar terrain. He had with him the basics for mobility — cash, credit cards, and his passport — and with these, he'd been able to leave the country before anyone was even aware he was missing. He had promptly made his way to Nassau via South America, where he knew both he and his money would be secure and anonymous. There he had taken stock.

Even if Penny had a change of heart, which he thought un-likely, there was now no going back. Perhaps he would be able to es-cape conviction on one or two of the deaths, but dodging all five, given the circumstances, seemed highly unlikely. His best shot would be to live out the rest of his life as someone else, far from any place where he might cross paths with anyone from his old life — his family, his friends, and, most painfully of all, Victoria. Deciding that this was his only real alternative, in one of his last acts as Jon Phillips, he had immediately transferred his recently stolen millions to a new British Virgin Islands bank account and begun establishing himself under a recently purchased identity in his new Bahamian is-land home.

In so doing, he found himself with a problem similar to the one Posarnov and Remini had started out with: once the money had been moved out of the U.S. and European banking systems, it needed to be laundered again for Jon to be able to either spend or invest it in the mainstream financial markets, so he was very limited as to how and where he could enjoy his new fortune. One of the ways in which he kept himself busy each day was to search for any potential cracks in the western banking system that would allow him to legitimize his tarnished funds, but the stringent new anti-terrorist measures were working effectively against him.

With far too much time on his hands for reflection in his self-imposed exile, he often dwelt upon the strangeness of the fact that it had been a genuine accident — the engine failure of his father's plane — that had provided him with a way to escape almost certain incarceration. In self-pitying moments, he sometimes tortured himself with thoughts of how little he was probably missed. He had been such a chameleon, breezing in and out of people's lives when and if it suited him, adapting all too well to wherever he was and whomever he was with, that no one, except possibly David and Vic-toria, had ever had any idea who the real Jon Phillips was. Having barely existed, at least not in any authentic way, it stood to reason that he would hardly be missed.

Still, as the months wore on, he wondered if he had made the right choice. Would even the prospect of the death penalty have been any worse than living out his days in this fearful isolation? Than losing Victoria at the very moment he'd found her? He was no longer sure of anything.

Penny wasn't on today's show. He watched for her until the program concluded, then held up his glass to the TV screen in an ironic toast, as the lengthening shadows merged into the gloom of early evening.